RUBY'S PRAYER

By Ronald H. Keyser

DEFIANCE PRESS
& PUBLISHING

Published in Texas by Defiance Press & Publishing LLC

www.defiancepress.com

Printed in the USA

For information about special discounts for bulk purchases or this author's availability for speaking engagements, contact info@defiancepress.com or 888-315-9446.

ISBN: 978-0-9962590-3-3 (Paperback)
ISBN: 978-0-9962590-2-6 (Hardback)
ISBN: 978-0-9962590-7-1 (Digital)

Editing by Janet Musick
Formatting by Debbi Stocco
Cover Art by Arnel Gregorio

Distributed by Hillcrest Media Group

Dedication

I would like to dedicate this book to my mom and dad who passed away in 2014. They could not wait to read every chapter as I finished it, and both would have been very proud to see Ruby's Prayer laying on their coffee table in a hard back cover. I wish they could have lived to see it.

Did you ever see the Devil? Have you ever been in hell?
Did you ever have an angel pay a visit to your cell
in solitary confinement where men are seldom fed?
I've seen it all in reality,
in the land of the living dead.

Excerpt from Seven Years in Texas Prisons
by Beecher Deason, circa 1900.

Table of Contents

CHAPTER 1

Leaving The Walls

"Wallace!" the guard barked as he came to a stop and gazed through the cold, steel bars at the prisoner. "You about ready to get out of here?"

With the uneven, heavy breathing of an overweight man, he selected a key from the large collection dangling from his hip and unlocked the cell door, which screeched and moaned a familiar, depressing sound as it opened. He walked in and placed a pair of shoes, socks, slacks, a shirt, a belt and a dress coat (all of them made in the prison fabric shop) on the end of the cot where Tom sat.

"I need you to put these on," the guard told Wallace. "Leave your black-and-whites on the bed. I'll be back to get you in fifteen minutes."

The mournful noise of the heavy iron door groaned again as the guard exited and locked it behind him. The sound was soon replaced by the fading echoes of his labored breathing and sluggish footsteps as he walked away.

Tom looked over the set of clothes for a moment before running a hand over his new possessions. The stack he was looking at was something he never would have worn before he came here. The shoes seemed to be the right size, but were truly ugly and obviously wouldn't hold up to any amount of walking before losing a sole. The belt was too big, the shirt was way too big, and the pants and jacket were made from a notoriously cheap cotton fabric the prison made and then sold on the outside. It was common knowledge that almost all the fabric produced by the prison ended up being worn by poor colored folk because most of them couldn't afford anything else.

The weave was so coarse that it seemed a man's skin would come off before he could wear a hole through it but, despite the fact that Tom knew they would probably make him itch for a week, he couldn't wait to get them on. Less than three minutes later, the folded black-and-whites were stacked neatly on the bed and Tom Wallace was wearing his new duds, courtesy of the state of Texas. He sat on his bunk and rubbed his rough, tanned hands together. Looking down at them, he realized they were the hands of a much older man and it would require a great deal of time before the large, ugly calluses wore off. His hands were trembling, too, just as they had when he first arrived.

When Tom came to The Walls in March of 1875, the prison didn't have enough cells and the state didn't have enough money to house the sixteen hundred-plus inmates in the system. Eight years earlier, the legislature attempted to solve the space and money problems within the prison by passing laws that enabled the state to lease all able-bodied prisoners for profit, so it was common practice for almost all prisoners to do their time outside the gates working for private companies. Those laws were still entrenched and, because Tom was able-bodied, he was no exception. He spent his first three years working on various railroad crews around the state, another at a granite quarry in Burnet, and did the last year of his time working the cotton fields at the Wynne farm in Huntsville. He was hoeing a row when he heard his name called, and he was told to get in the wagon because he was going back to The Walls.

As soon as he was back inside the huge, red brick building, they cleaned him up a bit by giving him a haircut and a shave and, for the last week, allowed him to eat as much food as he could during chow time. They also let him get away with not doing too much of anything in the shop he was assigned to during the day and, at night, he slept more than he could remember.

Even though he was still badly underweight, Tom had a notion his last seven days in the system were the State's way of fattening him up so the scars wouldn't show, and he wasn't far from wrong.

Sitting on his bunk as the worst sixty months of his life came to an end, a thousand thoughts went racing through his mind. The realization his time here was finally over engulfed him with grisly memories of a thousand guards yelling, untold numbers of men screaming, sledge hammers crashing in unison against impossibly hard stone, blasts of whips cracking against blood-soaked shirts, dispirited songs of the blacks sung all day long as hundreds of hoes slapped down on rock-hard clay, unbelievable stench, bleeding hands, shoeless feet, swarms of huge mosquitoes, scorching hot days, freezing sleepless nights, rancid water, rotten food, infected cuts, painful blisters, aching muscles, empty stares of broken souls, the baying of bloodhounds on the scent stopped only by the echoes of a rifle shot in the distance, and visions of lifeless bodies tossed into the backs of wagons like bales of hay.

A shudder came over Tom like it might shake him to pieces. He bolted off the bunk and replaced the silence in the cell with the sound of his own pacing. Rubbing his face vigorously, he reminded himself that any kind of noise was usually enough to drive the demons from his thoughts for a while and, right now, it would be the sound of his worthless, new brown shoes moving back and forth along the small cell floor.

The cell block Tom was in was empty except for him. He was the only one leaving today. All the other inmates had been rousted out at seven o'clock and put to work in one of the shops an hour before he got his new clothes.

Besides the cotton mill and shoe shop in The Walls, there were several other industries the state was experimenting with, including a furniture shop, a harness shop, a wheelwright shop and a wagon manufacturing shop. Tom had been assigned to the wheelwright shop during his brief stay inside, but he could not imagine how repairing busted-up wagon wheels could be considered hard work by the other men. They complained about anything and everything. Every prisoner inside The Walls had heard stories about the cruelty handed down to the crews working on the outside but, without experiencing it first hand, they would never know how lucky they were to be locked up inside, even if they all faced a long sentence or were crippled up somehow.

His thoughts were interrupted as the door creaked at the end of the block, followed by the sound of the guard getting closer with each step. When the guard finally arrived and looked in through the bars, he asked, "You ready, boy?" He unlocked the door and swung it open. The same depressing sound filled the air. "Come on; let's get you gone."

Tom didn't say a word, but at that precise moment he vowed to himself that, no matter what happened, he would never come back to this place and hear that noise again. After a second to let the thought sink in, he nodded once at the big guard and stepped out of his cell, stopping for a moment as the door was relocked behind him. He walked down the cell block ahead of the guard and exited out the side door into the exercise yard.

The yard was empty except for the two of them because all the other inmates were where they were supposed to be and weren't allowed to go anywhere else until it was time to eat or go back to their cells. If an inmate wound up in the yard by himself at this time of the day and didn't lie flat on the ground in a hurry, only one shot would whiz by his ear before the next one found the middle of his chest. Knowing this, a creepy feeling came over Tom as he stood there exposed. Out of nervousness, he turned to look back at the guard to make sure he was still behind him.

"You okay, boy?" the guard asked.

"Yes…yes, sir, boss," replied Tom. "It's just… it feels a little weird being out here right now."

"Don't worry. I ain't gonna run off behind your back and let you get all shot up right before you're supposed to get turned loose. Besides," he added, "your daddy's outside, and that just wouldn't be right."

Tom's heart nearly leapt from his chest at the news, but words escaped his grasp.

"You hear me, boy?" snapped the guard.

Tom's suddenly dry mouth managed to get the words out. "I'm sorry, boss. Thank you. I didn't know he was here."

"The state sends out a notice to kin whenever we're about to release a man," the guard said. "Looks like your daddy got his. Been in town since yesterday."

Tom suddenly felt like screaming at the top of his lungs. His dad was here! His mother and father stood by him throughout the ordeal of his trial and conviction, including his stay in the county jail before the state shipped him to Huntsville. He had received a few letters from home over the years, informing him everything was going all right at the ranch, even though his dad's leg acted up every time a norther blew through. But ever since his mother had taken ill and passed, the letters didn't come very often. Now his dad was right outside, not a hundred yards away from where he was now, and Tom couldn't wait to see him. As he avoided the large mud holes covering the exercise yard, it seemed to take forever to reach their destination.

"Stop here," the guard said. They were facing a pair of locked iron doors, except these didn't lead into another cell block; these led to the offices of the prison employees. They went through the first, the guard locking it behind them. They took a moment to wipe the mud off the bottoms of their shoes before the guard unlocked and entered a second door into a deep hallway with open doors on either side. Tom could see some of the people in the rooms out of the corners of his eyes as he and the guard moved past them. Even though he kept his head down, he could tell they all stopped for a second or two in the middle of a conversation or whatever they were doing to look as he passed by, and quickly went back to their business as if he never went by at all. It seemed as though setting a man free around here meant about as much to these people as missing the waste can with a piece of paper; it was a minor distraction at most.

They came to the front desk in the small lobby of the prison where a middle-aged woman sat behind a desk.

"Elly, you got Tom Wallace's walkin' supplies?" the guard asked.

"Yes, I do. They're right here." It was the first female voice Tom had heard in a long time and the first cheerful one he had heard from a state employee since he got here. She took a brown paper bag and an envelope out of the drawer in her desk and gave it to the guard, who handed them to Tom.

"Tom Wallace," said the guard, "you have successfully completed the sentence given to you by the state of Texas and are hereby free to go. In the bag, you'll find food to eat. In the envelope, there's five dollars cash money." He crossed his arms and rocked back and forth in his boots, leering as if he was about to give the best advice anyone could ever hear. "Don't come back here again now, you hear me, boy?"

Tom didn't pay any attention because he suddenly realized, for the first time in a very long while, *he didn't have to*. It was over. He was a free man. In a daze, he turned and raced out the front door, barely hearing the woman named Elly call after him, "Good luck, Mister Wallace!" It would be another week before he realized she was the first person in over five years who'd treated him with any respect at all.

CHAPTER 2

Reunion

"That'll be a dollar seventy-five," said the young man behind the counter. "How was everything?"

"Fine," said the guest, tossing his money down. He leveled a gaze at the clerk. "What's your name?"

Surprised, the man behind the counter pushed his long greasy hair behind his ears. "Paul," he said.

The guest had gone out of his way to avoid conversations with everyone for the last few days, and he wasn't going to let some dirty kid named Paul at The Keep Hotel, a run-down inn, trip him up now. It would feel real nice to tell him how uncomfortable the mattress was in his dusty, flea-bag of a room, or how the sheets smelled like a bad combination of sweat, beer and urine. It hadn't taken him but a minute before he pulled the sheets off the bed and threw his jacket down over the mattress so he could sleep on that instead. And the pillow was vile. He wound up using his lumpy travel bag.

To make matters worse, the room next door was used by men in town looking for a little female company, and they'd been in and out of there all night. To anybody else, that would have been plenty of reason to leave this rat-infested hotel and move to another establishment, Aunt Jane's, only a few blocks over, but that would have aroused even more curiosity in what was already an overly curious town. A white man staying in the most famous hotel for blacks in the state of Texas? Everybody in Huntsville would've stopped in the middle of the street and stared, which was exactly what the guest was trying to avoid — and the reason he stayed put.

After the miserable night he just spent, he would've liked nothing more than to replace the smirk on Paul's face with a bloody nose and make him eat the money on the counter. Instead, he gave the clerk a wry smile and a tip of his hat, knowing the greasy-haired kid must think him one hell of an idiot. He picked up his bag and headed for the door, chuckling to himself as he imagined what Paul's reaction would be when he found the sheets in the bottom of the outhouse and his mattress floating in mud out back in the alley. He reckoned that alone was worth the dollar seventy-five.

Jim Wallace stepped out onto the sidewalk in front of the hotel in late March of 1880 to a bright, spring morning. He was a distinguished-looking man, six feet tall and weighing a little over two hundred pounds. His hair, once a dark reddish-brown, now held a fair amount of gray. He kept it trimmed short in consideration of the hot weather, which was also why he never grew a beard, and he always wore the same dark Stetson that covered the small bald spot on the back of his head. His eyes were bright blue, and it had been said many times that he could use them to look right through to the middle of a man. That was true for the most part. A lot of people back home didn't care much for Jim Wallace because he either liked you right away or he didn't. But his ability to quickly read deep into another person's character had long since proven to be a great asset when it came to his business and his life.

He would tell you he was fifty-seven years young and, even though he walked with a noticeable limp, he could still get around nearly as good as anyone. He suffered the injury years back while in the cavalry during the Civil War. His horse was shot out from under him on a dead run and, when it fell, Jim's lower right leg was crushed against a large rock. If it hadn't been for his Colt revolver, which he refused to give up as he was taken to the field hospital, the doctors would have taken his leg off for sure. Although Jim never said a word, it only took a couple of times to show those butchers the business end of his gun before they understood he would shoot them dead if they tried to sneak up on him with their awful saws again. There had been plenty of casualties at the battle of Pea Ridge that day, and those doctors had a lot of other men to worry about, so they figured him for a basket case and set his leg the best they could, then stuck him in a corner to let nature take its course. But nature didn't take the course they thought it would.

After the longest, most horrific four days of Jim's life, one of the doctors finally tried to help with honey salves and quinine, lots of morphine and a rigid body cast that kept him from moving. From that time on, Jim started to improve quickly, much to the amazement of everyone. After a few weeks in the field hospital, and another month of care in a private home five miles south of the battle site, he let his wife Ruby know he could travel. She came by herself all the way from central Texas to the northeast corner of Arkansas to take him home.

There were several heated arguments between the two over what he should or shouldn't be doing with his busted leg but, within another two months, he was hobbling around trying to get the ranch going again. It was a year before he could walk without crutches and a few more to get to the point where he could depend on his leg on a regular basis. In the end, though, his injury probably saved his life, because most of his fellow soldiers in the 3rd Cavalry died that day, with the rest either severely wounded or killed before the end of the war, and he surely wouldn't have become the successful rancher he was if the accident hadn't occurred. By the time the South finally called it quits, the only real asset left in Texas besides timber was longhorn cattle. While most everyone else was off fighting in the war, Jim Wallace was working hard amassing the second largest herd in his part of the state.

Jim took a look around at the buildings in what he could see of Huntsville. The wet weather that followed him all the way to Huntsville had cooled things off, but now the streets all over town looked like one big pig sty. Early spring in Texas could be hot, cold, wet or dry, and it usually was, maybe just not in that order. People said if you didn't like the weather in Texas, stick around fifteen minutes because it would change, and this morning was solid proof. Even though it turned out to be a sunny morning, thick mud was everywhere and the streets were filled with a multitude of horses, people and wagons heading this way and that, which only made it worse. He was glad he'd arranged for a wagon and driver so he didn't have to stomp around in the muck on his way to the prison. Sure enough, his ride was waiting out in front of the hotel, just as the old man had promised.

Huntsville, Texas, was established by the brothers Pleasant and Ephraim Gray as an Indian trading post sometime around 1836. Presumably, they chose the spot because it was situated between the Bidai, Alabama and Coushatta Indian settlements, and the fact that it was on the highest hill they could find. Evidently there was not much point in establishing a trading post somewhere where no one could see it.

A few years later, when Huntsville was laid out as a city, all the streets going in and out of town went up the hill and then down and out the other side. Not a big deal really, but when the sky opened up and left the roads the way they were today, getting loaded wagons full of pine trees on their way to the mill made for a gigantic mess. That and the rest of the traffic on the streets was sure to keep everybody in town complaining about the state of things, even though a few days earlier, the residents had all been praying for a good downpour.

Jim had reasoned early on that a lot of people in this town were strange down to the bone, and there was something about the place he just didn't like. It wasn't because the folks of Huntsville all looked at him like he was a leper; a lot of towns were wary of outsiders. Huntsville, however, had a population of about seventeen hundred people, and it should have been easy for him to come and go unnoticed, but it wasn't. People here stared.

He didn't judge them to be disagreeable because of the nosy questions they posed as soon as he got off the stagecoach. He only smiled, and answered all questions with a simple "Howdy." There weren't many men who made it out of the war as well as Jim had, so he had made a habit of not talking about himself or his past, and that habit had served him well for eighteen years. He wasn't going to break it now.

Last night at the diner, however, it was about as much as he could stand. All he wanted to do was sit and enjoy his steak, which was surprisingly good, but every eye in the place was fixed squarely on him, and he knew that all he had to do was say one word to any of them and the onslaught would begin. Before he paid his tab, he caught the attention of an old man cleaning tables who didn't seem to care one way or the other who the hell Jim Wallace was, and he asked him to be out front of the hotel this morning at seven o'clock with a wagon, and here he was, and early, too.

In 1872, only a few years earlier, the Houston and Great Northern Railroad announced plans to put a rail right through Huntsville and had everybody excited about their great future ahead. Then the railroad company told the town it needed to put up one hundred thousand dollars to defray the building costs or the tracks would be laid elsewhere. There eventually were commitments for about half the money, but most of the townspeople became indignant; there was no way they would go along with legalized extortion, especially when everyone knew the railroad was coming anyway. After all, General Sam Houston was buried here and the prison was here. It only stood to reason that the state had to have a railroad to help support the prison. Plus, only twenty-two years earlier in 1850, Huntsville had lost to Austin in an election to become the state capitol. The railroads were bluffing, for God's sake; they had to be.

As it turned out, only a year later, the townsfolk raised over three hundred thousand dollars to build an eight-mile stretch of rail due east, to the very small town of Phelps, which is where the Houston and Great Northern tracks were laid instead. So, if people wanted to get to Huntsville by train, they had to go through Phelps. The railroads bypassed Huntsville completely, basically telling the people there to stick it in their ear.

No, the thing about these people that made Jim the most uncomfortable was the prison. In 1847, the Texas legislature chose Huntsville to become the site of the new state prison, and build it they did, practically right in the middle of town. "The Walls," as they called it, occupied four city blocks and sat two blocks east of the county court house.

When the prison first opened, it stood by itself, just off to the side of town, but it wasn't long before it was surrounded by saloons, several hotels, private homes and a host of other businesses, all built next door or a block or two over. Jim couldn't help but think it had to be mighty tough for an inmate to hear the sounds of free people going about their lives just a few feet away when all a man could do inside that big, brick cage was dream about those same sounds back home, wherever that might be. That had to be its own kind of punishment, and something the people in Huntsville didn't seem to care one lick about.

The prison made this town and they were proud of it, plain and simple. Maybe they felt that way because The Walls was the only penitentiary left standing throughout all the southern states after the Civil War, or maybe it was because almost every business in Huntsville depended on it in one way or another, but Jim couldn't understand it, no matter the reasons. He would rather spend the rest of his life punching cows all the way to Kansas and die flat busted than squander his years here without much ambition, sucking hind tit on an ugly government mule.

Jim knew he could never live in this town, among these people, but the ones who worked outside the gates and who relied on the prison for their existence were only half of what irritated him. The people who worked on the inside made up the other half of what irritated him.

Many times over the last five years, Jim thought it must take a certain kind of man to be a guard in the prison system, to deal in such human misery. That was the part that truly disgusted him. Granted, somebody had to do it, and there were some extremely bad men in there who deserved their fate, but he could not imagine closing an iron door behind a man and locking him away.

There had been plenty of stories handed down over the years describing the way the guards beat and tortured the prisoners, but there never was any proof. Most assumed these were only tall tales spoken from the mouths of spiteful ex-cons trying to get even with a guard or two who didn't let them read their mail or treated them a little too rough at times. Books had been published by ex-inmates describing the guards as being more violent than the prisoners they were guarding. Rumors circulated to the effect that the state was looking into these allegations, but not many cared in the first place so there wasn't much stock put into the idea that things would change.

Until five years ago, Jim hadn't cared, either. Sometimes, when worrying about his son, he wondered how a man could take the job. The pay couldn't be good, and there were all kinds of ways to make a living in Texas without having to settle for locking men up and beating the hell out of them, sometimes to death. No, it took a special kind of man to rob a bank and a special kind of man to be a prison guard. Jim knew that, if he had to choose to do one or the other, he would much rather spend his life robbing banks. The way he saw it, at least there might be a little honor in that.

"Why don't ya throw your bag in the back and climb on up here with me?" The old bald man tilted his head toward the back of the wagon. He gave Jim a wink. "The prison's two blocks yonder. Won't take just a little bit to get there."

"Thanks for coming," Jim said, tossing his travel bag behind the seat. He patted his bad leg. "Never would've been able to get around in all this mud."

The old farm wagon was fairly beat up from years of steady use, and looked even worse with mud all over the wheels, but Jim could tell by the coat on the red mare pulling it and the way the old man held the reins that he had made a good choice for his transportation. His driver had even pulled right up against the sidewalk so Jim didn't have to get down in the muck and dirty his boots, not that he ever wore fancy ones. The pair he had on now looked about as new as the wagon.

After a second to look it over, Jim pulled himself up and sat down next to the driver without a slip. He had to be careful climbing up and down anything. He learned the hard way never to take his leg for granted.

"What's your name, old timer?" he asked. He knew he was going to like this guy.

The man holding the reins was sixty-two years old and looked every bit of it. He was five-foot seven and about twenty-five pounds overweight, but he looked even heavier from the way he slumped forward in his seat. He didn't have a single hair on his suntanned head, but he had a couple of bushy, salt-and-pepper eyebrows creeping out from behind a pair of round spectacles. His face held the lines of a man who had been down a lot of roads in life, most of them maybe not so good. The jeans and shirt he wore were old but clean as a whistle, and the boots he wore reminded Jim of his own. The man's light brown eyes were alive, though, something that caught Jim's attention from the start. That and the excellent steak he ate last night were the reasons why he had hired the man for transport this morning.

"Call me Bear; everybody else does," the old man replied. "I kinda like the name 'cause it makes me sound like I'm big and ornery. Truth is, though, a long time ago I sorta lost all my hair all at once. Don't know why; just happened. Didn't take long before folks were calling me a batch of names, none of 'em too damn funny, either. Hell, I never even knew what a baboon was until my hair fell out, but somewhere along the way somebody called me bare, like b-a-r-e." He spelled it out slow and loud, rubbing the top of his head, and added, "I spell it b-e-a-r. The joke on me has been long gone, but I reckon I got everybody 'round here believin' I'm big and ornery. Well, ornery, least ways." Bear flashed a grin and laughed a little, as if he just remembered an old scrape he had been in that had made his name stick. "Ya ready?"

Jim was smiling, too. "Yeah, let's go."

Bear let out a couple of clicking sounds as he popped the reins on the back of the mare and the wagon lurched away from the sidewalk and into the muddy street.

"The name's Jim, Jim Wallace." Jim offered an outstretched hand. "It's a pleasure to meet you."

"Pleasure's all mine," replied Bear as they shook. "How'd ya like your steak last night?"

"It was damn good," Jim said. "You're the cook, too, aren't you?"

"That's me," Bear said proudly, and he winked again. "I do most everythin' in that place, but I like cookin' the most. I turn out a mean steak if I do say so myself. Ya know what they say…" he added, patting his oversized belly, "…never trust a skinny cook!"

"I'll keep that in mind," Jim laughed. "So tell me, Bear, how did you know where I was going? I didn't say anything about you taking me to the prison."

"Oh, that's an easy one," said Bear. "First off, somebody comin' to this town for only a night means they're comin' to gather up somebody out of the prison. Second, just about every nosy person livin' here knows somebody who knows somebody who knows who's gettin' out and who's gonna be here to pick him up. So, as soon as ya got off the stage yesterday, the talkin' got started." Bear pulled back on the reins and said, "Whoa."

The mare stopped so a wagon full of dry goods, probably on its way to a warehouse close by, could pass through the intersection. Once it passed, Bear sounded a couple of clicks and the wagon was moving again.

"Are you one of the nosy ones?' Jim asked. "You seem to know a few things."

"Naw. I'm a listener, not a talker," Bear said. "I do my level best to stay out of people's business but, where I work, I have to listen to nosy people all the time 'cause I can't get away from 'em. Seems like they feel most comfortable doin' their talkin' over a plate of good food, surrounded by others just like 'em, playin' a game they call 'whoever brags loudest wins.' Ya ever notice how talkers only talk about two things — themselves or somebody else? Whenever they talk about themselves, it's usually all a bunch of bullshit. If they're talkin' 'bout somebody else, they mostly can't say nothin' good at all. There's a few talkers in this town," he added. "Take a look. The ones starin' at us now are most likely them."

"I think you're right," Jim said, glancing around at the people milling on the sidewalks. He noticed that a few people on both sides of the street had stopped in the middle of whatever they were doing to watch the wagon as it passed.

Bear chuckled. "Either that, or it's been a while since anybody seen a couple of old farts like us in a wagon at the same time, and neither one of 'em in a pine box."

"That's probably more like it," laughed Jim.

"Speakin' of talk, they say you're a cattle man," Bear said.

"Yep. Like most everybody else in this state, I reckon," Jim replied. They were headed down the hill on 12th Street, the prison coming up on their right, so Jim pointed at the building and steered the conversation in another direction. "What time do the inmates get out when they let them go?"

"Usually 'tween eight and nine," Bear said offhandedly, then his mood suddenly turned sour. "'Course, that's if they come out at all." After a small pause, he sat upright in the seat and looked Jim square in the eye. "Mister Wallace, I'm sorry. I didn't mean nothin' by that, I swear. As soon as ya left last night, I asked a couple a questions and I know for sure your boy Tom is comin' out of there, yes, sir. Got it from a reliable account that he could stand puttin' on some weight, but he made it through okay. I'm terrible sorry. Sometimes I got a bad way of lettin' my mouth get ahead of what's left of my brain."

"That's all right," Jim said. Normally he didn't have much use for anyone who rattled off at the mouth, but Bear did it in such a way that Jim had to ask. "You knew somebody in there, didn't you?"

There was a stretch of silence before Bear answered, "My son."

Now Jim was the one who felt two feet tall. "Bear, I shouldn't have…"

Bear cut him off with a raised hand. "No, no, don't worry about it. It was a long time ago. Thing is, when I came to this town, I came for the same reason you have. Got a letter from the state sayin' my boy was gettin' out, so I came down here to fetch him, just like you are now. Traveled a long way to boot. There I was, sittin' right out in front of the prison, when one of them state officials came out and told me my boy was dead. Said they mailed me a letter, but guessed I hadn't got it yet. They even acted like they were real sorry, too. Said they had to shoot him out on one of the farms 'cause he was trying to escape. Please!" There was another pause. "Let me ask ya somethin', Mister Wallace, would ya try to escape if you'd been in there three years and ya only had six weeks before you was a free man? Ya wouldn't now, would ya?"

Bear stared off into the distance. "That's the story they stuck to, though. It was a hell of a thing." He shrugged his shoulders and sighed, then said with finality, "Never did find out what really happened, so that was that."

"I'm sorry," was all Jim knew to say.

"I appreciate that, Mister Wallace, but…"

"Call me Jim, will you?" Jim cut in.

Bear looked at him with a smile. "Jim it is, then. I just want ya to know, I'm happy for you and your boy to be gettin' together again today. I know it'll be somethin' that neither one of ya will ever forget, and it'll be a wonderful thing to watch."

"Why, thank you, Bear. That's kind of you. And here I thought you said you were ornery," Jim said.

"Oh, I am, just not right now," Bear said with a wink. "I ain't been drinkin'."

They made their way through the last intersection before Bear pulled the wagon over to a spot in front of a general store on the other side of the street from the prison and parked it neatly along the sidewalk. As they drew to a stop, Jim asked, "How come you're over here? Why not pull over there, right in front?"

"'Cause we ain't got nuthin' in this wagon they want. Sure as hell somebody would come out and run us off, so we might as well park it here," he said.

"What about this store we're in front of? Don't you think we might get run off from here, too?" Jim asked.

"Naw," replied Bear. "I guarantee ya right now somebody's in there just a hopin' that we'll hop off here and go in there and buy somethin'. He'll let us sit here, don't ya worry."

Bear set the brake and put the reins up. As soon as he finished, he rubbed the top of his head with one hand and started talking with the other. He was going on about how the town was growing in this direction or that, but Jim wasn't listening too much. The thought occurred to him that he was glad Bear considered himself a listener and not a talker because, if it was the other way around, he just might have to shoot himself. Jim liked the man, though, and was enjoying the company for a change.

"So what do we do now?" he asked as soon as he could chime in.

Bear's hands stopped in midair, and the expression on his face made it clear he had lost his train of thought, but he turned and nodded toward the front of the huge red brick building and said, "Nothin'. 'Til they let him walk out that door, we just wait."

A half-second later, his lips and hands were moving again because he remembered what he had been talking about before he was interrupted. Jim didn't pay much attention, though; his eyes and ears were focused directly on the front of the prison.

He thought about how most everybody in this town had become immune to the oppressive aura the building radiated because everyone came and went like they were entering or leaving one of the general stores over by the courthouse. They might as well be shopping for a pie or something the way they seemed to be so indifferent to the place. But Jim didn't want to step foot in there if he could help it; the idea gave him goose bumps.

The front of the Huntsville State Penitentiary was built facing north, two blocks long and made entirely of red brick. In 1880, the main entrance to the offices of the complex was a three-story tiered building, with a second-story balcony that covered the sidewalk, and was situated on the northwest corner closest to the town square. The infamous red brick wall from which the prison got its name started on either side and encompassed the rest of the four city blocks on which the structure stood.

A clock tower centered on the third floor, along with spires coming off all four corners of the second floor, gave a man a sense that it was built as a cathedral, and Jim was pretty sure the perception was a selling point of the designers so the people of Huntsville could go about their business feeling better about themselves, as if God's work was going on behind those walls of horror. He got an uneasy feeling in his stomach and wondered if that was the reason the people in this town were practically emotionless about the men inside.

He shook the thought off and glanced over at Bear. Ever since they had parked the wagon, Jim had kept his eyes glued to the front of the building, but every now and then he'd let his attention drift back to whatever topic Bear was rambling on about. He'd stick an "I know," or a "You're right" into the conversation so Bear would think he was listening, but every time someone came out the front door, Jim's heart skipped a beat, only to sink back in his chest when he saw it wasn't Tom. The process was wearing him out and it was only a little after eight o'clock. When he quit paying attention to the front door this time, Bear was right in the middle of another brain work.

"...and if this town didn't have as many good-lookin' ol' widows and if I wasn't as good-lookin' as I am, I'd a moved on a long time ago," Bear said, his head cocked to the side and a finger pointing off to somewhere.

"You're not married?" asked Jim.

"Me?" replied Bear, a little surprised. "Naw. I love to spend my fair share of time with the ladies, but I been by myself too long for the womenfolk 'round here to have anythin' to do with me for too long a spell. Besides, there'll always be only one girl I'll ever really love, and that was John's ma." He gave the street a vacant stare. "John was my boy."

A short silence followed, then Jim asked, "Did you have any other children?"

"Naw," Bear said, "we tried a bunch of times, but John was the only one who made it 'cause his ma didn't carry them babies so well. We lost one before John and two more after, God bless her soul. She was tryin' to push that last one out when she died." He paused, lost in memory. "She was a hell of a girl." He gave the sky a glance and pointed up. "Fact is, I'm sure she's up there lookin' out for all them kids right now."

There was another silence, with neither knowing what to say. Bear was thinking that he might have been a little too personal, and Jim was thinking about his wife, so neither one said anything.

Finally, Jim decided it was a little too quiet and changed the conversation. "You got a place around here somewhere?"

"You sure do ask a lot of questions for somebody who don't waste a lot of words." Bear raised an eyebrow in mock suspicion. "You sure you ain't one of them nosy people? I think you mighta been sent 'round here to spy on me, so's the rest of this town can learn all my secrets with the ladies."

Jim laughed out loud, then stopped abruptly. From the corner of his eye he saw the front door of the prison fly open and out ran a skinny, middle-aged looking man clutching a brown sack and an envelope. It was Tom.

Jim spun in his seat and jumped off the wagon into the mud, landing with most of his weight on his good leg. As soon as he hit the ground he knew he'd made a mistake because his left boot was instantly buried four or five inches deep in the wet Texas clay. He tried to pull it free, but he was glued to the ground, so he gave up and looked over at Tom, who was on the opposite sidewalk eagerly scanning the street. Jim started waving and yelling, "Tom! Tom! Over here!"

As soon as Tom saw his father waving at him, he took off across the street as fast as he could. He vaguely felt his right shoe get sucked off his foot by the mud, but that didn't slow him down at all. The look of pure joy on his father's face made him feel stronger the closer he got, and suddenly, after five long years, they were embracing. The bear hug that followed was one both felt could have gone on forever, but Jim finally pulled back and held Tom at arm's length, unable to stop grinning at his oldest boy.

As tears streamed down their faces, Jim looked into Tom's green eyes and said, "Let me look at you. Damn! It's been a long time, son. Too long."

"I know, Dad," choked Tom, wiping his face. "I'm so sorry this happened. I wish…"

"Now don't you even think about starting with that," snapped Jim, shaking his own tears off.

"But Mom…" started Tom.

"Listen to me," Jim cut in. "We've both come too far to get to this spot right here right now. It's over, every bit of it. All the way, through and through, it's over. So don't you ever tell me you're sorry anymore. You hear me?"

Tom dropped his head a little to the side and looked down meekly before nodding his head.

"Now come here," Jim said, pulling Tom in close for another sizable hug, lasting almost as long as the first. "We've a lot of things to do now that you're coming home, and none of them include you looking to the past and wishing you could change things. You understand?"

Tom nodded again, but this time his head was held high and he was looking his dad in the eye. They both wiped tears again before Jim said, "In fact, the first thing we need to do is get my boot unstuck from this mud so we can get the hell out of here. I can't move an inch."

All the tension that had built to this point between Jim and Tom evaporated and was replaced by the foolish sight of a grown man stuck in the mud in the middle of a city street. They started laughing so hard it made their bellies hurt and their eyes water up again. Even the mare flicked her ears and turned her head far enough to get an eye on them, then shook her head with a snort and flipped her tail in the air, as if she too thought the sight was funny.

Bear was laughing with them as he leaned over to the other side of the wagon, pointing at Jim and saying, "And here I thought *you* was the one supposed to get *him* out."

"I am…or was," Jim said. He finally caught his breath and he pointed at Bear. "Tom, I want you to meet Bear." He was trying to lift his boot out of the mud when he turned his head to the wagon and added, "I hired Bear to be our ride today, and I can tell you right now it's not going to be a boring one."

"I'm not so sure I know what that means," said Bear, "but I'm really glad to meet ya."

Tom noticed the delight in Bear's eyes and immediately recognized him as a friend. "Nice to meet you, too," he said.

Bear looked over at Jim. "You're goin' to have to get that boot off if ya want to get it out of the mud. The clay 'round here won't let go of a boot unless ya let go of it first."

"I figured as much," Jim said. "Tom, give me a hand, will you?"

"Sure thing." Tom stepped in front of his dad and leaned down to grab the straps of the stuck boot. Jim gingerly moved his weight over to his right leg and held onto Tom while he pulled his stockinged foot out, then watched

Tom work the straps back and forth until he got some air between the heel and the wet clay. With one final pull and a sucking sound, the mud-caked boot came free.

"There you go," said Tom with a smile. He banged the boot a few times on the metal rim of the wagon wheel to knock as much mud off as he could, then handed it back to his dad.

"Thank you, son," said Jim. "I think I'd best put it back on in the wagon. It'll be easier for me up there." Jim turned carefully, and tossed the dirty boot onto the floor boards. Then he placed his foot on the step and hoisted himself up onto the seat.

Tom climbed up next to him. "God, that shoe is ugly," Jim said, looking at his son's feet. "What happened to the other one?"

Tom looked down at his one shoe and chuckled. "It must be in the mud somewhere," he said. "The money, too. Hang on."

He hopped off the wagon before Jim or Bear had a chance to say anything and made his way to the white envelope laying next to his other shoe and the paper bag halfway across the street. On his way back, he explained, "I got an envelope with some money in it; might as well not leave it here."

As soon as Tom was back in the wagon with his gifts from the state in hand, Bear asked, "Where to now, gentlemen?"

Jim looked Tom over before answering. "I think we need to find a store somewhere so I can buy this man some clothes. I've seen better looking rags in the trash heap."

"Look at them shoes, too," Bear said. "I got bad news for ya, Tom. Ya won't be able to hang 'round me much with them ugly things on." He watched Tom pull off his muddy sock, toss it in the back of the wagon and put the shoe on his bare foot. "I'd have to tell my lady friends I don't know ya at all." He grinned and asked, "Y'all ready now?" and, without waiting for a response, he popped the reins one more time on the mare's back, turned the wagon around, and headed back up the hill toward the shops surrounding the town square.

"Yes, I am. More than ready," Tom whispered to himself, looking back and taking in the view of the cruel Texas prison as it finally started moving into his past. The front door to The Walls had been the entrance to a living nightmare that stretched to every corner of the state. Tom had traveled in neck chains across Texas, from one end to the other, before coming back here to where it all started. Now he gazed back as the portal to hell slowly faded away down the street.

When he'd arrived there five long years ago, Tom was twenty-five years old, not quite six feet tall, weighed a hundred and seventy-five pounds, had light brown hair and bright green eyes. His hair now held quite a bit of premature gray around the temples, his skin was tanned and tough as leather, he was twenty-five pounds underweight, and there were wrinkles around his eyes that made him look older than he was. He was also tired to the bone. He was still quick on his feet, which was an indirect reason he went to prison in the first place, but Tom knew it was going to take some time to get himself patched up physically to be the man he used to be. He also knew it would probably take more time to get patched up mentally because the dreams that hounded him at night were far worse than the aches and pains he had become accustomed to during the day.

He breathed a huge sigh of relief as the wagon rolled through the first intersection and the big, red structure slowly sank into the distance. For the first time, the thought crossed his mind that there would be another intersection, then another, then a mile, then a town, then a county, then a year and then a life between himself and his past. He couldn't wait to get there.

Jim noticed his son lost in thought so he nudged him with an elbow. "You hungry?" he asked.

"Famished," Bear said. "You buyin'?"

"I was asking Tom," replied Jim.

"Oh, right," Bear said with a sly smile.

Tom brought his attention back to the present. "I could probably eat something in a little while," he said.

Ahead of them were bustling streets and busy people heading this way and that, and he tried to take it all in. It was hard to believe. The only consistent topics of conversation among all the inmates Tom had ever known were those of women, food and what the first thing was that a man would do once he got out, and here he was, a free man out in the middle of Huntsville, talking about eating a decent meal and on his way to get some decent clothes. It was thrilling, and a damned good start. For the first time in years, he sensed a small piece of himself awaken from what seemed like a long, dark sleep, and he felt what it was like to be a man again. He also realized maybe the excitement of the morning was making the recent breakfast he ate not as filling as it seemed before.

"Can we get something to eat in an hour or so?" he asked. "I'm not real hungry now, but I think I'll be starving by then."

"Sure thing, son," Jim said. "You just let me know."

The prospect of food made Tom lean over to eye the paper sack sitting on the floor. He picked it up, looked inside and said, "Speaking of food, let's see what they put in my bag here." He reached down into the small paper bag. "Wow," he said sarcastically, holding up a badly bruised apple. "Look at this, too." He produced the final contents: four small pieces of jerky. "Not much, is it?" he declared. "I guess I shouldn't bad-mouth it, though. Wasn't long ago me and everybody else I knew would have been grateful for this."

"Well, ya don't have to be grateful now. Here, let me see that." Bear took the apple from Tom and tossed it into the mud, followed by the jerky. "Tell ya what," he said, "whenever ya say you're ready, we'll stop whatever we're doin' and head on over to where I work, and I'll fix ya somethin' up to eat that you'll remember for a long time. My treat."

"Bear, I have money," Jim protested.

"I ain't askin' you," Bear said. He nodded at Tom. "I'm askin' Tom here, and it would be my pleasure. Besides, I'll be getting hungry myself soon and y'all got a long trip home ahead of ya. Can't send ya outta this town on an empty stomach."

The more Bear talked about food, the more Tom forgot the semi-stale biscuit he had eaten earlier. Food considered good in The Walls was something no one in his right mind would eat out here unless it was all he had. The thought of a real, sit-down dinner made Tom's stomach rumble. "I don't think I can say no to an offer like that," he said. "I haven't had a good meal in ages, and all this talk about food is making me hungrier by the minute."

"Well, I can tell you from experience this man cooks a hell of a steak." Jim grinned. "I had one last night."

"We got a deal then?" asked Bear, reaching across Jim to shake Tom's hand.

"We got a deal," Tom said, sealing it with a hearty handshake. Suddenly they were all looking forward to it.

"Y'all takin' the train out of here, or the stage?" Bear asked.

"The train," Jim answered.

"Next one out's supposed to leave 'round noon, so sometime before then we'll chow down. Just tell me when, all right, Tom?" asked Bear.

"Sure. But, if we keep talking about eating I'm going to want that meal before we have a chance to get much further down this street," Tom said, removing his coarse cotton jacket and throwing it in the back of the wagon to join the muddy sock. He scratched his arms. "Right now, I'd like to get out of these itchy rags."

"Well, first things first then." Bear guided the wagon back up the two blocks traveled earlier, and just past The Keep Hotel when he looked over at Jim. "Tom here needs to get fixed up. We got all kinda shops 'round here. There's Gibbs Brothers next block over, Foster's on the other side of the square, and the J.G. Ashford store back down where we just came from. My bet is that y'all be needin' pretty much everythin', so I'd advise ya to go into Felder's right up here on the right. Some of the other stores 'round this town will try to charge ya an arm and a leg, just 'cause they know ya ain't one of the locals, but I know the guy that owns the place, and Felder's got a reputation for treatin' people fair."

Bear pulled the wagon over to the sidewalk in front of one of the shops. "Tom might be goin' in there lookin' like he found those clothes in a trash pile, but he'll come out lookin' good as new." He nodded toward a black man standing in front of the store. "That's a good shoe shine man standin' out front there, too. His name is Moses-Henry, and ya gotta say it like it's one name 'cause he gets offended if ya just call him Moses. He'll get that boot cleaned up for ya, Jim."

"Whatever you say, Bear. You're the scout," Jim said.

Felder's General Store was located a block off the town square and occupied the entire bottom floor of a two-story brick building, common to downtown Huntsville. Like most such places, the bottom floor was used for a business, while the upstairs housed the business owner and his family. A tin-covered awning spanned the entire sidewalk in front, and it was easy to tell that a man could either get or order most anything he wanted or needed inside. The windows and the sidewalk were packed with wares and it was easy to imagine the inside of the store would offer even more. Jim could tell right away they had come to the right place.

Tom hopped out first, then turned and gave his dad a hand as he got down. He had been doing that ever since he was a kid because of Jim's bad leg, and it made him feel good to do it once more. It was just one of a million little things that happened every day in Tom's former life that he had taken for granted, but now he knew he would never look at all those little things the same way again. He smiled as he looked into his father's eyes, and knew Jim was enjoying the moment, too.

"Thank you, son," Jim said as he stepped onto the sidewalk. "If I had gotten out of there slow and easy like that when we were in front of the prison, I wouldn't have made an ass out of myself like I did."

"If ya hadn't made an ass out of yourself like ya did, I wouldn't have had such a good time this morning." Bear flashed them a wide grin.

"Bear, let me see if I understand this," Jim said with a straight face. "I'm paying you, but you're insulting me. Is that right?"

Bear laughed and put on a face like he sincerely didn't understand. "You don't think there's somethin' wrong with that? Is there? Do ya?" He laughed again at the image of Jim stuck in the mud, but stopped abruptly when something caught his attention down the street. "Why don't you two go take care of your business in there and I'll be 'round here somewhere if ya need me. Just holler."

He set the brake and tied the reins in a flash, then was out of the wagon before Jim or Tom could say a thing. They watched him jog down the sidewalk to the corner and through the mud to the other side of the street where an older woman, adorned in a blue-and-white dress with a matching Sunday bonnet, was about to cross.

"Well, son of a gun. I didn't think the man could move that fast." Jim grinned as they watched Bear make a beeline for her.

"I didn't either," Tom said, "but I kinda like the guy. He's a character."

"He is that, son, he is that." They watched Bear help the woman choose a route around the worst of the mud holes in the street.

Jim turned to climb into the shoe stand chair, nodding hello to Moses-Henry. "Son, you go on in and pick out something to wear and I'll get this man to remove the mud from my boot. And hey, get yourself a new hat, too. I'll be in there in a minute."

"Okay. And thanks a lot. I appreciate this very much." Tom headed to the door. He stopped and turned to face his dad. "I need to ask you a favor, though," he said in a serious tone.

"Sure thing, son," Jim said. "What you got?"

"Do you think maybe we can get Bear to take us about a mile from here after we leave the store?" Tom asked. "I made a promise to someone that I'd visit before I left town and I want to keep it. It's important to me."

"No problem. Do you want to go before we eat or after?" asked Jim.

"Before, if it's all right with you," Tom replied. "It shouldn't take too long and we could be back here long before lunch time."

"Don't worry about it then. Just hurry up and get out of those awful-looking things." Jim settled into the chair. "Then we'll head off to wherever you need to go."

He turned his attention to the black man who was bent over inspecting his boots. "Your name Moses-Henry?"

"Yassa," said the shoe-shine man. "Juss one name, Moses-Henry"

"Well, Moses-Henry, my name is Jim and I got a little mud on one of my boots. I hear you're just the man to see about it."

Moses-Henry said, "Whoo, Lordy, you musta' got stuck in da' mud, didn' ya?"

On the same side of the street one block over, Sergeant Jack Pruitt tied his horse and was about to enter the courthouse to take care of a business matter when he caught sight of a newly released inmate going into Felder's General Store. Five years ago, he'd reached his rank with the prison system after ten long years of trying, and now he had his mind set on making lieutenant, which included a fairly decent raise. He had been trying hard to impress certain people who could appoint him to the position, and suddenly it looked like Lady Luck might have just shined down on him. Even though he was off duty, he thought it might look pretty good if he walked over to Felder's and caught a petty thief, or better yet, stopped a robbery. He suddenly felt fate was on his side, certain the events of this day would go a long way toward securing the roomy office right next to the warden's. He quickly crossed the muddy intersection to the row of shops on the other side of the street.

CHAPTER 3

Felder's Store

The jingle of the small bell above the front door, along with the echoes of footsteps on the worn hardwood floor, caught the attention of an older man wearing spectacles, a three-piece suit and a bow tie, his short hair parted neatly down the middle as he stood behind the long wooden counter stacked with merchandise. He stopped writing figures in the book laid out by the cash register, set his pencil aside, spread his fingertips atop the counter and leaned forward, surveying from head to toe the thin, brand-new ex-convict standing before him.

Everyone in this town recognized prison garb from a mile away, but usually that's what it was: a mile away. It wasn't very often he saw a new inmate in his store, although he could tell a few stories about some who thought they could steal a thing or two before they left Huntsville. Every merchant in this town knew the prison didn't give them enough to get very far so, until these newly freed men were on their way back to wherever they came from, they were all treated with more than a little contempt.

Peering over the top of his glasses, the man delivered his question in a holier-than-thou tone right out of a Sunday Baptist sermon. "May I help you?"

Except for the itching, Tom hadn't given much thought to the clothes he was wearing since he walked out of the prison, but now he suddenly felt extremely uncomfortable in them and would have stripped right there if he could. "I...I need some things," he said uneasily. Thinking the clerk might believe he was there to rob the place, he stuttered, "I mean buy...buy some things...clothes. I need a pair of jeans. And a shirt, a pair of boots, a hat, a belt...and maybe some socks, too."

"And how do you plan to pay for all that?" the man asked slowly, his tone implying that Tom didn't have the necessary funds for such a purchase.

"My dad's right outside; he's got money," Tom said, pointing to the sidewalk. "My friend Bear brought us here. He's our ride today and he said you'd treat us fair."

The man behind the counter took his eyes off Tom for the first time and quickly glanced out the window to the street, then turned back and asked Tom in an entirely new tone of voice, "You say you know Bear?"

"Yes. Ah, I mean yes, sir," replied Tom quickly. He felt the tension in the room lift and rushed to add, "I just met him this morning and all but my dad hired him last night to..."

"Ah, yes!" the merchant chimed in, rubbing his chin thoughtfully. "I remember now." He moved out from behind the counter onto the main floor, smiling. "I ran into Bear last night at Doorman's, and he told me about the two of you. I'm very sorry, but I simply forgot. I don't pay strict attention to everything that good man says because I'm afraid my capacity for remembering things is truly unworthy of Bear's gift for conversation." He shook Tom's hand vigorously. "The name's Felder. Welcome to my humble shop. I sincerely apologize for my initial greeting but, if you can forgive me, it would be my pleasure to be at your service."

"Yeah...yes, sir, sure." Tom felt relieved. All the stiffness between himself and the clerk vanished, but now he was even more aware of his decrepit prison clothes. He looked at his trousers, tugged a leg and added, "If you don't mind, I'd like to try some things on as soon as I can. I need to get out of these."

"I understand completely. Right this way." The shopkeeper placed a hand on Tom's shoulder and led him to the back of the store.

Walking among all the merchandise, Tom was comforted to find he was the only customer in the place, and he was quickly mesmerized by all the different items for sale. He passed hats, gloves, pelts, lanterns, rolls of cloth, tonics, brooms, mops, hammers, saws, pots, pans, pails, candles, canning jars, canned goods, picture frames, tobacco, bags of flour, beans, rice, and everything else he could imagine, all crammed together as tightly as possible and seemingly without any organization whatsoever. It had been a long time since he had been in a store like this and, even though he had no need for anything except clothes, it felt good to just stare at it all. He stopped to pick up an item or two on the way to the back, turning it over in his hands as if it was the first time he had ever seen anything like it. Each time, he received a patient and understanding look from Mister Felder as he set it back down.

"And what can we interest you in today Mister…my goodness, I'm terribly sorry, but I did not get your name," Mister Felder said, a bit embarrassed.

"Tom. Tom Wallace," Tom said, shaking Mister Felder's hand.

They reached the back of the store and Mister Felder waved his outstretched hand at the clothes along the wall. "Well, then, Mister Wallace, what manner of dress are you interested in today? A handsome suit, or would you prefer something a bit more relaxed?"

Tom gazed along the rows of clothing that stretched from one wall to the other. It was a wonderful sight. He hadn't seen this many new clothes since before he came to Huntsville and he'd forgotten how it looked and smelled.

Tom had spent the last five years in prison wearing the same pants and shirt he had been issued when he first arrived, and they weren't well made to begin with. He had taken care of them, though, and his clothes never got as bad as most of the other inmates because his sentence was short. He had seen hundreds of convicts during his stay in the system who wore black-and-whites that really weren't black and white at all because the rags they wore appeared to be solid black from years of dirt that had seldom been washed out. At every camp Tom worked at across the state, it was easy to spot the new inmates from the old by what particular stage of discoloration and stench their clothes were in.

"I'm really not a suit kind of guy," Tom said, looking up and down at the suit Mister Felder wore. He turned his attention to the clothes along the wall, fingering a new pair of heavy, cotton work trousers. "Just some comfortable pants, a shirt and some boots, if you got them."

"Relaxed it is then," Mister Felder said. He appraised Tom's frame. "I believe you'll need pants with a waist of approximately thirty inches, and a length of around thirty-one." He dug into a stack of pants, pulled a pair out from the middle and handed them over. "Here we are. I think these should do." Before Tom could respond, Mister Felder gave him a belt and was into another pile of garments from which he produced a white, short-sleeved dress shirt that buttoned up the front.

"Mister Felder," Tom protested, "I used to wear pants that were thirty-three inches in the waist. I think these may be too small."

"I can see by your frame that you used to be a larger man, Mister Wallace," Mister Felder replied, "but I'm afraid you will have to eat quite a bit to regain your physique and fit into your former clothes. Unfortunately, every single one of the inmates I have seen that come out of that building are in the same condition as you are now — or worse. I tell you what. I have a fitting closet right over there in the corner. Why don't you try those on? If you don't approve of the way they fit, I can assure you that you will leave my store with whatever size you wish. Oh, and one more thing," he said, tossing Tom a pair of cotton boxers, "you might appreciate these, too."

"Thank you, sir," Tom said, smiling as he headed to the closet. "I'll be right back." Closing the door, Tom shed his prison attire in a matter of seconds and it didn't take much longer to be dressed and admiring his new clothes in the mirror. Amazingly, everything was just a shade too big. Walking back into the room, Tom said, "I guess you were right. I might need to put on a little weight."

"Let me see," said Mister Felder, as he tugged at Tom's waist. "I think these will do nicely. I'm sure you'll outgrow them once you re-establish your weight but, if I were to sell you the clothes you'll grow into, they would be so big I imagine you'd be very uncomfortable in them, indeed. I'm assuming you have a trip to take soon and, if it were me, I would just as soon be comfortable than not."

"I think I would, too, now that you mention it," Tom agreed. "If you can fix me up with a good pair of boots and a hat, I'll be set. What have you got along those lines?"

"Right over here we have a fine selection of footwear." Mister Felder led Tom over to the side wall of the store. "This particular brand is put together very well. They are made right here in town and I personally know the man who makes them. I own two pair myself." He paused, put his hand on his chin and said, "I mean no offense but, my goodness, those are a hideous pair of shoes, aren't they?" He chuckled as he looked at Tom's feet.

"You're not the first person who's told me that this morning," laughed Tom.

"Well, thankfully for you, I'll be the last. You look like a size eleven?" asked Mister Felder.

"Twelve," Tom corrected.

"Twelve. My goodness, that is a large foot," he said. "But I happen to have that very size down here at the bottom of the pile." He pulled out a box, handed it and a pair of socks to Tom, adding, "I think you'll be pleased with these, too."

Seconds later Tom couldn't believe how good it felt to be standing there wiggling his toes in a brand new pair of boots. He went back to the fitting closet and gazed proudly at his new outfit in the mirror before walking back onto the main floor.

"Mister Felder, I saw some hats you have up there in the front window, but I didn't see any white straw Stetsons. Do you have any of those?"

"I certainly do," Mister Felder said as he adjusted his glasses, "but they just came in yesterday evening and I haven't had the opportunity to put them on display yet." He paused to take a good look at Tom's head, trying to gauge his hat size. "If you would give me a minute or two, I will be right back with a couple from which you can choose." Mister Felder turned and went through a door leading back into his store room.

Having everything else he needed to make the trip back home, Tom turned his attention away from clothes to the knick-knacks and novelties littering the tops of shelves, countertops and everything else that had a flat surface. His eye caught a crystal decanter with a set of matching glasses that closely resembled the set his mother displayed proudly in her china hutch back home. He couldn't ever remember anything being served out of them. Because of that, he didn't understand why she had gotten so upset when he accidentally broke one of the glasses when he was ten or eleven.

She didn't scold him much and he already felt bad about it, but he felt worse than he ever had in his whole life when she spent the rest of the day in her room crying, just loud enough for him to hear when he put his ear to the door. When she came out later that evening to put dinner on the table, she acted like she had just taken a nap and nothing in the world had happened, but Tom knew better. He told himself at the time he would never forget that day and, sure enough, he hadn't.

Tom heard the front door bell jingle as he sauntered across the floor to where the decanter was displayed and, without taking his eyes off it, he carefully lifted the expensive crystal bottle up in both hands and held it up, staring in wonder at the different colors of light passing through it.

"What the hell you doin' there, boy?" Jack Pruitt demanded.

Tom fumbled the crystal in mid-air, but somehow managed to catch it before it smashed to pieces on the hard wooden floor. He didn't know the man talking to him, but he knew the tone of a prison guard. He carefully replaced the decanter but, because his hands were trembling uncontrollably, the sound of glass jarring against the table top briefly filled the store.

"I see you got yourself a new set of clothes there, didn't ya, boy?" Pruitt barked as he unsnapped his holster strap, glaring at Tom and the decanter he had been admiring. "Whatcha gonna do with that? Need to get you a fancy bottle, too?"

Tom said nothing as he stared at the guard apprehensively.

The guard gave Tom a hateful grin as he continued. "Unless ya just robbed somebody on the way over, I know ya don't have any money. Maybe yer plannin' on robbin' this place. Which is it, boy, huh?"

His hand drew closer to the handle of his pistol as he asked again, louder, "Well, ya got any money, boy?"

Tom's right hand instinctively went to his hip where his gun would have been if he were home. He quickly raised his hands, not wanting to give the man a reason to draw, and stammered, "I...I don't have any money but..."

Tom's words were cut short as their attention was drawn to the sound of the bell as the front door opened.

"What's going on here?" Jim demanded. He had finished getting his boots cleaned and was making his way toward the door when he glanced through the windows to see a man about to draw down on Tom. Bad leg and all, Jim Wallace could move pretty quickly when adrenalin took over, and he charged through the doors with such force that the bell was knocked off its perch and went flying through the air before coming to rest with a clank on the floor behind the cash register.

"Mister, ya need to get the hell away from here. Right now!" Pruitt growled, trying to keep an eye on Tom and talk to Jim at the same time. "I got state business goin' on, and you got no part of it, ya hear?"

"That's where you're wrong." Jim closed the distance with long strides. "That's my son there and I sure as hell *will* have a part in it."

The situation suddenly changed for Pruitt. He had come over to Felder's hoping to stop a robbery, and he wasn't willing to let go of that idea just yet. Even though neither of these two men appeared to be armed and the father looked as if he could afford most anything in the place, Pruitt was outnumbered now, and Mister Felder was nowhere to be seen. They didn't give a lieutenant's office to a man who backed down much, and he was anxious to prove he could handle the situation. With his right palm still resting on the handle of his pistol, he looked at Jim, held up his left and said forcefully, "Stop right there, mister!"

Jim took a few more steps and stopped about six feet away. "Who the hell are you?" he demanded.

"Sergeant Jack Pruitt," the guard responded. He didn't mention that he wasn't a real lawman or that he wasn't on duty. He hoped if he said his name with enough force it might make the older man back off. It didn't.

Jim looked Pruitt over with disgust. "You're not the sheriff. You're a prison guard, aren't you?"

"What difference does it make?" Pruitt retorted. "I'm the one with the gun and I want to know how this here fella plans on payin' for all this. He looked at Jim suspiciously and asked, "You got any money?"

There were two things the guard had done up to this point that made Jim hopping mad. The first was to almost draw on his son for buying some clothes, and the second was the way he asked him if he had any money, implying he was some kind of poor white trash. Jim didn't know if he could take a third. Without taking his eyes off the guard, he reached around to his back pocket to pull out his wallet.

"Put your hands in the air!" yelled Pruitt, drawing and leveling his pistol at Jim.

Jim slowly raised his hands and glanced over at Tom, who stood still and white as a ghost. Looking back at the guard, Jim said through clenched teeth, "I'm not armed, you fool! You asked me if I had any money. I was going to show you."

"I don't know if you're armed or not and I sure as hell am not going to take your word for it," Pruitt said, keeping the gun aimed at Jim's middle. "Turn around and put your hands on that table. I'll be the one to see if ya got any money."

Jim slowly turned around, and bent over a small lamp table, carefully moving several glass curios out of the way to make room for his hands. Suddenly, they were all startled by the sound of the rear storeroom door opening.

"Oh, my word!" gasped Mister Felder, as he entered carrying three hat boxes and caught sight of the three men. "What in the good Lord's name is going on here?"

"I have reason to believe these two men here were goin' ta…" was all Pruitt had the chance to say. He had glanced at Mister Felder but when he turned his attention back to Jim, he saw a shiny flash from the corner of his eye and felt something that caught him square on the side of the head.

The ashtray shattered as soon as it made contact with Pruitt's skull and dropped him to the floor like a sack of flour. The wallop sent him down sideways, and he took out a narrow sideboard full of glassware that shattered in every direction. Fortunately, his gun didn't go off and landed with a thud on a sack of corn feed.

"Damn, that hurt!" yelled Jim, shaking his hand wildly as if that would stop the pain.

"Holy Mother of God!" said Tom in disbelief as he rushed over to the unconscious sergeant. "I hope you didn't kill him!"

"I didn't kill him. But I hope the horse's ass has a hell of a headache when he wakes up." Jim covered his bleeding palm with a clean white handkerchief.

They were all bent over looking at the unconscious man when they heard the sound of applause at the front of the store. They looked up to see Bear standing there with a huge grin on his face, clapping as hard as he could and piercing the air with a long horse whistle.

"I gotta tell ya — I'd a paid big money to see somebody do that, and I got to see it for free!" He wiped his hands together gleefully. Making his way over, he said, "What a great day this turned out to be! Howdy, Mister Felder," he added, pointing at Jim and Tom, "these two are the ones I told ya 'bout last night, but it looks to me like y'all met already."

It took a minute for Mister Felder to regain his composure. His face was still as white as Tom's. "I...I am...the name is Felder," he finally got it out, looking at Jim. "This is my store. You must be Tom's father."

"I am," Jim said as he shook hands. "I'm sorry for the trouble. We weren't looking for it," he said as he glanced down at the guard. "He's got a pretty good gash on the side of his head. Tom, why don't you get those clothes the state gave you this morning and bring them over here so we can stop the bleeding. And, Bear, hide that gun of his somewhere so he can't find it when he comes to."

Tom left his prison clothes in the fitting closet, but had them back in a hurry and soon his old shirt was tied around the unconscious guard's head.

"Bring that gun to me," said Mister Felder. "I'll put it in my safe for now and say I found it tomorrow, after you two are well on your way."

Bear picked up the pistol, then walked over and handed it to Mister Felder, who turned to Jim and asked, "How bad is it? Should we get him to a doctor?"

"He might need a stitch or two," Jim said, "but he'll be fine."

"I don't know why this jack ass pulled down on ya," Bear said to Jim, "but I can't even begin to tell ya how many times I thought about hittin' that fool over the head with something myself. It's about time he got laid out, 'cause he's had it comin' for quite a spell." Bear shook his head as he looked at the guard, whistled once again and added, "That was beautiful!"

"I don't care for violence myself," Mister Felder said, "but I have to agree with Bear. This man has been a menace to people around here since he was old enough to know better. And he's become intolerable since he was hired on at the prison. I knew someday he would go too far and he did, right here in my store."

He grinned and added in a playful manner, as though revealing a great secret. "This could be my lucky day. The bartender over at Doorman's is not too fond of Mister Pruitt, either, and he will be anxious to hear an eyewitness account of how this took place. That should be worth a few glasses of his best whiskey."

Tom couldn't believe this was happening. If he had knocked a guard out an hour ago, he would probably be dead right now, but everybody in the room was acting like the sergeant on the floor, blood flowing out of his head, was the highlight of their day. It was insane. After waiting five long years to get back out into the real world, he now faced the possibility he could be back behind bars in a matter of minutes. His heart racing, he asked, "What are we going to do now? Dad, I just want to go home and now you almost kill a guard. A guard!" Tom was pacing and staring at the man on the floor as he continued, "We need to get out of here!"

"Slow down there, son, slow down," Jim said, getting up and walking to Tom.

He held Tom's shoulders, looking him in the eyes. "Everything's all right. We'll leave here when we're good and ready, and there won't be anybody in this town coming after you or me. I promise. Let me tell you how this is going to play out…"

He led Tom by the arm back over to Bear and Mister Felder. "First off, this so-called lawman isn't wearing a uniform. Second, he never showed any badge, and third, his biggest mistake of all was making a move for my wallet while he pointed a gun at me. He could have been trying to rob me as far as I'm concerned and I wasn't going to let him do it. I defended myself, simple as that."

"Now that ya mention it," Bear said, rubbing the top of his head and pointing to the front door, "that's how it looked from where I was standin'."

The three men glanced over to the entrance and were startled to see a good number of people peering in through the windows, trying to get a glimpse of what just occurred. A few of the braver ones had quietly slipped inside for a better view. "They probably saw the same thing, too," he chuckled.

"Hopefully it won't get that far," said Mister Felder as he weighed the situation, "but, if I must, I will say the same thing in a court of law. Mister Pruitt held a gun on Mister Wallace and was reaching for his wallet. That *is* what I saw."

Tom relaxed a bit, wanting to believe them, but he wasn't convinced. "How can you be so sure?" he asked. "Nobody can just go around knocking out prison guards. I know how these guys think. He's going to be mad as hell when he wakes up and I'm sure he's going to want a piece of me to make up for the split in his head."

"That's not going to happen," Jim said. "There's nothing this idiot can do to you or me because too many people saw the whole thing, so relax." He could see the fear in Tom's eyes fade but asked one more time, "All right?"

"Your daddy's right," Bear said, nodding.

"He most certainly is," chimed in Mister Felder.

Tom could feel his anxiety start to evaporate. "So what happens next?" he asked.

Jim was a step ahead of him. He spoke loudly to the faces at the door, "Can one of you people run and get a doctor? This man's going to need a stitch or two." A few faces disappeared from the other side of the window pane.

Jim turned his attention back to his son. "Tom, did you find what you came here for?"

"Yes, sir. Everything except a hat," Tom said.

"Well, go pick one out," Jim said. "I know you're worried right now, but go on; everything's okay." He turned to Mister Felder, adding, "Let's get to the register and settle up. I need to pay you for the clothes and the damages."

"I can assure you, Mister Wallace, you will not be charged for any damages," Mister Felder said as they made their way to the register. "I am afraid, however, Mister Pruitt will receive an itemized bill for any merchandise that's in even the slightest state of disrepair." He had a sly smile and a gleam in his eye as he added, "The list will be quite lengthy, I'm sure."

"Do you think he'll pay?" asked Jim.

"He will eventually," Felder said. "Mister Pruitt has been on a cash-only basis for some time because I used to have to make him pay his overdue bills by showing up in the front office of the prison. At that point, he was always miraculously willing to settle his tab without delay."

Jim laughed. "That's not a big surprise, but total me up so I can pay you. Do you take cash?"

"Every day if I can help it," chuckled Mister Felder, moving behind the register. He bent down and hid Pruitt's gun under the counter, then straightened up and said, "Now then, let's see what we have here." He adjusted his glasses and went to work with his pencil. After a few minutes of calculations, he looked up and said, "Everything comes to a total of sixteen dollars and six cents."

"Sixteen dollars and six cents?" Jim repeated as he reached for his wallet.

"Yes, sir, and I can tell you that you will not find a better price in town," Mister Felder said proudly.

"I believe you," Jim said, handing over the money. "Mister Felder, it's been a pleasure doing business with you."

"Likewise," the store owner said. "I can tell you have been in a few scrapes in your time and, I must say, I was quite impressed with the way you handled yourself."

"It was nothing," replied Jim. "I've been in worse spots before with men who were a whole lot smarter than he is."

Bear joined them at the counter as Tom walked up wearing his new hat. "We've got a few more stops to make before we leave, so please tell the sheriff if he wants to talk to me about this, I shouldn't be too hard to find."

"I will, and thank you for coming by," said Mister Felder.

"I got a idea," Bear said with a mischievous grin, "that boy's about to wake up. You fellas wanna stick around a little so's we can see the look on his face when the pain hits him? That'll be worth a good laugh."

"Not me," Tom pleaded. "I'd like to get out of here right away, if we could."

"Fine by me. Let's go," said Jim. They all turned for the front door. "Tom wants to visit somebody about a mile from here so we better head that way if we're going to get back and have that lunch before our train leaves."

They hadn't taken three steps when the door opened and the town doctor came in carrying his bag and giving them all a slow stare as he walked by.

"Over here, Doc," Mister Felder said, coming from behind the counter and leading the way to Jack Pruitt. Looking back, he added, "Good luck to both of you, and don't hesitate to come back if you need anything before you leave."

"Thank you," Jim said as they went through the door.

"That's a good-lookin' hat you got there," Bear said to Tom as they came out onto the sidewalk and made their way to the wagon parked on the other side of the crowd now starting to break up. The people outside were all talking about what just happened and were slowly wandering off because the show was over.

Before Jim and Tom reached the wagon, Bear stopped them, saying, "Hold on, fellows. I'd like to introduce y'all to someone." They turned and walked to the older woman with the blue-and-white dress who stood waiting on the sidewalk. With a big grin, Bear said, "Jim, Tom — this here is Miss Berta Wortham."

"Ma'am," they said in unison, tipping their hats.

"Gentlemen, good morning," she said eagerly, nodding her head as she nimbly worked up a breeze with her pocket fan. "That was very exciting, if I do say so myself. I saw the whole thing and I can honestly tell you there won't be too many people around here upset over this. In fact, I hope it takes several years for Jack Pruitt to live it down. I swear, that man has been mean and rude to little kids and old folks alike, and everybody in between for near as long as I can remember. It's about time somebody came along and gave Mister Pruitt what he deserved. I'm sorry, but that's just how I feel." She added with conviction, "I'm going to have to say a few prayers this Sunday for saying that, but I know the Lord will forgive me."

Unsure how to respond, Jim said, "Well, it's nice to meet you, ma'am." They tipped their hats again before making their way back to the wagon.

"I'll be with y'all in just a minute," Bear said with a wink before turning to give his undivided attention to Miss Wortham.

Before they were out of earshot, Jim and Tom could hear Bear ask the lady in a sly tone, "Do you think I can come over later and *see 'em*?" The question made Jim jerk his head back to see Miss Wortham trying to hide her blushing face behind her fan, now moving faster than the wings of a hummingbird.

"Well…" she said slowly, as if thinking it over. Then she added coyly, "I suppose that would be all right. Say around six o'clock?"

"Six it is," smiled Bear. He lightly squeezed her hand, then turned and headed to the wagon. He was about to climb in when he looked up and saw the look on Jim's face. He laughed as he stepped onto the floorboard and said, "I can't help it if I'm charmin'."

All he got in return was a tongue-tied stare and a shake of the head, so he untied the reins, leaned over a bit to look past Jim and asked Tom. "Peckerwood Hill?"

"Yeah," said Tom.

"How did you know where he wanted to go?" Jim was surprised.

"You'll know why when we get there," said Bear. "It's not far." He popped the reins and the mare pulled the wagon away from the sidewalk and past Miss Wortham, who was steadily fanning herself as she continued to blush. Jim and Tom tipped their hats to her for the last time as the wagon started back down the street toward the prison.

Moses-Henry was standing at the edge of the sidewalk and yelled at Jim as they were moving away, "Mista, ya gotta free shine at this here stand any ol' time ya want."

Jim nodded at the man and mouthed the words, "Thank you."

Tom listened vaguely to Bear and his dad talking about something, but he wasn't much interested. His mind was still running a mile a minute over the episode in the store, forming a thousand different thoughts about what might happen before they left this town. His eyes were on the roof tops to see if they harbored a shooter. He gazed up and down the streets and sidewalks, scanning for anyone coming for them or laying a trap. His dad and Bear were yapping away like they had never been more relaxed in their lives and, even though Tom was trying to act like he was, he knew full well the apprehension he felt wouldn't ease until they were well on their way back home, listening to miles of railroad track clicking out a beautiful, steady tune beneath the wheels of a fast-moving train. Only then would he be able to breathe a true sigh of relief.

CHAPTER 4

Peckerwood Hill

Bear turned around and waved at Miss Wortham as the wagon moved back down the hill toward the prison, then glanced at Jim, who was still looking at him in disbelief. With raised eyebrows, Bear innocently asked, "What?"

"Well, I know it's none of my business…" Jim said, "…but did you just ask her what I *think* you asked her?"

"I sure did," Bear said, "we have a code: whenever we make plans to get together at her place, we pretend I'm going over there to see a couple of old vases she has in her room. She thinks it's more proper that way."

"She sounded like a church-going, God-fearing woman to me," Jim said.

"Church-goin', God-fearin' women need love, too," Bear smiled. "Besides, she'll be talkin' to God shortly after I get over there."

"Geez, Bear, I didn't need to know that!" Jim said, as if disgusted. "Hell! Now I'm sorry I asked."

Bear shrugged and winked. "Like I said, I'm charmin."

They all laughed as the wagon moved farther away from the store, then Bear changed the subject with a gleam in his eyes, "I gotta tell ya, Jim, that sure was somethin' to see! Remind me never to make ya mad in a saloon."

Bear reenacted the knock-out punch in Felder's. "Ol' Pruitt turned his head for about a second — and pow! that was the end of that! Bang, down he goes. He never knew what hit him!" He shook his head. "But I gotta a question for ya, now. Ya acted like ya been in some pretty tough spots before;

is that how ya got your leg busted up?"

"I suppose," Jim answered, as he unconsciously looked at his leg and rubbed it. "I got this in the war. It's a long story, but basically my horse fell on me."

Bear could see Jim didn't want to get into it, so he said, "What'd ya do, hit him over the head with your pistol 'cause he wouldn't stop?" He chuckled. "That's what happened, huh? Ya got mad at the damn horse 'cause he wouldn't stop, so ya knocked him out cold with your gun. That'll teach ya. Let me give you a simple rule: don't ever knock a horse out cold while you're ridin' it," he said, and pointed at Jim's leg, "and that kinda thing won't happen."

Jim couldn't help but laugh. "I guess I should have thought of that."

"Hey, Bear," Tom said nervously as they came to the first intersection, "we don't have to go right past the front of the prison, do we? Can't we go around somehow?"

"Sure thing. I understand," Bear said. He added with a reassuring nod, "I'll turn here and head south past the depot. I'll give ya plenty of room between the prison and this here wagon."

"Thanks," Tom replied as the wagon turned. He leaned back in the seat a little and was relieved for a few moments as The Keep Hotel temporarily blocked out the view of the prison, but The Walls was an imposing structure that could be seen clearly from miles around, and it wasn't long before Tom could feel the red bricks staring down at him again. He purposely tried to keep his thoughts from running rampant by looking at all the different people, businesses, homes and churches dotting the landscape south of town, and was soon lost in the sights of things he hadn't seen for some time. There were flowers in tended gardens, freshly washed laundry hanging from clothes lines waving in the breeze, small children playing hide and seek, and people going places like they had all the time in the world to get there.

He also noticed that those same people no longer stopped and stared as the wagon passed. Some would wave at Bear because they knew him, but now that Tom wore normal clothes, no one seemed to regard him as a carnival sideshow anymore and, for the first time, he felt he was no different than they were. It was a wonderful feeling and he silently soaked it all in. He knew the wagon made a left somewhere, and his dad and Bear never stopped talking but, for quite a while, all Tom could do was quietly drown in long-lost sights of the free world. He had no idea how much time had passed before they arrived, and he wasn't able to remember the route they took or recall a single word spoken along the way, but he would remember the ride to Peckerwood Hill for the rest of his life.

Tom came out of his trance at the sight of rows upon rows of white crosses lining a gentle hill on their right. He pointed and asked Bear, "Is that it?"

"That's it," he replied.

"Peckerwood Hill is a cemetery?" Jim asked, astounded.

"It's the prison cemetery," explained Bear. "All the inmates call somebody a 'peckerwood' if they come from a real poor family. They call this here 'Peckerwood Hill' 'cause the inmates who die in custody and get planted here either don't get claimed by anybody or their families don't have enough money to bury them proper."

"Is there anybody in there who's not a prisoner?" Jim asked.

"Nope, only inmates," replied Bear. "The story is, the land owners gave the land to the state in 1855, but the prison's been buryin' fellas in there since the beginnin' back in 1848. There's twenty-plus acres in Peckerwood Hill and the deed says the guards was plantin' the inmates there 'by mistake,' but let me tell ya, there was no mistake about it. They'd been puttin' fellas in there for quite a while 'fore the owners finally realized the land was worthless, and the only thing they could do at that point was to hand the tract over to the state 'cause the prison wouldn't stop diggin' fresh holes. There's seven years of unmarked graves somewhere in that cemetery, and the rest of 'em would be too if it weren't for the inmates. They're the ones that put up all them crosses ya see now. The state couldn't care less." There was a moment of silence before Bear looked at Tom and asked, "I guess ya came to see somebody?"

"Yeah, I got a friend buried in there," Tom said. "I promised I'd stop by before I left."

"How long ago did he die?" asked Bear, bringing the wagon to a stop.

"About a year and a half ago," Tom said. "He tore up his leg pretty bad working the rock quarry but it was a week or so before they sent him back to The Walls to get him to a doctor. He was in bad shape when he left and I didn't know if he was going to make it or not, so when I got back to The Walls, I asked some of the guys that worked burial detail about him and they said he passed on before the doctor had a chance to look him over. They told me where they put him, though, and we sort of had a pact with each other that if something were to happen to either one of us, the other would make sure to stop and say good-bye."

The men stared at the seemingly endless rows of sad wooden crosses covering the hillside.

"If y'all don't mind waiting, I'll be right back."

"Of course, son," Jim said. "Take all the time you need."

Tom was stepping down from the wagon when the sound of horses coming at them on a run made them all turn to look. Tom froze when he saw the three riders bearing down on them; Jack Pruitt was one of them. He looked at his dad in a panic. "It's the guard!"

"Sure enough is," Bear said calmly. "He's got Sheriff Zeb Coleman there on his right, and that'd be his deputy, Charlie Cobb, on the left."

"Well, I figured once that idiot woke up he'd try to do something," Jim said as he turned to look at his son. "Tom, don't say anything; just stand there and look relaxed. I'll handle this."

Jim watched the three men ride up to them, taking a good look at the two lawmen as they approached. The sheriff seemed to be around fifty years old, sported a white handlebar mustache and wore a wide-brimmed black Stetson. A brass badge was pinned to the dark vest he wore over a white, long-sleeved shirt. His face was weathered and, even though he was not a big man, he gave the impression he had seen most everything in his time and could settle any situation justly and without hesitation.

The deputy was a lot younger and bigger. He also wore a wide Stetson, only he wore no vest and his badge rested against his plain white shirt. Jim thought to himself, "*The old bull and the young.*" From habit, he also took a long admiring look at the two fine horses they rode.

"Howdy, Zeb," said Bear, as the sheriff and the prison guard pulled up along one side of the wagon and the deputy on the other. "What can we do for ya?"

The sheriff nodded at the prison guard, who now had neatly wrapped gauze on his head, and said, "This man here says he was in Felder's and one of y'all assaulted him." He pointed at Jim and added, "He says it was you."

"I didn't 'assault' anybody," said Jim, "and you're going to get the same story out of the three of us you got from everybody else who saw what happened. I don't know who that man is, but I thought he was going to rob me right there in the store, so I laid him out. By the way," he added, turning to look Jack Pruitt in the eyes, "he must have a real soft head because he went down faster than any man I've ever seen and I don't think it's a good idea for him to be up on a horse right now. He's probably real light-headed. There's a good chance he'll fall off and hurt himself again."

The guard's eyes were in flames as he blurted, "You sucker-punched me, you son of a bitch!"

"Shut up, Pruitt!" yelled Sheriff Coleman. "I told you we'd get to the bottom of this, but you have to shut the hell up. You hear me?" He looked at Jim again and said, "Tell me what happened from the beginning."

"Well, I picked up my boy from the prison this morning and took him to the store to buy some decent clothes," Jim said. "I sent him in ahead of me, and next thing I knew, this jack ass is about to draw down on him for not having any money. I guess he must have seen him go into the store and figured he was going to rob the place but, when I went in to show him I had money to pay for everything, he drew on me — and went for my wallet." Jim glared at the guard and added with disgust, "Never in all my years have I heard anybody claim they got sucker-punched when they were holding a gun on someone, but I guess there's a first time for everything. They didn't test him for smarts when they hired him on at the prison, did they?"

"So help me, God, I'm gonna make you pay before you leave this…" Pruitt began.

"The both of you need to stop right there," roared the sheriff. "I don't need any smart mouths right now from either one of you. You hear?"

"You're right, Sheriff," Jim said. He knew that now was the time to back off, but he still felt good about the fact that Pruitt was so mad he was about to blow out the blood vessels on both sides of his head.

Sheriff Coleman asked, "Bear, did you see what happened?"

"Saw the whole thing," Bear answered. "I was standing in the front of the store by the register when I saw that man," he pointed to Pruitt, "hold a gun on that man," he pointed at Jim. "Pruitt reached for his wallet. Looked to me like Jack made the mistake of tryin' to rob Jim here, but the only thing he's got to show for it is a busted-up head. I woulda done the same thing if it was me."

Bear stared down the guard, then glanced back to the sheriff and added, "Zeb, you know most everybody in town thinks Pruitt here is a horse's ass. Hell, I thought about hittin' him over the head with a skillet lots of times over at the diner, and I'da done it for sure if he pulled a gun on me the way he did Jim."

Tom was trying to act calm, but sweat was rolling off his brow and his stomach was in knots, so knew he wasn't doing a good job of it. It didn't help matters knowing the deputy was right beside him with his hand on his gun.

He could barely get the words out when the sheriff asked him, "You there, tell me what happened."

"I…I went in to buy some clothes, but…the next thing I know, that man," Tom stammered as he pointed at Pruitt, "came out of nowhere and…pulled a gun on me. My dad came in and stopped him."

He held his breath the longest ten seconds of his life before the sheriff finished eyeing the three of them and eased the tension by saying, "That's pretty much the story I've gotten from everybody so far, but there's one other issue. Pruitt here says one of you stole his gun."

"We stole his gun?" Jim asked in disbelief.

"Yes, sir." The sheriff looked into the back of the wagon. "I'm going to have to ask you to show me what you got in that there travel bag."

"Sure thing," Jim said, reaching behind the seat and pulling his bag into his lap. "That pistol's got to be in that store somewhere but we didn't give any thought in trying to find it."

"We couldn't find it," the sheriff stated calmly.

Jim threw his arms up in an exaggerated motion. "All I can tell you is, he went down so hard his arms went flying this way and that. Hell, that gun could be anywhere in that store. I'm sure it will turn up."

"I'm going to get my turn at you," Pruitt blurted as he tried to glare a hole through Jim.

"You already did," Jim said coldly. He opened the bag, exposing the contents to the sheriff. "See, Sheriff? No gun in here. It has to be in that store."

"All right, fellas, here's the deal," Sheriff Coleman said, adjusting himself in the saddle and looking them all over, "Pruitt here's got a busted head, all right, but he doesn't have a leg to stand on, so nobody's goin' to jail for…"

"Damn it, Zeb! You can't just let them walk away from this!" interrupted Pruitt, whose face had turned brick red. He pointed at Jim, "Not after he…"

"I told you to shut the hell up, Pruitt," yelled the sheriff. "If you open your mouth one more time, I'm going to let you cool off for the rest of the day in one of my cells. You got that? In fact, I want you to get away from here right now so I can finish what I need to say to these fellas."

The guard just sat on his horse, scowling at Tom and Jim with pure hatred, so the sheriff shouted again, "Damn it, Pruitt! I've had enough! If I have to tell you again, I'll be happy to explain to the warden why I locked you up."

He looked at the deputy and said, "Charlie, get Pruitt the hell away from me — or take him to jail. I don't care which."

"He's not the fastest horse in the barn, is he?" Jim asked as Charlie escorted the guard away.

"Never was and never will be," Bear said, grinning.

Tom felt a great deal better when the sheriff smiled, shook his head and said, "Lord knows that's right." Then he turned serious again. "But look here, men, I know Pruitt has everybody in this town wondering why he hasn't got his head split open long before now, and I'm sure he deserved it, but I can't put up with out-of-town folk, one of which just got out of prison, knocking the tar out of my citizens, no matter what."

Tom blurted, "I was only in there to…"

The sheriff raised his hand. "Relax. I know you were minding your own business, but you both need to listen to me — and listen good. This is my town, and these people pay me to make sure nothing like this happens to them so, if I get wind either one of you is causing any more trouble, of any kind, anywhere near my city limits, I'm going to make sure whoever is involved gets real familiar with the jail here in Huntsville. Do you both understand what I'm sayin'?" He was looking at Tom as he finished, so Tom answered first.

"Yes, sir," he said with relief. "I just want to go home."

The sheriff turned to look at Jim. "We clear?"

"Sheriff, I didn't come here to cause trouble," Jim said. "I'm just picking up my boy and taking him home, that's all. Mister Felder knows where his pistol is and he's going to give it back to that numbskull as soon as we're on our way out of this town. Who the hell gave that idiot a gun, anyway?"

"That's a good question," chimed in Bear. "I've wondered about that a bunch of times myself."

"You'll have to talk to the prison board about that one," said the sheriff. He sighed and shook his head as if to say it eluded him as well.

"Sheriff," said Jim, "all we want is to be left alone, so I need to ask you a favor."

"What kinda favor?" asked the sheriff.

"I need you to keep that moron away from us for the rest of the morning. I understand your position, but we'll be on the train at noon headed back home and nobody in this town will ever see us again," Jim said. "But that idiot over there needs to understand that if he comes after me again, I won't hesitate to bust up the other side of his brainless head."

Sheriff Coleman chuckled, but went back to his point. "I'll make sure

52

he stays away from y'all by letting him simmer down at the jailhouse with Charlie for a while," he said, "But, Mister Wallace, you've had people talking about you ever since you got off that stage yesterday and now you're in the middle of this mess."

He paused to peer at Jim closely. "Personally," he said, "I don't care how many head of cattle you got but, because of that, there's gonna be more than a few jealous people in this town wanting to know why I didn't throw you in jail for bustin' up a state employee. So right now you need to know — I don't care what your reasons are. If I find out you're involved with any more trouble, I'll lock you up, plain and simple. These lawyers 'round here can get mighty expensive, and we got a judge that hates rowdy types comin' into town causin' disturbances, so you'd best make sure I don't hear your name again today. Otherwise, you'll find yourself in Huntsville a lot longer than you planned, and you won't be stayin' in The Keep Hotel. This is the last time I'm gonna tell you. Ya got it?"

"I think we understand each other," Jim said calmly.

"Good then. Y'all can go on about your business." Sheriff Coleman tipped his hat. "Good day," he added. Then he turned his horse and rode off to join Jack Pruitt and his deputy.

"Don't worry," Bear said as they watched Sheriff Coleman ride up alongside the other two men, "he knows he can't lock ya up for anything. There was too many people that saw what happened."

"Do I look worried?" Jim asked.

"No, but your son sure does." Bear said with a laugh, but he suddenly stopped when he noticed that Tom was white as a ghost for the second time today as he stared toward the three receding horsemen. Bear turned to see the enraged prison guard abruptly turn his horse and head back for them at a full gallop.

"Guess he still has something to say," Bear said.

Neither Jim nor Bear flinched a bit when Jack Pruitt pulled reins alongside the wagon and snarled as he looked at Jim, "Let me tell you something, mister. Ya better make damn sure your boy don't ever wind up in prison again 'cause here's what's gonna happen if he does: I'll quit whatever post I have and transfer to wherever they send him just to make sure I get to make him dig his own grave and watch him fall into it. I swear to God, if he comes back for so much as kickin' a dog, you'll never find out what happened to him. Ever."

"Get the hell out of here, Pruitt," Bear snarled as he bolted from his seat.

"You no good piece of shit, you've gone too far. You come off that horse right now 'cause this time, I'm gonna kick your ass."

"He's not worth it, Bear," Jim said.

"You ain't gonna do nothin', old man," Pruitt hissed, focusing his rage on Bear. "Your boy's buried out there someplace in the middle of nowhere 'cause he deserved what he got. You ain't never gonna find him." He pointed at Tom. "And it'll be the same for that one if he ever comes back here. I can promise you that. And I'm gonna tell you something else, too, you might as well start lookin' for a new job 'cause I'll make it clear to your boss nobody from the prison is gonna eat at that run-down, rat-hole of a diner anymore unless you're fired. You're out of a job, old man."

"Pruitt!" Sheriff Coleman yelled as he raced up to the wagon with Deputy Cobb. "Damn, you're a pain!" was all he could say before Pruitt pulled his horse around and sped off in the direction of town, chunks of mud flying in the air. "Charlie, follow him and make sure he don't get out of your sight. I'll catch up." The deputy spun around and took off with a flash of hooves flinging mud.

The sheriff looked at Bear. "What the hell did he say?"

"Too damn much," Bear growled. "But I can tell ya this; ya don't have to worry about Jim here anymore 'cause if he wants to split open the other side of Pruitt's head, he's gonna have to pull me off him first, and that ain't gonna be easy. I can put up with his complaints about my food," he said, climbing back into the wagon, "but he told me about my boy bein' in an unmarked grave somewhere, and I sure as hell ain't gonna put up with that."

Bear took a series of long, deep breaths as he settled into the seat and looked the sheriff in the eyes to make sure he knew he was dead serious. "Zeb, ya need to keep that jackass away from me 'cause I'll hurt him. I don't care. I'm not from outta town, so I'll take my chances in front of the judge. Hell, the judge ain't stupid; I'm bettin' he'll know Pruitt deserves it."

"Just settle down, Bear," the sheriff said. "I'll make sure he won't bother ya the rest of the day. He's not gonna like spending the afternoon in jail, but he won't be any more trouble, at least not for y'all. I give you my word. Now, if you'll excuse me, I need to take care of some things. I hope the rest of your stay in Huntsville will be a little more enjoyable."

"Thank you, I'm sure it will," Jim said.

The sheriff tipped his hat to them again, turned his horse and headed back to town.

Jim looked at Tom. "You okay?"

Tom bent over, put his hands on his knees, took a deep breath and said, "Yeah, I'm all right." After a moment, he sat up straight and added, "Whew. It has been one heck of a morning. I'll sure be glad when we're finally on that train. That guard's got it in for us bad."

"You're wrong," Bear said, still worked up. "He's got it in for everybody."

"That he does," Jim said, "but I think the sheriff will keep him tied up for a while so we shouldn't have to worry about him anymore."

He patted Bear on the shoulder and tilted his head toward his son. "Bear, what do you say we give Tom here some time to take care of what he came here to do, and then we'll all head back to town for a bite to eat. All this ruckus has given me an appetite."

"Now you're talking," Tom said with a smile. "I could use something to eat now, too. You guys just give me a few minutes and I'll be back." He was about to head into the cemetery when he stopped and asked, "By the way, one of you guys got a pocket knife I can borrow?"

"Sure thing," Bear said. He dug in his pocket and tossed him a single blade.

"Thanks," Tom said as he caught it and headed into the field of white wooden crosses that marked Peckerwood Hill.

Tom wandered halfway into the cemetery, looking at the ground trying to find the grave he had come to visit.

Bear watched him for a bit, then said to Jim, "You got a good boy there. I'm glad I was here to see the two of ya get together again."

"Thank you, Bear. I'm honored you feel that way," Jim said. "I'm sorry you never had the chance to do the same."

"Me, too," said Bear.

"He's not buried out there?" Jim asked, motioning at the rows before them.

"No, or I'da claimed him and buried him someplace nice. But the truth is, I don't have any idea where he is," Bear said soberly. "Pruitt was right about one thing; my boy is one of hundreds of other convicts buried in unmarked graves all across this state. When I first got here, folks in the prison office told me his paperwork was missin' and they would let me know when they located his grave, but everybody 'round here knows that just means they put him in a hole somewhere, covered him up and moved on like he never existed. Happens all the time."

"I'm sorry," Jim said again, sadness and disgust in his eyes.

"Don't be," Bear said. "There's nothin' anybody can do about it now. But I'll tell ya how much I despise the prison — and everybody who works in it. They wrote on his death certificate that he died of natural causes: 'shot while trying to escape'. True story."

"Are you serious?" Jim asked angrily.

"Wish I wasn't," Bear answered. "Somebody in there must think he's a funny son of a bitch. I'd like to find out who wrote that 'cause I'd show him a natural cause he wouldn't never forget. Somethin' like a shovel up against the side of his head — that oughta be natural enough."

"I don't blame you. I'd feel the same way," Jim said. "If you don't mind me asking, how long ago did this happen?"

"Sometimes it's hard to believe, but come August it'll be six years." Bear rubbed the top of his head, then wiped at his eyes.

"What was he in for?" Jim asked.

"Stealin' a horse." Bear gazed into the distance, his eyes vacant. "He and a couple of buddies got liquored up one night, and one of the other fellas made him a bet he wouldn't take this good-lookin' horse tied up 'cross the street for a quick ride. John loved a dare but, as it turned out, the horse belonged to a Texas Ranger, and those guys don't have a sense of humor at all. Maybe it's 'cause he never really did have a ma, but my boy always had a knack for findin' trouble. I can tell ya this, though, he never did nuthin' to deserve anything like what he got in the end. He was only twenty-six when he died." Bear turned to look at Tom as he moved among the graves in the distance. "How 'bout your boy? How'd he end up here?"

"Manslaughter," Jim said quietly, as he too watched Tom move from grave to grave.

"He didn't shoot somebody, did he?" Bear asked. "He don't have them beady eyes like a gunslinger."

"No, nothing like that," Jim chuckled, "and you're right, he doesn't look like the kind of man who's handy with a gun, but don't let his looks fool you."

"No kiddin'. He pretty fast?" Bear asked.

Jim only nodded in reply, causing Bear to ask again, "So what happened?"

"Oh...he got into a fight with a man in a saloon," Jim said slowly, as if recalling the event for the first time in years. "But the fellow busted his head bad when he fell and never woke up." They both were quiet for a while. "It's amazing how a man's life can change forever in just a couple of seconds, isn't it?"

"You got that right," Bear said, "and most every time for the worse."

"I have to agree with you on that one, Bear." Jim absentmindedly rubbed his bad leg. He then added something that only two men their age could truly understand. "What a man wouldn't give to go back and change a few things, huh?"

"Well," Bear chuckled, "maybe you'd only change a few things, but my list is a whole lot longer, I imagine."

Jim laughed again. "Where you from?"

"Amarillo," Bear said. "Used to work the cattle drives. That's how I learned to cook. If you're putting out a meal for those guys, you better know what you're doin' 'cause they'll bring a bad steak back and beat you over the head with it."

"How many times did that happen?" Jim asked, laughing at the image.

"More 'n once," Bear chuckled, then added with a wink, "but only in the beginnin'. I learn pretty quick."

"What keeps you here in Huntsville, then?"

"Oh, I don't know," Bear said. "I guess nothin', really. After I got news that my John was dead, I hung around stayin' as drunk as I could, thinkin' they'd eventually tell me where he was buried so I could take him back home to be with his ma but, after a while, my money ran out so I've been cookin' for folks here ever since."

Bear pointed at the mare. "'Bout a year ago, I saved up enough money to buy Niki here, thinkin' I was finally gonna ride out of this town, but we're both still here, aren't we, Niki?" The mare flicked her tail at the sound of her name and snorted in response. "Damn, I almost forgot." He reached under the seat, pulling out two bright red apples. Climbing down from the wagon, he said, "She don't like pullin' wagons so much, but she'll do it if I give her a treat every now an' then."

"Guess my legs could use a stretch, too," Jim said as he got up and carefully made his way to the ground.

He walked over to Niki and rubbed her from hindquarters to head, admiring the way her coat shone in the sun. She wasn't a big horse, just over fourteen hands high, but she was a pretty sight standing there with her four white socks and her glistening red coat and mane. Jim respected any man who took good care of his horse and he could tell Bear took great care of his.

"What is she, five, six?" he asked.

"Yep, six," Bear said as he held the apples in front of Niki. The horse went after the treats right away as Bear rubbed her head. "That's my girl," he said affectionately. "I bought her off a blacksmith here in town who didn't treat her so good. He got her as a surprise for his daughter, but neither one of 'em ever took care of her, so it took me a while to get her as good lookin' as she is now. Niki's a smart horse, with a great disposition. Maybe it's 'cause she had a rough time of it at the blacksmith's, but it's funny sometimes how I know she'd like to leave this town as much as I do. For instance, she'll watch Tilley's train when it leaves 'til it's out of sight, but she couldn't care less when it comes back into town. Yep, one of these days we're leavin', me and her."

"How about today?" Jim asked.

"How about today?" repeated Bear, looking a bit surprised. "I've asked myself that question a thousand times, but I'm still here. And I'll probably be here to ask myself a thousand more."

"Bear, I'm serious. How about today?" Jim asked. "Why don't you come back with me and Tom? We're leaving at noon."

It took Bear a second to realize what the question meant before his perplexed expression changed and he answered, "Explain to me exactly what it is you're sayin'."

Tom followed the instructions he received to the letter. The inmate he had spoken to inside The Walls was assigned to burial detail for the last five years and knew the location of all one-hundred and sixty-seven inmates buried in Peckerwood Hill during that time. The state never kept any written records, so it was up to the inmates to keep track of their dead. That inmate told Tom to go to the top of the hill where the large headstone of the Indian chief Santana was located, head west past twelve rows of crosses, then if he turned right and made his way to the eighth grave from the end, he would be standing over his friend.

Tom took his time getting there, stopping frequently to look at the white-washed pine crosses, wondering how long it would take before the sun, wind and rain erased them all. The ground over some of the graves was sunken because the pine coffins six feet below had rotted and collapsed under the weight of the dirt above, and even the newer crosses bearing the deceased inmates' numbers were so poorly made they were already falling apart. Beneath every cross was a story of the forgotten, all dying at far too early an age at the hands of the most brutal men Tom had ever met, and all buried in a cemetery where no one in the country wanted to be laid to rest. It didn't matter where an inmate was born or where he came from, whether he was working in The Walls, rock quarries, railroad lines, or any of the other prison farms scattered throughout the state; the one thing every single convict in Texas had in common with each other was the fear of winding up in this place. No one wanted to die in the penitentiary; that was bad enough. But being buried alone in Peckerwood Hill, away from your loved ones and lying within clear sight of The Walls forever, was the worst ending to a man's life anyone could ever imagine.

Tom stopped to pick some wildflowers just starting to bloom in the spring sun before finally coming to the grave he was seeking. Standing over the white cross bearing the number "4361" in the middle, Tom bowed his head and said a silent prayer. He went down on one knee, laid the flowers next to the cross and said, "Well, Lee, I made it here to see you, just like I said I would."

He pulled out the pocket knife, saying, "I'll do the best I can," and started his task. "I'm sorry we didn't get to be friends on the outside, too. Hell, you would have only lived a day's ride from my house." After a long moment, he added, "It's a damn shame your leg snapped like it did, and you had to wind up here, but at least they put you in a good spot, far as I can tell. On this side of the hill, you don't have to worry about water collecting on you, and the view ain't that bad, either." He worked the pocket knife with concentration and in silence, talking to his deceased friend as his thoughts evolved. "It's too bad about your pa not having the money to come get you," he said, "but when I get the chance, I'll ride over to Pidcoke and tell him myself you're in a good place now. He might even remember it was me who wrote that letter for you."

It took a while for Tom to finish what he set out to do and, while he was working, he'd say things like. "I think you're going to like this," and "It's looking pretty good." When he finished, he stood up and smiled as he looked down at his handiwork. On the simple wooden white cross, directly over the prison numbers, was now the name: "Lee Potts" and, underneath, "Age 31."

"There you go, Lee. It even looks like whoever did it knew what he was doing," he said proudly. "I'm glad I could keep my promise. I know you'd have done it for me."

He surveyed the sea of woeful graves around him, giving thanks for his good fortune, and remembering his friend before he felt his task was complete. "Well, I guess I gotta go now," he said, tipping his hat to the grave. He looked toward the wagon to see his dad and Bear deep in conversation in the distance. "My dad came here to pick me up, and now we're off to get something to eat. Real food, too, how about that? After that, we're headed home, so I guess this is it." Tom stood there looking at the cross for a minute longer. "So long, Lee. You were a good friend."

He turned and walked away using a different path and taking time to look at other inmate numbers on other crosses, thinking how depressing it was that every single one of the different life stories buried here in Peckerwood Hill came to the same sad conclusion and were treated by the world as if they never existed at all.

"Let me see if I got this straight. You," Bear said as he pointed at Jim, "want me," he pointed at himself, "to go to Bell County and work for you as a cook. Is that what you're telling me?"

"Why not?" Jim said. "I got the idea last night at the diner. That's why I wanted you to pick me up in the wagon because I wanted to get to know you a little first." Jim chuckled. "I just wanted to make sure you didn't talk too much."

Bear grinned. "Guess I didn't do so good on that one, did I?"

"Look," Jim said, "you know as well as I do that the difference between a good outfit and a bad one is mostly the cook. The pay is about the same from ranch to ranch, but the top hands will always go to the outfit with the best chow. I'm going to do things a little differently now that Tom is coming home, and I'm going to need a good cook. So what do you say? I think you're the man for the job."

"What's the pay?" Bear asked.

"What are you making now?" Jim asked.

"Twenty dollars a month," Bear said, and added, as if he was driving a hard bargain, "Plus room and board."

"How about thirty? Room and board would be included," Jim said.

"Hmm." Bear rubbed the top of his head, "Okay, that part sounds good enough, but what kinda room would I be stayin' in?"

"The only thing I can tell you is that you'll be bunking in a room that's a good sight better than what you've been used to in this town," Jim answered.

"That part sounds good, too, but what about Niki here?" Bear asked.

"Bring her." Jim shrugged.

"Well, then, tell me this, how many widows ya got in that town?" Bear smiled.

"Plenty, I'm sure." Jim returned the smile. "Come on, Bear, enough already. How long will it take you to be ready to leave?"

"Well," Bear said, "I need a new job anyways 'cause that fool Pruitt will get my boss to fire me, so I guess we got a deal." They sealed the agreement with a hearty handshake. "I just need to collect my things over at the diner and then stop by the livery to get my saddle. Niki and me will be ready to leave at noon. No problem."

"Good then. You won't regret it," Jim said, satisfied. "The only thing we need to do now is get something to eat before we leave."

"I know just the place." Bear grinned. "My boss owes me a bit of money and I can't think of a better way for him to pay me. Even though it's a might early in the day for steak, I betcha Tom would love me for the rest of his life if my steak and eggs was the first meal he ate after doin' all that time."

"He probably would. Why don't you ask him yourself?" Jim said, nodding.

They watched as Tom strolled up, saying, "You guys about ready?" He could see a sly grin on their faces and a look in their eyes like they were trying to hide something. "What are ya'll up to? What's going on?" he asked.

"Come on, let's get in," Jim said, motioning to the wagon. "We'll tell you about it on the way."

CHAPTER 5

Lunch

"Here ya are, fellas," Bear said, as he set steaming plates on the table.

The quaint family restaurant they sat in was built on the bottom floor of an old two-story house that once belonged to the current owner's mother. Ayer's Diner was located one block off the northeast corner of the town square and two blocks north of The Keep Hotel. It was still too early to open for the lunch crowd, but Bear lived in one of the rooms above and assured Jim and Tom there was no cause to worry about being here during off-hours. Even so, his guests had been more than a little uneasy about entering the place before it opened.

They sat at one of the many tables crammed together on the worn wooden floor, and they looked down at medium-sized T-bone steaks, sizzling alongside three eggs cooked sunny side up. A basket with a pile of hot biscuits sat in the middle of the table, and the last thing Bear did before sitting down was to grab a small jar of honey to top off the early lunch. "One a ya gentlemen want to say prayers?" he asked.

"I will," Tom volunteered.

They took a moment to cross their hands and bow their heads as he began, "Lord, thank you for this wonderful meal we are about to eat, for this beautiful day, and for taking care of my dad while I was away. Thank you for seeing me through tough times, and for our new friend Bear. May we have a safe trip home and may you smile on our fortunes from this day forward. Amen."

"Amen," said Jim and Bear in unison. A half a second later, it was serious business as six hands reached for biscuits, knives, forks, salt, pepper and honey as they all got their food ready to eat.

"That was a nice prayer," Bear said as he poured honey on a split biscuit. "I hope ya guys don't mind the menu, but it was all I could come up with on such short notice," he added with a wink.

Tom cut a piece of steak and put it in his mouth as if it might be the last bite he would ever take. After he swallowed, he tilted his head back and muttered, "I haven't had anything that good in a long time." Before he bit into the next one, he said, "Bear, you're right, I'm going to love you forever."

"I told ya he would," Bear told Jim proudly.

"I hope you guys don't mind if I ignore you for a while," Tom said, diving into the steak again.

"Careful there," Jim cautioned. "You need to eat that nice and slow or you'll get sick. It's going to take some time for your body to get used to rich foods again, so if you don't take it easy, you're likely to lose your lunch before we get on the train."

"Your dad's right," Bear said. "I trimmed off all the fat I could, but your stomach is gonna get real mad if ya don't take your time."

"Whatever you say," Tom said with a bit of sarcasm as he took another bite. "I just forgot how good a steak can be."

They ate in silence for a while, with Jim and Bear occasionally smiling at each other after glancing at Tom, who looked like he had died and gone to heaven. He finally came up for air and reached for his glass of water.

"I told you what we were talking about at the cemetery," Jim said as he watched his son chow down on the splendid meal. "Bear's accepted a job as a cook with us."

Tom looked up, startled. Then he relaxed and started eating again. "Well, Dad, you sure picked the right man for the job," he said.

"I think so," Jim said.

"Speaking of the job, what am I getting myself into?" Bear asked.

"Well," Jim said, "I've always raised cattle. Before Tom went away, I got my cows to Fort Worth by hiring out the drives to another outfit but, now that he's back, we're going to take a different direction."

"You ain't plannin' on trail drives all the way up to Kansas, are ya?" Bear asked with a raised eyebrow, "'cause I might be too old for that."

"Oh, no," Jim answered, "nothing like that. I'm too old, too. We'll probably move them over to Waco now and then, but I'll still get one of the contractors to get them the rest of the way north."

"So we need a new cook just to drive cattle over to Waco once a year?" asked Tom. He looked at Bear and said, "No offense."

"None taken," Bear said. "Was wonderin' the same thing myself."

Jim finished chewing before he explained. "We need a new cook because we're going to fence in the ranch and build some stock pens on the north side. Over the next few years, the cattle business is going to change quite a bit. There's talk of the railroad coming through Belton soon and before you know it, devil's rope will be the reason why the only cows getting to market will be on a railcar."

Tom stopped eating. "Devil's rope? What's that?" he asked.

"Barbed wire," Jim said.

"That's what they call it, huh, the devil's rope?" Tom said.

"Yeah, the Indians gave it that name," Jim said.

"I've seen it around a few pieces of property now and then when we were laying down tracks for the railroads," Tom said, "mostly farms, though."

"Well, get ready; you're going to be seeing it everywhere before too long," his father said. "Farmers love it because it keeps open range cattle off their crops, but ranchers are starting to like it, too. Four years ago, I went down to San Antonio to see this kid named Joe Gates give a demonstration to a bunch of landowners. He claimed this new wire with metal barbs could stop a herd of cattle, so he built a stock pen right in the middle of town, filled it with thirty-five or forty head, then got them all riled up. But his fence held, just like he said it would. It was pretty impressive."

"What's that got to do with us?" Tom asked.

"Everything, really," Jim said. "First, I've got enough wire in the barn to fence in the whole ranch so we can keep the free grazers out and we don't have to worry about tracking our cattle down when it's time to take them to market. Plus, I think we'll be able to breed our cattle a lot better because we can make sure the cows only get bred by our bulls. Second, after we build our stock pens, there's going to be some steady money in keeping herds for other ranchers while they're waiting to get their cattle loaded onto rail cars."

"Why wouldn't they just walk 'em over like they been doin'?" Bear asked. "What makes you think everybody's gonna need a rail car to get their cattle sold?"

"Because barbed wire is going to change everything," explained Jim, picking up his fork and finishing off the last of his eggs. "I don't know one landowner who would rather have free grazers come across his property than not, and it doesn't make any difference if it's a farmer or a rancher; nobody wants herds of cattle crossing his property. Open range days are numbered, and soon everybody who has any land at all will have it surrounded with barbed wire. Trail drives won't exist anymore."

"That's kind of a gloomy outlook on things, don't ya think?" Bear said.

"Not really. The King Ranch has already done it and they've got over a hundred thousand acres. The thing is, most everyone can afford barbed wire, and the way settlers are moving into the state and gobbling up all the land, it won't be many more years before the Chisholm Trail itself will be nothing but a patchwork of fenced-in private property," Jim said. "When that day comes, my hope is that everybody in south Texas will know the only place to keep their cows while waiting for the stock cars is at the Four C's Ranch. We'll still raise our own cattle, but I'm hedging my bets that there will be just as much money down the road renting out our pens."

"How many pens ya gonna build?" Bear asked.

"Eventually, enough to hold a few herds," Jim answered, "around four thousand cattle."

"Sheeee! That's gonna be a hell of a lot of pens," Bear said, raising his eyebrows. "How much land ya got?"

"The Four C's is the second largest ranch in central Texas," Tom said, grabbing another biscuit.

"When we get finished fencing the lines," Jim added, "we'll have almost eighty-five hundred acres."

"Well, that's big enough, all right," Bear said. "But that's a hell of a lot of work to do. So let me ask ya this: how many hands ya gonna need for all these pens you're talkin' 'bout buildin'?"

"Six…seven, counting me," Jim answered.

Bear was about to take a bite when he paused, set his fork down on the plate and asked, "Are you puttin' me on? That's too easy! You're gonna pay me thirty-five dollars a month to cook for myself and seven cowpunchers?"

"No," Jim said, taking another bite of steak, "you're going to be one of the hands, too. It'll be me, Tom, you, Aya, Chas and a couple of others, once I get them hired on."

"Now wait a second. I can't cook and dig post holes at the same time," Bear said.

"I know," Jim assured him. "You're too old to be chasing cows around on a horse and building fences, but here's the deal. You can drive a wagon and that'll be about the most work you'll do outside of cooking. I expect breakfast at six every morning, lunch at noon — unless the boys are working the perimeters and then they'll need a lunch to take with them — and dinner at seven. If we need to run into town to pick up supplies or haul wire out to one of the pastures, that'll be your job, too. That's about it."

"Ya got this all figured out, don't ya?" asked Bear.

"I think so," Jim said as he wiped his mouth and set his knife and fork in the middle of his empty plate. "It's nothing you can't handle. Besides, if there's work requiring a strong arm, myself, Tom, Chas, Aya or the new hires will take care of it. You won't have to do any work that takes too much muscle."

"Now wait a second," protested Bear indignantly, "you're makin' it sound like I'm a washed-up old man! I can handle an honest day's work, too, ya know. If you boys need a strong back every now and then, I can help out."

"Good," Jim said, "but cooking and driving the wagon is what I'll be paying you for."

Bear nodded a few times and said, "Fair enough. Who's Chas and Aya, anyway?"

"You'll meet them when we get there," Jim said. "Aya's been with me for a while. He don't say much, but you'll like him. Chas is just a kid, though and, if I had to guess which one of you talked more, I think Chas might have a leg up on you. That boy asks more questions than there are answers."

"Chas...Chas Kane?" Tom asked. "Is that who you're talking about?"

"Yep," Jim said. "That boy was after me to hire him on ever since you left, so I finally gave in and let him have a shot."

"The last time I saw him he was only about that big," said Tom, holding his hand out chest high. "How old is he now, twenty, twenty-one?"

"He'll be twenty-one in the fall," Jim said. "God bless him; that kid don't know a whole lot, but he's just like a puppy with a stick. All you have to do is tell him what to do and point him in the right direction and he takes off on a run with a smile on his face, and don't stop till whatever needs doing is done. All of you should get along just fine."

"Sounds good; can't wait to meet 'em," Bear said as he finished his last bite.

"Bear, I think that was the best meal I've ever had, but I just can't eat another bite," Tom said, leaning back and wiping his mouth. He tossed his wadded up napkin onto what was left of his steak. "I tried to eat the whole thing, but I just can't."

"I didn't figure you would," Bear said. "You're too damn skinny right now, but don't fret none. I'll get ya fattened up 'fore summer."

"You have no idea how much I'm looking forward to that." Tom rubbed his belly. "That was great!"

"Glad you liked it," Bear said, rising and grabbing their dirty dishes.

"Let me help you," Tom said, rising from his chair.

"You just sit right there," Bear said. "I clean the dishes around here, too." He piled the three plates on top of one another and was gathering the knives and forks when they were all startled by the sound of the front door opening.

"Bear, what are you doing?" asked the stately man who entered.

"Hello there, Mister Ayres," Bear said, still gathering the utensils. "I brought these two men here to get something to eat. One of 'em hadn't eaten good food in quite a while and I couldn't think of a better place to go. Let me introduce you. This here's Jim Wallace and his son, Tom." They stood as he added, "And fellas, this here is the owner of the place, Owen Ayers."

"Nice to meet you," Jim said, a little uneasy. "I hope you don't mind us being in here."

"Oh, heavens, no," said Mister Ayers. He was a kindly looking old man with white hair sticking out from beneath a gray derby and a white goatee that hung four or five inches below his chin. His dark gray overcoat and slacks were sharply tailored, and the gloves he wore made it look like he had just been a pallbearer at a funeral. He had warm eyes, and he appeared genuine as he said, "The pleasure is mine. I think everyone in town has heard by now what happened to Jack Pruitt, so please, make yourselves at home. We're going to open soon anyway. Do sit down and relax." He was in the process of taking off his gloves when he asked, "Can I get you fellows anything?"

"No, thanks." Tom rested both hands on his stomach. "I'm about to pop as it is."

"Fine, then," Mister Ayers said. He became serious and motioned Bear to the kitchen. "If you two don't mind, I need to be excused for a moment. I need to visit with Bear privately."

"No need for privacy, Mister Ayers," Bear said, walking back and standing next to the table after having set the dirty dishes in the wash bin. "I already know what ya want to say 'cause I'm sure the first thing Pruitt did after he left us at Peckerwood Hill was find ya so he could get me fired. He was pretty steamed."

"Bear, you know I can't afford to lose any customers…"

"Hey, don't worry about it, Mister Ayers," Bear said, cutting him off. "I already got me a new job anyway. I'm awful sorry; you've been good to me and all, but I'm leavin' today to work for Mister Wallace here."

"Oh? Well…I thought you might stay on until I could find someone and you could find another job," stammered Mister Ayers, obviously more than a little surprised. "What about lunch today? Who's going to cook?" he asked.

"That would be you, I guess," Bear said with a shrug. "I hate to leave ya high and dry like this, but I been wantin' to leave this town since I got here. Plus Jim here made me a heck of an offer and I gotta take it."

Although everyone in the room knew that Mister Ayers had come to fire Bear, he looked as if he might go into a panic since Bear had made his own plans to leave. He was about to say something, but paused right before the words came out, then sighed. "Well, I guess it worked out for the best, then." He pulled the extra chair away from the table, spun it around backwards, and sat down, his arms folded across the back rest. "So are you going to cook for Mister Wallace?"

"Yep," Bear said. "He likes my steaks so I'm gonna cook for cowhands again."

"I have to tell you, Bear, I'm going to miss you," Mister Ayers said, giving his cook a rueful smile like he just lost a large bet in a card game. "We were getting busy around here since I hired you, but you know how it is. If the prison boycotts anybody in this town they can be out of business in a hurry."

"I know, Mister Ayers," Bear said, scratching the side of his neck. "I'd probably fire me too if I was you, so don't feel bad. I told ya me and Niki were gonna leave sooner or later, and today just happened to be the day. I'll always appreciate what ya did for me. I'm sorry, but I gotta go."

"Well, then, I wish you the best," Mister Ayers said with all sincerity. "Oh, yes!" He stood and reached into his wallet. "We have an outstanding matter of money I owe you, so let's take care of that now."

"Don't worry about it, Mister Ayers," Bear said, raising both hands. "I figure ya don't owe me nothin' 'cause of this breakfast I just gave away. Let's call it a draw."

"Don't be silly," Mister Ayers countered, as he stuffed thirty dollars into Bear's hand. "Before you came I was doing okay but, thanks to you, we now have the reputation of being one of the best places to eat in all of Huntsville. That's worth a lot more than thirty dollars, so take the money. Please, I insist."

Bear folded the bills and put them in his pants pocket. "Thank you kindly, Mister Ayers. You're a good man."

"I'm a business man," Mister Ayers said. He walked around the table, put his arm around Bear's shoulder and held up a fifty dollar bill, waving it in the air with a raised eyebrow. "I won some money in a wonderful card game last night. On the last card, I drew the queen of spades that filled a king high straight flush that beat an aces over kings full house, so I'll tell you what we'll do. You never did tell me what was in the spices you cook with, but I'll give you this fifty dollars if you tell me what's in them, and what you used them for. What do you say?"

Bear reached out, took the bill, folded it neatly and stuffed it into the lapel pocket of Mister Ayers' jacket. "I wrote them down already," he said. "The recipes are in an envelope in the knife drawer. There's enough spice in the cupboard to last ya through the week, too."

"You sure you don't want the money?" Mister Ayers asked.

"Keep your money. I'd just blow it anyway." Bear grinned. "Really, Mister Ayers, it's the least I can do. You've done enough for me already. You're the only man in town who offered me a hand when I was down and out, and I want ya to know I'll always be grateful for that."

"Thank you very much, Bear," Mister Ayers said. "Have you got your things together?"

"Yep," Bear said as he pointed toward the door. Sitting on the floor was an old travel bag with a few good-sized holes worn through, lying next to a dirty brown cowboy hat that wasn't in any better shape. They both looked as old as Bear. "I cleaned out my room soon as we got here and what I couldn't fit in that bag, I threw out in the trash. I'm ready to go."

After a moment of silence, Mister Ayers said in mock agitation, "Well then, ya'll get out of here. I've got a diner to open up here in a little bit, so you best leave now before I put you all to work."

Jim and Tom rose from their seats. Bear grabbed his worn-out travel bag off the floor and put his old hat on while his new employers took turns shaking Mister Ayers' hand and thanking him profusely for his hospitality before making their way out the door. Bear was the last to say goodbye.

"Good luck, Bear," Mister Ayers said. "If you ever get back this way, look me up."

"I will. And good luck to you, too," Bear said as they shook hands. "One more thing; don't over-do the spices, just enough to give it some kick and you'll be fine. Oh, and these," he said, tossing Mister Ayers his key to the front door and his room. "So long now."

"So long," Mister Ayers said. He watched the three men exit the front door, then stared through the window as they got in the wagon and moved off down the street. It was only after they turned the corner into the town square and were out of sight that he reminded himself he had worked hard before and he could do it again, at least until he found someone like Bear he could trust.

"Owen, you'd better get busy; you got some work to do," he said to the empty room. With that, he turned and made his way to the kitchen. He had a long day ahead.

CHAPTER 6

The Toast

"That's a heck of a hat you got on there," Jim said, as they walked out the door onto the sidewalk. "How old is that thing?"

"Don't really know," Bear said. He moved around to the other side of the wagon and added, "Probably as old as me and y'all can make fun of it if ya want, but this one'll keep the sun off my bald head just as good as those fancy ones you two got on. Besides, mine has character. At least, that's what Miss Berta says."

"I guess you could say it does," chuckled Jim as he looked the hat over. It used to be a dark brown color but had faded with the sun over the years and now had a permanent ring stained into the sides from countless times of being worn until it was soaked. The top had a few small holes in it that might let in a little sun and, overall, the thing looked like it might disintegrate into small dusty pieces if it got caught in a strong wind. But Bear was right, Jim thought, it did have character.

"Well, at least I know I'll be able to pick you out in a crowd," he said, "that's for sure."

"You wouldn't be able to do that if I had yours on," Bear said with a smile and a wink as he climbed into the wagon. He untied the reins and adjusted his hat proudly. "I think that meal ought to hold us 'til we get to suppertime. By the way, how are we gonna go about gettin' to Belton, and how long is it gonna take us to get there?"

Jim settled into his seat. "About a day and a half. The train out of Huntsville leaves for Phelps at noon but we won't catch the one from there to Houston until two o'clock. I think we get down there about five."

Tom took his seat next to his dad and Bear got the wagon moving as Jim explained, "We'll catch the early train from Houston to Austin in the morning, and the stage from there should put us back at the ranch by sundown tomorrow evening."

"Why don't ya just take the stage from here?" Bear asked. "Belton is pretty much due west, so instead of headin' south for an afternoon and back north for another, ya could make the trip in one day instead of two."

"For two reasons," Jim answered. "First off, I've got business in Houston I need to tend to and second, the way the sun is beating down on us, by this afternoon you won't be able to find any mud anywhere this side of Oklahoma and I don't like breathing in a bunch of dust off a dry trail all day. Besides, I rode the stage over here and the ride was so bumpy it made my kidneys hurt. It wasn't my idea of a good time. I guess I've gotten a little particular about some things in my old age."

"If you're so particular," teased Bear, "how ya gonna help out with all them cow pens you're talking about? That's a lotta work, and ya can't be too particular 'bout that."

"The question is, will you be able to keep up with me when the time comes?" Jim said. "Back home, at the end of the day, I'm usually the last one into the barn. But whenever I travel, my idea of roughing it is a bad steak and a slow bartender."

"A bad steak and a slow bartender..." Bear snickered.

"I can appreciate that," Tom said. "I don't care to breathe in any more dirt. I think I've inhaled enough in the last five years to cough up a mountain."

"Ya won't get an argument from me. The train's a better trip, no doubt about it," Bear said, still laughing. "Speakin' of slow bartenders, I gotta make a stop before we head down to the livery and get my saddle." He turned the wagon to his left into town square and pointed, "Doorman's Saloon is right over there on the south side of the courthouse. After I closed up the diner last night, I got pretty thirsty and I think I had more fun than I had money. I got a tab to settle before we leave; it'll just take a minute."

"You have a tab with the bartender?" Jim asked.

"Every now and then I run a little short on cash," Bear explained. "Last night was one of those nights." He shook his head. "I learnt a long time ago that whiskey and women are two of the worst investments a single man can make, but I just can't help myself sometimes."

Jim laughed and shook his head. "I suppose we have time for a quick stop, but I'd like to get down to the depot before too long so I can make sure that train doesn't leave without us."

"Trust me," Bear said, "we'll get there. Besides, old man Tilley don't have any idea what a schedule is. If that train pulls out on time today, it'll be a first."

"Let's not goof off too much, though, okay?" Tom said, apprehensive. "I'd rather be too early than too late."

"Don't worry," Bear said, "the livery's right next to the depot, so once we leave Doorman's, I'll have us standin' on that platform inside ten minutes."

They rode in silence, watching the activity in the town square as Bear maneuvered the wagon between all the others traveling in different directions.

On the way past the courthouse, they were startled by the sharp whistle of a train. In the distance, black smoke and a burst of white steam rose into the clear blue sky, announcing that the train was coming back into Huntsville. Bear looked off to the south and said, "There's old man Tilley now. He musta had a long stay over in Phelps 'cause most of the time he'd a been back about an hour ago. Probably stopped to do a little fishin'; he does that when things are slow."

"Who's Tilley?" Tom asked.

"He's the old man that runs the train," Bear said. "When the townsfolk put up the money to build the line from Huntsville to Phelps, they hired Tilley to drive it back and forth. The rail's changed hands a couple times since then, but everybody in this town calls that line Tilley's Tap, and most believe he owns it himself. I can't say for sure one way or another, 'cause he won't let on, but he sure drives it like he owns it. He don't know what 'on time' means."

They watched the thick black smoke as it rose to the north, carried by a gentle breeze gently swaying the top branches of the tall pine trees.

"It's going be nice to see that smoke falling away behind us once we're on that train headed south," Jim said, as Bear brought the wagon to a stop in front of Doorman's Saloon.

"Yeah, it is," Tom said, *"real* nice."

Bear set the brake and was tying the reins when he looked over. "Either one of ya want to join me for a toast? It'll be a good one."

"Why not?" Jim asked. They all got down from the wagon. "It's a great idea."

"I'll buy," Tom offered as they made their way across the wooden sidewalk to the swinging front doors. "I got five whole dollars, and I can't think of a better way to spend it."

He was the last to enter Doorman's because he stopped to listen to the steam locomotive blow its whistle one more time and clang its bell, announcing it had come to a stop. He knew the time was near for him to leave this town forever. He paused a moment to enjoy his new sense of freedom, then entered the saloon, the swinging doors closing behind him as he muttered under his breath, "I'm really going home."

"Howdy Barney," Bear said as soon as he stepped inside.

The middle-aged bartender looked up at the men making their way through the nearly empty saloon. "Hey, Bear. Back so soon?"

"Yep, but I ain't gonna stay long," Bear said. "Is Thelma up yet?"

"Nah," Barney answered, "you know how it is, All them girls were pretty busy last night, so I don't expect to see any of 'em come down the stairs for another hour or so. You can stick around or come back this afternoon."

"Can't," Bear said, "by this afternoon, I'll be long gone."

"Yeah, right," Barney said. "You've been saying that ever since I've known you. How 'bout a beer?"

"Yeah, three, and three shots of whiskey for me and my friends," Bear said as they lined up next to the bar. The bartender turned to pour the beers as Bear looked at Jim. "Barney's been here forever and he's the best bartender this side of the courthouse," he announced.

"That's right across the street, so that makes me the *only* bartender this side of the courthouse," Barney shot back with a smile. "You better watch it, Bear. I ain't poured your whiskey just yet. You keep it up and it'll be a real short one."

"Aw, you wouldn't do that," Bear said. Barney put three beers on the bar. "Not to an old man taking his last shot of whiskey 'fore leavin' this town for good, would ya?"

As he poured their three shots, Barney looked up at Bear. "You pullin' my leg again, or are you really leavin'?"

"Barney," Bear said proudly, "I want to introduce you to my new bosses. This here's Jim Wallace and his son, Tom. They're the ones I told you 'bout last night." Bear waved his hand at his guests. "Jim, Tom, this here's Mister Barney Lee."

"Nice to meet you," Tom said.

"Same here," said Jim, noticing the disappointed look in Barney's eyes as they shook hands.

Barney was a stocky man of medium height, with his short hair parted down the middle, sporting an unkempt, bushy handlebar mustache that looked way too big for his slender face. He dressed neatly, wearing suspenders and a pressed, long-sleeved striped shirt, topped off by a string bow tie.

"Bear told me he was pickin' y'all up this mornin'," Barney said, "but I wish he had told me one of ya was gonna knock the hell out of ol' Pruitt, 'cause I sure would've liked to have seen *that*."

"Didn't know I was going to do it 'til it happened," Jim said. "It sure seems to have made the day for a few folks in this town."

"I'm not sayin' I hate the guy," Barney said, "but I can tell ya that if you decided to run for mayor, you'd have my vote."

"I appreciate that," Jim said, "but I don't plan on coming back here any time soon."

"Can't say as I blame you there," Barney said. He glanced at Bear before asking Jim, "But tell me this, is he really leavin' or is he just tryin' to be funny?"

"Nope, he's serious," Jim said matter of factly. "As soon as we finish these, we'll be on our way. Well, boys," he added, holding his shot glass high and the rest of them following his lead, "Here's to…"

"Wait a second, fellas," Barney said as he poured another shot. "Hell, if Bear really is leaving, my income's gonna go down some. I deserve to be in this, too."

"Pardon my manners. By all means, get yourself one, too," Jim said as they raised their glasses again. "Here's to new beginnings."

"And bright futures," added Tom.

"And new friendships," said Bear.

"And lost old ones," Barney said a little sadly.

"Cheers!" They threw their shots back, slammed the empty glasses on the bar and quickly killed the bite in their throats with a quaff of beer.

Tom had a great deal more trouble getting his shot down than the rest and got a laugh from Jim and Bear when he wiped the beer off his upper lip, choking out, "That was pretty good!" He didn't mind them laughing at him because he thought it was pretty funny, too. He let the whiskey settle as he surveyed the inside of the first saloon he'd been in for years.

The ornate wooden bar stretched from the back of the saloon along the side wall and stopped about fifteen feet from the front window. They were the only ones leaning against it, but there were two older gentlemen sitting at one of the ten or twelve tables off to the side, talking privately and sipping on beers. Pictures of cowboys and horses hung on walls covered in flowered wallpaper, and the place smelled like alcohol mixed with stale smoke. Tom's attention was drawn to the eight or nine wooden framed mirrors hung on the back wall behind the bar that made the saloon look a lot bigger than it was. But it wasn't the mirrors that caught his eye; it was the reflection of the men in them.

The other three were deep into their conversation about Bear leaving and what he was going to do at his new job, but Tom never chimed in. He just relished the smiles on their faces. He then stared into the mirror at the face of the skinny man with the new hat and clothes solemnly looking back, and suddenly remembered all the nights when he couldn't sleep as thoughts raced through his mind of the things he would do differently if he only had one more chance. Five years before, he had made a pact with himself that if he survived the ordeal of prison, he would never be the same. He nodded at his image in the mirror, saying to himself, "I promise." He then took another swig of beer in a private toast with the innermost corner of his soul.

"What's that, son?" Jim asked. He had been watching Tom out of the corner of his eye.

"Nothing," Tom said. "Maybe I'll tell you later." He looked at the other empty beer glasses on the bar, so he finished his off with one big gulp and asked, "You guys about ready?"

"How about it, Bear? You ready to leave this town?" Jim asked.

"More than ya'll ever know," Bear said with a smile. "Barney, how much do I owe ya? For last night and this round, too."

"I wanted to get this round," Tom said, reaching in his pocket.

"Don't worry about it," Barney cut him off, "this one's on the house. Believe me, it's my pleasure to buy a round for any guy that knocks Jack

Pruitt out cold." He pointed a finger at Bear. "Just take care of this man for me. I'm gonna miss him."

"Nope…nope," Bear said stubbornly, reaching into his pocket and pulling out thirty dollars. "You gotta tell me what my tab is 'cause here's the deal; I pay people what I owe 'em and I expect to get paid when people owe me. That's the way it is."

Barney noted that Bear's intention was set. "All right, if you're gonna be a stubborn mule about it, you owe me seven dollars and fifty cents for last night, but I got this round 'cause it's your last and 'cause of Pruitt. Deal?"

"Deal, but seven dollars and fifty cents! That's outrageous," Bear teased. He winked as he threw a twenty on the bar and put the ten back in his pocket. "Did I have that much fun?"

"You said you did when you left," Barney said with a laugh. He took the bill off the bar and opened the register for change.

"Do me a favor, Barney," Bear said as he finished off the last drop of his beer, "tell all the girls I said goodbye, will ya, especially Thelma?" He tapped himself on the chest. "Something about her always did get me right here. And keep the change. If it's gonna be my last tip, it might as well be my best."

"I'll tell her, but that's too much. You don't have to do that," said Barney.

"Put it in your pocket before I change my mind," Bear said stubbornly. He held out his hand. "Maybe we'll meet up again sometime and I'll need to borrow it back."

"Maybe so," Barney said, shaking Bear's hand. "If you ever get back this way, you'll know where to find a good bartender with good beer."

"Like I said, you always were the best bartender this side of the courthouse," Bear laughed.

They headed for the door. Bear stopped before he went outside, looked back and tipped his hat. "Adios, Barney."

"See ya, Bear, and good luck," Barney hollered as they made their way onto the sidewalk.

"Let's go home," Jim said, as Niki pulled the wagon away from Doorman's Saloon and into the afternoon traffic.

"Yeah, I'm ready," Tom said.

"I'm gonna drop you fellas at the station," Bear said as he turned the wagon south toward the depot, "and then I'll run around the corner to the livery so I can drop this wagon off and grab my saddle. Shouldn't take more than a few minutes."

"Sounds good," Jim said.

"Ya did say ya won't be back in Belton until tomorrow 'round sundown, right?" Bear asked.

"That's right," Jim answered.

"Well, if ya don't mind," Bear went on, "I'd really rather just meet you two guys in Belton. It wouldn't take me more than a day and a half to get there, and I've always had this idea in my head that, when I finally did leave this town, I would do it on Niki's back."

"You sure?" Jim asked.

"Yeah. Besides, it'd be easier," Bear said. "Tilley's train is just for passengers so I'd have to ride her over and meet you in Phelps anyway, then I'd have to put her on and off trains for the next couple of days and that sounds like more trouble than it's worth. I'll just ride her over and meet y'all there."

"Are you really coming, or are you having second thoughts about leaving?" Jim asked. "I'll understand if you want to change your mind."

"Hell, no!" Bear exclaimed with conviction. He paused, then shook his head and chuckled. "Although, if you ever laid your eyes on Thelma Williams, you'd probably think twice about things, too. She can do that to a man. Made me forget who I was a couple a times. But no, I've been waitin' for this day too long, and ya ain't gettin' rid of me that easy. I'm goin' to Belton, all right."

"Do you have everything you need for the trip, money?" Jim asked.

"Yep," Bear said, "I had me a little put away in my room. Got what I need to get there."

"You know where you're going?" Tom asked.

"Hell, anybody that's ever had anythin' to do with cattle drives in Texas knows where Belton is," Bear answered with a smile. "I'll be bangin' on your door 'fore ya know it. I just gotta feelin' that Nicki here wants to leave this town on her own four legs, and I ain't spent any nights 'neath the stars in quite a while. It's kind of a personal thing twixt me and her is all. Besides, I should stop by Miss Berta's place and tell her the bad news. It's on the way out of town, and I can't leave her wonderin' what happened to me."

"Have it your way," Jim said, "but if you're not there in three days' time I'm going to start looking for a new cook the next morning, all right?"

"I'll be there," Bear said, giving Jim his word with his eyes. As the wagon came to a stop alongside the train station, Bear leaned into the back and pulled a holster and pistol out of his belongings before buttoning his bag up. "I might need this on the way, though." He looked at Jim and asked, "Think ya could take my bag with ya on the train? It'd save me the trouble of carryin' it all the way."

"Sure thing," Jim said.

"I know it don't look like nothin'," Bear went on, "and there ain't anythin' in there that means much to anybody 'cept me, but please make sure it don't get lost 'cause that happened once before when somebody reckoned it belonged in a trash pile."

"We'll guard it with our lives," Tom chuckled as he pulled both travel bags from the wagon.

"Well, gentlemen," Bear said with a tip of his old hat, "I'll see y'all in Belton in two days."

He guided the wagon away as Jim and Tom watched him move south across the tracks to the livery two blocks over.

"Have a safe trip!" yelled Tom.

"Y'all too. See ya day after tomorrow," hollered Bear as he waved.

"He'll be there," Tom said, watching Bear merge into the afternoon traffic and commerce of Huntsville.

"Yep, he will," Jim said. He took a long last look at the sinister, red brick prison on top of the hill above them. "You ready to get out of here? I've had a bellyful of this place."

"I thought you'd never ask," Tom said as they entered the one-story train depot and made their way to a middle-aged, red-headed lady behind the ticket counter. She looked up with a smile as she twiddled a curl in her hair and asked, "You boys look like you want a train ticket out of this town...am I right?"

CHAPTER 7

The Train Ride

The trip from Huntsville to Phelps only lasted about twenty minutes, but it seemed longer because Jim and Tom didn't say a whole lot along the way. Jim welcomed the quiet ride, though, especially after the events of the morning.

Tom stared out the window into the green fields and pastures they passed, thinking about how different things were the last time he traveled this stretch. Five years earlier, he had been transferred from the Belton County Jail over to the one in Austin on the back of a wagon. After a week there, he spent the next day and a half on top of a flatbed railcar, his hands and feet shackled and wearing a metal neck collar linked by chain to eight other prisoners. They had been given a few swallows of water, but none of them were given anything to eat during the entire trip. Tom remembered thinking at the time he couldn't wait to get to Huntsville because whatever was going to happen there couldn't be as bad as what they were going through on the rail car. He shook his head at the memory, recalling with disgust how naive he had been because he had never been more wrong about anything in his life.

His thoughts came back to the present as the train reduced its speed and came around a gentle curve. The locomotive pulled up slowly alongside tracks leading to Houston and spit up a high-pitched explosion of sound and steam from its whistle as it lurched to a stop in front of the depot in Phelps, Texas.

Since Jim and Tom were among only a handful people who made the trip from Huntsville, it didn't take long before they were off the train, across the other set of tracks and climbing the steps leading to the side of the small wooden platform in front of the Phelps depot. They looked around at the town, not much bigger than a bump in the road. Phelps was established in 1870 and now, ten years later, nothing much had changed at all.

Jim noticed a sign in front of a small building proclaiming it as a hotel, but thought to himself that, even though the room he was in last night was as bad as it was, he would've much rather stayed there than try any of the rooms in this town. A few hundred yards from the station was a small church, a few houses in the distance, and two beat-up dirt roads that crisscrossed what was supposed to be downtown Phelps. That was it; there wasn't even a post office.

Jim spotted the engineer making his way up the steps onto the platform. "Are you Mister Tilley?" he asked.

"That would be me," the man said as he walked over to stand before Jim and Tom. He was a middle-aged man wearing spectacles, light-blue pin-striped overalls with a matching engineer's cap and a pair of heavy boots. "Robert Tilley's the name," he said, taking off his work gloves and shaking their hands.

"I'm Jim Wallace, and this is my son, Tom."

"Nice to meet you," Tilley said. "I hope you don't mind me askin', but are you the one who laid out Pruitt?"

"I'm afraid so," Jim answered, now regretting the notoriety and how he had handled the situation.

"Well, next time you're on my train," Tilley smiled, "you and everybody with you rides free. Never did like that son of a bitch."

"Thank you. I didn't like him, either," Jim said. He knew he would never come back to take the engineer up on his offer and didn't want to waste another breath talking about Jack Pruitt. "I got a question for you, though. How many people live in this so-called town?"

"Phelps? About twenty-five, give or take," Tilley answered. "I guess the railroads were pretty hot at the people of Huntsville to lay their tracks through this place, but there's nothing anybody can do about it now. It's funny, though, 'cause if they hadn't, I wouldn't have a job."

"A job?" Jim asked. "Somebody told me you own this train."

"This train owns me," Tilley said. It was obvious the engineer used the answer frequently to neither confirm nor deny the question.

"What can we do here to pass the time while we're waiting for the train to Houston?" Tom asked.

"Well, there are two things: you can sit over there," Tilley said with a grin, pointing to a wooden bench on one side of the depot, "or you can sit over there," he finished, pointing to an identical bench on the other side.

"Figures," Tom sighed.

Another train coming around the bend from the south sounded its approach. "I woulda stopped to let you two do a little cat fishin' in that pond we just passed," Tilley said, "but there's some prisoners comin' I gotta take back to Huntsville right quick. Looks like I barely made it. That's them now."

They watched the northbound train round the long curve and puff its way toward the depot before Tom turned, walked to one of the benches and sat down. "I'll be there in a minute," Jim said. He looked back at Tilley. "I noticed you only have a passenger car behind your engine. Do you ever haul any freight back to town?"

"Not much," Tilley said. "I think they had high hopes of it, and had some plans to build a big rail yard and a turnaround for the locomotive in Huntsville when business got booming, but things didn't turn out like they planned. Far as I know, I'm the only train in the state that has to make return trips by backing up the whole way. I'd love to haul more freight, but most of the time, I only carry passengers heading to Houston and back."

"And prisoners?" Jim asked.

"Yep, and the prisoners," Tilley said with a regretful shake of his head. The northbound train was now a stone's throw from the depot. "Well, I gotta go an' get back to work, but I hope you and your boy have a safe trip home. It was nice to meet ya."

"It was nice to meet you, too," Jim said as they shook hands again. Jim watched Robert Tilley hop down off the platform and onto the white rocks surrounding the two sets of tracks. He darted in front of the slowly moving northbound train as it pulled in and climbed the stairs leading to the cabin of his locomotive. He stopped, waved and yelled something to Jim, but his words were lost in the whistle from the oncoming train. Jim flinched at the blast, as did everyone else standing there, but he waved to Robert, then shifted his attention to the huge black-and-silver steam engine as it moved slowly into town and came to a stop between Tilley's train and the depot. The train consisted of the engine, a coal carrier and ten or twelve boxcars headed off to who knew where, but the car hooked directly behind the coal carrier was nothing like the rest, and stood out like a filthy sore.

Jim walked to where Tom was sitting, put his travel bag down next to

Bear's and sat on the edge of the seat next to his son. "You all right?" he asked.

"Yeah, I'm okay," Tom said.

"Want to go for a walk?" Jim asked.

"Nah, I'm all right here."

"You sure?"

"I'm fine, really," Tom said.

Neither spoke a word as they listened and watched two armed guards on the flatbed rail car bark orders to the ten or twelve men who were chained together on the last leg of their journey into the Texas prison system. Judging by the way the prisoners stood in unison, it didn't take much imagination to realize they hadn't been able to stretch their legs for some time. All of them looked like they were worn out and could use a bath, and the stare in the eyes of most of them was the same Tom had in his when he made the trip five years past. Theirs was the look of totally defeated men who had lost everything and were hopelessly enslaved to the dark years ahead.

Out of reflex, Tom rubbed both his knees, remembering the aches and pains in them when he stood up in exactly the same spot those men now stood. His hands were sweaty and cold as he watched the guards tell the people standing on the platform to give them plenty of room until they had all the convicts off the rail car and loaded onto Tilley's train.

For the most part, the prisoners kept their heads down to avoid the stares as they walked past, and Tom remembered doing the same thing a long time ago. He recalled how people looked at them that day, how none of them showed the slightest bit of sympathy toward him or the men he was with. There were only veiled looks and whispers of speculation about what each man might be guilty of and which ones looked more dangerous than the others. He knew then if those same people had one of their own family members on that rail car, they wouldn't stare as they did, but evidently nothing had changed in the last five years. The people on the platform watching the convicts today acted the same as the people there five years before.

Tom wanted to walk over and tell the chained men to not give up because if he made it through hell, they could too, but those armed guards were serious about what they were doing and he couldn't get up the nerve, so he watched the process quietly from the bench. He looked on as the men were moved off the platform, around the front of the locomotive and over to Tilley's train. They climbed the steps into the empty passenger car one at a time. When the last prisoner was securely on board, one of the guards gave a wave to the engineer. Tilley sounded his horn once and put his locomotive in reverse. With a belch of steam, the train started backing away toward Huntsville, picking up speed around the gentle curve Jim and Tom had just traveled, taking the convicted men to their fate.

"That's how it was for you, wasn't it, son?" Jim asked.

"Yeah," Tom said quietly.

"I'm sorry," Jim said as he leaned back onto the bench and patted his son on the leg. "I really am. The sight of any man who lost his hope is one of the worst sights I think I've ever seen, and I know you must have had that look when you came through here. But you don't ever have to feel that way again. Not for any man, or for any reason. You hear me? What happened was a mistake that you paid a hell of a price for, but you paid it in full. Do you know what I'm saying, Tom?"

"I understand," Tom said.

"You don't owe anybody anything," Jim added, putting his hand on Tom's shoulder and looking him in the eyes.

"Thanks," Tom said. They sat quietly, watching the northbound train take on water, and neither said a word until long after its whistle blew and it moved slowly away.

Tom finally broke the silence. "You haven't mentioned Buddy. How is he?"

"Oh...he's fine, I guess," Jim answered. "Didn't you get his letters?"

"Nope," Tom said, "but that's not too surprising. I figured he never wrote because maybe he felt bad about the way things turned out. I don't know."

"He told me he wrote you all the time. You never got a letter?" Jim asked.

"Not a one," Tom said.

They sat in silence as Jim rubbed his hands together. "Well, you know how your brother is. He always wanted to make it big on his own and he's taken to that sheriff's job like that's all there is. I don't understand why he told me he wrote you, though." He paused for a moment. "Maybe he's just been too busy."

Tom looked at his dad like he was out of his mind. "Right," he said dryly. He looked at the bright blue horizon. "Was he there to help when Mom got sick?"

"Not much, but he came around now and then," Jim said. "He was there when she died."

"What happened to her?" Tom asked.

"Oh, about a year before she died, she started having headaches fairly often," he answered, his voice soft. "They kept getting worse. The doctor tended to her close, and tried everything he knew but, in the end, he said it was consumption that got her. Consumption, hell. That word just meant the damned doctors didn't know what the hell was killing her. Anyway, the only thing we could do was keep her full of laudanum for the pain." He sighed and gave his son a wistful smile. "She died in her sleep."

"I'm so sorry, Dad," Tom said. "I really wish I could have been there."

"I know, son, but speaking of your mother, I have something she wanted me to give you," Jim said. He reached into his travel bag, dug around a few seconds, then pulled out an envelope.

"Toward the end, your mom had some pretty bad days, but about three weeks before she died, she woke up from a nap one afternoon and said she felt great. She asked me to carry her out onto the porch where she could sit down and write you a letter. As it turned out, it was the last time she was able to do much of anything, and I think she knew it would be. She wrote this and made me promise I wouldn't open it until I had you with me on our way back home." Jim stood and handed the letter to Tom. "I'll leave you with it while I go inside and get the tickets. I'll be back in a bit."

Tom didn't say a word as he took the envelope and slowly looked at the beautiful handwriting he recognized as his mother's. He could tell her hands must have been weak and trembling when she wrote, "To Tom," on the front. He opened the sealed envelope carefully, pulled out two pieces of folded paper and read:

My Dearest Tom,

I'm terribly sorry for not being able to be a part of your homecoming celebration and I know you feel the same way for not being able to be here with me before I leave, so I guess that makes us even. I have longed for nothing else the last four years than to be with you again and the illness which will soon take me is the only thing in the world that could have kept me from it, much like your situation has stopped you. I'm asking you, please, don't carry the guilt of not being here with me for another day. Please? Before you read another word, I need you to promise me you will do this for me. Take a deep breath and do it now. All right? Thank you.

The doctor says there's nothing he can do anymore except to try and keep me comfortable, and I know when you read this I will have been gone for some time, but at least by writing this letter and making your father promise not to open it until you are safely on your way back here, I can smile knowing I might be able to reach through time and be a part of your happy day. You have constantly been in my thoughts and you have no idea how many evenings your father and I have spent sitting in the rocking chairs on the front porch discussing memories of you until the mosquitoes carried us off, but our talks are something I have looked forward to every day and I will miss them dearly. We have been very worried about your well-being and I pray when you read this you are in good spirits and in fine physical shape. Now that you are on your way home, I want you to promise me something else because I have been praying about some things that weigh on my soul considerably.

Tom, first of all, I want you to look after your father. He's a stubborn old goat who tries to do everything himself but I'm hoping you will see through his orneriness and stay here to help with the ranch. He will never sell it and all he wants to do anyway is give it to you when the time comes. I'm sure I can count on you for that, but I need your help on another matter that might not be so easy, yet it is just as important to me. Your absence has truly been your father's time of need, and even though he has managed to keep the place from falling apart, I'm positive he feels that Buddy has abandoned him because he has not come by the ranch at all to help out with the property while you were gone. Also, I want you to know that, after everything you've gone through, I fully understand the ill feelings you harbor toward your brother, but on my deathbed I pray the good Lord will help you put them aside and by doing so maybe there's a chance your father can settle his differences with Buddy, too. I do not want to leave this world wondering whether or not my family can get along with each other after I'm gone, and by praying for these things to come to pass, I know I will be able to stand in front of the Lord with a much lighter heart. Promise me now you will do your very best. Thank you, son, thank you very, very much.

I guess I need to close because I'm getting very tired. This letter has taken most of the afternoon to write, but I'm so happy I was able to talk to you today. Right now, I'm out on the front porch with the dogs watching the evening sunlight dance on Cowhouse Creek just before it settles below the horizon, hoping one day soon you will find yourself in this same old chair watching a sunset just like it. When that moment comes, I hope you will think of me and how much I love you. I'm sorry I didn't live to see the day you met the right woman or have the children I could always picture you with, but my last prayer on this earth is for that day to come soon, and for you to find nothing but happiness the rest of your life. You deserve it, son. I love you very much. Goodbye.

Your loving mother

Tom read the letter twice before folding it back into the envelope and wiping his eyes as he took long, deep quivering breaths. The last year had been by far the hardest of his five-year sentence, due in large part to the guilt he carried about not being able to see his mother before she passed away. Tom now felt that burden start to lift and was extremely grateful he had the chance to hear her thoughts one more time, even though the letter was written months ago. He leaned forward and put his elbows on his knees, then covered his face with his hands and quietly let his tears flow.

Jim stood inside the depot looking out the window at his son crouched over on the bench. He yearned to go out and tell him everything was okay but he didn't because he thought it best to give him a bit of privacy for his grief. Over the first few months following his wife's death, there were many times when he would sit by himself and cry much the way his son cried now, and he knew there was nothing he could do or say that would help. Part of him wanted to go talk to Tom about what Ruby had written in her letter so he could know for sure what was so important to her in her last days But not long after she died, he realized he didn't need to read it. In her last few months, every night he would close his eyes in the dark of their too-quiet house and hear her soft voice praying to God about the two things she used to worry about the most: himself and her boys. He didn't need to read the letter. It didn't take a big city lawyer to figure it out. He knew what Ruby wanted.

Jim watched from the window until Tom sat upright on the bench looking more composed. Then he walked out and sat down next to him. "Your mother was a hell of a woman," he said. "I miss her."

"Me, too," Tom said, and put an arm around his dad's shoulder. They sat quietly for a few moments before Tom held up the envelope. "You want to read this?"

"No," Jim said, shaking his head. "That's yours. Besides, I have a pretty good idea what she wanted to say."

"Yeah," Tom said, wiping a few more tears, "I suppose you do." He gave his dad's shoulder a squeeze. "You haven't said much. How have things been with the ranch? I've been worried."

"Oh, the ranch is fine," Jim said. "Aya and I have managed to keep the place glued together somehow, but we've had problems with rustlers trying to take whatever they can, whenever they can, since you've been gone. We really haven't done much of anything except keep an eye on the livestock."

"How long has that been going on?" Tom asked.

"About a year, I guess," Jim replied.

"Has Aya ever caught anybody?" Tom said with a bit of a smile. "He can sneak up on a ghost."

"He killed a couple of men over it," Jim said. "Been riding the lines at night since all this started."

Tom was shocked. "You didn't tell me any of this in your letters," he said.

"I figured you had enough on your plate to worry about. Besides, there was nothing you could have done about it."

"When did that happen?" Tom asked.

"The first one was on the north rim about a year ago, and the second time was on the west rim last summer," Jim answered. "Both times the rest of their gang high-tailed it out of there once they realized somebody was shooting at them, but we never could figure out who the dead men were or where they came from."

"Are they still messing with you?"

"Yep," Jim replied. "Aya runs them off all the time. Just last week he scared another bunch off the north rim again."

"Well, did Buddy ever find out who's doing it?" Tom asked. "He's *the sheriff*, after all."

"He seems to think some of Turner's men are behind it," Jim said softly.

"*Turner Bell?*" Tom asked in disbelief.

Jim shrugged. "That's what he says."

"That must leave Buddy in a tight spot," Tom said. "Turner got him elected sheriff, for God's sake. How is Buddy supposed to arrest his boss?"

"Well, your brother told me not to tell anybody because he was still working on it and wanted proof." Jim shook his head and stared into the distance. "But that was almost a year ago and Buddy still hasn't arrested anybody."

"I don't get it," Tom said. "Why would Turner want to steal your cows? It's not like he needs the money. Bell County was named after his father, for God's sake."

"I know it doesn't make much sense," Jim said, "unless you figure he's trying to get me to pull stakes and sell the ranch. Everybody knows he's been buying up most of the land around Belton, and I'm sure he'd love to get his hands on our place if he could."

"Have you asked him about it?"

"Hell, yeah," Jim said emphatically. "Do you really think I'd let that go once I got wind of it?"

"Well, now that you mention it, no," Tom laughed.

"It didn't take me long. I rode over to the Double T and knocked on his door after Buddy told me what he thought was going on," Jim said.

"What did he say?"

"Oh, he got upset. Said I had no right coming over to his house accusing him of such a fool thing and that if he wanted the Four C's he would've made me an offer, fair and square," Jim said.

"You believe him?" Tom asked.

"Part of me does and part of me doesn't. Turner and I haven't got along too well for quite a while now, so I don't really know."

"Did you let on that Buddy told you?" Tom asked.

"Hell, no," Jim said. "I wouldn't do that to your brother."

"Who else could it be?" Tom asked.

"Well, that's the thing, Tom. I don't really know," Jim said. "It might be Turner. Or it could be that the word's out that I've been running the ranch short-handed. Some might think it makes me easy pickings, simple as that."

"I'm sorry, Dad." Tom sounded genuinely distressed. "I'm really glad you're all right, but still, I should've been there to help out and…"

"I told you this morning not to apologize to me or anyone else, all right?" Jim said impatiently. "Things will get better now that you're back because we'll have another set of eyes on the place and, hopefully, the new fence will make the sons of bitches doing it realize we're not an easy target anymore, and they'll go find somebody else to steal from."

"I can see now why you want to close off the whole ranch," Tom said. "I had no idea any of this was going on."

"Well, things should settle down soon." Jim clapped Tom on the shoulder affectionately. "Don't you worry; by the middle of summer, we should have the fence up and that should help things considerably."

"I can't wait to get started." Tom had a new excitement in his voice. "How do you think the neighbors and the free grazers are going to take it?"

"The neighbors won't mind," Jim sounded confident, as if he had already spoken to a few. "In fact, they'll probably follow suit as soon as they see me get started, but the free grazers are another story. I've heard stories from different parts of the state that there's been some bad blood between the free grazers and fenced-in landowners. They say the grazers have cut down miles of fence, and there have been some killings over it but, the fact is, it's my property and I can do pretty much whatever I want with it. There's still plenty of open range out there. The bottom line is, free grazers don't own anything except cattle and they shouldn't be able to waltz them all over my fields just because they want to. Sooner or later, the law will come in and settle things, and I'm pretty sure they'll side with the landowners. They have to; can't see it getting squared up any other way."

"What if it doesn't work out like you plan?" Tom was skeptical.

"Then we're going to be doing a lot of work for nothing." Jim turned to look back at his son. "I've been thinking about all this for some time now, and every direction I look at it from I see the same thing: the cattle business is going to go through a drastic change over the next few years, and the ranchers who don't see it coming will be doing something else for a living when it gets here. I don't plan on doing anything else."

"It makes sense to me." Tom gave his father's shoulder a supporting squeeze. "When everything is said and done, you and I will make the Cowhouse Creek Cattle Company one of the largest outfits in Texas." He smiled. "What do you say to that?"

Jim raised his eyebrows. "Well, we sure have a lot to do. The only thing we've done since you left is round up the calves every spring and put our brand on 'em." He paused, thinking, then smiled. "But I can't think of a single thing I'd rather do in this whole wide world."

They passed the time waiting for the train discussing plans for the ranch before a whistle blew, alerting them to the arrival of the southbound train headed to Houston. Tom got up from the bench and walked over to the edge of the platform so he could look down the tracks and spy the locomotive headed their way.

"I guess we'll be moving out of this God-forsaken place in just a bit. By the way, you told Bear you had some business in Houston. Do you mind me asking what that's about?"

"I have to see an old friend of mine first thing tomorrow morning," Jim said. "There's talk about the railroad coming through Belton and I'm hoping he'll be able to tell me exactly where they're going to lay tracks, but you don't need to worry about any of that. His office is right around the corner from the train station so all I have to do is run in there for a few minutes and then we'll be off."

"The railroad is coming through Belton?" Tom exclaimed. "Bet that's got everybody excited."

"It sure does," Jim said as he stood. "There's plenty of folk saying it might make us as big as Fort Worth, but I doubt that. My guess is it will make the ranch worth more and the cattle business a lot better, but big as Fort Worth? That seems a might optimistic."

"Well, either way, it's got to be a great for us," Tom said.

"That it will, but I want to make sure they don't come right through the middle of our ranch," Jim said.

"I can see how that might not be such a good thing," Tom chuckled. He looked down the tracks again to see the southbound train slowing as it neared the depot. After the locomotive lurched to a noisy stop, they grabbed their travel bags and walked over to the last of the three passenger cars and climbed in.

"Where do you want to sit?" Tom asked as they looked down the row of seats, only a third full.

"As far back as we can get," Jim said, making his way to the last bench and sitting next to the window. Tom was right behind him, and was soon storing their bags under their seats. "I never did like to sit too close to the engines. There's too much noise, steam and ash flying around for me. We'll have a much nicer ride back here. Maybe we can even catch a nap."

"A nap sounds good," Tom said as he took off his hat, put it in his lap and leaned his head back against the wall behind him. He looked out the window and watched the signal man beside the tracks swing his lantern around in a wide circle, announcing to all that the train had officially departed as it lurched forward on its journey south.

He closed his eyes and was soon thinking about all the wonderful things that were in store ahead: his old room and the nice comfortable bed he'd be sleeping in, good food on a regular basis, the smiling face of an old friend or two, a good day's work for a good day's pay, riding a horse, watching the prairie grass blow in the breeze and simply making up for lost time with his dad. These were just a few of the happy thoughts that crossed his mind as the train moved farther down the tracks, but the clicking of the wheels as the train moved along the rails wouldn't let his past get too far behind him.

His thoughts wandered back to the men in chains on the flatbed rail car he had seen a little earlier. The trip he had taken to The Walls five years before was exactly the same as theirs, and he rubbed his neck as if he could feel the chains tighten on him again. He still remembered the dread that filled him when Tilley's train backed up around the last gentle S-curve into Huntsville and came to a stop below The Walls. All the men he was with that day knew exactly where they were going, but there wasn't a single word spoken between them. None of them were prepared for the sickening feeling in the pit of their stomachs as they looked out the windows at the imposing structure on the hill to see the sinister, red brick walls for the first time and realize their punishment was finally and truly at hand.

He remembered exiting the train and marching up the hill in the afternoon sun to the side entrance of the prison, with everyone staring as they passed. He could recount every long minute of the time he stood outside the gates, unable to swat the flies and mosquitoes because of his chains. Then the doors finally swung open and they were led inside like cattle to be processed and there they were introduced to a swarm of seasoned inmates who had gathered in the yard to give the "new meat" nicknames as they arrived to take their place among them.

The guards kept the other prisoners far enough away so they wouldn't pose a physical threat, but the hateful, chaotic chatter of name-calling could be heard throughout the interior of the walls. Tom had kept his gaze straight ahead, feigning indifference, but was as relieved as the rest when they were led inside to be checked in. Their teeth were inspected and their heads were shaved; they were deloused and given shoes, black and whites, an inmate number and the "do's and don'ts" of a new convict in the system. It was also explained very clearly to all that "a bullet will find you" as the harsh reality for not following orders at all times.

Afterward, and for the first time in two days, they were allowed to eat. Their plates were spotless when they finished, although the food they were given consisted of some kind of semi-spoiled meat and watery beans, food most of them never would have eaten in their former lives. They were seated together at one of the many tables lined up in a large, single-room mess hall and, although their malicious initiation into the prison from the other convicts was over, they were still met by stares and whispers everywhere they looked.

Tom ate in silence, staring down at the slop his mother wouldn't have fed the dogs as he listened in on conversations between the new inmates that ranged from where they called home and what they were in for to how they were innocent and framed for the deeds that sent them to prison.

Lying in his bunk later that evening, Tom knew he would never forget that meal because a realization hit him hard; he never wanted to become a man like those who made excuses for their actions. There were two things he held onto tightly as he began his time in prison: the love of his parents and the knowledge that he had a home to go back to when he got out. Because of that first meal inside The Walls and the bullshit stories he heard (from some of the worst people that mankind had to offer), he knew, no matter what, from that day forward he would be the kind of man who stood up and was accountable for his actions. It was clear to him why some of these men did time only to come back again later for something else, and Tom decided he would never, under any circumstances, allow that to happen to him.

He had been in his bunk for what seemed like an eternity, listening to the man below explain how, through sheer bad luck, he had wound up in trouble. Tom was never more relieved to hear the guards yell down the cell block that it was quiet time and everyone had to get some shut-eye. He thought he would finally get some much needed rest but, even after all the hardships and humiliations of the trip to this harsh new home, sleep didn't come to him. The loud echoes of men snoring up and down the cell block as soon as the chatter died was a cruel ending to two brutal days. No matter how hard he tried to ignore it, the noise was unyielding and drove him to the point of total despair. He tossed and turned in his bunk, wanting to cry out to God to give him the strength to see this through because he wasn't sure he was going to be able to make it, and this was only the first night. He wished he was home with his mom and dad so badly he could almost hear his father's voice in the distance call out, "Tom…Tom…Tom, wake up."

Tom opened his eyes and quickly sat upright. He looked at his dad, who was still shaking him by the shoulder.

"You all right?" Jim asked. "You dozed off, but it seems you didn't sleep so well."

Tom rubbed his face with both hands. "No, I didn't." He looked around to see an older couple sitting on the other side of the car staring at him as if he might have caused a scene. "Sorry, I had a bad dream, that's all," he said. With that, they turned their attention back to whatever it was they were doing, as Tom quietly asked his dad, "Was it bad?"

"I don't know," Jim said. "I dozed off myself, but you woke me up because you were talking in your sleep."

"What did I say?" Tom asked.

"You kept saying you wanted to go home," his father answered with a rueful smile.

"I was dreaming of my first night at The Walls," Tom said, as he moved around in his seat to stretch the sleep out of his body. He put his hat on, shook his head back and forth and added, "Whew."

Jim just patted Tom on the leg, then nodded to let his son know everything was fine. He decided it might be a good idea to stay awake the rest of the trip and help Tom keep his mind off bad memories. He stood, straightened his hat, stretched a bit and rubbed his bum leg to get the blood flowing, then sat back down and started a conversation that lasted all the way to Houston.

The miles went by unnoticed as they talked about Tom's mother, his brother, Bear, how his old horse "Deuce" had come up lame and had to be put down, the prices of cotton and cattle, how much Belton had grown, this new invention called barbed wire that was going to reshape the cattle industry and another new contraption that was starting to show up out in the fields called a windmill. It wouldn't be long before a man could get water to just about anywhere on his property by harnessing the wind to pump water from a well, and they both shook their heads, wondering how it was they didn't think of that.

They talked about the work needing to be done around the ranch, how the other families around the county had fared the last few years, and, lastly, they talked of Turner Bell. They spent the better part of the trip discussing the goings on around the Four C's and whether Turner was responsible for the stolen cattle, but they both knew there was nothing to be done unless they caught him red-handed.

Tom grew up not liking Turner Bell very much, simply because Jim always had a gripe about him somehow or another and, even after what he had been told the last few hours, he didn't think he could dislike him any more than he already did. Turner's ranch was over twice the size of the Four C's and it was just like him to try to grab all the land he could. Tom believed men like him never had enough. Their appetite for money and power was relentless, and they would go to any extreme to expand their kingdoms, even at the expense of stepping on less fortunate people who stood in the way.

Tom was so worked up at the thought that he acted as though he didn't care when Jim told him that Turner's daughter had returned to Belton six months earlier to live at her father's ranch. He hadn't seen her since she was a teenager and was truly sorry to hear she moved back home because of the horrible experience she went through when her husband was killed in some sort of robbery but, deep down, part of him was excited at the prospect of seeing her again.

He tried to dismiss the thought because of the bad blood between his father and hers, plus there was the cold hard fact he was a newly released ex-convict, which was something a proper woman like her would surely never be able to see past. Tom was certain there was too much smoke in the air to have anything come from an encounter between them, other than a polite yet distant hello. All he could think about for the rest of the trip was how, when and where he would cross paths with Jennie Lue after seeing her leave for Austin with her new husband, Henry Sloan, eight years ago. It occupied his thoughts from the moment his father brought it up to the end of the day, when they got off the train and stood on the huge wooden platform looking around at the hundreds of people milling around the passenger depot in Houston, Texas.

CHAPTER 8

Homecoming

"We're getting close," Jim announced as the stage wound its way north along the dusty road from Austin to Belton.

"Yeah, we are," Tom answered as he gazed out the window. He had traveled this route only a few times, and wasn't too familiar with all the landmarks along the way, but they had just crossed Salado Creek and Tom knew that put them only thirty minutes or so from stepping off the stage, finally bringing an end to his five-and-a-half year ordeal.

The night before, they had gotten a bite to eat around the corner from the depot, then retired early to the Capitol Hotel so they could enjoy a good night's rest. Tom hadn't slept much over the last few days, and was so tired after the events in Huntsville he figured it wouldn't take him long to doze off once he was in bed, and he was right. The first thought that went through his mind when he opened his eyes in the morning and saw his dad asleep on the other side of the room was relief, knowing he was able to make it through the night without dreaming of prison, and the second was the long-lost sensation of being able to bound out of bed to a wonderful day, feeling refreshed and in a great mood.

The meeting Jim had with his friend went as planned. It was over soon enough and they were on the train to Austin, having picked up the conversation about things back home right where they left off.

It was a pleasant trip as the miles went by and the weather was cool and clear. There were no bugs trying to eat them alive when the train stopped for other passengers and, although the trip lasted almost six hours, it didn't seem that long when they disembarked and made their way to buy tickets for the stagecoach. The windy, sunny weather that followed what was probably the last northeaster of early spring had already dried out most of central Texas. After a bite to eat and an hour wait, they were seated in the cramped coach making their way to Belton, getting closer and closer with every bump in the twisting dusty road.

For the entire trip, Tom had been anxious to cross Salado Creek, not only because it meant they were nearing home, but because the entrance to the Double T was just to the west and he was hoping he might get lucky enough to catch a glimpse of Jennie Lue out on horseback as they passed. He laughed at himself over his foolish adolescent thoughts because Turner's property was huge and the chances were small for him to see anyone in the distant fields or on top of the rolling hill where the two-story, white-gabled ranch house faced the road they traveled. Still, he strained his eyes to see if he could spot her somewhere around the barn or over by the guest quarters off to the side of the main building as they passed. Although he didn't see her, and felt disappointed, he didn't take his eyes off the horses and cattle grazing in the fields surrounding the house until it was all well behind them.

"Damn, that's pretty," he said when he finally brought his attention back inside the cramped, dust-filled stagecoach.

"Yes, it is," Jim said, admiring the view through the window. "I've had a few complaints about Turner in my time, but the way he lives sure isn't one of them. I gotta hand it to him; he does have a nice place."

"One day we'll be that big," Tom said.

"Yeah, we will," Jim said, "but it's gonna take a lot of work."

"That's the easy part," Tom said, with an earnest smile fueled by his excitement at his yearned-for homecoming. There wasn't much talk from then on between father and son as they got closer to home. Tom's heart quickened as they crossed the Lampasas River, because soon after, he knew the stage would come to the outskirts of his home town, the city of Belton.

Although much had changed in the last five years, he recognized just about everything, and was thrilled to gaze upon all the familiar places as they passed. He soaked in the sights of the usual stores lining both sides of the street selling everything a man could want or need. Here were barber shops, flower shops, churches, blacksmiths, livery stables and so much more, all thriving.

He read colorful signs along the way, advertising the shops themselves or events going on around town. A fancy one for the opera house caught his eye. It read: *'The Hanlon-Lee's World Famous Acrobats Coming Tuesday, March 28."* Surrounding the letters were scenes of men juggling, of someone getting shot out of a cannon, of a man flying through the air like a bird and another of a stagecoach wreck, with all the passengers spilling off to face certain death or serious injury.

Tom shook his head in amazement, realizing things certainly weren't the same around here because he couldn't imagine such a show taking place in Belton before he left. Belton had previously offered only mediocre plays at the opera house, or a washed-up singer or two who showed up from Austin to amuse the townsfolk. Now it seemed as if Belton was growing into a first-rate city, because shows like the one advertised on the fancy sign were surely not playing in any one-horse towns. For a brief moment, Tom thought it would be fun to see if the Hanlon-Lees could pull off the amazing acts they depicted, but his musing ceased as he felt the stage start to slow.

The driver coaxed the horses into a walk as the stage came into the center of town. Tom suddenly felt a strange mixture of excitement and relief that his ordeal was finally over, mingled with anxiety about facing the man who played the biggest part in sending him to prison in the first place. During his torturous years of imprisonment, he often thought of what it would be like to stand face to face with Buddy again, and now he was about to find out.

Since he was a child, Tom felt he and his brother were close but, as he grew older, it seemed as if Buddy didn't want or need a big brother, or anyone else for that matter. He believed Buddy started treating people the way he did because he was mad at the world for a reason that was out of everyone's grasp and felt, if he could only have a "eureka" moment and catch on to whatever it was bugging the hell out of his brother, his behavior might make sense, but try as he might, he was unable to figure him out. He had made sincere efforts to be close with Buddy as they grew up, and was under the assumption they were until five-and-a-half years ago. For some unknown reason, as soon as Tom left town in chains on the back of a wagon, Buddy abandoned Tom the same way he had abandoned his father.

The first few years of his sentence, Tom would lie awake at night in the filthy ditches used as sleeping quarters for the prisoners, trying to dream up an ingenious plan that would exact revenge upon his brother for what he had done or, to be more precise, for what he hadn't done. At the end of every day, he went to sleep thinking about it and always woke up the next morning with the exact same thought on his mind. It nearly drove him mad the first two years he was gone but, somewhere along the way, he knew he had to let it go because he couldn't let the rage overtake his every thought any longer. It was one of the hardest things he ever had to do but, eventually, he willed himself to drop the anger like a piece of unwanted baggage on the side of the road and walk away. He didn't want to be the kind of man who carried something like that around in his heart forever. Afterward, the rest of his time passed a little quicker and his labors weren't quite so hard because he was much more at ease with himself. He was proud of being able to forgive Buddy and purge that particular demon, and now he was nervous because he was about to find out if he had genuinely been successful or not.

As the stage pulled into the town square and stopped in front of the courthouse, Jim patted his son on the leg and said affectionately, "Welcome home, son."

Tom smiled. "Thanks. It feels good to be here." He looked out the window to see a handful of people moving about downtown Belton this late Saturday afternoon and, at first glance, didn't recognize any of them. He felt relieved. After the long trip, he wasn't in the mood to talk pleasantries with old acquaintances and would just as soon head to the ranch right away and deal with the unavoidable questions about his ordeal later.

He hopped out first, then helped his dad step down into the street before catching the travel bags that were tossed off the roof by the driver. They took a second or two to stretch, straighten their hats and look around before Tom asked, "What's next?"

"Come on." Jim sounded a bit irritated. He picked up his bag and headed across the street. "We have to walk over to the livery and hook up the wagon. Then we're going home."

Tom grabbed Bear's travel bag and jogged the few steps it took to catch up to his father. "Did you think Buddy was going to be here?" he asked

"Yeah, I did," Jim answered tersely. They reached the sidewalk on the other side of the courthouse and turned east toward the livery. "I wonder what he could be doing right now that would be more important than this."

"Well," Tom said, stopping and tapping his father on the shoulder, "looks like he was getting the wagon ready."

Jim stopped and looked down the street to see Buddy driving the wagon toward them. "Well, I'll be," he said, watching his youngest son get closer. "I guess he made it after all."

"I guess he did," Tom said, watching his brother draw near. He thought he would be nervous at this instant but, to his surprise, he was more calm and collected than he would have thought possible.

Even though Buddy was the Bell County sheriff, and Tom had done everything he could to forgive him, he still felt an urge to tackle his brother to the ground and wipe the arrogant smirk off his face with a thorough ass whipping. If this moment had happened three years ago, Tom would be doing just that, but right now he was content to watch his brother pull the wagon up next to them.

"Well...well, if it isn't the sheriff."

"Look what the cat drug in," Buddy quipped as he tied the reins and hopped down onto the sidewalk.

Buddy Wallace had dreamed of being a peace officer since he was twelve years old, and after pestering everybody he could for a year or so, he managed to get a job working at the county jail when he was sixteen doing odd jobs like feeding the prisoners, cleaning out the cells, sweeping the floors and running errands for the sheriff. Not many people in the town were interested in a job with the sheriff's department because the pay wasn't that good and cowhands had guns going off on a regular basis at all hours of the night but, because he was a large muscular kid, had a level head and was enthusiastic about everything he did, Buddy earned his deputy's badge by the time he was eighteen. Two years later, he had worked himself into the favor of then-Sheriff Bennie Leaks. Bennie had held the job for the last twelve years and was getting old, so he decided to retire. Even though Buddy was only twenty-one at the time, and because he had the support of Turner Bell and his son George, no real opposition and used the simple slogan of "Bennie likes Buddy," he won the sheriff's job handily in the next election. Just two months later, Bennie was found in bed with a hole in the side of his head and a gun in his hand, leading everyone to believe that the stress of the lawmaker's job finally took the ultimate toll. The general consensus around town was that no one in his right mind would want the responsibilities that came with being sheriff, so not long after Bennie Leaks was put in the ground, Buddy pretty much owned the job, and he knew it.

Buddy was a fairly tall man at six feet two inches, with a stout build that made the badge pinned to the front of his crisp white shirt look even more imposing. He always had a high-priced, wide-brimmed black Stetson hat on his head that amplified the color of his bright, shoulder-length red hair. Not only did Buddy have expensive tastes in clothes, he also had most of the townsfolk wondering how he could afford a lot of the other fine things in his life as well. His large collection of hand-made boots always had a sparkling shine, and the horse he owned was one of the finest examples of a palomino in this part of the state. His light brown saddle was made especially for him by Frank A. Meanea, who just happened to be the most sought-after saddle maker in the country, and it matched the color of his horse almost perfectly. Buddy figured if the famous, young scout Buffalo Bill Cody owned one, it was good enough for him, and would give a lengthy, detailed commentary about what a fine piece of craftsmanship it was to anyone who happened to be unlucky enough to comment on it.

Soon after Buddy became sheriff, there was talk around town that his spending habits were either funded by his father, bonuses from Turner Bell or by discounts from the various shop owners who might be trying to get in good with the sheriff, but nobody knew for sure.

His sunken, pale-blue eyes were almost hidden behind a constant squint but, for the most part, people in town never really knew what color they were because it was hard to talk to Buddy without staring at the waxed handlebar mustache stretching from one side of his face to the other. Tom believed the reason Buddy grew his wavy red hair to his shoulders and his large red mustache the way he did was because he wanted to hide the millions of freckles covering the pale-white skin on his face. His brother told him it wasn't that way at all and said he wore it to make him look meaner, which could only help him in his job. Tom always thought it made him look a little insane, but now, five years later, Buddy evidently still didn't think so. He walked directly over to Tom, wrapped his arms around him as if he was genuinely glad to see him and said, "It's good to see you; been a long time."

Tom stood there for a moment, still clutching the travel bags, but finally dropped them to return his brother's hug. They stayed that way for a moment, then Buddy backed away to take a look at his brother from head to toe, still chewing on the toothpick in his mouth. "They didn't feed you at all, did they?" he asked.

"Oh, yeah, it was a regular feast the whole time," Tom said, his sarcasm getting the better of him. "I got tired of eating so good."

"Well, you're home now so you'll be fat as a pig heading to the slaughterhouse before you know it," Buddy said, playfully faking a punch to

Tom's stomach.

"Yeah…I suppose," Tom said, flinching a bit.

"You two wanna head over to Dayna G's, get a drink and maybe a bite to eat? My treat," Buddy asked, with raised eyebrows and the arrogant smirk Tom was all too familiar with. "And Tom, I might even be able to get one of the girls to take you in for the night if you got the notion. I know it's been a while." With a mischievous grin and wide eyes, he said, "What do you say?"

Tom looked at Buddy and shook his head. He picked both travel bags off the sidewalk and tossed them into the back of the buckboard. "No, thanks," he said. "The only thing I want to do now is go home and sit out on the front porch with Dad for a while."

"I'm with you," Jim said, looking at Tom. "It's been a long day."

"What about dinner?" Buddy asked. "Aren't y'all hungry? I told you I'd buy."

"We'll eat at the house," Jim said. "Aya's probably got something on the table right now."

"How is Aya, anyway? He doing all right?"

"Why don't you come with us and ask him yourself?" Jim said.

"I'd love to, but I have some things I have to clear up over at the jail." Buddy feigned regret. "Maybe next week sometime."

"Whatever," Jim replied. He stepped up and into the wagon with obvious annoyance. "It would be nice if you finally started coming around the house every now and then."

"I will…I will," Buddy promised. "I've been so busy with all the crap going on around this town that I just don't have any free time for myself. Hopefully, one of these days I'll get things settled down, then I'll be by to see you so much you'll think I moved back home. You'll see."

Tom followed his father up into the buckboard, sat down, and said, "Dad, I want to get out of here. You ready?"

"I am if you are." Jim untied the reins.

"Oh, yeah," Buddy added, "I almost forgot. I heard you might be looking to take on a hand or two and…"

"I don't want to talk about that right now," Jim said. "It's been a long day and I just want to go home."

"Okay," Buddy said, "but if you're thinking about hiring some help, make sure you talk to me first."

"We'll see," Jim said, "but not today. I do appreciate you getting the wagon ready, though."

"No problem. I figured it might make the last leg of your trip a little easier, that's all." He paused and took the toothpick out of his mouth. "And Tom, I'm sorry for how things turned out, I really am, but I had to do my job. You understand, don't you?"

Tom gave his brother a scathing look. "We gotta go. I'll see you around." He then turned to his father. "Come on, let's get this thing moving."

"If there's anything I can do, you let me know, okay, Tom?" Buddy said as their wagon moved into the street. "Stop by the jail anytime. You still remember where that is, don't you?" He laughed loudly and spitefully before they moved too far away, adding, "Ah…you know I'm just kiddin', right? Really, Tom, I'm glad you're home. Would have been nice if you had made it back before Mom died, 'cause I'm sure she would've liked that, but better late than never, I guess."

Tom looked at his brother, standing there fingering his toothpick, and shook his head in disgust. He finally looked away as they moved down the street, wondering why Buddy was such a horse's ass. Even though he had promised, the request his mother made of him in her last letter might be the hardest thing he ever set out to do. Tom was determined to try the best he could, but no matter how many times Buddy said or did the things that riled him to the core, he was never quite prepared for it. It always felt like a sucker punch when moments like this happened. Even though the words hurt Tom to the bone, he decided then and there he wasn't going to let his guard down with his brother anymore.

It might have been different if he felt Buddy was genuinely sorry about the way things turned out and wanted to make amends, but the words his brother spoke that afternoon made Tom realize he was never going to be able to trust him again. If they both buried the hatchet, lived to be a hundred years old and never got sideways over a single thing for the rest of their lives, Tom knew it would never be the same between them as it was when they were kids. From now on, he'd have to keep an eye on Buddy at all times. He remembered his father telling him once that, as long as you held a snake by the head, it couldn't bite you, but he never thought he would have to apply that lesson to his brother.

Father and son rode in silence for a few minutes before Tom asked, "Why do I get the feeling that Buddy has a chip on his shoulder you couldn't knock off with a ball peen hammer?"

"I wish I knew," Jim answered. "If you find the answer to that, you need to let me know."

"I will," Tom said, "but I don't like my chances."

When they reached the outskirts of downtown Belton, Tom said, "This place has changed, but maybe not all that much, has it?" When no response came, he glanced over to see his father holding his hand up in a slow wave to one of the shops they were passing. On the sidewalk in front of the women's clothing store she owned stood Miss Emma Lawton, who waved back as they went by. Jim's smile disappeared quickly when he realized his son was watching. Tom didn't think anything of it, though, happy to see a friendly face. When they were well past Miss Lawton's store, Jim popped the reins, sending the horse into a trot. They made their way into the darkening countryside, heading for home at last.

Buddy watched his dad and brother until they were out of sight, then turned and walked over to the courthouse and up the steps to where George Bell now stood.

"He's back," Buddy said, stating the obvious.

"Yeah, I saw from my office upstairs," George said. "You think he's gonna get wind of what's going on?"

"Hell...you're kiddin' me, right?" Buddy asked. "You mean Tom?"

"I'm serious," George said. "Do you think he'll get in the way?"

"No," Buddy answered. "I handled him once and I can take care of him again if we have to. I figure the only thing he wants to do right now is stay the hell out of trouble but, if he wants to get caught up in the middle of what we're trying to do, trouble won't take long to find *him*. Don't worry. I can play Tom like a fiddle."

"Okay, but we have to get this deal done soon," George said. "Time is running out."

"Look," Buddy said, "you're the mayor. You just worry about your job. I'm the sheriff and I'll worry about mine. I still got a couple of tricks up my sleeve."

"All right," George said, "but that rail will be coming through here in just a few weeks."

"I know where we stand," Buddy said, "and I've been thinking that maybe we can use Tom to our advantage." He turned and started walking toward the livery. "I gotta go, but I'll keep you posted."

"You better," George said. "Let's get this wrapped up once and for all."

"It'll be over with soon enough. Don't worry. And tell your sister I'm still waiting," Buddy called back. "She needs to know a handsome guy like me won't be single forever."

George laughed loudly. "I betcha Jennie Lue stays awake at night losing sleep over that one." He watched Buddy until he was well down the sidewalk before he heaved a nervous sigh and went back inside the courthouse. There was a council meeting tonight and he needed to go over his notes.

After a forty-five minute ride down the dark, dusty road, Jim and Tom came to the fork leading into the property. The brightly painted, white metal arch straddling the entrance with *"Four C's Ranch"* spelled out across the top had never looked so good to Tom as it did right then. Neither said a word as they crossed Ruby's Bridge, a simple wooden structure built by Jim and the boys years ago to span a narrow bend of Cowhouse Creek. The sounds of the horse and wagon moving across the boards alerted the dogs that started barking and running out to see who it was.

As soon as they saw Jim driving the wagon, they let out a few happy yelps and escorted them the last hundred yards up the gentle hill toward the lighted ranch house. The two men on the porch stepped off and made their way over to greet them as the wagon came to a stop. Jim felt the weight of the world finally lift as only a parent could, knowing he finally had his son back in the fold, safe and sound.

Tom was just as elated and wanted to climb out of the wagon so he could get on his hands and knees and kiss the earth but instead he walked past the excited dogs and went over to wrap his arms around one of the men, who returned the hug as if he was going to squeeze the life out of him.

"Aya," Tom whispered, his eyes watering up, "you have no idea how good it is to see you."

The man stood back and held Tom by the arms, looking at him with a smile that beamed from ear to ear. Aya was around fifty years old, near as anyone could figure, had coal-black eyes, with jet-black hair always worn in a ponytail down the middle of his back. There was a trace of gray creeping into his brows, and miles of wrinkles from a lifetime under the sun were engraved into his weathered, gentle face. He only stood about five-and-a-half-feet tall, and always wore the same leather vest over a long-sleeved shirt, but anyone could tell the man was in remarkably good shape. His strength never failed to outmatch all takers in the friendly arm wrestling contests that sometimes took place around the ranch.

"It is…good," he said in his deep voice. He wiped the moisture from his eyes and gave Tom another bear hug, this time lifting him off his feet.

When Aya finally let go, Tom dried his face again and looked over to see the heavy young man waiting patiently and said, "You must be Chas."

"That's me, Mister Tom," came the energetic reply as Chas stepped forward. Chas Kane had always been a big boy growing up but, even now as a young man, he still looked like a huge, clumsy kid who never got out of the baby-fat stage. He was a few inches shy of six feet and weighed over two hundred pounds, not all of it lean muscle, especially around his midsection. He wore thick glasses over a pair of green eyes that sparkled from a freckled face surrounded by a head of thick, sandy blond hair worn short. He beamed a smile at Tom, displaying a set of teeth as crooked as Cowhouse Creek itself.

"I haven't seen you since you were a kid." Tom reached out to shake hands. "You're all grown up, aren't you?"

"Yes, sir," said Chas, returning his handshake vigorously, "and, if you need anything, Mister Tom, you just…"

"Whoa there…just call me Tom."

Chas stammered for a second and glanced at Jim to see if it was all right to call Tom by his first name. Getting a nod from his boss, he said, "Ah, okay then…Tom…if there's anything I can do for you, just let me know. I'm a darned good hand and, if you need somethin' done, I want you to know you can count on me to do it, whatever it is."

"So I've heard," Tom replied. "My dad told me you were working out just fine."

Chas looked like he was going to burst with pride at the compliment.

"Really? Wow. Well, anything you need, okay?"

"Why don't you take the wagon over to the barn and put the horse up for the night?" Jim said, "and grab those travel bags, too. Bring 'em up to the house on your way back."

"Yes, sir, Mister Jim!" Chas responded with the enthusiasm of a dog going after a stick. He grabbed the bridle's cheek strap to lead the horse and wagon around back to the barn. As he disappeared into the dark they heard him call back, "Aya's got some dinner for y'all, so don't go to sleep, okay? I'll be back in just a few minutes and maybe we can visit."

"I like that kid," Tom said.

"Me, too," Jim said, "but come on. Let's get inside and see what's for supper."

"Now you're talking," Tom said as the three men made their way onto the porch. Jim and Aya went into the house first as Tom stopped to rub each of the excited hounds behind the ears. He looked at his mother's favorite rocking chair and smiled, knowing it was from there that she wrote his letter. He reached over and pushed the back of the rocker, then listened to the crickets sing as he imagined his mother sitting there, moving back and forth with a smile on her face, welcoming him home at last.

"I'll do my best," he said quietly, gazing at the chair until it was still. He opened the screen door to enter a house smelling of freshly fried chicken. After a home-cooked meal, an hour or two with his dad and a couple of old friends out on these same chairs, he figured he would be more than ready for a good night's sleep in his own comfortable bed.

CHAPTER 9

Sunday Morning

Tom woke the next day bright and early. After he got dressed, he walked through the quiet house and out onto the porch to find his dad sitting in one of the chairs sipping a hot cup of coffee.

"I figured you'd be up soon," Jim said, pointing to another steaming cup that sat on a small table by his mother's chair.

"Thanks, Dad." Tom shooed off the dogs and sat down. "That smells good…and good morning."

It sure is nice to be home, he thought to himself. The morning dew covered the ground and almost looked like snow. He listened to the birds sing as they started their day. Taking a moment to notice the last of the stars slowly disappearing into the blossoming blue sky, he turned his attention to the wildflowers that were everywhere. He smiled, remembering how his dad once told him this was the time of the year when God took his paintbrush and splattered all the colors of the rainbow across the earth.

"Did you sleep okay?" Jim asked.

"Yeah, I did. It was great being in my own bed," Tom replied, taking his first sip of coffee. He wasn't being quite truthful, thinking it best not to share the dream that had come again last night about returning to prison and finding that Jack Pruitt was now the face of the guard welcoming him at the gates. He shook the thought off.

"Where's Aya and Chas?" he asked.

"Chas is down at the barn, but Aya's probably still sleeping," Jim said. "He usually gets up a little later because he rides the lines every night."

"Everything all right?" Tom asked.

"Yep. He said he didn't hear or see anything."

"That's good." Tom held his cup with both hands to keep them warm. "Looks like it's going to be a nice day. What are we going to do?"

"Not much, I hope," Jim said. "We usually don't do much around here on Sundays, but I need to ask you a favor."

"Sure," Tom said. "What is it?"

"Follow me." Jim got up from the chair and slowly stepped off the porch and into the yard, taking time to work the stiffness from his weak leg.

"Let me get my hat; I'll be right back." Tom ran inside. It wasn't long before he was out of the house and into the yard, trying his best not to spill his coffee all over the front of his shirt as he caught up with his father.

They walked around the corner of the one-story house to the barn. Jim originally built it as a big shed after he and Ruby bought the place, but added onto it a few times as the ranch grew larger. Now it stood large enough to house animals in ten different stalls, with a loft so big a person could get lost in it. The two large doors were already open, letting in the morning light. so they both walked inside to the sight and smell of horses poking their heads out of their stalls to see who was coming. There were the usual three wagons that were always parked in there: the old work wagon they used as their heavy hauler, the buckboard they rode in last night, and the one in the back corner, a single-horse, candy-apple red surrey that belonged to his mother. Tom could tell it hadn't been used for some time because it was covered in dust, but he couldn't see much as his view was blocked by what seemed like thousands of rolls of barbed wire, neatly stacked from one side of the barn to the other.

"Holy cow!" he said, as he walked to the back to get a closer look at what they were going to be spending a great deal of time on over the next few months. "You weren't kidding, were you?"

"Nope." Jim made his way to the middle of the barn as he sipped his coffee. "But pay no mind to that now; we'll worry about the fence tomorrow." He walked to one of the stalls and said, "Tom, come on over here. There's something I want to show you."

Tom knelt to poke the metal barbs on the strands of wire with his thumb before he stood and said, "You were right, this is going to keep us busy for a while — and it's sharp!"

With a whistle and a shake of his head, he rose and went to his father, who was gently rubbing the forehead of a paint stallion.

"This is Clever," Jim said, watching Tom's reaction carefully.

"Wow!" Tom said. He reached out to the horse, his palm up.

Clever stood a shade under fourteen hands high, and had the most remarkable coloring of any paint Tom had ever seen. His intelligent brown eyes were set in a mostly white forehead that ended with dark gray lips and pink nostrils. Brown markings started at his ears and went down one side of his head to encircle his left eye, which gave the impression of an eye patch. He had a chocolate-brown chest, belly, forelegs and the forward half of his hindquarters, but the rest of him was white mixed with a few brown spots on his side and flanks. He had a long brown tail with a hint of white close to his rump and a totally white mane, except for a touch of brown hanging over the top of his forehead.

Clever took one whiff of Tom's hand, then snorted and nibbled on him a bit with his lips to show him it was okay to rub his ears.

"He's beautiful," Tom said. "Where did you get him?"

"There's a new horse breeder over in Round Rock by the name of Isaac Norton. He has a bunch of good animals, too. But I heard a lot about this one prize stud he had, so I went over there with Clever's mama to see for myself. I took one look at that horse and decided then and there I was going to breed her with him. We got lucky, too, because it took the first time. Not one problem with the birth, either. He popped right out, and was on his feet in just a few minutes. Almost like he couldn't wait to be a horse and, ever since Clever hit the ground, he's been curious about everything. I didn't name him that because he's stupid, I guarantee you that."

"Dad, I know you didn't want to get into it on the train," Tom said, eyeing Clever's glistening coat, "but what happened to Deuce?"

"Well...I guess you deserve to know." Jim sighed. "Your brother never came around here much, but one morning he showed up and said he wanted to take Deuce out for a ride, so off he went. He was gone for quite a while, then got back here later that afternoon on foot. We found Deuce way out by the little falls on Cowhouse Creek with a broken leg, so we had to put him down right there."

"Buddy left Deuce out there all that time with a broken leg?" Tom asked, sickened at the thought.

"Yep." Jim shook his head as if he couldn't understand it, either.

"Did he say what happened?" Tom asked.

"Not really. He just said the horse lost his footing, which was probably true, but that was only part of the story. When we got out there, Deuce was lathered up pretty bad," he explained. "It didn't take a genius to figure out that he'd been ridden too hard for too long, and lost his balance because he was played out."

"Son of a…" Tom began. Sadness and disgust filled him. "Buddy did that?"

"I'm afraid so," his father said. "I'm sorry. But there's nothing anybody can do about it now, except maybe…" He didn't get the chance to finish his sentence.

Both turned, startled by the sound of someone moving around by the front of the barn. "Good morning, Tom!" yelled Chas as he came out of the tack room carrying a saddle and a blanket.

"Good morning, Chas," Tom said. "You going for a ride?"

"Me? No… these are yours," Chas said. He paused, looking at Jim. "Uh-oh, you haven't told him yet, have you?"

"Told me what?" Tom asked.

"That favor I wanted you to do," Jim said with a smile, "is to take your new horse out. You need to get to know him."

Tom pointed at Clever as he looked at Jim in shock. "You mean…he's mine?"

"Yep." Jim laughed out loud, proud of the homecoming gift he was offering.

"I didn't mean to spoil it, Mister Jim. I promise," Chas said. "I thought for sure you woulda told him by now."

"Don't worry about it, Chas," Jim said. "Besides, after all the time you spent cleaning up Tom's saddle and getting it to look as good as new, you deserve to see the look on his face, too."

"I don't know what to say," Tom said. "He's…beautiful."

"Just get your saddle on him and get out of here for a while," Jim said.

Tom gave his dad a grateful hug. "Thank you…wow." He looked at the saddle Chas was carrying to see it was his, but it was in far better shape than he had ever kept it. "Wow, Chas, That saddle looks brand new. You didn't have to do that."

"Oh, it was my pleasure, Mister Tom…I mean…Tom," Chas said, beaming. "I enjoyed it. Really. But this thing's getting heavy. Let's get it on his back. What do you say?"

"Let's do it," Tom said.

He opened the stall and walked in with Chas. Ten minutes later, he was leading Clever out of the barn by the reins as his father told him about the horse and what he should look out for, but Tom wasn't listening very closely. Before his dad could finish what he was saying, Tom was in the saddle and moving into the field behind the barn, heading north to see at last some of the familiar scenery he had missed so much. He could tell Clever was just as excited about the prospect of an early morning run as he was, but he held the horse to a trot at first because he wanted to make the ride last a while and he needed to show Clever who was boss.

Even though Tom hadn't been on a horse in over five years, riding Clever turned out to be one of the easiest things he ever did. The horse seemed to know beforehand what Tom wanted him to do. Not only was he sure-footed with a smooth gait, but he had stamina and was as fast as any horse Tom had ever ridden when he finally let out a piercing whistle, slapped Clever on the rump with the end of the reins and turned him loose on a full, thundering run. Watching the rolling hills spotted with grazing cattle, trees, brush and wild flowers race by was a feeling Tom had long forgotten and wanted to last all day but, after a short while, he slowed Clever to a walk and let him cool down.

Tom pulled up at one of the gullies leading into Cowhouse Creek so Clever could get a drink of water and, as soon as Tom was on the ground, the horse checked his pockets with his nose to see if he was carrying any treats like an apple or carrot. Tom laughed when Clever discovered there were none, put his forehead against Tom's side and nudged him away, as if saying the next time he should bring something. A long scratch behind the ears turned out to be the next best thing to a treat, though. By the time Tom got back in the saddle and turned for home, he felt like the horse was just as happy to have him for his master as he was about having him for a horse.

Tom wasn't in any hurry on the ride back and, when the ranch finally came into view, he pulled Clever to a halt so he could admire the Four C's as it spread out before him. The ranch took up thirteen-and-a-half square miles, which included most of the basin Cowhouse Creek flowed through on its way to join the Leon River north of Belton. The sight of his family's property as he rode over the gently rolling hills surrounding the valley always made him smile. The big red barn stood out more than the rest because it was roughly twice the size as the house, but the four-bedroom home on top of the gentle slope was a prettier sight. The back was built to look like a log cabin, but the front, sides and two chimneys that stood at opposite ends of the house were made of white limestone brick. Covered white porches ran the length of the house on all sides, offering shade no matter the time of day, and the roof was made of dark wooden shingles, creating a stark contrast from the white brick that surrounded most of the place.

The smokehouse was off to one side of the barn, and the log cabin bunkhouse, which slept eight hands, was fifty yards or so away on the other. There were three privies, one close to the house, one behind the barn, and another close to the bunkhouse for the hired help. Butting up to the barn and completing the panoramic view were three corrals. The largest one was used to break their horses, a medium-sized one was used for keeping an eye on an animal or two coming out of a sickness or injury, and the small one they used for branding, all connected to each other. His father had told him the only thing here when he bought the place was an anthill and, even though Tom had heard the story countless times, he had to give his dad credit because their land was surely a beautiful place to call home.

As he rode closer, Tom spotted a small, wrought iron fence close to one of the large oak trees, a few hundred yards from the house. He steered Clever that way, knowing it must be where his mother was buried.

Up until now, he had never given a thought as to where his family might one day all be laid to rest but, as he tied Clever to the fence and stood on the gentle hill looking at the new family cemetery, he knew his mother must have chosen this spot because it was perfect. He had the feeling she had been hoping for plenty of grandchildren because the pointed, wrought iron fencing surrounded an area far too big for Jim, himself and his brother. Tom unlatched the small gate and walked inside the cemetery to stare at the lone headstone, which stood just offset from the very middle and next to the plot that would one day hold his dad. It read:

Ruby Nell Wallace

1824-1879

She Always Led Us

Even Into Heaven

He took off his hat, bowed his head and said a silent prayer before sitting down on the grass at the foot of the grave, leaning back on his hands and talking to his mother as the leaves in the nearby oak, along with the wildflowers on the hill, gently swayed with the first hint of a morning breeze. He told her of the ordeals he went through in prison, things he had learned about life and about himself, but the most important thing he talked about was what he was going to do now that he had been given the second chance he had longed for. Until he found himself in prison, with everything he loved in this world stripped away, he never knew exactly what mattered most and what kind of man he really wanted to be. He did now, though, and he could never go back to the way he was before that fateful day in Dayna G's Saloon. His time in prison allowed him to search his soul and nurture a part of himself that was certain to govern the rest of his life and, ultimately, to make amends for the mistakes of his past.

He told his mother, when everything was said and done, he would hold tightly to what was now more essential to him than the very air he breathed. He was determined to live out the remainder of his days trying to be nothing more than just a simple, good man. He vowed to her, as he had to himself, when he was on his deathbed he wasn't going to have to look into the eyes of anyone and wish he had done it differently. He had seen far too many of those dying stares while working on the chain gangs and, from now on, nothing would be more important to him than that.

When he ran out of things to say, he got up and brushed the grass off the seat of his pants, now wet with dew, and stood a little longer, staring at the headstone and listening to the sounds of the gentle wind and the birds in the field. He put his hat back on and said, "This sure is a nice place you picked, Mom. I'll be back to see you tomorrow." He left the enclosure, closing the gate behind him, untied Clever, and climbed into the saddle. Gazing at the headstone one more time, he mouthed the words, "I love you, Mom."

Suddenly realizing he had lost track of time and most of the morning had passed, he put Clever into a trot toward the house. He smiled all the way home, knowing the guilt he'd carried in his heart for the last five years was now completely gone, and how exciting it was that he now could move on with his life.

CHAPTER 10

Sunday Afternoon

"You ready?" Jim settled himself on the seat of the buckboard.

"Sure," Tom said, climbing in, "let's go."

When he returned to the barn after his morning ride, Tom brushed down Clever and turned him loose in the big corral, then headed up to the house only to see his dad and Aya getting the wagon ready for another trip into town. Jim told him he needed to see if he could rustle up another hand or two to help with the barbed wire, so Tom grabbed a quick bite to eat and shortly after was sitting next to his father in the buckboard looking back at Aya in the front yard, waving as they moved away. As he looked back, his thoughts raced through a hundred different memories of growing up in that same yard, but his mind fixed on the one that stood out far more than any others. As he held up his hand in a slow wave to his old friend, that particular memory came back stronger and clearer than it had in years.

Every person in the county knew Aya was an Indian, but nobody was quite sure what tribe he belonged to because he never said a word to people he didn't know and not many more to the few he knew and trusted. He showed up at the Four C's a little over twenty years ago, repairing things around the ranch nobody asked him to fix but needed fixing, nonetheless. Jim tried to run him off at first because of the language barrier and the fact there were more than just a few Comanche raids taking place only twenty-five miles or so to the west.

There hadn't been a great deal of bloodshed during those raids but, if a rancher didn't watch his livestock closely, especially his good horses, they'd come up missing pretty quick. An Indian coming around, for any reason, was cause to grab a rifle. Jim must have chased him off a dozen times, only to see Aya stop and sit down on a far hill then come back after an hour or two and pick up where he left off. Finally, after a week or so, Jim got tired of the whole mess and invited him down to the house where they worked out a deal in simple sign language that allowed Aya to become a hand at the Four C's. Ruby wasn't too happy about the whole thing at first, thinking Aya might be some kind of scout taking reports back to his tribesmen, but it was only a few months before she and most other people stopped feeling that way because Aya's reputation at the ranch and around town became that of a man who could be counted on like no other Indian anyone had ever known.

It was less than a year later, when the war broke out and over Ruby's strenuous objections, Jim decided to become part of the 3rd Cavalry. Like most all other people in Bell County, Jim thought the war would be over quickly, and that he could do his duty and be back home tending to the ranch before the next spring. But, as it happened, in September of 1861, just a few short months after Jim left to join the Confederate Army, four well-armed men rode up to the house looking for food and a place to rest their horses. They soon realized there wasn't a man around to defend the place and, even though Tom and Buddy tried to act as if they could, they were only thirteen and twelve years old at the time. Their shaking rifles were quickly pulled from their grasp by three of the men who dismounted and fanned out around them. He and Buddy stood helplessly in the grasp of the filthy bearded men as the older one, who had done all the talking, grabbed their mom by the hair and tried to drag her into the house. A shot suddenly rang out and echoed down Cowhouse Creek as the leader clutched his chest and fell over dead, spilling Ruby back into the front yard.

More shots were fired in rapid succession, and before anybody knew who was shooting or where it was coming from, the other three men were lying on their backs with large pools of blood spreading out on the front of their tattered, dirty shirts. Tom would never forget the look in Aya's eyes after he charged up to the house, leapt off his horse and pulled a revolver out from underneath his vest to fire one point blank shot into the chest of the only man still writhing on the ground gasping for breath. Aya didn't say a word, but the stern, cold glare in his eyes when the gun went off made it perfectly clear to all there should never be any mercy for any men such as these.

Tom and Buddy were unable to speak, but would talk to each other for years about whether or not either one of them would ever have the nerve that blazed in Aya's eyes that day. Ruby never said anything as she nodded with tears streaming down her face, but words could never describe the feelings of relief and gratitude the look in her eyes made known.

Although the language barrier improved only slightly through the years, from that day forward, Ruby made sure Aya was always treated like family, never once mistrusting him again. For Tom and Buddy, Aya became like a second father after the shootings. The story of how he saved them all single-handedly soon spread far and wide, which not only gained him the respect of Ruby and the boys, but everyone else in the surrounding area.

"Where's Chas?" Tom asked, his thoughts coming back to the present.

"Over at his favorite fishin' hole," Jim said. "I swear that boy must be mad at every fish in that creek because he'd try to catch 'em all day every day if he could get away with it. He's pretty good at it. Dinner on Sundays is almost always fried catfish."

"Well, I hope his luck doesn't change," Tom said, rubbing his stomach. "Catfish sounds great."

"It won't change," Jim laughed. "I got a lot of confidence in him."

"Yeah, I do, too," Tom said, echoing his dad's laughter. He could picture Chas by himself out on Cowhouse Creek, getting up and running from beneath a shade tree as one of his cane poles doubled over after the bobber disappeared, and letting out a triumphant yell as he successfully wrestled his finned victim onto the muddy bank. Tom looked forward to a day when he could leisurely wet a hook but, as the wagon pulled out of the yard, he knew it wouldn't happen soon; there was too much work to be done.

"You think we'll be able to find a couple of guys willing to work?" he asked.

"I think so," Jim said. "Word's been out around here for the last few weeks that I was going to put the fence up when you got home, so I imagine once people in town see us, we'll have more than two or three men wanting to talk to us about it."

"I hope so," Tom said. "We got a lot to do."

"Yes, we do," Jim said. After the wagon passed loudly over Ruby's bridge and reached the dirt road on the other side, he asked, "Let me ask you about something — are you nervous about heading into Belton so soon?"

Tom squirmed. "I guess so."

"You don't have to go if you don't want to," Jim said. "I can go by myself."

"No…I might be a little uncomfortable with a few people, but I might as well get it out of the way now." Tom let out a deep sigh.

"You sure?"

"Yeah, I'm sure." Tom turned to watch their house disappear behind the bend. "I don't know what I'm going to say, though. I mean, how am I supposed to answer a question like 'Hey Tom, it's been a long time. How was prison?'"

"Well…you can say whatever you want but, if it was me, I'd reckon only an ignorant son of a bitch would ask something like that," Jim said, "so I wouldn't say anything. I'd just walk away."

"You're probably right."

Jim clapped Tom's shoulder. "Don't worry, Tom. You coming home will only be on people's tongue for a couple of days at most. Next thing you know, they'll be jabbering about something else and you'll be old news. Trust me."

"I hope so," Tom said, "but right now I feel like I'm heading into town as the new circus clown."

"Well, just remember, no matter what you might see or hear today, when a man pays a debt in full, he doesn't owe anybody anything anymore." Jim looked down the road into the distance. "If you feel like someone's trying to look down at you, just look them right in the eye until they find something else to stare at. You don't have to say a word to let them know you don't care what they think." He rubbed his bum leg. "I know what I'm talking about. I've had a few people stare at me."

Tom was struck by the comment because, even though he had seen his dad walk with a limp for as long as he could remember, he had never once considered him a cripple. The thought other people might came as a shock, and he understood for the first time in his life how remarkably strong his father must be to have accomplished what he had in the last nineteen years with only one good leg. He let the thought sink in, then turned to his father. "Thanks, Dad. I love you."

Jim glanced over at him. "You're home now, son. Everything's going to be all right." Then he added with a chuckle, "And I love you, too."

The anxiety that had crept up on Tom lifted and the rest of the trip went by quickly as they talked about the work ahead, who they might be able to hire on, and what they were going to do for a cook if Bear didn't make it like he said he would. They both had the feeling he'd turn up somewhere but, as a rule, cowhands weren't the most reliable bunch in the world and it wouldn't be the first time one of them was a no-show. They did have his bag, though, which was a little encouraging, if nothing else.

As they pulled into the outskirts of town on this early Sunday afternoon, Tom was taken by the sight of all the people on the sidewalks going about their business dressed in their fancy Sunday clothes. He and Buddy grew up being very familiar with the Bible, only because Ruby read from the book almost every night before bedtime, but neither she nor Jim could ever belong to any of the congregations around town. Like any other city, Belton had its fair share of reputable churches, but Jim and Ruby always believed the only reason there were so many preachers in the area was that people could feel good and pious about themselves on the Lord's Day when the rest of the week they were up to things entirely different.

There were roughly three times as many brothels in town as there were churches, and it was common knowledge that no self-respecting lady would be seen anywhere downtown except for Sunday during the day. The town had prospered from a reputation for cattle drives, women, gambling and saloons that drew every sort of person from all over the state, and not a single one was ever seen or heard talking about how they were drawn to Belton because of all the fine churches or the rousing Sunday sermons.

Bell County was formed on January 22, 1850 and was rich in a plentiful supply of deer, wild turkey, bear, buffalo, wild horses, ducks, wild hogs, and a generous amount of water coming from four different major sources. Cowhouse Creek flowed into the Leon River in the northwest part of the county, which then ran into the Lampasas and the Salado Rivers in the southeast, which then became the Little River farther downstream.

The people who settled the area tried to get county status from the state the year before but were turned down for no apparent reason, even though there were over six hundred residents at the time, with more moving in on a daily basis. When they tried again a year later, everyone figured it would be helpful if they named their new county after an influential man of the state, and they were right. They chose to name it after Peter H. Bell, who was the current governor of Texas but had never lived in the area. He was evidently flattered about the whole thing, though, because the state legislature was soon carving out a fairly large piece of the state and naming it after him.

They also chose the small settlement of Nolan Springs as the county seat, which was to become Belton a year later, with the first sale of town lots taking place on August twenty-sixth the same year. Merchants opened stores almost immediately in the new town square, and one of the favorite stories told throughout the years was of a man by the name of John Henry, who picked out the closest elm tree he could find and opened up a saloon beneath it with nothing more than a barrel of whiskey, a board laid across the top and a single tin cup for his customers to drink it with. The town's reputation started at that moment, because it was said that John Henry had quite a business, and it didn't take long for others to follow suit. Of course, with the influx of new shop owners, cotton farmers, ranchers, cowhands, blacksmiths, prostitutes and every other kind of man or woman moving into town trying to find a place where they could eke out a living, the fire and brimstone preachers weren't far behind. The churches didn't spring up as fast as the saloons did, but they all seemed to be full on Sundays with the same people that were prospering the rest of the week off the women, drinking, cattle and gambling the town had an illustrious reputation for.

As the wagon moved slowly through the streets, Tom watched the people strolling around in their fancy clothes, remembering many a time when his parents made it clear they didn't want their boys to grow up thinking that doing the same thing was a dignified way to live.

Whenever talk of religion came up, his mother invariably found a place in the conversation for her favorite expression about the matter, which was: "It's better to wash your hands every day than once a week." Coming back after five long years, Tom could see most of the people in this town still felt otherwise.

"Where we going first?" he asked, as his father turned the wagon into the town square.

"I thought I'd take us over to the hardware store on First Street," Jim said, working the wagon around a few of the others moving about the square. "There's usually a man or two hanging around over there looking for a job."

"Sounds good to me." Tom gazed across the courthouse lawn to the hardware store on the other side. "Hopefully, we'll find a few who aren't afraid of an honest day's work."

"I hope so," Jim said, less than hopefully, "but you know how that goes; we'll probably have to run a few off before we find the ones who'll stick." As they got closer he added, "Doesn't look like there's anybody out front, but

I bet if I go in there and tell old man Peyton we're here in town, we'll have people chasing us down the street before we leave to go back home."

Jim pulled the wagon to a stop and tied the reins in front of the Smith and Peyton Hardware Store and Buggy Shop.

"You coming with me or you want to stay here?" Jim asked, slowly stepping down into the street.

"I'll come with you." Tom hopped down onto the sidewalk.

They hadn't made it halfway to the entrance of the store when Tom heard a familiar scratchy voice, "Tom! Tom Wallace! Is that really you?"

Tom looked to see an old friend sitting on a bench in front of the clothing store two shops down who quickly rose and made his way toward him, a toothy grin spread across his face.

Tom let out a friendly laugh and said, "Yeah…it's me…come here." He reached out to hug the man who was obviously glad to see him. "I'll be damned — Church Davis," he added, a gleam in his eyes. "It's good to be home and it's *really* good to see you."

"Well, I guess so!" Church said as he lifted Tom off the ground in a bear hug. When he finished trying to squeeze the life out of him, he put him back down on the sidewalk and added, "It's good to see you, too. But I understand how you feel. Who wouldn't miss me if they didn't get to see me for five long years? I don't see how you stood it."

"Somehow I managed." Tom laughed again. He backed away a step and straightened his hat with one hand while pointing at Jim with the other. "You remember my dad, don't you?"

"Sorry for my manners," Church said, reaching out to shake Jim's hand. "Mister Wallace, how are you, sir?"

"Fine, Church. You doing all right?"

"Well…to be honest, I could be a little better," Church said, putting both hands in his pockets, shaking his head and glancing down at his feet. He looked up and squinted at Jim with a no-nonsense expression on his face. "Tell you the truth, I heard you might be needin' a good hand or two, so I been sittin' over there on that bench for the last couple of days waitin' to talk to you. Mister Wallace, sir, I'm hoping you'll gimme the chance to help y'all out."

"You've been sitting over there for two days?" Jim was astonished.

"Yeah, yeah, I have," Church said seriously, looking Jim in the eye. "Word's out y'all are gonna fence in the Four C's, and I reckon that's gonna take some time. Seems to me that could keep a man like me in work for a pretty good spell." He rubbed his chin in a nervous twitch. "Personally, I'm tired of hoppin' from one trail drive to the next, and my forty-year-old bones are tellin' me I shouldn't be lookin' at the rear end of any more cows while they shit all the way to Kansas. Don't get me wrong; I can still put in a good day as well as anybody, but workin' the trail is a young man's game, and I don't feel like I have enough spring chicken in me to do it anymore."

He paused, glancing down at the sidewalk again, then looked Jim square in the eyes and said with as much sincerity as he could muster, "Mister Wallace, I would be grateful if you would take me on. I can promise you won't regret it. I'll be a good hand."

"Where you staying?" Jim asked, looking Church over from head to toe.

"I got one of the rooms over at Rachel's Boarding House, south of town."

"You really want to work for us?" Tom asked, not quite sure his friend was serious.

"Yeah…if the pay's decent…yeah, I do," Church said. The look on his face sold Jim and Tom both.

"I'm paying everybody the same," Jim said, "twenty-five dollars a month, three squares a day plus room and board."

"Sounds good to me," Church said with a gleam in his eye.

"Fair enough, then." Jim smiled and shook Church's hand to seal the deal.

"All right!" Tom whooped. "Who would have thought Church Davis would one day quit chasing cows and come work for us?"

"I guess people change," Church said sheepishly "Maybe it's just my time."

"Well, Tom and I both know a little bit about that," Jim said. "Where's your horse?"

"Rachel's got an extra stall she's been lettin' me use," Church said. He snapped his fingers, "and that's another thing. I was hoping you'd have some extra room in that barn of yours that I could get ya to throw into the deal."

"No problem," Jim said. "How long will it take you to move your things into the bunkhouse out at the ranch?"

"Whenever you give the word, I'm ready," Church said. "I could head out to the Four C's right now if you want me to."

"Well, why don't you get going then?" Jim turned and walked to the entrance of the hardware store, stopping before he entered and turning back. "Tom and I have some business in town this afternoon and I'm not sure when we'll be back at the ranch. When you get there, tell Aya you're working for us now. He'll get you fixed up. Fair enough?"

"Fair enough," Church said. "and thanks again, Mister Wallace. I really appreciate it."

"And one more thing," Jim said with a smile, "call me Jim, okay?"

"Okay, Jim it is." Church returned the grin. "See you out at the ranch." He looked at Tom. "Well, you don't look so bad; a little skinny maybe, but you seem to have made it through okay."

"Yeah, well, you don't look so bad either, 'cept you must still be smoking 'cause your voice sounds worse than ever," Tom replied.

"Thanks for remindin' me." Church reached into his shirt pocket and pulled out a tobacco pouch. After expertly rolling his smoke, he struck a match off the bottom of his boot, took a long pull off the cigarette and slowly exhaled a small blue cloud into the air as he flipped the spent match into the street.

At six foot three and weighing well over two hundred pounds, Church Davis was a fairly big man. Even though he was in his early forties, most of it was still lean muscle, with the exception of a noticeable beer belly. His worn black hat hid most of the short, curly gray hair underneath, and his clean-shaven face bore the usual lines of a man who had spent a number of years working cattle under the hot Texas sun. His boots, pants and trousers all looked as though they had seen better days, which made Tom ask, "Have you been working?"

"Not really," Church said, shaking his head and taking another puff. "I been livin' off the little money I put away 'cause I just can't get the steam up to join any of the drives outta here. Had me some offers, but I just can't get myself to go." He paused a moment. "Well, actually, the big reason is that I been seein' this girl pretty regular, and she'd rather have me 'round here than out on the trails. I gotta tell ya, though, I sure am glad your dad hired me 'cause I'm about broke, plain and simple."

"Why didn't you try to hire on at Turner's place?" Tom asked, adding with a grin, "They hire old, broke-down cowpokes like you, too, ya know."

"Hey! Watch it, skinny man." Church laughed. "Truth be told, I did. A couple of times, but I think his son George always killed the deal. For some reason, that little weasel never liked me." He raised his eyebrows, shook his head and took another puff. "Don't know why; never did nothin' to him."

"That's George," Tom stated. "I don't think he likes anybody unless he gets something out of the deal." He patted his friend on the shoulder. "But it doesn't matter now since you're working for us, and I'm really glad you are. How long has it been since you quit chasing cows?"

"About five months," Church answered. "Word's been out that y'all were gonna need some help, so I figured I'd just lay low and try to get you guys to hire me on when the time came."

"Geez, Church," Tom said, "what if my dad had said no?"

"Don't know. I reckon it would've been back to the trails." Church frowned, then let his worried look fade away.

"Well, it worked out good then, I guess." Tom glanced down at the sidewalk.

"What do you mean, you guess?" Church asked, playfully shoving Tom on the shoulder.

"I mean it'll probably be pretty hard for you to take, having some skinny little guy like me run circles around you out at the ranch." Tom shoved Church the same way. "If you think you're too old now, wait until you see how work is really done."

"Yeah, well, we'll see about that," Church said, his cigarette dangling from the corner of his mouth. "It's great you're home, Tom. I missed you." He took another puff and turned to walk down the sidewalk. "I gotta get. Need to round up my things, but I'll see you at the Four C's this afternoon."

"See you there," Tom called, watching his most trusted friend outside of the family disappear behind a small crowd of people who gathered at the far end of the covered wooden sidewalk. Tom was about to enter the hardware store when his dad came out the door. "Hey, did you find anybody else in there?" he asked.

"No, but I left word," Jim said, adjusting his hat. "Old man Peyton said he'd send a couple of guys our way before we left town."

"What are we going to do now?" Tom asked.

Jim looked around, "What do you say we just take a little walk."

"Okay by me."

They headed down the sidewalk, watching the residents milling about in their fancy clothes, shopping and visiting in small clusters. "Is it me, or does this town look different?"

"No, it's different. They had a fire here last year and it damn near burned everything down," Jim said, tipping his hat to a passing lady. "It didn't take long to rebuild, and now people go about their business as if it never happened."

"That must be it," Tom said. "I was going to say that most of these places look better than I remember." They turned the corner and were walking down East Street when Tom pointed. "Ah, hell, there's Buddy."

His brother was walking their way and no sooner had Tom spoken when Buddy saw them, too. As he neared, he said, "Hey, I've been waiting for y'all to show up."

Tom wasn't in a hurry to see his brother again after what he had said the night before and didn't really want to hear why he was looking for them now. "How'd you know we'd be in town?" he asked.

"That's an easy one," Buddy said, chewing on his eternal toothpick. He looked at Jim. "Dad, word's out you're going to be hiring help and I need to talk to you about it."

"You want to quit being sheriff and get a real job out at the ranch?" Tom asked his brother with an impish grin. Normally, he would never say such a thing, but after last night it felt good to sling it in the other direction.

"Good one," Buddy said, "but no."

"What you got, then?" Jim asked with resignation as they stood in the middle of the sidewalk.

"I got a couple of men in mind for you that I'm sure will work out," Buddy said. "I know them both real well."

"I don't need two men," Jim said. "I already hired somebody, so I only need one more."

"Oh, no. You didn't hire Church Davis, did you?" Buddy asked, as if Jim had made the biggest mistake of his life. "Hell, he hasn't worked in God knows how long and besides, he's too damned old."

"You let me worry about that," Jim said. "I think he'll work out just fine."

"I do, too," Tom said, resenting the attack on his friend.

"Well, at least he'll probably outwork you," Buddy said, looking scornfully at Tom. "You're too damn skinny to be much good around a ranch."

"You two stop it, now," Jim said. "Look, Buddy, Tom and I are just out for a little walk and I don't really feel like arguing with you over who I'm going to pay my money to. If you're trying to be a Good Samaritan by helping these fellows out, just send them to talk to me before we leave town today. No promises, though, you understand?"

"All right," Buddy said, fingering his toothpick. "I wish you'd just sell the place, though; I'm worried about you. I've been trying to tell you that fencing in the ranch is going to cause a hell of a stir with the free grazers, and

I'd really hate to see you get caught up in all that mess 'cause…"

"Not now, Buddy," Jim said sternly. He tried to walk around Buddy, only to be cut off as his son moved in front of him.

Jim halted and gave his son an impatient stare. "Look, Buddy, I've been listening to you press me hard to sell the ranch for the last six months and the answer is still no. It's not going to happen."

"You don't seem to understand," Buddy said. "People are likely to get hurt over this barbed wire mess, and I don't want it to be you."

"What about me?" Tom asked dryly.

"Neither one of you," Buddy said, giving Tom a go-to-hell look.

"If you're so worried about us getting hurt, maybe you ought to look out for us. That's your job, isn't it?" Tom stared his brother down.

Buddy ignored the remark. He jerked the toothpick out of his mouth and waved it around, focusing on Jim. "I'm trying to look out for both of you. I know people who would pay a hefty price for that place. If you sell, this so-called 'range war' on the horizon won't involve either one of you. Dad, once you start putting up that fence, there's gonna be trouble, and I don't think a man your age should put yourself at risk."

"A man my age?" Jim fixed his cocky son with a smoldering glare. He grabbed Buddy by the shoulders and shoved him out of the way so quickly and with such force that Buddy lost his balance. "The answer is no. And I don't want you to bring it up again, ever. You hear me?"

Jim Wallace moved past his startled son and down the sidewalk, not looking back, his limp belying his strength.

Buddy stood there watching his father walk away, then put the toothpick back in the corner of his mouth. "You should talk to him."

"I *do* talk to him. Maybe *you* should try it sometime." Tom turned and went after Jim, who was fifteen or twenty paces in front of him and, like his father, didn't look back. If he had, he would have seen his brother staring a hole through him with a hateful sneer, the likes of which he had never seen before.

"Hey, Dad!" Tom caught up to his father at the corner. "You okay?"

"Yeah…I'm fine," Jim said in a softer but still aggravated tone of voice. He stopped and turned back to face Tom.

"What was that all about?" Tom asked.

"Ah…your brother's been trying to get me to sell the ranch for some time now," Jim said, letting out an irritated sigh, "and the more I tell him 'no', the more he bugs the hell out of me about it."

"I don't understand. I mean, why would he care?" Tom was confused about his brother's attempt to get his dad to sell their farm.

"I don't know, but I wish he'd leave the subject the hell alone."

Tom saw his father staring past him in the direction of Buddy, so he turned to see his brother stomping his way to the other side of the street. He glanced to see where Buddy might be headed, only to feel a large knot suddenly form in his stomach and his heart skip a beat. Not a hundred feet away was Jennie Lue Sloan, standing on the far sidewalk next to her father, Turner Bell.

Buddy scowled as his brother and father walked away and, if anyone had been close enough to see the look on his face, they would have known it was not a good time to try to talk to him. His teeth were clenched and his body was rigid with the frustration he felt from trying to talk his father into selling the ranch for over six months now. He had people lined up who were anxious to pay top dollar but, the more he brought it up, the more stubborn his dad became.

It was one thing to get snubbed by his father when all he was trying to do was talk some sense into him, but it was another altogether having to put up with insults from his brother. If anyone else in this town were to talk to him that way, he would wind up in the county jail with more than one nasty bruise on his face, but now he was going to have put up with insults from an ex-convict, and that was something he couldn't swallow easily. He took a deep breath and let it out forcefully as he looked around, then changed his demeanor instantly when his eyes caught sight of Turner Bell and his daughter walking around the corner and standing in front of the general store directly across the street.

He knew it had to appear to everyone in this town, especially Turner, that he was glad to have his brother back home, so he quickly put on his best face and hurried to the other side of the street where he tipped his hat and said, "Howdy, Mister Bell, Jennie." He took the toothpick out of his mouth. "How are y'all doin' today?"

"We're just fine, Sheriff," Turner said, shaking Buddy's hand. "And you?"

"Couldn't be better," Buddy said, returning the handshake vigorously. "Out doing a little shopping?"

"Not much." Turner put his arm around his daughter's shoulder and chuckled. "Jennie Lue here wanted to come into town and dragged me with her but, so far, we haven't bought a thing. But it's such a lovely day, we've been enjoying ourselves anyway."

"A beautiful day it is," Buddy said, turning his attention to Jennie Lue and adding with as much charm as he could muster, "and a beautiful daughter, too."

Jennie Lue glanced at Buddy in a way that let him know his remark did nothing for her, then looked at her father. "I think I'll go in the store and look around." She turned and entered without saying another word, leaving Turner and Buddy on the sidewalk, alone in an awkward moment. They both stood there a minute or two, exchanging polite hellos with a few of the townsfolk that strolled by, but most people on the sidewalk gave them a wide berth.

Turner Bell was only five foot six, not much of a physical threat, but he always appeared in a perfectly pressed, three-piece suit and a bow tie, topped off with an expensive derby that didn't hide that his salt and pepper hair was as well-kept as his neatly trimmed handlebar mustache. He invariably walked with a fancy cane, and his large collection of expensive boots made it appear that he never wore the same pair twice. He exuded the confidence of the most influential man in the county and was someone who was not to be bothered, especially if he was having a conversation with the sheriff.

As soon as there was a break in the pleasantries with the people passing by, Turner asked, "Did your brother make it home yesterday?"

"Yes, sir," Buddy said proudly as he pointed across the street. "That's him over there, and it sure is good to have him back."

"Oh, I see. How is he doing?" Turner eyed Tom from a distance.

"I think he'll be fine," Buddy said. "He's a little on the thin side, but he made it through okay. I knew he would. We wrote to each other quite a bit while he was gone. I was plenty worried about him going in, but from his letters he made it sound like it was a pretty easy stretch. I guess all this talk about how hard it is on those chain gangs is just that: talk."

"Well, I'm sure it was a tough situation for you and your father to go through, anyway," Turner said as he tipped his hat to another passerby, "but I'm happy for your family that the ordeal is finally over. I know you've all got to be very relieved."

"We are," Buddy said. "It's been hard worrying about my only brother every day for so long. For me, it's like there's been a black cloud hanging over the family for a long time and it's finally gone. I'm sure my dad feels the same way."

"I bet he does," Turner said with a nod, "and Buddy, I'm not sure what it could be but if there's anything I can do to help, don't hesitate to ask."

"Thank you very much, sir. I appreciate that," Buddy said. He hooked his left thumb under his belt. "Ah, now that you mention it, there is one thing I'd like to ask you, but it doesn't have anything to do with my brother. I was wondering, do you think y'all might be interested in a bite to eat before you head back home? It would be my pleasure to treat you and your daughter."

"I don't think so, Buddy," Turner said. "We had a big breakfast before we headed over here and, besides, I don't know if you're aware of this or not, but I don't think Jennie Lue would enjoy sitting down and having a bite to eat with you. No offense."

"None taken," Buddy said quickly, putting the toothpick back in the corner of his mouth and swirling it with his tongue. He moved his head around, trying to get a glimpse of Jennie Lue through the store windows. "I don't know why she won't give me the time of day, but it'd be nice if she'd give me the chance to show her she's wrong about me."

"Are you interested in my daughter?" Turner asked, raising an eyebrow.

"No, sir," Buddy stammered, changing his tone to one of complete respect. "No, sir. I just don't know why she won't say two words to me. That's all."

"Well," Turner said, looking bored, "maybe one day you can ask her but, for now, if I were you, I'd let it be. Once Jennie Lue has her mind made up about something, it doesn't change easily." He reached into the side pocket of his vest, pulled out his gold watch and opened it to glance at the time. "It's getting late. I guess I better get in there and see what Jennie Lue is spending my money on." He tipped his hat. "Good day, Buddy."

"You have a nice day, too, sir," Buddy said as Turner went through the swinging doors to the store. "If you need anything at all, you just let me know."

"I'll do that." Turner didn't look back.

Buddy stood there for a bit longer before gazing back across the street to give his brother another long stare. He took the toothpick out of his mouth and flipped it into the dirt. Glancing into the window one more time, he tried to catch a glimpse of Jennie Lue as he walked past the front of the store. He paused at the corner, then started toward Dayna G's Saloon a couple of blocks away to see what was going on over there.

Tom vaguely heard his dad saying something about how Buddy wanted him to sell the ranch but, as he looked at Jennie Lue, he wasn't much aware of anything except the sight of her. He instinctively took off his Stetson and straightened his hair, then stood there motionless, his hat in his hands, soaking up the sight of the prettiest girl he had ever known. She was four years younger than him, a little over five feet tall and weighed around a hundred and fifteen pounds. She wore brown boots, navy blue slacks, and a white blouse that buttoned up to a small white bow around her neck. Her white straw cowboy hat with a simple brown leather band covered her shoulder-length blonde hair, which was tucked behind her ears. Even from where he stood, Tom could tell her smile was still just as beautiful as her bright hazel eyes, which continued to shine with the fiery determination he always admired her for, but she soon turned and walked into the store, leaving him wondering if he would be lucky enough to see her again today.

"What?" he asked, putting his hat back on and turning to see his dad looking at him with a knowing grin.

"Hmm," Jim muttered, as he looked down and scratched the back of his neck. He looked at Tom and said with a smile, "Well...well...Jennie Lue Sloan, huh?"

Tom put on his best poker face, but it wouldn't have fooled anybody, "What are you talking about?"

"Come on, son," Jim said, laughing as he turned to head down the street, "let's go see if we can find somebody who can help us hang some wire."

Tom looked back one more time to see Buddy glaring at him from the other side of the street, but he didn't look at his brother long because his eyes were drawn to the store front's wide window. For a brief moment, he thought he saw Jennie Lue standing in the sunlight on the other side of the paned glass, watching him with those beautiful hazel eyes, but he soon had to turn and walk away to catch up with his father.

"Jennie, you see something you want?" Turner asked after he walked into the store and found his daughter by the cash register reading the label on one of the bottles of medicine stacked on the counter.

"No. I didn't come in here to buy anything," said an irritated Jennie Lue as she put the bottle back down. "I was just trying to get away from Buddy, that's all. He's far too self-important for me."

"I know he can be," Turner said with a shrug, "but I believe that's how he thinks he needs to act, being sheriff and all."

"Well, sheriff or not, he's a jack ass and I don't like being around him." Jennie Lue walked to the window to see if Buddy was still outside. "You don't mind if we stay in here a minute or so until he leaves, do you?"

"Of course not," Turner said. "In fact, now that we're here, I can pick up those matches your mother has been nagging me about for the last couple of days."

Jennie Lue heard her father ask the man behind the counter where he kept the cases of matches but, as she looked through the window, her attention was drawn to another figure on the far side of the street. She froze when it turned out to be the man she was secretly hoping to run into. It was the first time she had seen him in eight years, but she felt a deep rush of excitement because he seemed to be looking right back at her with the same handsome smile that always made her lose her tongue when she was younger. Her heart skipped a beat as she watched Tom from the shadows inside the store, wondering if that honest yet guarded connection might still exist between the two of them. She didn't take her eyes off him until he put his hat on and walked away down the far sidewalk to catch up with his dad.

It was no accident that she had talked her father into coming to town today, and she was elated at the chance to see Tom again, but she also felt a momentary twinge of sadness because her first opportunity to lay eyes on him since she moved to Austin was so fleeting. Jennie Lue ducked from the window as Buddy walked by outside, and was somewhat relieved when she glanced over at her dad to find him occupied at the cash register. She wouldn't have been able to explain to her father exactly what it was across the street that had gripped her attention if he had been watching. She exhaled slowly, waiting for Buddy to move well past the store, then took another long glance at Tom through the store's lettered-paned glass, a gleam in her eyes and a soft smile spreading across her face. When Tom was finally out of sight, she walked over to her father, grabbed his left hand with both of hers and asked in a much happier tone, "Are you ready, Daddy?"

"Sure," Turner said, "where would you like to go?"

"I don't know," she said, squeezing his hand and tugging him to the door with a spring in her step, "but I sure am glad you came out with me today."

"Me, too," Turner said with a bewildered smile, "me, too."

"Mister Wallace!" a voice called out as Jim and Tom walked beneath the covered sidewalk. They both turned to see Curry Hampton hurrying after them. "Mister Wallace," he said, a bit out of breath, "I'm glad I caught up with y'all."

"What can I do for you?" Jim asked, although he suspected what Curry wanted.

"Buddy told me you'd be needin' work done around the ranch and I should talk to you 'bout it," Curry said, a little uneasy. "Fact is, I sure could use a steady job."

Jim studied the man in front of him. Curry Hampton was in his mid-thirties, with long brown hair that looked as if it hadn't been washed in some time. His five-foot-ten frame was overweight by about forty pounds. Curry had scratched out a living in Belton for years and had earned a reputation for being a handy man who could repair most things around a place for not much money, but everybody in town also knew that if it was something important to be fixed, Curry's work was never up to snuff. His clothes were dirty and worn, giving testament to the fact that his income was a reflection of his reputation.

"Buddy told you to come see me?" Jim asked, not even remotely surprised that his youngest son would send him this less-than-savory character.

"Yes, sir," Curry said, a bit more confident now. "He said he'd worked it out that you'd hire me on."

"He did, did he?" Jim said. He paused for a long moment. "I'll tell you what. I'm paying my guys twenty-five dollars a month…"

"That sounds great!" Curry said.

"Hold on there," Jim said, raising his hand. "Listen up, Curry, you've made a name for yourself for not doing good work, so here's the deal: I'll pay you ten dollars a month to start and I'll increase it when you show me you're not going to expect pay for sitting on your ass all day."

"But, Mister Wallace," protested Curry, "I can do just as good a job as anybody else around here and, besides, that's not even fifty cents a day."

"Take it or leave it," Jim said, his arms crossed.

"Does that include a bed and meals?" Curry asked weakly, scratching the side of his head.

"Do you want the job or not?" Jim asked with finality.

"Well...I...I need the money," replied Curry.

"All right, then. Be at the bunkhouse by dark," Jim said, "and be ready to work at sunup tomorrow."

"Yes, sir, Mister Wallace," Curry said. He took a deep breath and opened his mouth as if he wanted to say something in protest, but evidently changed his mind at the last second. He shook his head once, then tipped his hat and quietly walked back the way he came.

"Why did you hire that guy?" Tom asked when Curry was out of earshot.

"Hell, I don't know," Jim said. "I guess I'm hoping it might keep your brother off my ass for a spell, and that in itself would be worth keeping him around."

"There's no way he'll work out," Tom said, watching Curry disappear around the street corner.

"You and I both know that," Jim said, "but at least we can use him for the time being. We can always get somebody else the first time he shows up late for breakfast."

Tom laughed. "That might be tomorrow."

"You know, you're probably right. I never thought about that."

"Lucky I'm around," Tom said.

"You're damned right about that." Jim put his arm around Tom's shoulder. "Come on. I think there's a chance I might know where our cook could be."

They started walking down the street when Tom was struck by something that hadn't occurred to him before. "Dad, why didn't you hire help before now?"

"I thought about it," Jim said. "I just wanted to make sure you made it back first before I did anything."

"What do you mean 'made it back first'?"

"Don't take this the wrong way," Jim said quietly, "but I've heard some pretty grim stories about men in this state who don't make it home after they get shipped off to prison, and I knew I wouldn't have it in me to run the Four C's unless you made it back safe and sound."

"What would you have done if I hadn't?" Tom asked. "You can't just quit."

"That's exactly what I would've done," Jim said with conviction. "I've had more than one offer to buy the ranch, and I'd already made my mind up to sell the place and be done with it if you didn't come home. Hell, even Henry Sloan made me an offer."

"Really! Jennie Lue's husband?"

"Yep," Jim said.

"I'll be damned," Tom said, "I guess it's true; Turner does want our property."

"I'm not so sure about that," Jim said. "Henry came by the ranch late one afternoon and tried his level best to talk me into selling the place to some outfit he knew out of Austin. Told me they wanted it pretty bad, but we'll never know for sure because he was robbed and killed later on that night, just outside of Belton as he was heading back home."

"You're kidding," Tom said in disbelief. "You didn't tell me that."

"Didn't think about it until now," Jim said with a shrug.

Tom looked away to hide the shock in his eyes and, for a few moments, the only sound between them was their boots on the sidewalk. "Did Buddy find out who did it?" he asked.

"He said so; hung a black kid over it," Jim said. "That kid swore up and down he didn't do it, though, and I kinda believed him because there were some things about the whole mess that didn't add up."

"What do you mean?"

"Well," Jim said slowly, "first off, they never found any money on that boy and second, Henry had this real expensive gold pocket watch he was always showing off that came up missing. They never found that, either." Jim let out a heavy sigh. "But Blondy Harbison said he saw the kid fire the shots, so that was that."

"Who's Blondy Harbison?"

"Buddy's deputy," Jim said, "has been for about the last three years. Word is he used to be up in Fort Worth, but evidently was a little too quick with his gun, so they ran him off. Buddy hired him on, but there's something about the guy that doesn't sit well with me. I don't know what it is, and nobody in town seems to care much about him, except the women, that is. The young girls around here all swoon over that long blond hair like it was sent from heaven."

Tom's mind raced through the news. He was suddenly sure there was no way Jennie Lue Sloan would ever give him the time of day. Not only was his past a huge ball and chain around any hopes he had for her, but her husband had been killed after leaving his family's ranch. He felt like a stupid fool and shook his head in disgust, certain he had been kidding himself ever since her name came up on the train. "She must hate the whole lot of us," he said quietly, as they turned north to cross the street.

"What was that?" Jim asked.

"Nothing," Tom answered. He took a few short disappointed breaths, then changed the subject. "Let me ask you then; what would you have done if I hadn't made it back?"

"Oh, I don't know. Maybe traveled some," Jim said. "Makes no difference now, though. The storm's passed for both of us."

Tom smiled at his father affectionately and nodded once to let him know he felt the same way.

They were moving into the one part of town that was busy at all hours of the day and didn't get far before a small group of cowboys spotted Jim and tried to talk to him about a job. They were quickly disappointed when Jim told them he already hired the men he wanted and didn't need any more hands right now. Tom wished that one of them had gotten to his father before Curry, but he knew that once his dad made his mind up about something, nobody was going to change it. Tom scratched his head over the futility of the situation while Jim shook the hand of each dejected young man. He let out a small disgusted "Humpf" as they walked away, trying to imagine what it was Buddy could be up to that would make his father hire Curry Hampton over one of these other eager cowhands. He didn't say another word for a while as the idea kept running through his head, but he changed his train of thought quickly when he realized why his dad figured he knew where to find Bear. They were walking into the northeast area of town that housed most of the saloons and brothels.

Tom let out a chuckle. "I think you might be on to something."

"This ain't my first rodeo," Jim said as they looked around at the busy intersection. There were horses and wagons tied up in front of every building, with people coming and going into the different saloons, with loud noises coming from the inside of every tavern. Pianos were playing, loud voices in the background boasting of who knew what, and occasional squeals from the working girls that gave the whole scene a carnival-like atmosphere. It was a scene Tom purposely hadn't thought of for a long time, and a chill came over him as he spotted a horse tied up in front of Dayna G's that was, without a doubt, Niki. "Over there," Tom said, pointing her out.

"I told you," smiled Jim, taking a few steps into the street. He stopped when he realized Tom hadn't joined him, and turned to see the worried look on his son's face. "You okay?" he asked. "You don't have to come with me. I can be back in a minute."

Tom had long thought about the day when, sooner or later, he would have to face the one place on earth he should have stayed away from on that fateful day, and how he would feel when he did. He hadn't expected it to be right after he got back to Belton because one of the promises he made to himself was that he would no longer frequent any establishment like the ones in this part of town. Not only did walking through those doors cost him over five years of his life, but he had often wondered how much money he would have put away if he had only spent half of what he did on liquor, poker and one of the girls every now and then. He eyed the two-story building Niki was standing in front of for what seemed like an eternity, then let out a deep breath. "No. I'll go with you."

"You sure? When you get down to it, there's no point in you going in there, too." Jim gave his son a hard look, trying to gauge the situation.

"No. Let's go get our cook." Tom stepped into the street, looking at his dad in a way that let him know he was ready to face this part of his past. "I'm all right. Besides, I kinda miss the guy."

"You know what?" Jim said with an easy laugh, putting his arm around Tom's shoulder, "It's only been two days, and I kinda miss the guy, too." They started their way over but hadn't made it halfway across the street when they noticed all the lively sounds coming from Dayna G's had come to an abrupt halt.

"Bartender, I'll have another," Bear said as he put his empty mug down. He was standing at the bar in Dayna G's, which was said to have the prettiest girls in town and sounded like just the place to stop for a cold beer or six after a long hot two-day ride in the saddle. "What's your name?" Bear asked, as the bartender expertly slid the frothy mug down the bar top where it stopped right in front of him.

"Gilmer Mure," said the bartender. He walked over and held out his hand. "Everybody 'round here calls me Gil. What's yours?"

"The name's Bear. Pleased to meet ya," he said as he shook Gil's hand. "I always thought it was a good idea to be on a first-name basis with my three Bs."

"Oh, yeah?" Gil said, laying both palms down on the bar and leaning forward to better hear the coming story. "And what are the three Bs?"

"My banker, my blacksmith and my bartender," Bear said with a smile, "and, since I don't have a banker or a blacksmith for the time bein', I guess you're it for now."

Gil laughed. "I suppose there's some truth in that, old timer. You don't mind if I use that, do you?"

Bear held his mug aloft in a toast. "Consider it yours. Just don't call me an old timer in front of these girls." He took a long quaff of beer, wiped the foam off his upper lip and set the mug down. "I prefer to think of my age as an asset 'cause it's taken me years to get to the point where I understand the three Ws perfectly."

"Okay," Gil said, knowingly taking the bait. "And what are the three Ws?"

Bear stood up as straight as he could and held his chin out in a mock aristocratic pose. "My good man, I'm gonna let ya in on a little secret. In my travels, I have acquired the knowledge that any man who knows what the three Ws stand for will always attract the ladies, because most every pretty girl you'll ever meet is interested in a man either *wise, wealthy,* or *well-proportioned.*"

Gil laughed louder this time, "I'm gonna use that, too," he said as Bear took another long swig from his beer.

"Only on one condition." Bear set the mug on the bar. He pointed at Gil, a sly smile on his face. "Ya can't let on to these girls that I'm not wise or wealthy; I only tip like I am."

"Your secret's safe with me," Gil assured him with a smile, "but what about the other W?"

"One out of three ain't bad," Bear said with a wink, smiling proudly.

Gil laughed even louder as he walked to the beer taps to pour Bear another. "This ain't the first time you been in a place like this, is it?" he said.

"Can ya tell?" Bear asked.

"Yeah, I can," Gil said. He brought another full mug and set it in front of Bear. "But I won't let on like I know. Here. This one's on me."

"Why, thank you," Bear said with surprise. He lifted his new glass in another toast. "I got a good feeling about you bein' my new bartender. Yep, I think you and me are gonna get along just fine."

Gil smiled. "Likewise. So tell me, what kind of a name is Bear, anyway?"

"Hell, that's a long story. How 'bout if I tell ya next time?" Bear put his mug down and looked around the saloon. Although it was Sunday, the place was surprisingly busy. There were twenty-five or thirty cowboys drinking at the fifteen or so tables spread out on the hard, wooden floor, each with his eye on one of the girls that stopped by every now and then to take one of them upstairs. There were another ten or twelve cowboys lined up at the smoky bar alongside him, and four or five card tables in the back of the room were full of gamblers more interested in watching their game than any of the women. The notes of "Oh, Susanna" were banged out of a piano against the far wall by a gray-haired, bow-tied black man, an empty tip jar next to his sheet music.

Bear had been swapping stares with the same pretty brunette who sat at a table in the corner with a man with long blond hair wearing a deputy sheriff's badge. He was just about to have Gil send her a drink in the hopes of introducing himself when the sheriff came in and sat down with them. He looked at her again, saying to Gil, "Right now, I'm a little more interested in finding out the name of that pretty little thing over there."

"That's Jessie," Gil said as he looked her way. "She's about the prettiest girl in the place. You obviously don't have anything wrong with your eyes."

"Send her a drink on me," Bear said, as he looked at Jessie and hoped she would come over and talk to him.

"I don't know if I would do that just yet, if I was you," Gil said.

"How come? It's my money."

Gil put his hands on the bar, leaned forward and said in a low voice, "'Cause that's the sheriff's girl. Maybe ya ought to wait until he leaves."

"What do ya mean, the sheriff's girl?" Bear asked. "She's a workin' girl, ain't she?"

"Well…yeah," Gil said, "but the sheriff don't like anybody messin' with her while he's in here. I guess he figures it makes him look bad."

"But I don't know how long I'm gonna be here," Bear said. "All I want to do is buy her a drink, so ya go ahead and take whatever it is she likes right on over there."

"I don't know…ya sure ya wanna do that?" Gil asked.

Bear nodded. "Go on now. Just say it's from the gentleman at the bar, and make sure ya play up the words 'the gentleman'."

"Oh-kay, then. Whatever ya say," Gil said as he poured a shot of Amaretto, walked around the bar and over to the far table. He set the shot down in front of the girl.

Bear watched all three people sitting at the table turn to look as Gil pointed back to him, then raised his glass in a friendly toast. Their reaction wasn't what he expected. The sheriff and his deputy talked to each other as they sized him up from across the room and it was obvious from the way Jessie was reacting she was trying to talk them out of whatever it was they were about to do.

Gil returned to his station behind the bar, leaned to Bear and whispered, "I tried to tell ya," as the sheriff and his deputy got up from the table.

"Howdy, Sheriff!" Bear said as Buddy and Blondy walked up and stood, one on each side of him. "Nice town ya got here." Neither said a word as they stared at him until finally Bear added, "Either one of ya like a drink? I'm buyin'."

Buddy slowly wiped down his long mustache while giving Bear a cold stare. "I don't drink on the job and, besides, I don't think I've ever let a drifter buy me a drink," he said.

A few of the customers standing at the bar quit talking to each other and listened in when they noticed the sheriff's conversation with the old man wearing the ugly hat wasn't about anything friendly.

Buddy took his time looking up and down at the dusty clothes Bear wore and said with a smirk, "I always figured it'd be better if drifters saved their money. Maybe then they could afford clothes that didn't smell like cow shit. What do you think?"

Bear looked to his left at the deputy, then to his right at Buddy and said with a grin, "I think anybody has the right to be whatever it is they want to be…like a sheriff…or even a deputy." Bear held his mug up in a toast and took a swig.

"What the hell is that supposed to mean, old man?" Blondy asked.

Bear turned to get a good look at Blondy Harbison. He could tell right away he wasn't a man to be messed with. He looked to be about the same age as the sheriff, five feet ten or so, clean shaven, and in good physical shape. He already had his right palm on the butt of his pistol, flicking the side of it with his trigger finger and making it clear to all he was ready to wield it.

Bear looked him in the eye and could tell he had used it before and, not only that, he liked using it. "Here, let me do this." Without taking his eyes off Buddy, he unbuckled the belt to his holster, took it off and laid the gun on the bar, making it known he wasn't there for a fight.

"What I mean is, people ought to have the right to do whatever it is they want, as long as it don't hurt nobody, and I ain't hurtin' nobody. In fact, I'm feeling downright neighborly."

Buddy eased the tension between the two of them a little by showing a little smile, but raised it more when he said, "Yeah, I bet you are. But the problem is, *you ain't my neighbor.*"

"Oh, but I am," Bear said as friendly as he could. "Belton's gonna be my new home and, up until now, I was thinking I'd come in this place quite regular."

Buddy's jaw tightened as he sucked air through his teeth, and exhaled slowly. "You need to think twice about what you're saying. If I was you, I'd find another town a ways away from me."

Bear noticed there were more customers in the saloon following the situation at the bar, and the noise level in the place was dropping as they tried to get an earful. He picked up his mug, finished the last of his beer in one big gulp and set it back down.

"Look, Sheriff, I was just tryin' to buy them two girls you had over there at the table a drink; that's all. Is there anything wrong with that?"

"What two girls?" Buddy asked.

"Why, that pretty brunette over there and the blonde one that was with her," Bear said with a friendly smile. "Where'd she go anyway?" he added as he looked around the saloon as if he was trying to pick her out of the crowd.

More than one customer snickered over Bear's remark, which made Blondy grab the butt of his pistol as if he was going to draw. "You son of a bitch," he snarled.

"Hold it, Blondy!" Buddy said, loud enough to get the attention of the rest of the patrons in the bar. He stared his deputy into letting go of his gun, then turned back to Bear. "You think you're funny, old man?"

"I don't know. Maybe," Bear said, as if he didn't know what was going on. "Why do you ask?" He turned to look at Blondy, who was so mad it appeared smoke would blow out of his ears any minute. He reached up and slowly held out his spectacles while squinting his eyes, "Oh! I'm sorry. You ain't a blonde girl, are ya?"

By this time, the piano player had stopped playing and even the card players had taken their eyes off their money, turning to look at the bar to see what was going to happen next. Blondy's face was beet red. He was breathing heavily and his eyes looked as if they could shoot fire.

"Look here, old man," Buddy growled, "I don't know where you came from and I don't care, but you've finished your beer, so it's time you walk out that door and head on back to whatever dump it is you call home and stay there. And it'd probably be a good idea if you don't come back around this town, if you know what's good for you."

"You might be right," Bear said, nodding and appearing to ponder the sheriff's advice. He took his old hat off and rubbed the top of his head, then looked at Buddy, adding, "I'll be right back."

Before Buddy or his deputy could say or do anything, Bear walked away from the bar and over to the table where Jessie sat. He spoke just loud enough for everyone to hear, "My name is Bear and I hope I have the chance to meet ya proper. I'm sorry about today." He reached into his front pants pocket, pulled out a small wad of money and handed her a five-dollar bill, saying with a wink, "It was a pleasure just watchin' you smile. I hope to see it again real soon."

He turned and strolled back to the bar, unaware of the look of admiration on Jessie's face, but he knew it was time to leave because the sheriff and deputy appeared to have had enough. "Well, Sheriff..." he began.

Buddy reached over, grabbed Bear's holstered pistol off of the bar and seized him forcefully by the arm as he half-led, half-dragged him toward the door, with Blondy close behind. He was madder than a hornet. "You don't listen so good, do you?" he sneered.

Bear didn't want to leave so easily, and was trying to wrestle his arm out of Buddy's grasp when he and everyone else in the place were taken completely by surprise by the two men who walked into Dayna G's and stopped dead in their tracks. The last thing anyone expected was for Bear to look at them and say, "Why, Jim! Tom! Good to see ya!"

There were other reasons they were all shocked. For one, Jim Wallace had lived just outside Belton for years and, like all the residents, knew full well about the saloons and brothels that littered this side of town, but never once had anyone actually seen him in one. Secondly, Tom had only been home for two days and here he was, already back in the same saloon where he killed that man over five years ago. But the last and most surprising thing of all to the people in the saloon that day was the question that came out of Jim's mouth.

He pointed at his youngest son and asked, with no small amount of indignation, "Buddy, what the hell are you doing with my cook?"

"*Your cook?*" Buddy asked.

"Yeah, my cook," Jim said with a curt nod.

"Bear, what's going on?" Tom asked.

"I don't know. All I wanted to do was have a couple beers and buy a girl a drink," Bear answered, wrenching his arm free of Buddy's grasp. "Next thing ya know, the sheriff here and his deputy are tryin' to run me outta town."

"Buddy?" Jim raised an eyebrow as he glared at his youngest son.

"It's my job to run off vagrants like this one," Buddy said, giving Bear a disgusted look, trying to make his excuse sound reasonable. "I don't like this guy; he's too much of a smart ass for me."

"I wasn't bein' a smart ass," protested Bear as he pointed at Blondy. "I just don't see so good and I mistook that feller for a pretty blonde girl, that's all."

More laughter came from the crowd as Blondy said viciously, "You need to let me have my time with him, Buddy. I'm a deputy sheriff and I don't have to put up with this shit."

"Well, maybe you should get a haircut or grow some hair on your face," Jim said.

A few more chuckles went through the crowd but stopped abruptly as Blondy hatefully stared everyone down. He glared at Bear and hissed, "You and me are gonna have a little go round down at the jailhouse."

"Come on, son, are you really going to arrest him just for being a smart ass?" Jim asked.

Bear looked back and forth at all three Wallaces with an amazed look on his face, then pointed at each, saying, "Ahhaaah...the sheriff here is your son...and your brother?"

"Yes," Tom said. "Guess we forgot to mention that."

"Wow. Now, that's right interestin'. Guess it makes no difference to me, though," he said with a shrug. "I don't get into trouble with the law, so I don't mind him bein' the sheriff nearly as much as I mind him bein' so ass-holic this early in our friendship."

This time it was Buddy's turn to stare down the laughs that went through the room but, after a moment or two, Jim broke the silence. "Buddy, why don't you just let it go? Bear's here to stay. You two might have gotten off on the wrong foot, but he's going to be my cook, no matter what. So I'm going to ask you again, do I need to follow you down to the jail to get him out or are you going to let us leave now?"

Buddy never took his eyes off Bear as he answered, "No…y'all can go, but before you do, I want to know your name."

"The name's Bear," he said, offering a hand. "Pleased to meet ya."

Buddy stared at Bear's outstretched hand for a long moment without shaking it, then looked him in the eye. "Bear, huh? That's a stupid name. Well, let me tell you something, Bear," he said, "first off, it's time for you to go, and second, I don't care if you work for my dad or not. Next time I see you in here, you ain't gonna be so lucky."

"Shut the hell up, Buddy." Jim glared at the people who were watching the situation and listening to their every word. He held up both hands as he tried to make eye contact with as many as he could and asked them all loudly, "As long as he doesn't hurt anybody, he can go anywhere he damned well pleases. That's the law, right?" He got approving nods from most everyone, then turned back to Buddy. "That's the law. Right?"

Buddy briefly nodded, but didn't say anything.

"I guess that's it, then," Jim said. He turned to the door. "Come on, fellas, let's go."

"Hold on there a minute, Jim," Bear said, as he walked back to the bar, "I got me a bar tab to settle up. Here ya are, Gil," he added with a wink, tossing a gold coin on the bar, "I think that ought to cover it."

"Thanks, Bear," Gil said, picking up the coin with an appreciative smile on his face. "You take care."

"Will do. Oh, and one more thing," Bear said as he started back toward the door. He stopped before Buddy and asked real friendly, "Can I have my gun back?"

Buddy handed it over, but grimaced as Bear continued while buckling it on. "I can't shoot worth a damn, but I like havin' it around in case I need to throw it at somethin'." After he tied the leather string around his leg, he tipped his worn-out hat to the sheriff, "You have a good day, now."

As they left Dayna G's, the piano player started a lively tune to take the tension out of the air, which made Jim stop and take a look at him before he joined Tom and Bear out on the sidewalk. There was something about the way the gray-haired black man returned the stare that made Jim think they knew each other, but he couldn't immediately recall when or where.

Bear lingered long enough to see that, before the crowd went back to their conversations and the place returned to its normal noisy state, Blondy went over and sat down at the table with Jessie to glare at everyone in the place with a dumbstruck, yet infuriated look on his face that would be the hot topic of conversation in Belton for a few days to come.

Buddy followed Bear, his dad and Tom out the door and watched with calculating eyes as they walked down the street. He leaned against a pole beneath the sidewalk awning and reached into his shirt pocket to pull out a fresh toothpick and stick it in his mouth. He contemplated the events of the last two days, none of which were going his way, and stood there a while thinking it over, deciding now wasn't the time to make any rash mistakes. He turned to go back inside, knowing the first thing he needed to do was to get Blondy to calm down. The second would be to visit the courthouse tomorrow morning because he was certain he'd have new instructions for his deputy after he had a long talk with the mayor.

"Y'all got any other family members I need to know about before I go makin' anybody else in this town mad enough to shoot me?" Bear asked from the back of the wagon as it lurched into the street and away from the hardware store. He thought it would be much more comfortable making the final leg of his trip in the wagon, so he tied Niki to the rear, sat down behind the seat and leaned comfortably against the saddle his horse made clear she was more than happy to be out from under.

"I think that's about it," Tom said, laughing. "Can you think of anyone else, Dad?"

"No. Not right off hand," Jim replied.

"Look here, Jim, I'm awful sorry 'bout all that," Bear said. "I didn't mean to…"

"Bear, if you apologize to me one more time, you're going to have to walk," Jim said. "Don't worry about it. If it makes you feel any better, Buddy's been a big rock in my boot lately, so why don't we change the subject? How was your trip?"

"Hot, dry, sweaty and wonderful." Bear immediately launched into lengthy details about his entire ride to Belton, starting in Huntsville.

Tom listened in a little at first but, as his father turned the wagon north onto Main Street, he found himself lost in thoughts about Jennie Lue, the way Henry died, and how in the world he ever let himself get excited about her in the first place. Even though Bear was talking non-stop in the back, Tom had no idea what he was saying because he was busy kicking himself over his lame-brain idea that there might have been a way to make his pipe dream come true. He took his hat off, closed his eyes, leaned forward in the seat and scratched the top of his head, feeling resigned of any hope she could ever look at him again with that angel's smile he remembered so well. As he sat up and put his hat back on, he opened his eyes to see none other than Jennie Lue and her father standing on the corner they were approaching.

Tom realized, while he was holding his head down and kicking himself over his foolish ideas, Jennie Lue Sloan had already spotted them as they came down the street and was staring right at him with a soft smile as he looked up. There was something about the way she was looking at him that made him forget in an instant all the things he had been beating himself up over. Her eyes were even more beautiful than he remembered because, not only did they still shine like a young girl's, they now also held the look of a grown woman, and her smile still radiated the saintly glow that could make his heart stop in his chest. As they grew closer to the corner, Tom nearly fell out of his seat as she raised her hand and slowly waved at him with a wide smile. He waved back with an astonished look on his face as they passed not twenty feet away.

He glanced at her father and noticed he hadn't seen them coming until they were already passing through the intersection. Tom was reminded of the deep differences between Turner and his father, because Turner's chat with Jennie Lue came to a sudden end as he looked at Jim without emotion. He was vaguely aware Bear was still in the back yapping about something, but Tom's eyes returned to Jennie Lue's and stayed until he could no longer see her.

Tom turned around in his seat after she was out of sight and his thoughts came back from the clouds.

"Now that little girl back there has it bad for ya, Tom," Bear chuckled. "I know what I'm talking about 'cause I seen girls look at me that way lots of times."

Tom turned to look at Bear, uncertainty written all over his face. "Oh, I don't know about that."

"Shoooooot," Bear said, drawing out the word and letting out another chuckle. "You got it bad for her, too, don't ya? I saw the way ya looked at her, ya know."

Tom said nothing, feeling the flush of embarrassment creep up into his face.

Bear went on, "If I was you, I'd hop down off this wagon and head back there as fast as I could and tell that pretty little thing whatever it took to make her want to spend the next fifty years or so with me. If I'm guessin' right, that shouldn't take much." He let out a long cat whistle. "She was somethin', Tom and, if you don't make a move on her real soon, I'm gonna be extremely disappointed in ya."

"Do me a favor, Bear," Tom said softly without looking back, "let it go, will you?" He looked at his father, who was gazing at him with a question in his eyes. "Trust me; there's a lot of reasons why I need to leave her alone."

Jim's eyes softened., "No, there's not, son. None that concern you anyway." He popped the reins on the horse's back and said to Bear, "What he means is, me and her daddy don't get along so good."

"Why is that?" Bear asked.

"Like Tom says," Jim sighed, "a lot of reasons."

"Do either one of ya have anything else to tell me about this town before I get in any deeper?" Bear asked. "Whoo-wee, I only been here a couple of hours and I already got a headache from all the nonsense 'round here."

"Is that from the nonsense or the alcohol?" Jim grinned.

"Well, now, I don't rightly know," Bear said, leaning back against his saddle and pondering. "That's a good question. I do know I'm hungry, though. How long 'til we get to the ranch?"

"About thirty minutes," Jim answered, "and, with any luck, some fried catfish will be on the table when we get there."

"Now there's some great news," Bear said. "My first day on the job will be my first day off."

They all laughed as Jim drove the wagon down the winding dusty road to the ranch. But it wasn't long before he and Bear were engaged in another conversation about Belton, widows, saloons and whatever else it was that rapidly crossed Bear's mind.

Tom didn't catch much of it. For the rest of the trip, he was wrapped up in thoughts of Jennie Lue and any clever ideas he could come up with that would allow him to see her again. It was almost as if he slept the entire way because the next thing he knew, the buckboard was rattling across the boards on the bridge named after his mother and the yelping dogs were running out to greet them. The front door opened, and Aya and Chas stepped out onto the front porch as they came to a stop in the front yard.

They climbed down and were immediately surrounded by the excited hounds but, as soon as they were finished checking out the new guy, Bear walked up and held out his hand to the freckle-faced kid and said, "Howdy. My name's Bear. You must be Chas."

"Pleased to meet you, sir," Chas said, blushing as though he was shaking hands with Rutherford B. Hayes, the president of the United States.

"Pleased to meet ya, too," Bear said, "only don't call me sir, okay?"

"Okay…Bear," Chas said.

Bear turned to Aya and looked him over slowly from head to toe, then uncorked the biggest surprise of the day when he reached out with an outstretched hand and asked, "Albaamaha? Kosaatiha? Comanche?…eh?"

Jim, Tom and Chas had their jaws on their chests as they looked back and forth between the two men.

Aya held out his hand to Bear and said, "Albaamaha."

"Sahmi Aya?" Bear asked as he took Aya's hand and shook it earnestly with both of his.

"Anoolo Aya. Ayapaali," came the reply.

"I see, the quiet man who sneaks up on things, huh? Istinkano ittabaaka isna," Bear said.

Aya used sign language to help himself explain, "Nice…to…meet… you," he said in his raspy, deep voice, showing he could speak at least a little English. "Iyyowwa tankoolimpa takka?" he asked, putting a hand on Bear's shoulder and pointing to the door.

"Yaama…aliila, mmmm. Catfish sounds great," Bear responded, patting his stomach. He took his eyes off his new friend and noticed the gaping stares of the other men. "What? What the hell are y'all starin' at?"

CHAPTER 11

Dinner At The Double T

"Thanks for taking me, Daddy," Jennie Lue said.

The black two-horse, four-person covered surrey came to the end of the winding private road leading to the front of their large Victorian home nestled amid the expanse of the Double T Ranch. Jennie Lue and her father had a worn-out look to them as the buggy came to a stop because, even though the ride from downtown only lasted a half-hour, they left for Belton shortly after church that morning and both were now relieved about the prospects of relaxing at home.

Turner bought the fifteen-thousand-plus acres in the summer of 1851 with the money he made from selling off his dry goods business and his land holdings in Austin. He was thirty-six years old at the time, and had no idea he might be worth so much but, when the transactions were said and done, he thought it was a good idea to reinvest his wealth in the new county to the north that bore his family name. Turner was tired of the big city and would rather be a big fish in a small pond rather than the other way around, so he came to Belton armed with a wagon full of money to get into the cattle business. He arrived with his new bride, built her the prettiest home in the county as he had promised and, within three years, everybody for miles around knew he owned the largest herd of cattle in the county.

There had been talk of him running for governor like his famous father, but people were surprised to find that he couldn't care less about the job.

Even as a young man, Turner never showed the slightest desire to become a politician, and his father had been extremely disappointed in him because of it. Although Turner was well educated and making a name for himself as a successful businessman, Peter Bell struggled with the fact that his only son had no desire to follow in his politically ambitious footsteps. After listening to far too many stories about his father's boring exploits delivered from a fancy leather chair behind a large oak desk, Turner decided to go his own way, being of the philosophy that it was far better for public offices to be served by other people who just happened to owe men like himself more than one huge favor.

In the midst of a heated argument, Turner had made the mistake of saying he would rather die skinny and his own man than get fat like his father and be indebted to someone else, which infuriated Peter Bell to the point that he severed their relationship for good. Even though Turner's father was still alive, they never came to terms over their differences because neither made any effort to correspond with the other after Peter Bell vacated the governor's office in November of 1853 and moved to Washington, D.C. to fill an empty seat in the United States Congress.

Turner felt regret that they were still at odds twenty-seven years later, but knew he wouldn't be the one who tried to make amends. His father was too stubborn and in no way would he would ever make the slightest effort to understand Turner's own, more practical point of view.

"Jennie, I can't think of anything I would rather have done today," he said with a loving smile as he set the brake and tied the reins. "But I'll never understand why you women say you have to go shopping and then don't come back with a single thing."

"I couldn't find anything I wanted, that's all," she protested. "Besides, are you saying you're disappointed I didn't spend any money?" She stood to climb out of the wagon with a raised eyebrow, hands on hips.

"Oh, no, no," he said, "I'm not saying that. You women are different, that's all."

"And you men are, too," she said. "Here we went and spent the whole afternoon together, which is something we don't get to do very often, and all you do is complain."

"I'm not complaining, my dear. You know I had a great time. All I'm saying is that y'all are different from us men." He turned the surrey over to his stableman, Cornelius, who ran out to meet them as they pulled into the yard.

"Thank God!" she said in mock exasperation. She met her father in front of the surrey, took his hand in hers and started walking with him to the front door. "If it wasn't for us women, you men would have already argued and complained yourselves into killing each other off by now."

"You think so, do you?" He grinned as they climbed the steps to the huge white, covered porch surrounding their fine home.

"Down to the very last one of you," she laughed. She opened one of the two front doors leading inside, yelling as she closed it behind them, "Momma, we're home!"

Their house was built like most two-story homes of the time, in that the main support timbers were driven deep into the ground and, except for the large master bedroom in the rear, both top and bottom floors were identical. The two spacious living rooms, kitchen and large dining area downstairs were located on either side of the stairway, the landing of which ended close to the front door in the foyer. The house was cooled in the summer months by large, wooden vents in the walls above every door in every room, which when opened helped circulate the air, and warmed the house in the winter when closed. The entire structure was white except for the polished steps and the ornate mahogany banister leading up the staircase, with varnished wooden floors upstairs and down and oak-stained wooden slats nailed snugly against the high ceilings occupying every room.

They took off their hats, hanging them on the large hat rack by the front door, as the sound of footsteps moving across the floor above filled the quiet house.

"Is that you, Turner? Jennie Lue?" Judy Bell asked.

"Yes, Momma!" Jennie Lue said, running her fingers through her blonde hair and shaking it out to settle around her shoulders.

"Have you got new goodies to show me?" her mother asked, coming into view as she made her way down the wide stairs.

Judy Bell was a short woman, only five feet tall, with a solid head of gray hair that never seemed to be even a tiny bit out of place. The wrinkles around her light-blue eyes were those of a happy person, and were partially hidden by the weak spectacles she insisted on wearing at all times, claiming she couldn't see a thing without them. She always wore some sort of full-length, flowery summer dress around the house, even if she worked a bit outside, which wasn't very often, and the dress she wore today was no exception. It was sky blue with pink roses on the front.

"She didn't buy a blessed thing." Turner smiled as he hung his jacket cn the hat rack. "I swear, she pestered me for a week about wanting to go into town, but she comes home empty-handed. I don't get it."

"I didn't see anything I wanted, Momma," Jennie Lue explained.

"Turner, you men just don't understand, do you?" Judy said, walking over to give them a welcoming hug. "You don't pay him any mind, Jennie Lue. You and I both know what Sunday shopping is all about, and we don't have near the time to explain it to him, so just let it be. Maybe I'll take you next week and, between the both of us, we'll make up for what you didr't spend today. How does that sound?"

"Oh, God," Turner said, looking as though he needed a good place to hide his billfold.

"I'd like that, Momma," Jennie Lue said. "I did see a few things that looked nice, but I just couldn't get myself to say yes."

"Well, next week I'll be the one that says yes," Judy laughed. She gave her husband a serious look. "Turner, I suggest you sell off a sizable number of your cows this week so Jennie Lue and I will have enough money come next Sunday."

"How'd I get myself into this?" Turner groaned as he loosened the top button of his shirt and untied his bow tie.

"Oh, quit your whining," Judy said. "We both know it's spring, and we could all use some new clothes. I'll even do a little shopping for you when we're in town. There, does that make you feel better?"

"I could use a new white shirt or two," Turner said, thinking about it. "If you could pick those up for me, I'd consider the whole thing worth it."

Judy looked at Jennie Lue with a smile. "I guess we're going to town next week. How do you like that?"

"It'll be fun," Jennie Lue said with a gleam in her eyes. "Don't let Daddy fool you, either. He already told me he enjoyed our time today."

"You don't say?" Judy said, as if confounded. "Well, you just run upstairs and get yourself ready for dinner because we're eating in thirty minutes. You can tell me all about it when you come down."

"All right, Momma," Jennie Lue said before bounding up the stairs.

As her daughter neared the top, Judy called out, "Your brother will be here for dinner, too. Isn't that great?"

"Oh...sure," she called back sarcastically. "That way we can spend the next few hours listening to every boring little thing that's going on in this town."

"I hope not," her mother said. "This is the first time in three months your brother's stopped by the house, so we're bound to have something else to discuss. Besides, if they talk about Belton for more than five minutes, I'm going to take their dinner and feed it to the hogs."

"You promise?" Jennie Lue yelled down. She laughed as she opened the door to her room.

"I promise," Judy called out. She turned to look at her husband. "Turner, you don't have to talk about Belton tonight, do you?"

"Maybe a little bit," he said, "but I'll try not to let George get carried away."

"Why do you think I'm referring to George? It's you I'm worried about."

They walked into the living room. "Did you get those matches I asked you for?"

"Yes, I did," he said as they sat in their favorite chairs. "I told Cornelius to put them in the kitchen. I'm sure he's got them in the cupboard by now."

He picked up and unfolded the newspaper and talked over the top of the page, "Jennie Lue was in a great mood today. It was nice to see for a change."

"Yes, I noticed," she said. "Maybe she's getting to the point where she can get on with her life."

"I hope so," he agreed, his head down in the paper. "I sure do hope so."

Jennie Lue closed the door behind her, went straight for her bed and fell on her back, arms above her head. She couldn't remember the last time she was so excited about anything and she closed her eyes to replay over and over the two encounters she had with Tom Wallace today. The first one was just dumb luck, even though she had a pretty good idea he'd be in town this afternoon, but the second was planned. There wasn't a store she wanted to go into anywhere near the corner she was on when Tom passed in the wagon, but she had pleaded her best case to her father to be there. She knew Tom would have to go down Main Street to get home, so she figured the odds were good that she'd get to see him again if she stood there long enough and she was right. Fortunately, one of the store owners recognized her father and kept him occupied as they talked about who knew what, but she didn't have to wait long before Tom, Jim and the man in the back she hadn't seen before passed by.

Lying with her eyes closed, she pictured Tom's handsome face as she stared at him through the shop window and the way he waved back at her as they went through the intersection. It looked to her as if he was glad to see her again, or was he just trying to be nice? Even though he looked back at her until he was well down the street, he didn't smile much.

Doubts started creeping into her mind as a host of reasons why Tom wouldn't have anything to do with her quickly materialized, the main one being that she had left town eight years ago with a ring on her finger. She tried to shake the thoughts off, so she got up and walked to her vanity where she sat, put a brush to her hair and asked herself a series of silent questions while staring at her reflection. How would she feel if the shoe was on the other foot and he was the one who got married and moved off? Could she forgive him? Could she trust him? Would she be able to give him her heart? How would her father feel about Tom and his past? How would both their stubborn fathers ever get over their differences and agree to such a thing? The answer to all these questions was the same; she didn't know.

Lost in her thoughts, Jennie Lue slowly went from having simple doubts about her and Tom to feeling sorry for herself as the excitement that filled her for the last few hours was replaced by the depressing idea that she might be wishing on stars that were much too faint. She put her brush back on the vanity table, put her hands in her lap and sighed as she pondered the same questions over and over.

"Jennie Lue!" her mother called from downstairs, "your brother is here. He's pulling into the yard."

"I'll be there in a minute," she called. But, instead of leaving, she walked across her room and fell back down on the bed. This time, she landed on her stomach with her arms outstretched, and vacantly stared at the lamp on her night stand, not bothering to wipe away the small tears that ran down the sides of her face.

"Don't be too long!" her mother yelled. "Dinner will be ready in just a few minutes!"

"I'm coming!" Jennie Lue listened to the front door open and her parents step outside. She lay on her multi-colored patchwork quilt for a brief moment longer, gloominess overtaking her at the thought of all the obstacles that stood in her way. When she got up, she went back to her mirror to dry her cheeks, then took a deep breath as she practiced putting on a happy face.

After a minute or two, a look of determination started to glow in her eyes and her smile was no longer forced, because the answer to the most important question of all entered her mind for the first time. She turned away from the mirror and walked out of her bedroom. Before she reached the top of the stairs, she once again had a spring in her step because she knew that, no matter what happened or how it looked to anybody else, it was her life and she was bone tired of living with regrets. She still had no idea what to do to make Tom see how she felt, or what she would say when her father reacted to the news, but the simple solution to what road to take next rested on the knowledge that she wouldn't make the same mistake again and spend another eight years wishing she had listened to her heart.

"Dad, Mom, how are y'all today?" George walked up the steps and met them with a hug. George Bell wasn't long in stature, like everyone else in his family, and stood five foot six with boots on. He was born only two years before his sister, but appeared to be much older because he was overweight by thirty pounds and had been smoking fat cigars on a regular basis ever since he was old enough to have his own money to pay for them.

George loved being the mayor of Belton, and tried to look the part by spending a great deal of time in the barber shop making sure his handlebar mustache and light-brown hair were perfectly in place. He didn't seem to mind that, no matter what expensive three-piece suit or top hat he wore, his outfits never seemed to fit or match just right. The sleeves on his jackets were either a bit too long or too short; his pants were always too big because he never bothered to get the legs tailored to fit the size of his stomach, and he never took off his vest in public because most people correctly guessed that, if he did, it would reveal a shirt that had not been pressed. His jacket was perpetually unbuttoned because his belly stood out a bit too far, but it didn't bother him since he liked to play with his silver-chained pocket watch and believed it helped his image to be a bit portly.

Whenever his mother or father showed concern over his weight, George argued that great politicians should be far too busy behind a desk doing great things for the people than being concerned with their own fitness but, the truth of the matter was, he just liked to eat too much and hated the idea of doing anything that might work up a sweat.

At twenty-eight years old, George was more than likely too young to be the mayor of even the smallest town in Texas, much less Belton, but he had run for office the same year Budcy ran for sheriff, and had won with more than a little help from his father. He was only twenty-one at the time and there was a great deal of concern among the townsfolk about the prospects of a mayor that age, but everyone knew whatever decisions came out of that office would really be coming from his father, which probably wasn't such a bad deal. Turner had played a large part in making Belton thrive the way it had over the years, and everyone there was prospering because of it. After a few town meetings and some heated debates between Turner and his soon-to-be-swayed opponents, his son won by a landslide over two other men. George had run unopposed in every election since and it was common knowledge among voters that he would be mayor as long as his father was alive.

In spite of the ease of his victories, George had come to find his own town had become boring, and juggling the same old job for six years made the politics in Austin look like a new lease on life if he could just play his cards right. Secretly, he was devising a plan to win a seat in the Texas legislature and one day make a run at the governor's office because, whatever political ambitions his father lacked, he was bound and determined to make up for.

"We're fine, just fine. Come on in," Judy said, as she led her husband and son to the front door.

"I heard you were in town today," George said to his father.

"Yes, we were," Turner said, as he closed the door behind them. "Your sister dragged me down there."

"Oh, Turner, knock it off," Judy said, "we both know you had a good time." She looked to the top of the stairs. "Speaking of your sister, here she comes now."

Jennie Lue emerged at the top of the stairs with a bright smile on her face, saying, "Hi, George." When she reached the landing, she walked over to give him a hug. "How is the mayor today?"

"Well, you know," George said, trying to sound important, "it's all I can do to keep my head above water with everything that's going on. I've got the cattlemen on one side of me, the landowners on the other, the…"

"George, I love you, but I'm sorry I asked," she said cheerfully as she left her brother with an unfinished thought and turned for the dining room. "Is dinner ready?" she asked her mother.

"Yes, it is," Judy said. She motioned to her husband and son. "You two come on now."

Turner waited in the foyer as his son hung up his coat. As they walked toward the dining room together, George asked quietly, "What's with Jennie Lue? She seems to be in good spirits for a change."

"I don't know. Maybe she just needed to get out of the house," whispered Turner with a shrug. "We're hoping she might finally be getting back to her old self."

"I hope so," George said. "It was a terrible thing, but it's time she got over it. What's it been, a year, a year and a half since Henry was killed?"

"No," Turner snapped, "six months."

"That's all? Seems like it was a lot longer than that. Either way, it's high time she got over it," George whispered. As they walked into the dining room, he added in a normal voice, "Well, at least we're going to eat good food. I never once walked away from this table hungry."

"You never walked away from any table hungry," Jennie Lue laughed.

"Very funny." George frowned at his sister without humor.

Turner sat in the cherry wood chair at the head of the table. "Judy, what's for dinner tonight?"

"You'll see." Everyone at the large, ornate dining table placed napkins in their laps. She glanced at the kitchen door as it opened and out came two servants, each carrying a tray with platters and bowls of steaming food, immediately filling the room with the aroma of a hot southern meal. There were string beans, mashed potatoes and gravy, sliced tomatoes, freshly baked cornbread and a roast that looked as if it could be cut with a fork, all to be washed down with either a glass of water, sun tea or homemade lemonade.

After the servants went round the table filling the glasses and plates to each person's liking, they retired to the kitchen and left the family to enjoy their meal.

"George, why don't you say grace," Judy said.

They all bowed their heads as George began, "Thank you, God, for this food, and thank you for all we have." He opened his eyes, making furtive glances around the table as he tried to come up with something else to say but, when the pause lasted a bit too long, he closed his eyes and said, "Here's to the Father, the Son and the Holy Ghost, whoever eats the fastest gets the most. Amen!" George uncrossed his hands and clapped them once with a big grin on his face as he reached for his fork, then looked at his mother who was shaking her head, a disapproving look on her face.

"Was that bad?" he asked, smiling as he chewed his first bite.

"Remind me not to let you say prayers anymore," she said, annoyed.

Everyone ate in silence before George looked up at his father and said, "Dad, I don't want you to think I came over here just for business, but we're at the point now where I'm definitely going to need you to make up the difference in the hundred thousand."

"What hundred thousand?" Jennie Lue asked.

"The money the railroad wants," answered Turner. He laid his fork on the table and sipped his tea before adding, "They want the city of Belton, and other cities the lines go through, to pitch in money to offset their costs; otherwise, they threaten to go around."

"One hundred thousand dollars?" Jennie Lue exclaimed. "That's an awful lot of money. Sounds like blackmail."

"It is," George said, picking up his fork and resuming the attack on his food. "But the railroads know every town along the way prospers a lot more than that so, most of the time, they get their money."

"How much have you collected so far?" Turner asked.

George swallowed a large bite and took a sip of water before answering, "Sixty-one thousand."

Turner glared at his son. "You told me you had commitments of eighty-five. What happened to that?"

George was clearly shaken as he put his fork down and tried to explain, "As God is my witness, I had everyone swear up and down they were in, I promise I did but, when it came to handing over the money, it was a different story. Everybody who pulled out gave me the same excuse."

"And what excuse was that?"

George took a deep breath. "Everyone said you should foot the bill because you're the one who stands to profit most." He shook his head as if he couldn't understand. "I told them it was all a bunch of bull, and everyone in town is going to stand in high cotton because of those rail lines, but they just wouldn't listen to me."

A long silence settled at the table as Turner gave the issue serious thought.

"When do they want the money?" he asked.

"By Friday. They're only forty miles to the south of us, and I only have five more days," he explained. "If I don't get them the money by the end of this week, those tracks are going to be laid down to the east of us."

Turner took a deep breath through clenched teeth. "I'll talk to the bank first thing tomorrow. Am I safe to assume they'll take a check?"

George scoffed. "I wish, but no. They want cash."

"I see. Well, how do I know they'll keep their word?" Turner asked, frowning. "What's the guarantee?"

George leaned forward and put his elbows on the table. "The only guarantee we have is, if we don't pay the money, we don't get the lines, plain and simple."

Turner leaned back in his chair and nodded. "All right, then. I'll make up the difference. It will take a few days to put together that much in cash, but you'll have it by Friday."

"You won't regret it," George said hastily. He was obviously relieved. "My bet is the railroad is going to make Belton the biggest town in the state, which should make you the richest man in the state…maybe the country."

There was still aggravation in his voice as Turner held up his hand and said, "George, it would probably be best if you didn't say anything else about this tonight." He picked up his fork, adding, "A common street beggar could have done a better job than sixty-one thousand, but…I guess it is what it is."

"I promise…" George began.

"I already told you; you'll have your money by Friday," Turner said. He shook his head in dismay. "You don't have to sell me anymore."

"Well…" Judy glared at her husband, "I thought the two of you said there wasn't going to be any talk of business tonight. Yet…here we are."

They ate in silence again until George put his fork down and reached into his coat pocket to pull out an envelope with Jennie Lue's name on it. Relieved at the chance to talk about something else, he handed the gift across the table to his sister. "I almost forgot. I got these for you today. I hope you like it."

"You got something for *me*?" she asked. The tension in the room lifted as she reached to take the envelope. "That was awfully nice of you. What is it?"

No one could tell if George's sudden happy mood was because the conversation with his father was over or if he was genuinely glad he brought his gift. "Why don't you open it and find out?"

Jennie Lue tore the envelope open and exclaimed, "Oh, my! George…

you didn't have to do this!"

"What is it?" Judy leaned toward her daughter to get a glimpse.

"Two tickets to the Hanlon-Lees! You know, that show coming to the opera house this Tuesday?" she said, beaming.

"That's the acrobats, isn't it?" Turner asked. "That show's been sold out for a month now. Those tickets had to be hard to come by."

"They sure were," boasted George, "but I was able to talk my way into these from somebody who owed me a huge favor, so I decided to give them to Jennie Lue." He looked at his sister. "I thought it would do you good to have a nice night out." He picked up his fork and resumed the siege on his plate.

"That was a nice thing to do, George," Jennie Lue said, holding the tickets up for all to see. "Who should I take?"

Judy put her fork down and smiled at George to say thanks. "Anybody you want to, sweetheart. But you should go. It sounds like a nice time."

"I'm so excited," Jennie Lue beamed, clutching the tickets to her chest. "George, thank you so much!"

"You're welcome, and it was my pleasure," George said through a mouthful of food. "It should be a good show. These Hanlon brothers do all sorts of tricks."

"I've heard they're more than just tricks," Turner said. "I heard they're amazing. They even do something like a stagecoach wreck, right on stage, right there in the opera house."

"That's right," George said, acting like an expert, "but I'm sure it all has to do with ropes and pulleys."

"Have you seen them before?" Jennie Lue asked.

"Well…no," George said, "but I've talked to a few people about it, and they all say the same thing."

"And what is that?" Jennie Lue asked.

"That the acrobats are fun and all," George said, "but that no one could possibly do all the things they do without help from ropes and pulleys. They do make it look somewhat believable, though."

"I see," Jennie Lue said, rolling her eyes to make it known that she doubted his supposed expertise. "Are you going?"

"No, I'm going to pass," George said. "I have other more pressing commitments."

"Well, I'll let you know how it is then." She smiled and laid the tickets in her lap.

George held up a forkful of mashed potatoes as if he were making a toast. "I hope you have fun," he said, then buried the pile in his mouth. He took a gulp from his water glass to wash it all down before adding, "Speaking of fun, did you two have a nice time in town today?"

"Yes, we did," Turner answered. "I had a chance to talk with a few of the shop owners for a while, which was a good thing. It helps me to keep an ear to the ground and listen to what their concerns are."

"Turner!" Judy said, frowning at her husband from across the table, "is that *really* why you went into town today? To talk to the shop owners? What about the wonderful time you had with your daughter? The two of you haven't spent much time together these last few months, and I for one was glad to see you have the afternoon together."

Turner raised his glass of iced tea to Jennie Lue. "She knows I had a great time. And that I look forward to doing it again," he said, winking at her.

"Really, Daddy?" she asked, giving him a big smile.

"Why, of course." He took a long sip.

"Well, you're going to have to wait your turn," Judy said, "because I'm taking all the money I can fit in my handbag and taking Jennie Lue next weekend."

"I have to tell you," George interjected, "I'm glad to see you in such good spirits, Jennie Lue. It's about time you started getting over that whole mess."

"George! You stop right there," his mother scolded. "You don't have any idea what your sister has gone through."

Jennie Lue said nothing, preferring to glare at her brother. "All I'm saying is I'm glad to see her in good spirits," he said defensively. He put his fork down and threw his hands in the air. "It's a good thing! And it's time…that's all," he said.

"Just ignore him, Momma," Jennie Lue said, giving her brother another hateful look. She put her fork down and wiped her mouth. "George, I thank you for the tickets and all, but we all know that if we have to have a conversation with you and the topic isn't about sucking up to people, you have no idea what you're talking about," she said.

"Now, now," Turner said. He looked at his son. "George, don't mind your sister's business." He looked at his daughter, "…and Jennie Lue, firing off insults at anyone in this family is not going to be tolerated, besides not being very lady-like."

"I'm sorry," she said, letting her expression tell her brother she wasn't.

Everyone ate quietly for a while, but eventually George got the conversation going again as he neared the end of his meal. "I heard Tom Wallace is back in town."

Jennie Lue glanced up around the table with a look of surprise but, as her eyes found her mother's, she immediately realized if she wasn't more careful, she was certain to give herself away. She hoped her mother had no idea what the look was about as she quickly turned her attention back to her plate and pushed her green beans around with her fork.

"Yes, I saw him with his father today," Turner said. "I suppose they were in town to hire on some ranch hands. That's what the word is, anyway."

"I hear they're going to start fencing in the Four C's tomorrow." George put his knife and fork on his plate and leaned out of the way so the servant could remove it. He rubbed his stomach to show he had his fill. "I know why they're in such a hurry to do that, too. Most everyone around these parts think it's the Wallaces that are stealing your cows, and now nobody will be able to ride through there to see if any of our brands are in his herd."

"You don't know it's them. And no one has ever found our brands anywhere near their place," Jennie Lue said, careful to conceal her anger.

"Who else could it be?" George turned to his father. "How many times in the last year have you had trouble with rustlers?"

"I don't know exactly," Turner said, giving the question some thought. "Three or four, I guess. You'd have to ask Cornelius to be sure, but it's been too much, I can tell you that."

"I'm thinking the only reason Jim Wallace has been able to keep the Four C's going since Tom got shipped off is because he's been selling off our cows to pay his property taxes. Everybody knows there hasn't been a damn thing going on at that ranch for the last four or five years."

"George, watch your mouth at my table," his mother warned.

"Sorry, Mother," George said. "I just wish we could run the lot of them off and be done with their kind, that's all. This town would be a whole lot better off."

"George, correct me if I'm wrong," Jennie Lue began as she reached for her water glass, "but don't you have to have some sort of proof before you can accuse somebody of something like that?"

"I have all the proof I need right here," George said with conviction, pointing at his head.

"There's your mistake," she said sarcastically. "You don't have anything up there to keep your proof in."

"At least I'm out there every day trying to do something good for this town," George snapped at her, giving her a mean look, "not sitting at home all the time crying over things that should have been settled a long time ago."

"I'm not going to tell you again, George," Turner said, raising his voice. "Leave your sister alone."

George glared at Jennie Lue as he took a long, deep breath, then turned to his father and said, "All I'm saying is, Jim Wallace has caused enough trouble around here. I wish you would go over there and buy him out so we could get rid of him once and for all. Besides, that ranch would make a great addition to the Double T."

"Jim Wallace will never sell," Turner said as he fiddled with his napkin. "Unless you can come up with some solid evidence that he's the one behind the rustling in these parts, this entire conversation is a waste of time."

"You do need proof, don't you?" Jennie Lue asked. "That's *the law*, isn't it?" She was getting more than a little irritated with her brother.

"Why am I the only one who sees it?" George said. "Hell! That one stinking Indian they got over there probably stole more cows in his life than anybody could imagine. And I'm not the only one in town who thinks that's all his kind is good for."

"George!" Judy said, "that's enough! I will not allow that kind of talk in my house! That man, Indian or not, saved the lives of those kids and their mother. He deserves a lot more respect from you."

"I'm sorry, Mother," George said insincerely, "but that was a long time ago, and there's a lot of people nowadays who think that Indian is just as responsible as Jim Wallace for the rustling that's been going on around here. I'm not sure how they do it, but I know they have a heck of an operation going on. I can just... *feel* it. I wish Buddy had more guts in him, but I think he's gone soft. I think, deep down, our town sheriff doesn't want to send his father off to prison like he did his brother."

"What do you mean he sent his brother off to prison?" Jennie Lue asked, sitting up straight. "You always said it was that circuit judge, what was his name? Judge Arthur...Arthur Danly. That's it. You told me he was the one who wanted to make an example of Tom."

George's face lost all expression. He looked around the table at all their faces and finally said, "I guess it doesn't matter anymore. But there's no reason for what I'm about to say to leave this table. Fair enough?" George got a nod from the rest of his family before he continued, "Buddy was the one who pressed Judge Danly for Tom to do time."

"Why on earth would he do that?" Jennie Lue asked, appalled. "His own brother? He should have been the one to help him! Everybody knows that fellow he killed had been drinking half the day and charged him with a knife. He never should have been arrested, much less sent off to prison!"

"We all know the story," Turner said, "but the fact is, there wasn't a knife found and Tom had been drinking, too. Under the law, it was a simple case of manslaughter. I have to say, though, I was surprised at the time that Buddy didn't do much to help his brother."

"Buddy will tell you to this day he was only trying to do his job and stay out of the way of the legal process," George said as he leaned back in his chair, "but, the truth is, he felt he had to send his brother up because he was the new sheriff, and it was critical to let the townsfolk know he was all business."

"You mean Buddy thought what people in this town thought about him was more important than the welfare of his own brother?" Jennie Lue asked in disbelief.

"No…" George paused to choose his words, "Buddy felt his responsibility to the town was greater than his own feelings."

"My God!" Jennie Lue said, collapsing back against her chair, a look of exasperation on her face. "His *feelings*? *What* feelings? And another thing: Are you defending him? Because it sounds like you are."

"No, I am not," George said. "Buddy and I have been friends for a long time but, when it comes to our jobs, I draw the line."

"Like Buddy did?" she said with a smirk, folding her arms across her chest.

"Look, it's not like there was a chance that Tom would get hung over the deal," George said, leaning forward and putting his elbows on the table. "Buddy had it all worked out with Judge Danly. He knew his brother would only get five years. Besides, there was no question in anyone's mind that he killed the guy. In the end, justice was served and Tom would be back in five years. Buddy sent his message to the townspeople, and that was that."

Jennie Lue stared at her brother as if he had lost his mind. "*That was that?*"

"Yep," George said, "and it's all water under the bridge now. We have other things to worry about, like Jim Wallace and how we're going to get him to stop stealing cattle. Buddy might go down in history as the greatest sheriff to ever live if he just had the guts to arrest his father and send him away like he did Tom."

"The greatest sheriff to ever live? You're kidding, right?" Jennie Lue asked, her eyes blazing.

"No, I am not kidding." George stared down her defiant gaze. "At the very least, I'm positive that the cattle rustling business in this county would be done for."

"But we don't know for sure that Jim Wallace is doing it," Turner said as he pushed away from the table and leaned back. "It could be drifters. God knows this town attracts them like flies to manure."

"Turner...not at the table, please," Judy said, rolling her eyes and heaving a sigh.

Turner looked at his wife without emotion, and nodded to let her know he got her point. "Maybe Buddy's all wrong about his dad being behind it," he continued. "It wasn't long ago that Jim Wallace came to me and asked me straight out if I was the one stealing from *him*."

"That doesn't mean anything," George snapped, his aggravation flaring. "It could have been his way of trying to throw you off his scent. I'm sure if we went over there right now we'd catch them eating a piece of meat for dinner with our brand on it. Is that what it's going to take before anybody will believe me?" He shook his head in wonder. "Now Jim Wallace has his murdering son back to help him, so no telling how bad things will get."

"George, again, thank you for the tickets...but you're an idiot," Jennie Lue said. She threw her napkin onto the table, grabbed the tickets off her lap and stood.

"Where are you going, young lady?" Judy asked.

Jennie Lue strode away to the foyer, saying over her shoulder, "I'm going to my room."

"You have not been excused from the table!" Judy hollered after her.

"May I be excused?" asked Jennie Lue loudly as she climbed the stairs.

Judy looked at her husband, sighed and raised her eyebrows as they listened to Jennie Lue's footsteps on the wooden floor above them end with the slamming of her bedroom door.

"I guess her mood hasn't really changed all that much, has it?" George said. "I knew it was too good to be true." He leaned back in his chair. "Maybe I should've given those tickets to somebody who would've appreciated them a little more."

"You did a good thing, George." his mother said, aggravated with the entire conversation, "Don't go ruining it now."

"Your mother is right," Turner said. "Your sister's going to have to take it one step at a time." He sighed as he rose from the table. "Why do you have to argue with her every time you see her? Your views on things will never match hers. It's time you realized that." He nodded to the front door. "Now what do you say you and I go out on the porch? There's a few things I need to go over with you privately. You can even smoke one of those nasty cigars if you want. I know you have them on you."

"Sure thing," George sounded relieved. He stood and walked out of the dining room. "Do you have matches?"

"We do," Turner said. He looked at his wife. "Have Cornelius bring a box of matches and an ashtray around front, will you? We'll just be a few minutes." He kissed the top of her head, then followed his son out the door onto the porch.

"Right," Judy said sarcastically. She got up from the table and turned toward the kitchen to find Cornelius. "Last time the two of you were going to be 'just a few minutes' you stayed out there half the night," she muttered, resigning herself to the knowledge this evening would be no different.

Jennie Lue lay beneath her covers for hours that night thinking about Tom Wallace. She listened to the crickets outside mixed with the mumblings of her brother and father downstairs on the porch. Every once in a while, she even caught a whiff of that awful thing George called a cigar as it wafted through the screen of her open bedroom window. She couldn't care less what they were talking about. All she could think of was how she could see Tom again tomorrow, but between the recollections of the day's events, her anger at her brother over his ridiculous remarks, and the news that Buddy intentionally sent Tom to prison, her mind wandered far too much to come up with a solid plan. She didn't know what time George finally left, even though it seemed as if he might stay out on the veranda all night yapping away, but she finally fell asleep dreaming of happy days to come, and didn't wake up until the sun was approaching the noon sky.

When she got out of bed, she immediately got dressed and headed down to the stables to get Cornelius to saddle up her horse. She had no idea what she would say to Tom once she arrived at the Four C's, or what kind of an excuse she'd use to justify why she had come, but as soon as she was in the saddle, she headed north in a hurry, hoping she would get to the Cowhouse Creek Cattle Company before she lost her nerve.

CHAPTER 12

Our Turn

"Okay, everybody, lift! Now hold it right there," Jim instructed the others. He maneuvered the pins of the wrought iron gate into the hinges mounted on the large side post set firmly in the ground just to the right side of the entrance road. "Okay. Now ease it down."

A small cheer went up from the hands as the new front gate to the ranch settled into position. Everyone took turns swinging it back and forth; it worked perfectly.

Jim decided that hanging the gate would be the first step in fencing in the ranch, so he and the hands tackled it first thing. Not only did it require a lot of labor to set the sturdy side posts and braces, but the gate itself was so heavy it took four men to lift. They started right after breakfast and, even though it wasn't quite noon, they had invested a day's worth of sweat to get the job done in time for lunch.

"Chas, how are you with a paintbrush?" Jim asked.

"Near as good as anyone else, I guess," he answered. "How come?"

"There's some white paint and primer on the floor of the tack room. You know what I'm talking about?"

"Yes, sir," Chas responded, removing his hat and wiping the sweat off his freckled forehead with a sleeve.

"After lunch, I want you to put some primer on this," Jim said, wiping his own face. "Then, later on this afternoon, I want you to make this the prettiest white gate in the county. You think you can do that for me?"

"Yes, sir!" Chas said, as if talking to an officer. Nothing was missing but a salute. "You can count on me, Mister Wallace."

"Good." Jim put his hat back on and glanced around the group. "We'll all come out here later this evening and have a toast when it's done. What do you fellows say?"

Everyone reacted like it was a great idea except Chas, who looked more than a little unsure about the whole thing. He glanced at the rest of the men, hoping they wouldn't make fun of him.

"Are ya talking about a real toast? With real whiskey?" he asked.

There was a brief moment of silence as everyone looked at him. Chas hadn't pestered Jim for months about getting hired as a hand at the Four C's just because he wanted to be a cowboy. They all knew there were two main reasons he had tried so hard. One was he had to get away from his father, who was widely known as the most abusive drunk in town, and the other was, even though Chas had never set foot in a church, he had shared with all of them about how he used to pray to the Lord every night that he wouldn't have to live another day in the tiny, broken-down, one-room shack he was forced to call home. Throughout his childhood, he was frequently seen around the outskirts of town wearing clothes so dirty and tattered that even the poor colored folk would stare at him. And there was always a bruise or a cut on him somewhere, compliments of his father and a cheap bottle of whiskey.

Due to his excess weight, red hair, crooked teeth and his father's horrible reputation, Chas had also been the butt of countless jokes among the townspeople most of his life. But Chas hardly ever let on it bothered him. He wasn't necessarily a stupid kid, but he wasn't the brightest, either. He never spent a single day in school, couldn't read or write, and the fact that he spent the first eighteen years of his life practically blind didn't help matters. It was only after he'd gotten hired on at the Four C's that Jim bought him his first pair of eyeglasses, which enabled him to see the world clearly for the first time. It didn't take much for anyone to realize that, along with his sense of belonging at the Four C's, his spectacles were his most prized possession.

The thing about Chas that Jim respected a great deal, though, and was the main reason he gave him a job when no one else would, was that he had made it abundantly clear there was no way anyone would ever get him to swallow a drop of alcohol because, as he said, no matter what happened in his life, he would rather stab himself in the chest with a dull knife than wind up being a drunk like his father.

"You don't need to worry, Chas," Jim said with a wink, "I got a bottle of sarsaparilla up at the house just for you."

All the men laughed and the anxiety written on Chas's face was replaced with relief as he let out a deep breath, nodded his head and said with a smile, "Okay. We'll have a toast, then."

Everyone patted Chas on the shoulder, making him visibly proud to be one of the boys. After a moment or two of good-natured ribbing, Jim said, "Why don't we pick up our tools and throw them in the buckboard so we can head over and see how Curry and Church are coming along? After that, we'll break for lunch."

"Sounds good to me," was the unanimous hearty reply. They picked up their tools, tossed them into the back of the wagon and climbed in to go find the other hands. When they located Church and Curry ten minutes later, it didn't come as a surprise to anyone in the wagon that they hadn't accomplished nearly as much as they should have.

Jim's plan to fence in the property was simple enough in that they were going to start setting posts on the west side of the front gate and make a circle around the eighty-five hundred plus acres, finishing from the east. After breakfast, Church and Curry were chosen to fill the work wagon with posts and rolls of wire and begin laying them out to the west along the property line, while Jim, Tom, Aya and Chas would hang the new iron entrance gate that would span their road a hundred yards or so in front of Ruby's bridge. Once they were finished, they would all meet up and start setting posts in a straight line fifteen feet apart. Even though he didn't complain when Jim laid out his plans to everyone, Church hadn't been too thrilled about the prospects of working alongside Curry Hampton and grew even less so as the morning wore on.

Church stopped what he was doing to wipe the sweat off his face and grimaced as he heard another complaint.

"Geez, these are heavy," Curry said as he pulled one of the few rolls of barbed wire he had lifted today out of the back of the wagon and dropped it on the ground.

"Aw, quit your whinin'." Church said as he grabbed a roll off the back.

Nobody was real happy with Curry, because not only did he show up late at the ranch last night so drunk it amazed everyone he was able to stay in the saddle, but it wasn't even noon yet and he had complained about the bunk he slept on, the food he ate for breakfast, the paper in the outhouse, how hot it was going to be later on and how he had to sit down and rest because of his bad ankle, which nobody knew about until it was time to get up in the morning and go to work.

No one was quite sure if it was because he was feeling sick from the large amount of alcohol he consumed in town the night before, or whether it was because he was just naturally a pain in the ass, but everyone who got up that morning looking forward to a good day's work was not liking Curry Hampton at all, especially Church. "If ya can't handle the hangover, don't put your hands on the bottle," Church spat, carrying his roll of wire to a stack of posts.

"My drinkin' is none of your concern," Curry snapped, breathing heavily and stopping to fan himself with his hat. The temperature was only in the mid-eighties, yet Curry's unkempt hair and clothes were already soaked in sweat and he smelled like a sour barrel of rot-gut whiskey, even from a distance. He was the last one out of bed that morning and would probably still be snoring if Church hadn't thrown a pitcher of water on him. The only time anyone had a laugh courtesy of Curry was then because, even though he awoke in a tirade, it didn't last long because he was soon out behind the bunkhouse heaving what was in his stomach out into the tall grass. He wouldn't listen to the rest of the hands when they told him to get a shovel and turn the grass over, but when Jim finally stepped in to settle the matter, he reluctantly complied.

"Your drinkin' is my concern when I have to do my work and yours, too," Church said, making his way back to the wagon for another roll of wire.

"Come, on, Church," Curry said as he replaced his hat, "don't be so hard. Hell, I know you been drunk a time or two. And besides, the longer it takes to do this, the longer we'll have a job."

Church picked up another roll and grunted. "Well, I know one thing; the longer you stand there doin' nothing, the better your chances are to find one of my boots buried in your ass. And my bet is that, after this morning, it'll look a lot worse for you than it will for me if we get into a scrape our first day on the job," he said hotly.

"Is that how you're gonna be?" Curry asked, as if he was the one put out.

"I'll tell ya how I'm gonna be." Church said as he carried the large roll to the property line, set it down and turned back to the wagon, "if you don't say anything else to me for the rest of the day, then I'm not gonna have any more ideas about poundin' your face into the dirt. How's that?"

Church was startled when Curry suddenly started moving like a real ranch hand for the first time and wished for a second that he had threatened him earlier. He soon realized, though, the reason Curry got to working as quickly as he did was the sound of the buckboard, loaded with Jim and the rest of the crew, headed their way.

"Figures," he said, loud enough to get Curry to look over at him.

"How are you fellows doing?" Jim asked, as the wagon came alongside and stopped next to theirs.

"About as good as 'a' man can do," Church said, letting Jim know he hadn't gotten much help.

"What do you say we all head in and see what Bear's got ready for lunch?" Jim asked. "Then we'll get back out here this afternoon and start setting some posts."

"Sounds great," Curry said, as if he had worked up a mighty appetite.

"You two follow us on back," Jim said.

Church took one look at Curry, then turned to Jim. "If you don't mind, I'd like to ride in with you guys," he said.

"Sure thing," Jim replied, knowing the reason why. He looked at Curry. "Stay right behind me, nice and slow," he instructed.

"Yes, sir, Mister Wallace," Curry chimed, hopping into the seat and grabbing the reins.

They made the short trip back to the ranch house where Bear was inside tending the flames of the lazy column of smoke rising out of the stove pipe and into the clear sky.

Church had driven the wagon all morning, and now that he was holding the reins, Curry believed Jim must think highly of him, because not even Chas was allowed to drive the wagons and he had been here a lot longer. He was feeling pretty good about himself all the way to the house, but his mood changed quickly when he tried to follow the others inside. Jim stopped him on the porch and told him to sit down because they needed to talk.

After they were alone, Jim reached into his pocket and pulled out two dollar bills and handed them to Curry. "Curry, this is not working out and I have to let you go. I'm going to pay you for three days, but I don't want you to ever set foot on my property again, you hear me?"

The expression on Curry's face went from shock to anger in less than a second. "You didn't even give me a chance," he griped.

"I gave you all the chance I needed." Jim stood to let Curry know the conversation was over. "Now clean your things out of the bunkhouse and get."

"This ain't right," Curry protested, as he stood, stepped close and glared at Jim.

Jim backed away, not because he was intimidated, but because he couldn't stand the way Curry smelled in the hot mid-day sun.

He pointed at the bunkhouse. "Go on, Curry. Aya's getting your horse saddled right now and will have it here in just a minute. We all expect you to be on it as soon as he brings it around." Jim opened the door to the house and yelled inside, "Tom! I want you to take Curry to the bunkhouse and see that he gets all his things." He turned back and looked at Curry as if he couldn't figure out why he was still there. "You heard me. Go on, now, get."

Curry stared at Jim before he turned away in a rage and stormed to the bunkhouse. When he came out, he glared at Tom like he wanted to kill him, knowing the only reason Tom was there was because his father thought he might steal something from one of the other hands. The idea of it made him even madder and, by the time he reached the front yard and climbed into his saddle, he was infuriated to the point of glaring at the rest of the hands like he wanted to kill them all. His eyes spit fire at the men who quickly gathered on the porch to make sure he left peacefully.

"Y'all are no better than me!" he yelled. "Y'all be sorry for this, mark my words!" With that, he turned his horse, kicked it in the sides and disappeared in a cloud of dust down the road leading out of the property.

Without turning away from watching Curry, Jim said, "Tom, I want you to take your horse out and follow him. Make sure he doesn't double back and try to do something stupid."

"Sure thing," Tom said.

"I had Aya file out a piece of his horse's shoe last night," Jim said. He pointed out some distinctive horseshoe marks on the ground. "He ought to be easy enough to tail. Just make sure he winds up in town and not back here, okay?"

"You did that last night?" Tom asked, then grinned. "You knew you were going to fire him, didn't you?"

"Well, I never have trusted that fellow, and some things are just inevitable," Jim said. "And there's one other thing I need you to do, though. Stop by Dayna G's while you're in town and either find that black piano player or leave a message for him. I'd like to see him, soon if possible. His name is Percy. Can you do that for me?"

"How do you know him?" Tom asked, surprised his father knew anyone employed in a saloon.

"You'll know soon enough. I thought I recognized him yesterday," Jim explained, "and it came to me when we were about halfway home. Anyway, I owe him a big favor, so I want you to bring him here if you can. You up to that?"

Tom didn't want to go anywhere near Dayna G's saloon, but he knew a ride into town beat the heck out of the prospects of setting posts in the ground on a hot afternoon. "Yeah, I can do that. I'll get Clever saddled up."

Bear was watching the situation unfold from just inside the front door and stuck his head out. "Ya want something to eat before ya go?" he asked loudly.

"No, thanks," Tom said. "To tell you the truth, I'm still full from this morning."

"Well, if you fellers are done runnin' that fool off, ya better get in here and eat while it's hot or I'm gonna throw it all out the back door." Bear let the door slam as he headed back inside.

Tom looked at his father. "I should be back in a couple of hours," he said.

"Be careful," Jim said. "If Curry's tracks turn off the road anywhere between here and town, don't do anything except high-tail it right back here to get us. Don't get yourself into any trouble, you hear?"

"Don't worry, I won't," Tom said, smiling to reassure his father. "Besides, I kinda like it here, and I plan on sticking around a while."

"Good," Jim said with a grin, "I kinda like having you around myself."

Ten minutes later, Tom had Clever saddled and was crossing Ruby's bridge at an easy lope. His father was right about Curry being easy to follow because the back left shoe on his horse had been filed out so deeply even Chas without his glasses might be able to track him. Tom looked down into the dirt every now and then to make sure Curry was still heading into town but, for the most part, he took every chance to look at the scenery as it passed. Even though Clever made it known he wanted to run, Tom held him to a trot for the first five minutes or so because trailing Curry was turning out to be easy enough and he didn't want this trip to end too quickly.

The sight of thick brush and multi-colored spring flowers lining each side of the road, reaching up to the small white clouds floating across a blue noon sky, made Tom grateful his father had chosen him to make this trip. As he took in the sights of spring and listened to the birds singing to each other in the trees, it struck him there was plenty of time to set posts in the ground, but he also had five long years to make up for. Realizing his chance was in front of him at last, the thought brought to mind a few men he had known who would never have that luxury.

As Tom kept one eye on the scenery and the other on Curry's trail, his mind wandered back to the nightmare he had last night. It was so vivid Tom thought for sure he was back in prison, working for the railroads again in some unknown part of the state, and he woke up in a cold sweat far too early. He lay in bed, wondering if he had made enough noise to wake his father, and couldn't get back to sleep because he kept thinking about the man in his dream.

Leonardo Hernandez wasn't even a man really; he was just a small Mexican kid, only sixteen years old at the time, and had just started serving a two-year stretch for forging a check at a general store because his family needed groceries. Not a day went by where Hernandez didn't get a beating from the guards because he wasn't fulfilling his work quota, so he decided they might finally leave him alone if he ratted out a fellow inmate who had stolen a few pieces of jerky. His plan didn't work. The guards still beat him during the day for not working hard enough, and the inmates got their revenge by holding him down at night and taking turns putting their own marks on him.

Only a month into his sentence, he asked one of the guards if he could go into the bushes to relieve himself. When he didn't come out, the guard ordered Tom to go in there and drag him out, finished or not. Tom walked into the thick brush to find Leonardo hadn't intended to relieve himself at all. He had only been out of sight for a few minutes, but had managed to tie one leg of his trousers around a branch of a tree and the other around his neck. The way his eyes bulged out of his head was a vision Tom would never forget, but the heart of the nightmare was the determination it must have taken for that kid to hang himself like that, not twenty feet away from everyone else, without making a sound.

Tom was forced to dig the unmarked grave they buried Leonardo in beneath the tree where he was found. One leg of Leonardo's pants remained around his neck and the other around the sawed-off branch he hung himself from. The guards all thought it was funny to bury him in such a way, and a few even got off their horses to urinate in the grave before Tom shoveled the dirt over his body. It certainly wasn't the first time Tom had seen an inmate die; he had already worked the rails for two years but, for him, the way Leonardo Hernandez killed himself epitomized the depths of hell a man could experience when forced to do time in the Texas State Prison System.

Trying to get these thoughts from his mind, Tom pulled Clever to a step, put his hat over his saddle horn and poured water from his canteen over his head. He put the canteen back in his saddle bag and ran both hands through his hair before putting his hat on again. He decided it might not be a good idea to take too long tracking Curry because he didn't want his mind wandering any more than it already had, so he looked down at the dirt one more time to make sure Curry's tracks were still heading into town, and whistled loudly to signal Clever it was time to run.

The horse was more than ready and took off without wasting a second, getting to full speed just as they reached a blind turn in the narrow road where the corner was blanketed by thick brush spilling from the base of a steep hill. Tom was looking at the ground and not paying attention to the road ahead when Clever almost threw him out of the saddle as he went from a dead run to stopping in his tracks.

Tom's first thought was that his new horse must have some kind of serious mental problem his dad didn't tell him about but, as he regained his balance and looked up, he realized he had picked the worst moment of his life to look like such a brainless idiot. Before him was Jennie Lue Sloan, white as a ghost and trying to keep her startled horse under control, but laughing so hard she looked as if she might cry.

Tom realized he must have scared the hell out of her as he came flying around the bend, so after an awkward moment that seemed to last forever, he asked, "Are you...are you all right?"

"Yes. Yes, I'm okay," Jennie Lue said between giggles.

"I'm awfully sorry," he said as he rubbed the side of his excited horse's head. He felt like a fool, and took his hat off and tried to let her know. "I wasn't paying attention. I..."

"Please," she said, raising a hand to cut him off, "don't worry about it. I was riding a bit too fast myself. But I have to tell you; that's the most exciting thing that's happened to me in years." She exhaled deeply and patted her chest. "Woo! I don't know if my heart can stand another scare like that. I thought you were going to run me right over, Tom Wallace. Where are you going in such a hurry?"

"I was...I'm headed into town," Tom said, still deeply embarrassed. "I got my new horse yesterday and I was just letting him run. I'm terribly sorry."

"Please don't say that again," she said, giving him a reassuring look. "Really, it's all right...okay?"

"Okay. Well...good, then." Tom nodded.

Jennie Lue looked at his horse. "My, what a beautiful animal. Is he yours?"

"Yeah," said Tom, grateful for the change in subjects. "Thanks. My dad gave him to me. I was taking him into town." There was a brief pause between them before Tom asked, "So where are you headed on such a beautiful day?"

Suddenly, it was Jennie Lue who was embarrassed. She hadn't decided what excuse she was going to use, and hadn't planned on running into Tom just yet because, if the truth be known, the closer she got to the Four C's the more she felt like a fool for heading this way in the first place. Sitting on her horse and looking at him now, she realized that if they hadn't run into one another like this, she almost certainly would have looked at their ranch from a distance before turning around and heading back home. It was too late now, though.

Hoping Tom wouldn't notice the flush she felt creeping to her face, she said, "I was just out for a ride and...I was...just coming down this road when all of a sudden..." she paused, searching for words, but finished with a shy smile as she threw her hands open, "...and here you are!"

"Huh," was all that came out of Tom's mouth as he looked at her smiling face. He beamed from ear to ear as he repeated, "...and here you are." They both grinned at each other, not knowing what to say before Tom finally asked, "May I ask where you were headed?"

"No place, really," she lied. "I was just riding."

"Well, would you like to ride with me?" Tom asked. The look on his face made it clear there was nothing in the world he would like more. "I mean, if you don't have anything else to do."

Jennie Lue smiled. "I'd like that...but only on one condition."

"What's that?" he asked.

"You don't charge headlong into any more blind turns, okay?" she smiled sweetly.

"It's a deal," Tom said, with a humble shake of his head.

As Jennie Lue turned her horse around and they both started slowly for town, he added, "I'll try not to do anything that stupid the rest of the day, I swear."

"I hope so," she said playfully, "we don't want that horse of yours to throw you off into a creek or something."

Tom laughed at himself. "No...that wouldn't be pretty." He paused a second, grew serious and added, "Jennie Lue...really...I feel rotten about that."

"Oh, don't worry." She waved it off. "Actually, it was kind of fun. I mean, I thought we might run into each other sooner or later...just not like that." They laughed over the idea before she added, "I spotted you in town yesterday."

"Yeah," he said, "It was nice to see you."

"You, too," she replied, again with a bright smile.

"I heard about your husband," he said. "I just want to tell you, I'm very sorry. It must have been a terrible thing."

Jennie Lue glanced down at her saddle before looking up at Tom with a squint. "Thank you. I...I appreciate that...very much." After a moment she said, "I heard you and your daddy were looking for hands to help build a fence around your place. Is that true?"

"Yep. Started on it this morning," he answered.

As they rode along easily, their horses content with the pace, he told her all about the plans he and his father had for the ranch, his mouth on one subject and his mind on another. He heard himself talking, but all he could think about was how beautiful she was and how he could see so much life in her eyes. He had to look away a few times because he felt she might get a little uneasy the way he was staring, but each time he looked back into those eyes of hers, he was amazed. He felt just as he did years ago, as if he could see forever in them. He felt relief as he concluded his news about the Four C's because it occurred to him that he had done most of the talking and he would much rather listen to her.

"How is your family?" he asked.

Jennie Lue let out a short laugh. "My family...well, where do I start? Let's see...my daddy is doing all right except he stays tied up with all his business dealings and doesn't have much time for anything else. My brother is the same, only worse now that he's been the mayor for so long. And my

momma is doing well, but I wish she'd quit worrying about me so much."
She paused to chuckle. "Sometimes I think she believes fretting over me is
what God put her on this earth for and it sure can be annoying. She means
well, though."

"Enjoy it while you can," Tom said softly.

"Oh, Tom…I'm so sorry! How thoughtless of me," she said quickly. "I
heard about your mother after we got back to Belton. I'm terribly sorry."

"Thank you," he said. They rode in silence for a few minutes, both afraid
to say something that might open a wound in the other, until Tom broke the
mood and the silence.

"Jennie Lue, I have to tell you that riding alongside you today is about
the best thing that's happened to me since I can remember, but I need to ask
you a huge favor."

"Sure," she said with an uncertain smile, "what is it?"

"Please don't tell me you're sorry about anything. Really, there's nothing
you need to be sorry about," he said, gazing into her eyes. "I know what I'm
talking about. If I've learned one thing in this world, it's what lies ahead that
matters, not what's behind."

The anxiety on Jennie Lue's face as she waited for Tom to ask his favor
was quickly replaced with a smile as she realized he was telling her she didn't
need to apologize or explain why she married Henry Sloan and moved away
those many years before. A flood of relief swept over her, knowing the last
eight years of her life weren't something for which he wanted or needed an
explanation for. She also knew there was a good chance he was saying he
wasn't quite ready to talk about his past, but that didn't matter to her because
she never felt she needed any answers from him, either. Tom was right, too;
the past was the past and the one thing she was sure of was she wanted no
more part of it.

She straightened herself in the saddle and held out her hand. "I've recently
learned that lesson myself. So I won't if you won't. No more apologies. Deal?"

"Deal." He smiled as he reached over to seal their pact with a handshake.
It suddenly occurred to him that it was the first time he had touched Jennie
Lue since she was a child and, although he had dreamed about it for as long
as he could remember, he was shocked at the way it gave him a jolt that went
straight to his core. He had never experienced a feeling like that from any
other woman, and found himself mesmerized by the gleam in her eyes. Then
he quickly realized that, if he didn't let go, she might feel a bit uncomfortable,

so he reluctantly let her soft hand slide out of his.

After they had ridden down the road a bit, he said, "It's good to see you again. You look nice. Beautiful, really."

She blushed and said, "Thank you. You look pretty handsome yourself."

"No kidding?" he said. "You really think so?"

"Yes, I do. You've always been," she added, shyly looking away.

"Wow," he said as he gazed into the distance at the outskirts of Belton. He looked back at Jennie Lue to see her gazing at him with those deep hazel eyes and suddenly felt like a school kid in front of the prettiest girl in the class, without a clue what to say. They rode in silence until they were almost to town when he blurted out the first thing that came to mind. "That's a good-looking horse you got there. What's his name?"

She reached forward and rubbed the gelding behind his ear. "Pancho. My daddy gave him to me when I moved back home. I guess he wanted me to start getting out some, but I haven't really ridden him all that much. He's a real sweetheart, though, never in a hurry to do anything, and he gets along with just about any kind of animal there is, including humans."

"Yeah? Well, he's real nice," Tom said as he looked the horse over. Pancho was a paint like Clever, but was a shade taller because he was a gelding. He was mostly brown with a few white spots along his body and four white stockings to go along with a white stripe running down the middle of his forehead. He had a soft quiet look in his eyes that was a sharp contrast to the alertness in Clever's, but the two horses had gotten along beautifully since almost running into one another.

He rubbed his own horse behind the ears. "It looks like Clever's got a new friend."

"And Pancho, too," she said, as she pulled up just north of town. Tom reined in Clever as Jennie Lue said with a happy frown, "I guess I need to go. I didn't let anyone know where I was going, and I don't want my momma to get too worried."

Tom took a disappointed breath. "You sure you don't want to ride into town? Oh! Never mind; I get it." Before she could answer he said, "It's probably not a good idea to start the rumor mill down there, is it?"

"No, it probably isn't," she said, looking dejectedly toward Belton. The expression on her face slowly evaporated as she turned away from the buildings in the distance to look back at him. With a mischievous grin and sparkling eyes that made him think of her for the rest of the day, she added,

"Not yet, anyway."

Her statement was far more than Tom could have hoped for. He took off his hat and held it in his lap to hide his fingers that were tightly crossed, and asked, "Can I see you again? Soon? I'd like that a lot."

"I would, too. When?" she asked with a smile, blushing at the speed of her response.

"How about next Sunday?" he asked. "I'll have the whole day off. You just tell me where and when."

Jennie Lue thought for a second. "How about if we go for a ride? I can bring a lunch and we can even have a picnic somewhere, if that sounds okay to you."

"I know just the place," he said eagerly. "What time?"

"I won't be finished with church until around noon, but I can meet you right here on this road at one o'clock," she said, and started laughing. "Back where we almost ran each other over. We can call that 'our turn'…how's that?"

"I'll be thinking about it all week," he said with a beaming smile. "You bring a basket and I'll show you my favorite spot in the whole world. Fair enough?"

"I'm looking forward to it," she said. She turned her horse away from town and took one more long look at Tom. "I'm sorry I have to go, but I'll see you at our turn this coming Sunday at one o'clock."

"I'll be there," he said.

He watched as Jennie Lue gently kicked Pancho in the sides and headed off in the direction of the Double T. She didn't turn around and let him see the happy look in her eyes or the way she excitedly mouthed the word 'Yes' to herself as she rode away.

When she was completely out of sight, Tom turned Clever toward town and startled his horse for the second time that day by letting out a yell that might have been heard all the way to the other side of Belton.

Buddy Wallace leaned back in his chair, hands clasped behind his head and boots propped on the corner of his desk, spending a quiet Monday at his jail. Things had been surprisingly slow. The only thing he had done for the last two days was babysit a couple of cowboys who had a little too much to drink over the weekend. That was the good news; the bad news was he had far too much time on his hands to think about what he was going to do about his brother and his dad.

He had gone over to the courthouse first thing that morning to visit George and, although they both came to an agreement about what to do next, he had a nagging feeling that he was being pushed into a corner from which he might have to fight his way out.

What started only a few months ago as a simple plan to make a lot of money had become much more complicated with the return of his brother. The fact his father was dead set against ever selling the place made Buddy feel as if the prize was slipping through his fingers. He had made the decision to get in boots-deep from the beginning, but lately it seemed like he was getting in deeper by the day.

He let out a slow breath, reached into the front pocket of his jeans and pulled out a small key. He used it to unlock one of the side drawers of his desk. Pulling the drawer open, he stared into it for a few minutes before he was startled by the sound of the front door flying open. Buddy slammed the drawer shut and locked it quickly as Curry Hampton burst into the jailhouse.

"What are you doing here?" asked Buddy as Curry brought an end to his quiet morning.

"You gotta do somethin' about your pa!" Curry growled, leaning over with both hands on the desk.

"My pa? What the hell are you talking about?" Buddy said. "You're supposed to be…"

"I know where I'm supposed to be!" screamed Curry. "That son of a bitch ran me off like a stray dog!"

"All right, settle down. What happened?" Buddy asked, leaning back in his chair. "And start from the beginning."

"I'll tell ya what happened," yelled Curry, leaning a little further over the desk, "I worked my ass off all mornin' long while Church Davis rode me the whole way, telling me I wasn't doin' nothin'. He didn't do shit hisself, but somehow managed to talk your pa into cuttin' me loose. In front of everybody like I was scum! I don't know who I'm more mad at, Church or your pa."

Buddy clasped his hands behind his head, slowly put his boots back on his desk and stared at Curry for what seemed like five minutes before he reached into his shirt pocket, pulled out a toothpick and stuck it in the corner of his mouth. With anger in every word, he took every bit of steam out of Curry as he said, "Don't you ever barge in here and talk to me like that again. Do you understand?"

Curry stood straight and backed away from the desk, the color draining from his face. "Well, uh, I ain't hollerin' at *you*, Buddy. I'm sorry…didn't mean nothin by it. But your pa didn't give me a chance, and now he's made me look like the biggest fool in town!"

"You don't need my father to do that," Buddy said, his eyes burning a hole into the man who stood cringing before him. "Hell, I guess it's my fault. I never thought you were real smart, but I did assume at least part of that pea brain of yours was working."

"Buddy, I…" Curry started.

"You only had to do *one* thing," Buddy said, his feet crashing to the floor. He stood and stalked around the corner of the desk, "one lousy thing, and it didn't even take you half a day to foul it up." He backed the visibly shaken Curry into a corner. "What am I going to do with you now, hmm? *We had a deal*. But now you need to give me one *good* reason why I should let you keep breathing…and it best be convincing."

Tom tied Clever in the nearly empty street in front of Dayna G's and stood there for a few moments looking at the front door trying to get his nerve up. He hadn't thought much about walking into the place again until just now because his mind had been on next Sunday ever since he parted company with Jennie Lue. Thankfully, the place looked about as empty as he had ever seen it, so he took a deep breath, walked across the sidewalk, through the swinging doors and into the place that had changed his life forever. It took a second or two for his eyes to adjust to the lack of light, but soon he could see there was only one other person besides Gil in the place and it was the man he had come to see. The two men stopped in the middle of their conversation and eyed Tom as he walked over to the older black man who was sitting backward on his piano bench facing the bartender on the other side of the room.

"I understand your name is Percy," he said.

A look of surprise came from the piano player. "That it is." He studied Tom for a moment. "You were in here yesterday, weren't you? Who might you be?"

"My name is Tom Wallace." Tom held out his hand.

"Well, Mister Tom Wallace," Percy said as he shook Tom's hand, "pleased to meet you. What can I do for you? Something tells me you're not gonna ask me to play a tune."

Tom laughed and shook his head. "No, I'm not. My father asked me to come down here and talk to you. His name is Jim Wallace."

"He was in here yesterday, too, wasn't he?" Percy asked.

"Yes, he was," Tom replied.

Percy chuckled to himself as he looked out the front window like he was looking into the past, then turned his gaze back to Tom. "You know, you're the spittin' image of your old man. If I didn't know any better, I'd swear somebody set my watch back twenty years and it was your daddy standing here in front of me. How's that leg of his?"

"Oh, it's fine. He's fine," Tom said. "He wants to visit with you, though, and sent me down here to see if you can make it by the ranch sometime, soon if you can, maybe for dinner or something."

"I'd love to, but those are the hours when they want me around here the most," Percy said, "so I don't think I could do it then."

"When can you?" Tom asked.

"Well, let's see," Percy said, "how far from here is this place of yours?"

"Little over a half-hour ride," Tom answered.

"Monday afternoons are my slowest time of the week," Percy said with a wink, "so how about right now?"

Tom grinned. "That would be great. I know my dad's anxious to see you."

Percy stood and started for the stairs and said, "I'll meet you out front. Give me a few minutes to get my horse." Taking off his bow tie and vest as he walked past the bar, he told the bartender, "Gil, tell Dayna I had to leave for a while but I'll be back before this evening. I guess your old jokes are gonna have to be the entertainment while I'm gone."

"No problem. I'll tell her," Gil said from behind the bar as he watched Percy climb the stairs to his room. When he was out of sight, he turned to Tom, a sad look on his face. "Tom, I'm...I'm real sorry how things turned out. I really am," he said.

Tom held up a hand. "Gil, I never thought you and me weren't friends, so don't start thinking I've ever held anything against you, okay?"

"That may be, but I feel like I let you down," Gil said, looking down and shaking his head.

Tom walked over to the bar. "It doesn't matter now, right?"

Gil looked up at Tom and pointed at the floor, saying, "I saw that knife right there, Tom. I don't know what happened to it in all the confusion, but I saw it. I told your brother I saw it. I told everybody I saw it, but nobody seemed to care. Your brother even told me that unless I delivered that knife to the courthouse in person, it would be in my best interest to keep quiet. I've wondered to this day why he would tell me something like that."

Tom reached over the bar and put his hand on Gil's shoulder. "Me, too, Gil, but don't you worry about it…it's over. And we're still friends, right?"

"I'd like that, Tom…I really would. I just don't want you to spend the rest of your life thinking I didn't try to help you."

"I appreciate that," Tom said. He held out his hand. "Friends?"

"Friends," Gil said, as he shook Tom's hand in earnest, relief in his eyes. "So you're taking Percy with you today, huh?"

"Yeah, my dad knows him from a long time ago," Tom said. "We're going to ride out to the ranch, but I'll have him back before you know it."

"No problem," Gil said. "I don't know how he makes it, anyway. Not many people in this town have ever given him a nickel, even though he knows a lot of good songs, probably the best piano player we ever had."

"How long has he been here?" Tom asked.

Gil shrugged. "Six, eight months or so. Came from New Orleans. I always figured him the type to not stick around very long, but he's still here. He's a good man."

Tom talked to Gil for a while longer, but his mind and eyes kept drifting back to the exact spot where that man lay dying on the wood floor five-and-a-half years ago. The faint yet noticeable stain where the blood pooled beneath his convulsing body was still easy to see for anyone who knew what happened that day, giving Tom a cold shiver and telling him it was time to go. Gil was in the middle of something about the beautiful sound the piano made when Tom interrupted him.

"I'm sorry, Gil, I need to get some fresh air. If you see Percy before I do, tell him I'll be out front, would ya?"

Gil stopped in mid-sentence, looking a bit confused, but said, "Sure thing. I'll tell him."

Tom turned and walked away but, before he got to the door, a young woman yelled at him from the stairs, "Excuse me! Mister Wallace! Before you go, can you do me a favor?"

Looking back, Tom saw it was the same young girl Bear bought the drink for the day before, standing half-way down the staircase, leaning over the rail and clutching a blanket around her that showed the haste she was in to make it down the stairs before Tom left.

"Sure, ma'am," he said, "what can I do for you?"

She used a free hand to push her long, brown morning tangles out of her face. "I just ran into Percy. He was on his way out back to get his horse and said he was going with you out to your place. Is that true?"

"Yes, ma'am," Tom said.

"Could you please give Bear a message for me?" she asked.

Tom stood there and nodded as she continued with a giggle, "Tell him that Jessie, that's me, would like to see him again. But tell him this time he needs to come here around nine o'clock on Tuesdays or Thursdays. I can make some time for him then 'cause those are Buddy's poker nights, and he won't be here for sure. Can you tell him that for me?"

Tom tipped his hat to her. "Yes, ma'am. I'll tell him today."

"Thank you kindly," she said with a smile. She stood for a second longer looking at Tom, but suddenly realized she was standing there without too much clothing on, so she clutched her blanket closer and ran back up the stairs giggling like a child, yelling, "Thank you very much!"

Tom looked at Gil with a grin. "Something tells me that girl and Bear are going to get along just fine."

"Their secret is safe with me," Gil said with a chuckle. He watched Tom head for the door, but before he had a chance to walk out, he added, "Oh... and Tom, thanks for coming in today. I'm really glad we had a chance to talk."

"Me, too," Tom said.

He walked out onto the sidewalk to take a breath of relief just as a horse and rider raced up to the front of the building and stopped in a cloud of dust. The eyes in Curry Hampton's ashen face were enraged as he jumped off his horse like his saddle was on fire. He didn't say a word as he threw his reins over the rail, but he gave Tom a cold, baleful stare as he stormed past on his way inside the saloon. His voice was clearly heard demanding Gil set him up with a bottle of whiskey, making Tom feel sorry for him because he knew it had to be tough on a man to live his life going from one drunken catastrophe to another. Even though he knew it was Curry's own fault, and there was no doubt he deserved it, Tom shook his head at the thought as he glanced up and down the street, not really looking at anything.

He decided to shake off the chill he had gotten inside with a walk down the sidewalk and to put some distance between himself and Dayna G's, but he didn't get twenty feet when he heard Gil yell out his name. He froze at the unmistakable sound of two pistols being cocked behind him, one after the other.

"Curry! If you don't put that gun down right now I'll drop you where you stand!" he heard Percy yell.

Tom turned around to see Percy on horseback pointing his gun at the back of Curry Hampton's head. Curry was on the sidewalk between the two of them, his revolver leveled at Tom's chest. Evidently, the man was so mad that he didn't make it to the bar before he turned around and followed Tom back out onto the sidewalk to shoot him in the back. Percy must have come around the corner on his horse and saw what was happening just in time. Curry obviously couldn't care less that Tom was unarmed and totally defenseless but, as soon as he turned his head and saw Percy staring at him over the barrel of his gun, he knew his life would be over if he didn't back off. Curry still had his pistol pointed at Tom as he turned to face him again and for a moment had a look in his eyes as if he was considering whether or not it was worth it to shoot him anyway.

Percy told him to drop it one more time so he slowly bent over and put his gun down. He stood straight, holding his hands up. "This ain't the end of this...not for neither one of ya," he snarled.

"It will be for you if you reach for that pistol," Percy said, climbing off his horse. Keeping his gun leveled, he walked over and picked up Curry's.

"You never were too bright, were you?" he asked. Curry sneered. "What were you gonna do, shoot a man in the back in broad daylight? In front of everybody?" Percy asked. They looked around and noticed a few people across the street watching the incident unfold. Percy held up the revolver just out of Curry's reach. "You can pick this up at the sheriff's office tomorrow. Might be a good idea to wait until that drunk you're about to tie on wears off."

Curry stared, hatred in his eyes, then stormed back into Dayna G's without saying a word, leaving Tom and Percy on the sidewalk staring at each other in amazement.

"Thanks," Tom said.

"You're welcome," Percy said, putting his own pistol back in his holster and sticking Curry's in the front of his pants. He turned to climb back on his horse, saying, "Sorta looks like I might'a saved both father and son."

"What do you mean?" Tom asked as he climbed on Clever.

"Your father didn't tell you?"

"Not yet," Tom said as they started riding down the street.

"Well…" Percy said, with a far-away look in his eyes, "I met your father back in the war. At the time, I was owned by a wealthy family in Arkansas and the Rebs brought him to us to take care of. He was no use to them anymore 'cause his leg was busted up bad, and it was left to me to change his bandages, feed him and what not." He laughed as a memory crossed his mind. "I didn't think any man could be that stubborn or ornery but, in all my days on this earth, your father wins the prize when it comes to those two things."

"Yeah," Tom said with an affectionate chuckle. "God bless him."

Percy shared the whole story from years before as they rode two blocks over to the sheriff's office, then pulled Curry's pistol from the front of his pants as they reached their destination. "You want to do this? I know he's your brother and all, but I'd just as soon stay out here."

Tom saw there was something Percy wasn't telling him, but he didn't ask. He took the gun and hopped off his horse. "Sure. I'll be right back."

Buddy had done nothing since Curry Hampton left his office except sit in the chair behind his desk and wonder what the hell he was going to do about him. It wasn't like the idiot had to do anything difficult, except maybe get his hands calloused a bit from putting up a fence, but he couldn't even do that. Now, after telling him part of the reason why he wanted him to go work for his father, he knew it was only a matter of time before Curry opened his drunken mouth and said the wrong thing to the wrong person, and that just couldn't happen. Buddy's mind ran through ten different ideas on what he might do, and he was about to start on number eleven when he got up from his chair and looked out the window to see who had ridden up outside.

"Great," he mumbled, "this day just keeps getting better and better." He reached for his hat and put it on, changed the aggravated expression on his face as he opened the door and walked outside. "Well, well," he said with a smile, "what do I owe the privilege of you two coming by here to see me this day?"

Tom walked over and handed his brother Curry's gun butt first. "We had a bit of trouble with Curry. Looks like that fellow you knew 'real well' and would work out 'just fine' didn't pan out at all. In fact, if it wasn't for Percy here, he probably would've shot me in the back a few minutes ago. Here's his gun."

Buddy reached out to take the gun from Tom. As his hand wrapped around the grip, the gun pointing at his brother, he briefly wondered if he could successfully explain it away as 'an accident' if the gun went off right then. He thought better of it, though, dropped the pistol to his side, and looked at Tom with a serious expression. "You two all right? He didn't hurt you, did he?"

"No. We're fine," Tom said, "thanks to Percy, anyway."

Buddy looked at Percy and tipped his hat. "Thank you for watching out for my brother. If there's anything I can ever do for you, just let me know… ya hear?"

Percy didn't say a word as he looked down at Buddy. He tipped his hat once, as Tom told the story of Curry Hampton's brief relationship with the Four C's to his brother.

When he finished, Buddy pointed at Percy. "How does he fit into all this?"

"Dad knows him from the war," Tom said, walking to his horse. "Percy's riding with me back to the ranch to see him."

Buddy sounded sincere when he said, "No kidding? That's great."

Tom was back in the saddle when he looked at his brother and said, "I guess that's it, then. You might keep an eye on Curry this afternoon. No telling what he might do."

"Hopefully," said Buddy with a grin as he watched his brother and Percy move their horses away, "he's already so drunk the only menace he'll be to anybody for the next day or so is me while I have to listen to him snore in my jail."

"Well, good luck with that," Tom said.

Buddy grinned and hollered as they rode away, "Yeah…thanks a lot!"

As soon as they were well down the street, Buddy walked back into his office carrying Curry's pistol in one hand and straightening the big red mustache covering his clenched jaw with the other. The smile he wore while talking to his brother would not appear again for the rest of the day; he was busy making plans, only this time, he was absolutely sure whatever he was going to do about Curry would happen quickly.

"I take it you don't care too much for my brother," Tom said as they rode down the street.

Percy looked at Tom with a half grin. "You noticed, huh?"

"None of my business, I guess," Tom said, and shrugged, as if he shouldn't have asked.

"That's okay," Percy said. "Buddy's never done anything to me personally, but only because I do my best to stay as far in the background as I can. I've watched your brother teach people the hard way it's not a good idea to get too well known in this town for anything without his approval."

"Like Bear yesterday?" Tom asked.

"Exactly," Percy said, nodding, "Like Bear. I guess you could say Buddy doesn't like anything or anybody unless there's something in it for him."

Tom shook his head at the thought, knowing Percy was right. They continued on with nothing else to say until reaching the outskirts of town when Percy asked, "What's the name of your ranch?"

"The Four C's," replied Tom.

"You tellin' me Jim Wallace owns the Four C's," Percy asked, "and all this time I didn't know it?"

"He doesn't go into town much," Tom said, "or saloons, for that matter."

"Well, that explains why I never saw him," Percy said.

"We'll change that soon enough," Tom said. "What do you say we get these horses moving and get out of here?"

"Sounds good; lead the way," Percy said. They put their horses into a gentle run, making the last few buildings on the outskirts of town fall away behind them.

Tom admired the way Percy handled his horse as they rode alongside each other and knew he must have spent a great deal of time in the saddle over the years, but the closer they got to the blind curve in the road, the more his thoughts wandered back to his accidental meeting with Jennie Lue and their conversation afterward. As they reached the bend and rode through, Tom looked down to see the hoof prints they had left behind earlier, which brought to mind the gleam in Jennie Lue's eyes when she called it "our turn." Although he was already excited about the prospect of spending next Sunday afternoon with her, he suddenly felt like he might be the luckiest man alive because he realized the double meaning of the name, and wondered if she had, too. He knew if "their turn" meant a wonderful new life together, he was more than ready to make it count because if, by some fantastic stroke of luck, Jennie Lue was indeed the answer to a mountain of prayers, he was certain he wouldn't blow his chance this time around.

He always believed she was a prize that would make him cherish every minute of every day for the rest of his life and, after wasting five long years in prison, he was keenly aware she was the kind of woman a man might have a chance at once in a lifetime, if at all. Although he tried to calm down and stay level-headed about the whole thing by telling himself he shouldn't think too far ahead, take everything one day at a time and make sure Jennie Lue felt the same way he did before he fell in too deep, to say he wasn't having much luck would be a huge understatement.

As he and Percy engaged in friendly conversation while riding the rest of the way to the house, Tom never once stopped feeling like an excited young boy on his way to his first county fair or thinking about meeting Jennie Lue next Sunday at the narrow blind bend in the road they had agreed to call "our turn."

CHAPTER 13

Trouble

"Tom?" he heard his father calling through his bedroom door, "are you going to stay in there all night, or are you going to come out and join us?"

He had been lying on his mattress with his door closed for a few hours thinking of nothing but Jennie Lue and their rendezvous on Sunday but now, with his father knocking on his door, he thought it might be a good idea to go join the rest of the fellows who were out on the porch shooting the breeze. They had been out there since dinner was over, yapping about who knew what. Tom put his boots to the floor, sat on the edge of his bed and groaned, "I'm coming! Be out in a minute!"

"You feeling okay?" his dad asked through the door. "You don't feel sick or anything, do you?"

"No. I'm fine," Tom said, leaning forward and tousling his hair. "It's just been a long day, that's all. I'll be right out."

"Okay," Jim said, "see you in a minute."

Tom listened to his father's footsteps fade away, then straightened his hair with his fingers and stood. On his dresser was a small picture of his mother. He picked it up and studied her image. A contented smile spread across his face before he set it down and stepped into the living area of the house.

The ranch home Jim built for Ruby wasn't fancy or huge by any stretch, but it was extremely well-built. Tom and Buddy's modest bedrooms were on one side of the house, opposite the kitchen and dining area, while the master bedroom was in the back. The living room in the front stretched from one side of the structure to the other and the two fireplaces on either side made a comfortable place for Tom and Buddy to sleep when the winter nights turned cold. With the exception of one piece, Jim made all their furniture himself and always talked down the quality of it when a conversation turned that way. But the truth was, all of it looked as though it came from the finest furniture stores in town. The one item he didn't build was Ruby's upright piano, which stood against the wall outside Tom's bedroom.

As Tom made his way to the front door, he stopped for a moment to look at the fine, dark walnut-colored wood of the piano and smiled, knowing his mother never would have allowed the dust to collect on the shiny finish as it was now. He moved his finger along the top, then held it up to the light before reaching down and opening the cover that hid the ivory keys, revealing the manufacturer's insignia that he remembered so well:

B. Shoninger
New Haven, Conn
Estabished 1850
+ New York +

Although his mother tried her best to interest him in playing, Tom never seemed to have the time for it and suddenly realized how much he regretted not sitting down with her and learning. He put a finger on one of the keys and felt a jolt go through him when it rang out as the songs she used to play suddenly echoed through him and brought back fond memories of happy evenings. He closed the cover and stepped back to look at the instrument one more time, again telling himself that one day he would learn to play. Then he walked through the living room and out the door onto the front porch where the rest of the hands were laughing.

"Hey," Jim said as he looked up from his rocker, "look what finally crawled out of bed."

The rest of the men stopped in the middle of whatever they were talking about as Tom feigned aggravation, asking, "What the heck is going on out here?"

For a second or two, he was greeted by nothing but the sounds of crickets keeping time with the crackling logs in the front yard fire, lit to keep the bugs away and throw light on the porch. Aya and Bear were sitting in two chairs that matched the small round table next to the porch rail. Chas sat by himself in the two-person swing at the corner of the house, while Church and Jim sat in the two rockers on the other side of the door.

"Just what is it that's so important it keeps you fellas chattering away out here for hours?" Tom asked, grinning.

"Not a damn thing," Bear responded quickly with a wink. "But 'twixt me and you, I think they're all captivated by my incredible good looks and my amazin' gift of storytellin'."

There wasn't a laugh or a moan that didn't escape the mouth of every man there before Church stood and asked, "You wanna sit here?"

"No, you go ahead," Tom said with an appreciative smile. Church knew the chair he had been sitting in was Ruby's, but Tom waved him back down and settled into the swing next to Chas. "Bear, I know firsthand that tongue of yours never stops moving, but I'm pretty sure those good looks you're talking about might be your imagination getting the best of you."

There was good-natured agreement from all as Bear feigned insult. "So that's how it's gonna be, huh? Well, I got news for ya'll. Whoever thinks I'm handsome gets a nice, big fat steak tomorrow, and whoever thinks otherwise will get a dish I like to call 'Bear Surprise'."

Everyone laughed as they realized what they needed to say next, but Chas didn't quite catch on and asked innocently, "What's Bear surprise?"

Bear laughed out loud and shook his head. "Oh…a little of this and a little of that. I make it different every time and I won't tell ya what's in it until after ya eat it, but when I do I can promise you'll be surprised enough to want to head out back and give your best imitation of the Curry Hampton spew."

"Ohhhhh," was the unanimous groan as they remembered the way Curry started his first and last day at the ranch. After the commotion died down a bit, Church looked at Bear with a straight face. "Bear, I don't know ya that well yet, but if ya keep puttin' meals on the table like ya have been," he said, "I just might draw a big ol' heart on the ceiling above my bunk and put a picture of you right in the middle of it."

"With Cupid's arrow going though?" Tom asked.

"With Cupid's arrow going through," Church said with conviction.

They laughed and agreed with the sentiment, but the friendly ribbing was soon directed at Church because all the hands knew he wasn't on the trail anymore due to the girl he had been seeing in town. As a consequence, he had endured a few jokes over the whole thing since arriving at the ranch.

Their undivided attention was pointed squarely at Church when Jim asked, "What do you think that lady friend of yours is going to say when she finds out you go to sleep at night looking at a picture of Bear and not her?"

Church waited a moment for the laughter to die down. He looked at Jim like a judge would look at a prisoner right before handing down his sentence. "Hopefully she won't find out but, if she does, she's just gonna have to understand."

"There's one man who's eatin' steak tomorrow. Anybody else?" Bear said over the sound of laughter.

"I don't know," Tom said, "can I have a day to think it over?"

They all laughed except Chas, who looked a little uncomfortable with the whole idea, uncertain if everyone was serious or not. As soon as the chatter died, he stuck his nose into the conversation, asking, "Bear, I didn't get to hear how ya know how to speak Injun. Can you tell me?"

Bear rubbed the top of his bald head, then turned to Chas. "I guess so. My wife was Indian…Coushatta…almost the same language as Aya's here."

"Really?" Chas said. "You was married to an Injun lady?"

"Sure was," Bear said.

"How'd ya meet her?" Chas asked.

"I won her in a poker game," Bear said.

"What? A poker game?" Chas sat straight up in the swing.

"Yeah," Bear said, "all I had was a pair of threes, but I figured it was enough 'cause that ol' boy just had to be bluffin'. Turned out he was."

"You can't gamble with people, can ya?" Chas asked, as if he couldn't comprehend the idea.

"Not so much anymore," Bear said, "but thirty-five years ago things was different. She had run off from her tribe 'cause the chief wouldn't let her marry his son, and she wound up getting picked up by the bastard I beat in cards. He had her 'bout six months or so, but wanted to get rid of her anyway 'cause she wouldn't have nuthin' to do with him. She told me it was 'cause he wouldn't take a bath, but I think it was 'cause she was strong-willed; if she didn't like ya, that was all she wrote. For that matter, if she didn't like *anything* she could sure make your life hard over it. She was the toughest woman I ever met."

Chas had a look on his face that let everyone know he didn't understand what Bear was saying. "She was tough? You didn't fight her, did ya?"

"No, no," Bear explained with a grin, "not tough like that. Tough like…

she was tough inside, like you."

The puzzled look on Chas' face was replaced by one of awe. "Like me? Really?"

"Sure, like you," Bear said as he looked around at the rest of the hands. "These boys here told me all about you and your pa, and they say ya came out of it just fine and can handle just about anything. Takes a man who's tough inside to do that."

Chas leaned back into the swing looking like he would burst with pride. Ever since he found out Jim was going to hire on new hands for the work ahead, he wanted nothing more than to be one of the boys. Tonight, after spending only one day with them, he realized he was. The rest of the men were looking at him with smiles on their faces and nodding in agreement.

He squirmed in his seat. "Well…thanks, Bear. That's mighty nice of ya to say, but…can ya…can ya tell me about Mister Aya? I know him and all, but I don't know nuthin' 'bout him. The two of ya talked Injun with each other all night last night, so ya gotta know a lot more than me."

"I'd like to hear that, too," Tom said.

Bear looked around at everyone before he glanced at Aya and asked, "Meyka cha innaatiika chisnoola istiila?"

Aya nodded indifferently before raising an open hand and saying in his low, gravelly voice, "Yama."

"Well," Bear said as he rubbed his hands together, "first off, his full name is Ayapaali, which means 'the quiet one who sneaks up on things.' Seems when he was little he was always playin' jokes on his people by sneakin' up and scarin' the daylights out of 'em. He must a had a knack for it, though 'cause, even as a young man, he was always the one chosen to lead the huntin' parties. Says he can still walk up on a deer any old time he wants."

"That's right," Tom said, "I can't remember a time when Aya didn't come back with a deer when he set out to find one, or anything else, for that matter. He was always good at that, but what I'd like to know is, where did he come from?"

"From the Alabama tribe in east Texas," Bear said, looking around at the bunch. "Twenty-two years ago this summer, Aya's wife and babies died in childbirth."

"Babies?" Tom said, "you mean 'baby', don't you?"

"Nope," Bear said. "She was carryin' twins. Boys. Lost 'em both. He took it real hard, too."

"Oh, my God...that's terrible," Tom said. He looked at Aya and added, "I'm very sorry."

Aya nodded, knowing what Tom was saying, and Bear continued. "Told me he spent the next six months or so doin' nuthin' but getting drunk and feelin' sorry for hisself."

"Aya got drunk?" Tom said in disbelief.

"Not only drunk," Bear said, "belligerent, too. Wanted to fight just about everybody, and it got to the point where his own people pretty much run him off."

"Wow," Tom said, looking at Aya and trying to imagine him drunk. "I've never seen him touch a drop."

"Well, that was before he had his vision," Bear explained.

"What kind of vision?" Chas asked.

"Said it come to him in a dream." Bear shrugged. "Evidently, at the lowest point of his life, after he got run off by his tribe, he got liquored up real good one night and passed out on the banks of a small creek. Sometime during the night, the spirit of an ancient warrior came to him disguised as a deer and told him he had failed the test of the passing of his wife and sons, but he had one more chance to redeem himself. Showed him a valley where he was to go and stay until he had completed two *real* important tasks. One would set things right for the way he lost his faith after the death of his wife and sons, and the other would pardon him for the way he treated his own people. Only after he completed these tasks would he be allowed to return and live with his tribe again."

"What were the tasks?" Church asked, who along with everyone else was captivated by the story.

"He don't know," Bear said. "The spirit told him he would return and tell him when it was time to go home, but there was two things he was not allowed to do in the meantime."

"What's that?" Chas asked.

"Well, he can't swallow another drop of alcohol," Bear said, holding up one finger and then another, "and two, he can't talk in any language other than his own."

"Why?" Church asked.

"Doesn't know for sure," Bear said, "but he thinks that by only speakin' his native tongue it will help keep him in touch with his tribe. Maybe a better way to put it is, he thinks if he doesn't keep that part of the bargain, he won't be able to find his way back when it's time to go home. At the end of the day, I guess it's his way of stayin' an Alabama Indian and not becomin' a white man."

"Must have been a hell of a vision," Tom said.

"It was." Bear nodded. "He woke up with a start and told himself it was all just a dream, but found himself starin' at the biggest white-tail buck he had ever seen, standin' on the other bank lookin' him right in the eye. Told me that buck was no more scared of him than if he was an ant crawlin' 'round in the dirt, and it stood there 'til Aya knew the dream was real. Only after that did the deer turn and head off into the brush."

"That's a heck of a story," Chas said.

"And that's not all," Bear said, clapping his hands and rubbing them together, "he got up from where he had passed out, waded over to the other side to look at the prints that big ol' deer left in the mud, and had no sooner crawled up the far bank when a flash flood swept through, swallowin' up everythin' in that creek. Aya would have drowned for sure if he hadn't woke up when he did, so that very morning he set out to find what turned out to be this valley and do whatever it was that spirit had in mind for him."

"But how much longer is he supposed to stay here?" asked a wide-eyed Chas.

"Don't know," Bear said, "but he's pretty sure one of them tasks is complete."

"I'll be damned," Tom said, as he looked at the spot in the yard where the four dead men lay years before and realized the connection between Aya's vision and the shootings. It took Tom's breath away when he suddenly understood that Aya had a chance to regain his faith that day by saving the lives of a woman and her two boys after losing it with the deaths of his own wife and sons. A shiver went through him as he thought about what might be if Aya hadn't gotten up off the bank of some far-off creek long ago to crawl out the other side. Tom glanced at his father and saw a look on his face that made it plain he couldn't believe his ears either.

Everyone on the porch knew the story of Aya and the four bandits. They all sat quietly, not knowing what to say but, after a minute or two, Chas felt a little uncomfortable with the silence.

"Mister Jim, when is Mister Percy supposed to be back here?" he asked.

"Any time, I reckon," Jim said, looking down the road toward Ruby's bridge. "He said he needed to talk to Dayna over at her place and gather his things. I figured he'd a been back by now."

"Tom told me you knew him back in the war," Chas said.

"Yeah, I did," Jim said absently, still looking off into the distance. He looked at Chas and smiled. "Things didn't look so good for me after I busted up my leg, but at the time Percy was owned by a family in Arkansas who took me in and did their best to doctor me up. Percy was the one that did all the doctoring. He did a hell of a job, too. I always felt I owed that man something...shoot, I couldn't even stand up to relieve myself or wipe my own ass, but that man never once complained." Jim chuckled. "After all he had to go through trying to get me patched up, the least I can do is give him a chance to get out of that smoke-filled cave I found him in."

"Maybe he can play us a tune or two on your piano when he gets here," Bear said. "I was listenin' to him in Dayna G's yesterday, and he's pretty damn good."

"Maybe so," Jim said. The dogs got up and ran out of the yard, barking at the sound of hoof beats echoing off Ruby's bridge. "Why don't you ask him yourself?"

They all got up at the sound of the approaching rider and walked into the yard as Percy rode into the light surrounding the front of the house.

Percy pulled his horse to a stop and stayed in his saddle as he looked at everyone. "Good evening, gentlemen. I hope you boys aren't sittin' out here waiting for me to liven things up, 'cause y'all are liable to be in for a disappointment."

"Well," Jim said as he stepped off the porch, "we were just talking about you." He pointed at Bear. "Bear was hoping that before the night was over you might be able to play us a tune on that piano inside; says you're pretty good."

Percy tipped his hat to Bear then looked back at Jim as he swung his leg over the back of his horse on his way to the ground. "I guess I could do that. I suppose that ain't a bad way to start my first day on the job," he said.

"I thought you were going to bring all your things," Jim said, noticing the small bedroll on the back of Percy's horse.

"I did," Percy said with a smile. "By the time I squared up with Dayna, I didn't have much left to call my own." He paused and looked at the ground for a second before he added with a laugh, "I tell ya, she's one mean ol' lady. You know, she even took the rest of my clothes just to settle the last fifty cents I had on my bill."

"She was a little mad, huh?" Jim said with a chuckle.

Percy grinned as he swatted the dust off his shirt. "I guess you could say that." They both laughed at the thought before Percy asked, "Is it all right with you if I turn my horse loose in that corral of yours?"

"Sure," Jim said. He looked over at the porch. "Chas, can you take care of that for me?"

"Sure thing, Mister Jim," came the reply as Chas leapt off the porch, ran to the animal and led it around back to the barn by the reins.

After Chas was gone, Jim held an outstretched hand to Percy and said with genuine sincerity, "I'm glad you came, Percy."

"Thank you. I'm glad you asked," Percy said as he gave Jim a hearty handshake. "It was kinda funny how we ran into each other again like we did but I can tell you I'm real happy to be here. You'll get your money's worth out of me, I promise."

"Hmm," muttered Jim with a chuckle, "seems to me I already have. I believe I'm the one who owes you."

"That was a long time ago," Percy said. "Besides, somehow I feel you would have done the same for me."

"Maybe you're right," Jim said as he put a hand on Percy's shoulder. "Now, why don't you come join us on the porch for a spell and get to know the rest of the boys."

"Sounds good to me." Percy followed Jim up the steps and onto the covered porch, passing out handshakes all around as he was welcomed to the Cowhouse Creek Cattle Company.

"Have a seat right here," Church said as he motioned Percy to the rocker he had been sitting in.

"Thank ya," Percy said as he took Church up on his offer. "I believe I will."

Jim sat in the rocker next to him. "Did you have an uneventful ride over?"

"Yeah," Percy said, watching the rest of the men take their seats around the porch, "except I left Belton with considerably less than when I arrived, thanks to Dayna G."

"Don't worry about that," Jim said with a chuckle. "We'll get you into town over the next day or so and get some new clothes for you."

"I appreciate that," Percy said. He looked around, acknowledging everyone there. "Church...good to see ya. And you must be Bear. I'm sorry we didn't get properly introduced yesterday."

"We can fix that right now," Bear said as he rose, walked over and shook Percy's hand. "Pleased to meet ya."

"The name's Percy Goff, and pleased to meet you, too," Percy said. "I think a lot of folks in this town want to meet you after the way you embarrassed the hell out of ol' Blondy." Percy changed his expression to one of concern. "You might want to watch your step around town for a while, though. Blondy Harbison don't take lightly to anybody treatin' him like that."

Bear sat in his chair, his expression stunned and worried. "That kid in the saloon yesterday was Blondy Harbison?" He rubbed the top of his head and gave a tired chuckle. "I'll be damned."

"You know him?" Jim asked, now more interested in the conversation.

"I know *of* him, sure do." Bear sighed. "Didn't know that was him yesterday, though. Ah, hell! I can be dumb as a stump sometimes."

"How'd you hear about him?" Jim asked.

Bear sat shaking his head for a few moments as he looked into the distance, then turned to Jim. "All over, I guess. I mean, I don't know him personal-like. We never had beers together, that's for sure, but I started hearin' stories 'bout that kid way back when I was in Amarillo. Talk made its way up from Fort Worth about this kid taught to shoot by ol' Longhair Jim Courtright hisself."

"Jim Courtright…he's the sheriff of Fort Worth, isn't he?" Jim asked.

"Some call him that," Bear said with a wave of his hand, "others call him a murderer for hire, a drunken gambler and a blackmailer behind his back, but everybody calls Longhair Jim "Mister" in public 'cause of that gun on his hip." Bear paused. "Ain't nobody goes in or out of Hell's Half Acre wantin' anythin' to do with that man."

"What's Hell's Half Acre?" Tom asked.

Bear rubbed the top of his head again, as if trying to find the right words to describe it. "Well, now, there's a part of Fort Worth they call 'Hell's Half Acre' that's a lot like the part of Belton we was in yesterday, 'cept it's a whole lot bigger and a whole lot worse. It didn't get that name for nuthin'. See… Longhair Jim got hisself elected sheriff and cleaned the town up, but he did it by shootin' just about anybody that got out of line or didn't pay him for protection or pay their gamblin' debts. Hell, I heard a story one time that he shot and killed a guy for beatin' him fair and square in a card game!"

"And he's the sheriff?" Tom asked, amazed.

"Well, you never been to Fort Worth, have ya?" Bear asked. He shook his head. "Fort Worth's a cow town sittin' right in the middle of the Chisholm

Trail, and that town gets its share of rowdys comin' and goin'. I'm not sayin' there's a big halo floatin' over Belton, but this town ain't nuthin' compared to what goes on up there. Anybody that wants to live anywhere near Hell's Half Acre in Fort Worth ain't plannin' on reaching a ripe old age, that's for sure."

"And you're saying that Blondy Harbison was trained to use a gun by Longhair Jim Courtwright?" Jim asked.

"Yep," Bear said. "Not only that, but I heard the reason Blondy lit outta there was because Longhair Jim knew the day was comin' when he was gonna have to kill his understudy. Rumor had it that Blondy got wind of it and decided Longhair Jim was the only man he couldn't beat, so he high-tailed it." Bear shook his head in disgust. "Just my luck my smart mouth would run into him here."

"There was a lot of talk when Blondy came here that he got run off from Fort Worth," Jim said, "lots of rumors about questionable shootings. People say he killed his first man when he was fourteen. Talk was, he enjoyed it too much."

"He been involved in any killin's that don't add up since he got here?" Bear asked.

Jim nodded. "There's been a few," he said, "but there's never been enough proof to do anything about it. People around here don't like Blondy much at all, but I guess they aren't ready to believe their deputy enjoys going around killing people."

"I don't think there's any doubt about it from what I hear," Bear said, "and maybe that was the reason Longhair Jim had it in for him. But the short version is that Blondy knew Longhair Jim was gunnin' for him, so he lit out. It's not so much that he got run off; he got scared off, and there ain't but a handful of people on this earth that can scare Blondy Harbison." He took a deep breath and exhaled slowly. "And he just had to wind up here…I'm about as dumb as they come."

"I wouldn't worry about it so much," Jim said, trying to downplay the situation. "You need to remember my son is also the sheriff. I'll talk to him tomorrow and make sure you and Blondy get a chance to patch things up, all right?"

"I'd appreciate that," Bear said with a somewhat relieved look, "'cause if them stories are true, that Blondy Harbison fella is almost as fast as Longhair Jim, madder at the world than Bill Longley and meaner than John Wesley Hardin."

"I met John Wesley Hardin just last week," Tom said. "Right before they turned me loose. He was in prison at The Walls. There was a new story going around every day about another man he killed, and most of the inmates talked about him like he was some kind of hero. To me, he didn't seem much different than anybody else, except he's a lot smarter than most. He's studying on being a lawyer now that they got him locked up."

"Well, I got news for ya. The only thing different about those kinda men is that they're a lot bigger cowards than most when they don't have a gun in their hands," Bear said, "but something about them ain't quite right in the head when they do. I'm sure our friend Blondy is the same way but the problem is, who's gonna get the nerve up to take that gun away from him? That's the question."

"I'll talk to Buddy tomorrow and get this straightened out, Bear," Jim repeated.

Bear got up and leaned against the porch rail as he looked out into the yard, then turned and nodded at Jim. "Thank ya, and I'll do my best to keep my damn mouth shut from now on." He glanced around at the worried expressions. "But lookee here, y'all don't need to worry about my ass gettin' shot off 'cause I can't keep my tongue from flappin', so let's change the subject."

Bear walked back to his seat. "Tell ya what, Percy. Jim here told us all how you patched that leg of his up in the big war. Why don't ya explain to us how ya did that with him bein' so bullheaded and all." The tension lifted considerably as everyone laughed at the remark, but they all listened intently as Percy related his side of the story about how he came to know Jim a long time ago.

When he was finished, Bear asked, "How'd ya find yourself in Belton?"

"Well, when the war was over and I became a free man, I did a whole lot of odd jobs as I worked my way to New Orleans," he said. "Once I got there, I met up with a bunch of musicians who taught me how to play the piano. I guess I had a knack for it 'cause the next thing I knew I was makin' a livin' at it, playin' in saloons and whatnot."

"How did ya wind up out here?" Bear asked.

"I don't know. Maybe I got tired of the bars." Percy shrugged. "That, and the woman I was in love with ran off with a rich man who lived over in Fat City. I guess I just needed a new town to call home, so I left. About the time I ran out of money, I was pullin' into this little town called Belton," Percy added with a grin. "You boys ever hear of it?" They all chuckled at the familiar ring to Percy's story, because similar events happened to each of them, making it possible for them all to wind up on the front porch of the Four C's.

"Speakin' of Belton," Percy added, "I have to tell ya that little girl Jessie sure wants ya to stop by and see her. She made me double-swear I'd tell ya that first thing."

Bear laughed. "That's what Tom here was telling me." He shrugged as he sat back in his chair. "Don't hold it against her, now. She's not the first girl who ever got enchanted by the three Ws."

They howled as Bear told them the meaning but, as soon as the laughter died down, Jim got them going again. "Bear, are you sure those three Ws don't stand for a wayward, washed-up old water-rat?" he said.

Bear rubbed the top of his head as they howled again, and said, "I don't know. It very well may be. Just don't go telling Jessie that. I want her to believe my version."

"You keep cooking like you have been and I won't breathe a word," Jim said.

"Deal," Bear said. He looked around at everyone. "Speakin' of cookin', anybody want a slice of apple pie? It's probably cooled off enough to eat by now."

"That sounds good," was the reply from most everyone.

Bear got up and walked to the screen door. "Why don't you boys follow me? After ya'll take a bite of this pie, all of ya will have a picture of me by your beds, surrounded by a heart pierced by Cupid's arrow."

"I'm right behind ya," Church said. They wasted no time following Bear into the house.

Percy was the last of the hands to go inside leaving himself, Jim and Tom alone on the porch for a few moments. "I just want to thank both of you gentlemen one more time for giving me the chance to get myself back on my feet. It means a lot to me," he said.

"You'd have done the same for me," Jim said.

"You're right," Percy said, "I suppose I would have."

"Well, get on in there, then," Jim said. "Bear's got some leftovers for you and you can top it off with a piece of that pie he's been so anxious for everyone to try."

"Yep. I believe I'm gonna like it here," Percy said with a grin, then turned and disappeared through the door.

"We got a good group," Jim said as he looked back at Tom. "A little motley maybe, but overall I think we have the hands we need."

"I think you're right," Tom said with a chuckle. "We've got an Indian, a former slave, an old bald man that used to be married to a squaw, a washed-up old cow hand, Chas and me, an ex-con. What a group!"

"Don't forget about the old crippled man," Jim said with a laugh, patting his bad leg.

"Oh, yeah, him, too," Tom said as he put his arm around his dad. "Come on. Let's go inside and see how that pie turned out."

As they started for the door, Chas came around the side of the house asking, "Where'd everybody go?"

Tom was about to tell him they were all inside when all the dogs suddenly stood up and growled, their attention focused down the road and into the darkness toward Ruby's bridge.

Jim, Tom and Chas stood quietly, trying to get a glimpse of what the dogs were warning them of, but they knew it had to be something out of the ordinary when all three started barking and leapt into the night. Without a word from Jim or Tom, Chas started running after the hounds, saying "I'll go down there and see what it is."

"Hold up there!" Jim yelled before he could get too far, "you might need this." Jim reached in behind the front door and pulled out the double-barreled shotgun he kept loaded with buck shot. As he walked off the porch and into the yard, he added, "You don't want to run up on something you can't scare off."

Chas turned and ran back to Jim, an astonished look on his face clearly showing he was proud he could be trusted with the shotgun. "Yes, sir, Mister Jim. I'll be real careful with it, I promise."

"I know you will," Jim said. "Just be careful with yourself, too."

Chas stood looking the gun over as he held it carefully, then looked at Jim one more time as if to say thanks before running off into the darkness after the barking dogs.

Tom came off the porch to join his father. "I think you just made that boy's day. You ever let him handle one of your guns before?"

"Oh, yeah," said Jim as they walked to the other side of the fire so they could see into the darkness better, "only he's never done it on his own before; I've always been close by."

"What do you reckon it is?" Tom asked.

"Probably just a coyote or something," said Jim.

By now Jim and Tom had put the fire far enough behind them that they could see the silhouettes of Chas and the dogs under the stars as they neared Ruby's bridge, and watched as the dogs stopped halfway across but continued to bark loudly at whatever it was on the far side. They were puzzled when a sparkling light appeared on the other side of the creek, but Jim caught on quick and started running as fast as he could, yelling, "Chas! Get away from there!" Neither Jim nor Tom could do anything except watch as the lit fuse arced through the air and came to rest on the bridge, glowing for a few seconds before the clear, half-moon night suddenly turned into day.

In the briefest of moments, Tom and Jim were horrified as the shapes of Chas and the dogs went flying through the air, the explosion ripping the quiet night apart. Although they were still fifty yards from the bridge, the shock wave was so strong it nearly knocked them off balance when it hit them a half-second later. They ran on blindly, their eyes readjusting to the dark with shards of flaming timber raining down all around them as they fruitlessly called Chas's name.

Nearing what was left of Ruby's bridge, they saw a flash of light on the far side of Cowhouse Creek and Tom heard what sounded like a bee go past his ear. He lunged and grabbed his father by the shoulder, pulling Jim down with him as another flash appeared, instantly followed by the same buzzing sound, which would have passed right through his chest if he hadn't thought to reach out and bring his father to the ground.

They laid there a moment, then rolled over to see if they could spot who it was that was trying to kill them, only to see other flashes of gunfire coming from a slightly different spot on the other side of the bridge. A few seconds later, all was quiet when they heard Buddy's voice ring out, "Dad! Tom! Ya'll out there?"

"What the hell is going on?" yelled Jim as he lay on the ground, "Who's trying to kill us?"

"It's okay. It's over," called Buddy. "Y'all can get up."

"What happened?" Tom asked as he got to his feet.

"Curry Hampton," was the reply. "I guess he wanted to get even for you running him off earlier today. He was drinking all afternoon."

Tom stumbled his way down the steep embankment and crossed the creek before he frantically climbed up the far bank to find Curry Hampton on the far side, lying dead on the ground, gun still in hand and two pools of blood spreading out across his shirt, plainly visible even in the faint moonlight.

"Jesus!" Tom said, "I can't believe it!"

"It's a good thing I came along when I did," Buddy said as he looked down at Curry's body. "Are y'all okay?"

"Yeah. Oh, geez — Chas!" Tom said, spinning around and making his way back to the other side of the creek. He combed the ground looking for his friend.

He was close to a panic when he heard his dad say, "Tom, over here. I got him." Tom ran over to find his father kneeling over Chas, unconscious but alive. "Run up to the house and get a wagon," he said urgently, "tell Church to ride into town and get Doc Carrington out here right now. He's hurt bad."

Tom raced back to the house, running into the rest of the men on his way; they had rushed out at the sound of the blast. It didn't take long for them to understand what happened or what to do next and, within a few minutes, Church was off in a fury to get the doctor while Chas was lying on his side in the back of the wagon, being taken back to the house.

Tom felt sick to his stomach when he first saw the twenty-four, inch-long piece of shredded timber poking out the front and back of Chas's left shoulder next to his collarbone, but had seen enough injuries during his time in prison to not let his shock show when Chas came to.

"How come you blew the damn bridge up?" Tom asked with a grin when Chas finally opened his eyes.

"I didn't...I promise I didn't," Chas said, trying to clear his head as Percy and Tom leaned over him. Searing pain swept through the young man. He instinctively reached over to see what was causing it when the look of agony on his face was replaced by one of shock as he saw the piece of wood sticking out of his shoulder.

Tom and Percy each took one of Chas's arms to keep him from moving and calmly told him to lay still, but Chas brought a smile to everyone's face as he stammered in short, broken breaths, "Well...lookee here...I gotta tree growin' outta me."

"It ain't a big tree, though. And you'll be fine," Percy assured him.

"It's a good thing, too," Tom said as he brushed Chas's curly red hair out of his eyes, "otherwise we couldn't tell which is your head and which is the tree. They're both pretty hard, you know."

Chas choked out a couple of chuckles. "Guess ya might be right. You ain't the first one I heard that from," he whispered.

"Just lie there and be still," Jim said from the front seat, "The doc is on his way and we'll have you good as new before you know it." He turned to Aya. "Get this thing as close to the porch as you can." Aya nodded once as Jim turned back to Tom. "We'll carry him into Buddy's old room so Doc can work on him in there."

"Wow," Chas muttered, "I get a bunk in the main house?"

"Yeah, you do," Jim said, smiling, "but only if you don't move around anymore, you hear me?"

"Yes, sir, Mister Jim," Chas said, as though drunk. He stopped looking at the wood sticking out of him and blinked his eyes a few times trying to clear his vision. "Hey, where's my glasses…I need my glasses."

"Don't worry about those," Tom said, "I'm sure we'll find them in the morning."

"But it's important. Mister Jim got those for me," he said.

"Don't you worry about those glasses," Jim said with authority. "I'll get you another pair if I need to. You just lie still for now."

"I'm sorry, Mister Jim. I didn't mean to be no trouble. I'll do whatever ya say," Chas said with great relief and settled down onto the floor of the wagon as if he needed to sleep.

They lurched to a stop in front of the house and in a flash Jim and Aya were out of the front seat helping Tom and Percy carry Chas through the house, laying his limp frame on Buddy's old bed. Bear had been busy all this time getting the room ready and, when they all stepped back to take a look at the injured young man under the lights of several lanterns, the extent of his injuries became fully apparent. For the moment, there wasn't too much bleeding from his most obvious wound, but it was clear whenever the two-inch wide piece of lumber did come out of his shoulder, he was going to lose a lot in a hurry. He had cuts and gashes all over his face, none of which seemed too serious, but his left ear was bleeding profusely, turning his bright red hair even redder, soaking the left side of his tattered shirt and filling the room with the unmistakable smell of fresh blood.

Everyone was in shocked silence as they stood around the bed looking down at Chas. Jim turned and said, "Boys, I'm going to stay in here, but we've all got some work to do." The rest of them lit out to different parts of the house with grim expressions on their faces, looking for anything that might come in handy for the gut-wrenching job ahead.

"What was *that*?" Jennie Lue said, bolting upright in her chair and looking to the north. She had been talking with her mother and father on their front porch, her usual custom before turning in for the night, but was suddenly alarmed at the ominous boom in the distance. If it had been a cloudy evening, it would have been easy to mistake the noise for thunder as it overwhelmed the rest of the night sounds, but the weather was clear, so all three people were unnerved as the echo rolled through the skies from what appeared to be somewhere close to the Four C's.

"Sounded like an explosion…a big one. Hell, half the people in the county probably heard that," Turner said as he stared in the direction of the explosion. "Sounds like it might be close to the Wallace place," he added, folding his newspaper and setting it down on the table next to his chair. "I wonder why they'd be using dynamite at night, in the dark."

"No telling what they're up to," Judy said, as if she wasn't surprised. "Maybe George was right about them. Nobody uses dynamite at night unless they're up to no good."

"Maybe it wasn't them who used it," Jennie Lue said nervously.

"My guess is that they didn't," Turner said.

"What do you mean?" she asked.

"I hope I'm wrong," Turner mused as he stared into the darkness, "but they started putting up that fence today and that sound you just heard might very well be the first shot of the war."

"The war? What war?" she asked.

"The one between the free grazers and the land owners," replied Turner with a sigh. "There's been more than a little concern over that fence they're putting up and what it's going to mean in the end for the free grazers. I for one think it's a great thing for the land owners and have half a mind to fence in our place, but there's a whole bunch of cattle grazers out there who think otherwise and have made it known they'll take action if they're forced into a corner."

"But they just started fencing in their land today," Jennie Lue said. "You wouldn't think the free grazers would do anything so soon, would you?"

"I don't know." Turner rose from his chair. "I'll find out about it in the morning, but there's nothing we can do right now, so I think I'll call it a day. Maybe we all should."

"I think you're right," Judy said as she also rose to go inside. "Come on, Jennie, it's time for bed."

Jennie Lue stood and, without saying a word, followed her mother and father to the front door. After they entered, she looked back to the north and stared. She had a nervous habit of biting her lower lip when she was troubled by something and was doing so now. She walked into the house and up the stairs into her room, lying awake for several hours, unable to stop thinking about the menacing sound she heard and the sickening feeling it brought to the pit of her stomach. She knew she had to ride out first thing in the morning to find out what caused the explosion, but had no idea how she was going to slip away without letting her mother or father know. But, by the time she fell asleep, she didn't care and was determined to fly out of bed before the first rooster crowed.

Forty-five minutes after the explosion, Tom watched his brother drive his wagon past the re-stoked fire and park in front of the house. "So, Buddy...you think Curry had it in for us just because Dad let him go?" he asked.

"Of course, what else could it be?" Buddy said as he tied the reins and looked around at the rest of the hands on the porch. He glanced at Curry Hampton's body in the back, then slowly turned to look at Tom, Aya and Percy, who were waiting for Church to return with the doctor. "It's a good thing I came along when I did, otherwise things might have been worse. He had a few more sticks of dynamite on him. By the way, how's Chas?"

"He's alive. Dad and Aya are in there with him now," Tom said. "He's not doing so good. I hope Church brings Doc Carrington soon."

"Is it that bad?" Buddy asked.

"Yeah, I think so," Tom said.

Buddy took a quick look around the yard. "What about the dogs...they all right?"

"I'm sure they didn't make it," Tom said with a shake of the head. "From the looks of it, they were on the bridge when it went up. I'll get up at first light and head back down there with a shovel."

"That's a damned shame." Buddy turned to stare into the darkness toward the blown-out bridge. "Well…if ya'll need anything, just let me know. I got to get back to town and take care of Curry here. Thought I'd come up and make sure you and Dad were okay, but it would make my skin crawl if I just left him in the back of the wagon while we all wait for the doctor."

"I can see your point," Tom said, taking another look at Curry, but he soon glanced back at his brother. "Now that you mention it, there is one thing you can do. Tell me, how did you manage to get here just in the nick of time? Dad tells me you hadn't been out here for months, so why tonight?"

"Seems to me you ought to be more grateful to somebody who just saved your life," Buddy said, "but, if you gotta know, I came out here to check on the progress of that fence of yours. That, and the fact that I heard Curry was down at Dayna G's all day claiming he was going to head out here and try to kill the whole lot of you because of the way he'd been treated. I never thought he'd try it, though." He took off his hat and straightened his hair. "'Course, nobody ever took him too seriously. Everybody figured he was just letting off steam. Wouldn't be the first time Curry made an ass of himself."

"Hey, Sheriff," Bear said as he stood up from his chair, cracked his knuckles and walked over to the wagon. He offered an outstretched hand. "I sure am grateful for ya bein' out here this evening, and I wanna tell ya I'm sorry 'bout the way we got off in Dayna G's yesterday."

Buddy waved the thought away and shook Bear's hand. "Don't worry about it. I didn't know you at the time, but now I do. Jessie's just a whore, anyway."

"Ah…now don't go sayin' things like that. It ain't nice," Bear said. It was obvious to everyone he was trying his best not to get aggravated over Buddy's last remark as he paused for a moment, rubbed the top of his head and asked, "but I got a question. How'd ya get that wagon of yours cross that blowed-up bridge?"

"Downstream a ways there's a shallow crossing, almost where Cowhouse Creek joins the Leon River," Buddy said as he pointed to the southeast, "just takes a while to get down there and back. That's why my momma had my dad build the bridge. When it floods, that crossing is the first place to go underwater. This house is set far enough away from the creek where it won't flood up here but, even if what used to be that bridge down there goes underwater for a day or two, it's not like downstream where it can stay flooded for a week or more."

"How did Curry get all the way out here?" Bear asked, walking around to the side of the wagon and peering into the back where Curry's body lay. He took a loud whiff. "Wooweee! That man smells like he musta drunk all the whiskey in town."

"I saw his horse when I came up to the bridge," Buddy said. "I guess the sound of the explosion must have run him off. I'll probably find him when I get back to town." He looked at Tom. "I'll bring him out here tomorrow and give him to y'all. It's only right; payment for the bridge, I guess."

Tom wiped his face and sighed, then looked at his brother with an outstretched hand. "I'm sorry, Buddy. Thanks for being here…really."

Buddy shook his brother's hand. "Don't worry about it."

"It's just that Chas is hurt bad," Tom said with a deep breath, "and it's been one hell of a day, that's all."

"Well, it's over now. And I gotta go," Buddy said as he climbed back up into the wagon. He popped the reins and the wagon started moving. "Tell Dad I'll be back out here tomorrow to see if there's anything else I can do."

"Can ya tell that long-haired fella, that deputy of yours, that I'm sorry we got off to a bad start?" Bear said.

Buddy laughed. "Sure. I'll tell him. He ain't so bad once you get to know him."

"Well, tell him I ain't so bad, neither," Bear called out with a nervous laugh, "and thanks for coming by when you did!"

"Sure thing. Good luck with Chas. Tell him I'm pullin' for him," Buddy called back as he drove the wagon into the darkness.

Tom and Bear walked back onto the porch and sat down next to Percy, who had been listening quietly to the conversation.

"Ya don't like the sheriff too much, do ya, Percy?" Bear asked.

"It's not that so much," Percy said, "it's just…there's something I can't put my finger on. I've never been able to trust him."

"What do you mean?" Tom asked.

"Well," Percy began as he adjusted himself in his chair, "for one thing, I don't think I've seen Buddy go anywhere driving a wagon. He always takes that fancy horse of his. 'Course, you boys wouldn't know that cause y'all ain't been around, but I'm just wonderin' why he would be in a wagon tonight."

"That could be anything," Bear said, "but personally, I'm glad he showed up. He coulda rode up on a camel out here and it wouldn't make no difference to me. One of us woulda had to shoot that Curry fella, and I'm just glad it was

Buddy that did it."

"Maybe you're right," Percy said softly, "maybe you're right."

They all sat silently, listening to the sounds of the night, but stood abruptly as the crickets went quiet, replaced by the rumble of hoof beats making their way up the road to the house. "That's got to be Church and the doc," Tom said as he rushed inside to tell his dad.

Ten minutes later, Tom, Percy, Bear and Church were all quietly seated on the porch, determined to stay there as long as it took for the doctor to finish his task but, after grimacing at the grizzly screams coming from inside the house, Tom got up from his chair. "I can't sit here and listen to that. I'm going to find those dogs," he said.

Bear stood without hesitation. "I'll get us a couple lanterns from inside."

Church immediately followed, saying, "Hold up, Tom. I'll go with ya. Where do ya keep your shovels?"

"We've got a few in the barn. Follow me," answered Tom. He stopped before he rounded the corner of the house, looked back at Bear and added, "give us a minute or two and we'll meet you right out here."

Bear flinched at the sound of another scream coming from inside as he opened the screen door. "You boys better hurry then. Won't take me that long." He looked at Percy, who hadn't moved and asked, "Ya comin?"

"Nah. I'd best stay here," Percy said with surprising calm. "They might need something in there."

"Okay then," Bear said before he disappeared inside.

A short time later they were combing the dark with lanterns and shovels, whistling and calling in vain. It took a while to find each of the three hounds in the shin-deep bluebonnets that covered the ground. All the dogs were on the bridge when the explosion happened and were thrown in every direction, but it was obvious they never knew what happened by the way their bodies were ripped apart.

Two hours later, the three tired men trudged their way back up the road to the house, having accomplished the grisly task of burying the mangled dogs where they lay. Their shock over the events of the evening had been replaced by extreme anger. Even though Tom was the only one who had an emotional tie to any of the animals, by the time they finished burying the last one, they all would have given just about anything to make Curry Hampton come back alive just so they could kill him again.

They walked past the embers of the fire in the front yard and climbed onto the porch. Bear set the two lit lanterns on the table while Church leaned the shovels against the railing before they all returned to their seats. No one spoke because there was no need. Percy knew the fate of the dogs by the looks on their faces, so each man sat in silence, hoping the news from inside would be much better. The house was now uncomfortably quiet and, except for the occasional muffled voices of the doctor or Jim, all four men would have guessed no one was alive in there. After another hour or so, they all stood up in unison as the bloody, haggard group of Jim, Aya and Dr. Walter Carrington stepped outside.

"How is he, Doc?" Tom asked.

"I think he'll make it, Lord willin' and the creek don't rise," he said with a tired sigh. He set his bag down and unrolled the sleeves of his bloody shirt. Doctor Carrington stood only a shade over five feet, but what he lacked in stature he more than made up for in respect among the people of Belton. The fact that he was old enough to have delivered almost every baby in town for the last twenty years was enough for him to be the most trusted man with a medicine bag in the county. He also took his work personally and, if someone didn't follow his instructions to the letter, he wasn't afraid to cause such a ruckus over it that even the most stubborn person wouldn't dare ignore him again. "He's busted up pretty bad. He'll never use that arm again and won't hear another thing out of that left ear most likely but, all in all, he's rather lucky...everything considered."

"How's that?" Tom asked.

"Well..." The doctor paused as he pulled a pipe from a pouch in his back pocket. He struck a match on the heel of his boot and the flame briefly illuminated the tired look on his face before he blew it out and flung the spent stick into the yard. After he took a long pull from the glowing tobacco he said, "If that piece of wood had caught him just a little lower or to the right, he would have died then and there. I got the wound cleaned out as best I could and he's doin' fine for now, but the biggest threat to him for the next few weeks is going to be infection. Make no mistake about it. So I'm going tell you boys a few things that are going to have to be law around here if you expect him to get through this."

They listened intently as the doctor asked, "Any one of you got experience treating wounds?" Everyone turned to look at Percy as he raised a finger in answer, so the doctor turned his attention to him. "Do you know how to administer morphine?"

Percy nodded. "I've used it before on a few men…during the war."

Doctor Carrington rubbed the side of his face and said, "Okay, then, first thing is there's a bottle and a syringe in Chas's room. I already told Jim how much to give him but don't you be shy about using more if you think you have to. I'm going to keep you in a generous supply of laudanum and morphine, and I want you to use it. I want that boy so drugged up he won't know what's happened to him for at least a week, all right?"

Percy nodded as the doctor continued, "Second: for the next two or three weeks, you need to keep those hands of yours clean as a whistle. I know you boys are trying to put up a fence around here, but Percy, I don't think it's a good idea for you to work outside. You've got to keep those hands germ-free. Third: I want you to be the only one that goes into that room. You'll need to feed him, bathe him, relieve him, the works. Fourth: he'll probably get a fever, so you need to be ready to not get any sleep for a while. You'll need to keep a bucket of real cold water and some towels in that room at all times. Don't let the fever get him."

The doctor paused and pulled another long puff on his pipe before he finished. "And last and most importantly, you need to be ready to hit him over the head with something heavy if he wants to get up and move around without my permission. The truth is, he'll bleed to death before I can get back out here if he rips those stitches open." Doctor Carrington looked Percy hard in the eyes. "You think you can handle all that?"

Percy looked at Jim who was staring at him with a smile and said, "Yeah, Doc. I've done it before."

Doctor Carrington looked confused for a moment as he glanced back and forth from Jim to Percy, then shrugged and picked up his bag. "Good. Then, if you gentlemen don't mind, I think I'll take my leave. It's been a long night."

Jim followed him out into the yard. "How much do I owe you?"

"I don't know yet," Dr. Carrington said as he climbed into his saddle. "I'll send you a bill. But we'll have to see how things go. I got to tell you, Jim, that boy's got a long way to go before he's out of the woods."

Jim reached out, shook the doctor's hand in earnest and said, "We'll do everything we can. And thanks, Doc. I'll send word every day to let you know how he's doing."

"Well, I'll be back in a couple of days to check on him, regardless," the doctor said as he turned his horse away, "but I want those instructions followed to the letter…you hear?"

Jim let out a tired chuckle and said with a wave of his hand, "I got it, Doc. We'll do exactly like you said."

"Good. Then I'll see you day after tomorrow." He kicked his horse in the sides and disappeared into the shadows of the night.

Jim stood there until the sound of hoof beats completely faded away, then made his way up to the porch where everyone was sitting, patiently waiting for his firsthand account of how Chas was doing. "Hopefully he'll be fine, fellas," he said as he slumped into his rocker, "but it's going to be a while before Chas is healthy enough to do much around here."

"What do we do now?" Church asked.

"I guess we need to find those dogs," Jim said as he looked down the road to what used to be the bridge.

"Already did," Tom said bitterly. "None of them made it; never had a chance. We buried them all."

"Thanks...thanks a lot," Jim said sadly as he stared off into nowhere. "I figured them for goners, but...it's a good thing Chas doesn't run any faster than he does; otherwise, we'd be burying him, too. And Tom, thanks. I heard those bullets go past us."

Tom nodded. "Somebody around here has to look out for you."

"Maybe so," Jim said, "but I guess, all things considered, it could have been a lot worse, especially with Chas."

"Is he sleepin'?" Bear asked as he scratched the side of his head. "Hell, with all that screaming going on in there, I was thinking he wasn't gonna make it."

"It was only that way in the beginning," Jim said, "but I got to hand it to that boy. After Doc got that piece of wood out of him, he went right off to sleep. I couldn't believe it, but he did. The morphine must have knocked him on his ass."

"He's going to be okay, though, ain't he?" Church asked.

"Doc seems to think he'll pull through as long as we do what he told us," Jim said, "but we'll have to make a few changes. Tom, it's best for now if you stay in the bunkhouse and let Percy have your room."

"Sure," Tom said as he stood and walked across the porch to the screen door. "I'll go get my things."

"You don't have to do that," Percy said. "I can sleep on the sofa in there."

"It's no big deal," Tom assured him, and walked into the house.

"Tom's room is right next to Buddy's. That's where you need to be," Jim said. He pointed to the bunkhouse, "so go on…get your stuff."

"Okay, then," Percy said as he stood, "but I ain't been here one full day and you're already movin' me into the main house. People around here will be thinkin' you've lost your damned mind lettin' a black man do that."

Everyone laughed. "Wouldn't be the first time the neighbors looked at me a little funny," Jim said.

"No, probably not," Percy said with a chuckle as he stepped off the porch and headed for the bunkhouse.

"The rest of you boys might want to call it a day," Jim said as he stood. "Come sun up, we got a bridge to rebuild."

Without a word, the rest of the men left the porch and walked over to the bunkhouse, leaving Jim alone with his thoughts. To say he felt bad about what happened to Chas was quite an understatement because, deep down, Jim knew he was responsible and should have known enough to take the necessary precautions. Although he hadn't figured Curry Hampton to have the nerve to kill, the simple fact was that he should have been prepared for it. He vowed to himself then and there nothing like this would happen again.

All the talk about what the free grazers might try if he fenced in his property suddenly became a lot more real after the events of this evening, so Jim decided he wouldn't sleep until he had it worked out in his mind exactly how he was going to defend the Four C's and his men from any more attacks from anyone, for any reason. He was about to go inside when he was startled out of his thoughts by Aya, who had walked back onto the porch carrying a rifle and a blanket.

Aya laid down on the porch swing, wrapped himself in the blanket, adjusted a corner of it behind his head and set the rifle on the wooden deck within easy reach. He nodded his head once to let Jim know this night watch was his, then stared off into the darkness, listening and watching for anything out of place. Jim took a long look into the darkness as well before letting out a tired sigh, then turned and walked into the house, past Ruby's piano and to the entrance of Tom's room.

"Hey," Jim said as he watched his son take the small picture of his mother off his dresser and put it in the small travel bag laying on his bed, "you almost done?"

"Yeah," Tom said, "give me a minute and Percy can make himself at home."

"That's not what I meant," Jim said. "The time has come for me to show you something important."

The tone of his voice made Tom pause for a second and, in that brief moment, he knew whatever his dad needed him to do demanded his immediate attention, so he grabbed his bag off the bed and said, "Sure, where we going?"

"Follow me." He pointed at the kitchen floor on the way to the door of his bedroom. "Go ahead and set your bag down here. You can get it on your way out."

Tom did as he was told. He knew where they were going and tried to recall the last time he set foot in his parents' room. He wasn't quite sure how long ago it had been, but was certain he got in trouble when he did because he and his brother were never allowed in that room, for any reason whatsoever.

When they entered, Tom looked around, mildly surprised to see everything clean and in its place, knowing his father on his best day could never match his mother when it came to battling dust or keeping the house tidy. He smiled, realizing his dad put time and energy into keeping the memory of his mother alive between these four walls. Jim had made all the furniture in this room as well, which was just as impressive as the furnishings throughout the rest of the house.

But Tom wasn't drawn to his father's impressive woodwork or the beautiful patchwork quilt on the bed his mother had stitched years ago. His attention was focused directly on the forty to fifty small glass figurines inhabiting the room. Most were arranged neatly on the dark oak dresser, but there were many more standing on top of the matching bedside cabinets and on the shelves in a large bookcase, leaving no doubt who was responsible for collecting them. The only piece of furniture in the room that didn't have some type of curio on it was the large wooden rocking chair sitting on a small throw rug next to the window facing the corrals in back.

Tom walked over to the chair and ran his fingers down the smooth armrest before he turned his attention back to the assortment of collectibles. He slowly walked around and eyed the different pieces. "I guess you haven't changed things in here much since Mom died," he said.

Jim looked around as if he hadn't noticed them in some time. "No. There's been a time or two when I thought about putting them up, but I just can't get myself to do it. Your mother sure had an eye for that kind of stuff," he said.

"They're beautiful," Tom said as he moved over to a bedside table and looked at the small collection there. "I don't believe it!" he stammered as his heart skipped a beat and a tear formed in his eye. "You have no idea how many times I've thought about this tiny little glass!"

Jim nodded and smiled. "That was her favorite. She was mighty upset when you broke it because that was her favorite set of crystals in the whole world. She stayed in here all afternoon crying about it, but the next day took out some glue and put it back together as best she could. She never did put it back out on the china cabinet with the rest of the set because she reasoned that little glass there held more memories than all these other things combined." He added with a laugh, "That, and maybe she didn't want you to break it again."

Tom wiped the moisture from his cheek as he looked at the piece. "You're probably right about that, but she didn't do such a good job fixing it, did she?"

Jim laughed. "No, she didn't. She spent a lot of time on it, though, and did the best she knew how, but a blind man could see that little glass won't ever hold another drop of water. She sure loved it, though."

Tom carefully set the small glass back where it was, then looked at his father. "Thanks. I never knew."

Jim took another quick look at the glass and smiled again, enjoying the memory one more time, then glanced up at Tom. "She was going to tell you one day; she just never had the chance. But that's not what I need to show you. Come over here and give me a hand."

Tom followed his father to the end of the bed where they picked up and carried the heavy cedar chest to the side of the room, then rolled up the rug that was beneath it and set it against the wall. "What are we doing?" he asked.

"You'll see," Jim said. He got on his hands and knees and pushed down on one of the wooden slats in the floor. Although it looked as if the polished board would never budge, it came up easily and revealed a handle to a much larger cellar door. Jim pulled it open, exposing a small wooden staircase leading into the ground below the house. "Grab me that lantern over there in the corner," Jim said, pointing. "There's some matches on the back of the dresser, too."

Tom did as his father asked, and soon was following him down the steep stairs, holding the lantern high. "Be real careful with that light. I built this next to the storm cellar, which is right on the other side of this wall here," Jim said, tapping his fingers on the hard wood at the bottom of the stairs.

The small room looked as though it hadn't been used in some time, but must have been constructed very well because it was neither damp nor very dusty. Tom never would have guessed it was here, and felt somewhat insulted at first because his dad hadn't told him about it before, but the feeling was quickly replaced when he stepped off the last stair and saw the full contents of the small vault.

There were approximately twenty-five carbine rifles lining the full length of one wall, and on the other there looked to be a hundred boxes of ammunition. Everything a man needed to reload it all was stacked on top of a wooden work table with a lone decrepit stool in front. Tom counted twelve Colt revolvers with holsters full of bullets hanging on pegs that covered the far short wall, with several small barrels of gun powder sitting on the hard wooden floor beneath. "Good Lord!" he said as he took in the sight, "I never knew you had all this."

"I've been collecting it for years," Jim said as he looked around. "Never really felt the need to tell you or your brother about it, though, until now."

"What do you mean?" Tom asked.

"Well," Jim said with a heavy sigh, "if there's going to be any more trouble, we need to get everyone prepared for it."

"What trouble? Curry Hampton's dead," Tom said.

"I don't know for sure. Free grazers, maybe," Jim said, "but, after tonight, I'm not going to take any chances. Part of our workday from now on is going to include target practice for everybody."

"You really think that's necessary?" Tom asked.

"Yeah, I do. And we're going to start tomorrow. I don't want anybody unarmed anytime. Hell, I sent you off into town today defenseless as a newborn calf," Jim said. He shook his head in disgust as he left his thought unfinished, knowing how close Tom came to catching a bullet in the back in front of Dayna G's.

"This isn't all I need to show you, either," he added. He moved around Tom in the small room and made his way under the stairs. "Bring that light over here."

Tom watched as his father got on his knees, used his hand to wipe a thin layer of dust off the wooden floor and opened another small, hidden door in the slats. He pulled out a metal chest about twice the size of Doc Carrington's medical bag. Jim slid the chest across the floor a couple of feet so Tom could get a better look inside, then opened the lid, revealing a small stack of paper money next to a burlap bank bag that contained a large handful of gold coins that glistened in the lantern light as Jim reached in and pulled them out.

"What's all this for?" Tom asked.

"There's not much in there now, but it's time you know it's here," Jim said. He looked Tom in the eye. "In case something happens to me."

"Don't say that," Tom said. "Nothing's going to happen to you."

"I hope not," Jim said, "but, after tonight, I'm not taking any chances."

"How much money is that?' Tom asked as he gazed at the contents of the chest.

"Oh…I don't know," Jim said. "It used to be full. I've always made it a rule to stash away ten percent of whatever I make in this box and it's come in mighty handy at times. I paid for all that barbed wire in the barn out of this. And I've had to dip into it quite a bit these last few years for a lot of other things. I didn't do a whole lot of ranching while you were gone, plus your mother being sick and all." Jim sighed as he looked up at Tom. "Gotta pay the tax man, too. Anyways, at least now you know about it."

Jim closed the lid, slid the chest back across the floor and set it back in its hiding place with a grunt before adding, "Nobody knows about this except you and me, not even Buddy." He slapped his hands together to knock the dust off, then took a deep breath. "Maybe that's the reason he's been trying to get me to sell the place. I don't know; probably can't understand how I can afford to just sit here doing nothing, but the main thing is, as long as he isn't part of this outfit, it's none of his business. So nobody, I mean nobody, ever knows about this, understand?"

"As God's my witness," Tom said, giving his father a look that instantly let him know he could be trusted. "I won't tell a soul."

"Good," Jim said, "I'm glad I got this out of the way. But it's high time you and I started putting money back in here. We can't afford to keep pulling it out anymore, or soon we'll wind up selling off chunks of this place just to pay the taxes."

"That isn't going to happen," Tom said with a proud smile.

"I'm glad to hear you say that," said Jim. "Now go on up and get some sleep. It'll be a long day tomorrow. I'm going to stay down here and clean these guns; got to make sure they're all ready to go."

"Let me help," Tom said as he pulled a rifle off the rack. "We can knock it out a lot quicker together."

Jim almost told Tom to get back over to the bunkhouse and crawl into bed, but stopped and grinned before the words came out. "You'll need to move over, then. I need some room to work on that bench, too."

For the next few hours they meticulously cleaned the barrels and oiled the firing mechanisms of every gun in the cellar while discussing everything from Curry Hampton, Chas, the dogs, the fence, Ruby, Buddy and whatever else came to mind, until Tom finally asked, "Dad, exactly how did you bust up your leg?"

Jim set the rifle he had been cleaning down on the bench and took a deep breath. "I guess I never told you the whole story, did I?"

"No, you didn't," Tom answered. Unsure if he went too far with his question, he added, "You don't have to tell me if you don't want to, though. It had to be a terrible thing."

"It was." Jim pulled the worn-out stool around behind him. The old chair protested with creaks and groans but held his weight, even though a betting man would have guessed otherwise.

Tom put the pistol up he just finished cleaning to focus on the story he had always wanted to hear but never had the nerve to ask about until now.

"Your momma threw a fit when I decided to enlist," Jim started. "Everybody thought the war wasn't going to last very long. They wanted to make me a lieutenant in the 3rd Texas Cavalry, which was a great honor at the time, so I felt I couldn't turn it down. Anyway, it was the seventh of March in 1862 and my outfit wound up on the edge of Arkansas. The Battle of Pea Ridge was supposed to keep those Union boys out of Missouri. Even though we had them outnumbered almost two to one, it sure didn't turn out that way. It was snowing and cold, real cold. A lot of our infantry didn't even have shoes, and I heard later on our reinforcements followed their bloody footprints in the snow to find us. Our commanding officer was Major General Earl Van Dorn, and I hope he goes down in history as the worst field general who ever lived because he made a decision to cut his own supply lines just so he could get us all to the fighting a few hours quicker. Figured we could march faster if we didn't have to wait on such mundane things like ammunition."

Jim looked away from Tom for a moment, staring into the past. "A lot of our boys died because of that. We lost the battle because, after the first day, we didn't have anything to shoot back with."

"I never knew that," Tom said.

"Things like that don't get in the papers too much," Jim said. "In any event, my outfit got into the fray right away. We were behind an artillery unit that was pounding the hell out of our boys in the field. Caught them completely by surprise and took command of all six cannons in less than five minutes. 'Course, that drew a lot of attention our way; those Union boys didn't take kindly to us turning their own guns on them. Half hour later, we came under fire from what seemed like a hundred soldiers coming up on us through a ravine. We left a few men there to guard the cannons while the rest of us remounted and charged that gully trying to drive those northern soldiers out of there." Jim cocked his head as if listening to hear a far-off noise. "You ever hear the sound a bullet makes when it hits horse flesh?" he finally asked.

"No," Tom said quietly.

"Sounds almost like the smack you hear when you clap your hands together real hard," Jim said. "I can still remember hearing that sound, plain as day." He shook his head. "My horse went right out from under me. I didn't really feel any pain when my leg crashed against that boulder, but I knew I was in trouble because I heard it snap. Well…I heard it getting crushed; sounded like a June bug sounds when you step on it. I don't know how it happened, but I never blacked out and, as soon as the fighting was over, they came and got me out from underneath that horse. Couple hours later, they had me in a field hospital. When they carried me into the operating room — that's what they called it — I called it the saw room, they told me my horse took a bullet right in the chest and I was lucky to be alive, but the only lucky thing that happened to me that day was I didn't pass out."

"You had to be in a lot of pain," Tom said with a concerned expression, "seems it would have been better to be unconscious than to go through all that awake."

"If I had passed out, I wouldn't have this," Jim said, tapping his right leg. "I wasn't going to let anyone take my pistol from me." Jim pointed to the last pistol on the wall. "It was that Colt revolver right there."

Tom reached over and pulled the holstered pistol off the peg. "This is the gun you used in the war?"

"That's the one," Jim said, nodding.

"You ever kill anybody with it?" Tom asked.

Jim solemnly nodded. "A few. After we got close to those cannons, I took out a couple of those Union boys, and they were just boys, too. None of them could have been more than twenty years old." Jim let out a deep breath. "That's how it was, though. That war was a hell of a waste for both sides."

"And this gun saved your leg?" Tom asked as he pulled the pistol out of the holster and turned it over in his hands.

Jim chuckled. "Thank God it was early in the fighting and there were plenty of wounded coming in. Once I pointed that gun in a few faces, they decided to leave me alone. Guess they didn't have enough time to disarm me with everything else going on, so they just stuck me in a corner. I still remember the look on that old doctor's face the first time I pointed that barrel at him and pulled back the hammer."

"What did you do? Threaten to kill him?" Tom asked.

Jim chuckled again. "I guess you could say that." He paused a moment before he added, "To make a long story short, I got to keep my leg and old saw-bones got to keep his life. Seemed like a fair deal at the time."

"It must have been awful," Tom said.

"It wasn't the most pleasant thing I've ever been through, that's for sure, but it all worked out. Your momma came all the way from Belton to fetch me and bring me back home, and we've been here ever since."

"What happened to the Union soldiers in the ravine?" Tom asked.

"They got their cannons back," Jim said. "I heard later on we lost about half the unit in that charge."

"And I thought I'd been through some tough times," Tom said as he set the Colt on the work bench.

"Make no mistake, you have," Jim said. "We both have. But it's the rough times that make a man know who he really is and teaches him what's most important in this life."

"Was this ranch the most important thing to you?" Tom asked.

"No," said Jim without hesitation, "Not even close. This ranch supports my family; that's all it does. I knew as soon as that horse fell on me all I wanted out of life from then on was to be a good husband and father. I hope I can look at St. Peter when the time comes and have him tell me I did a good job at those things."

"Well, I hope that day is a long way off," Tom said, "but, in the meantime, I can vouch for you."

Jim smiled at his son as he stood and stretched. "Thank you, son, thank you. But now, story time is over; we still have these guns to look after."

"We're almost finished," Tom said as he picked up the pistol and went to work. "I appreciate you telling me what happened in the war, Dad. And I think you're right; rough times do make a man realize what's important to him."

Jim smiled and resumed cleaning a rifle. "What about you, Tom? What's important to you now that you're home?"

"About the same thing as you," Tom said. "I just want a peaceful, simple life."

"Jennie Lue is a beautiful girl," Jim said with a knowing grin. "I always did like her. The two of you would make a great couple."

Tom blushed, looked at his father and nodded. "Thanks, Dad."

They turned their attention back to the firearms and not another word was spoken between them until each gun was perfectly clean and certain to work as good as new. It was only a few hours until sunrise once they finished and returned the rug and cedar chest to their original positions at the foot of the bed.

They got a laugh out of the idea that Percy must have thought they disappeared into thin air when he brought his things into the house earlier. He was sitting in a chair beside Chas's bed, his nose in a book, when he peered over the top of a pair of reading glasses "Where the hell did you two run off to?" he asked.

"Tom and I had some things to talk about," Jim said. "Everything all right?"

Percy let out a deep, exhausted sigh as he removed his glasses. "Yeah. So far so good, but I am glad to see ya. I was afraid that sheriff of yours might come back and wonder why the hell a black man was all alone in this house."

"You're not alone; you got Chas here with you," Jim said.

They all turned their attention to the sobering sight of the heavily bandaged figure on the bed, the small amount of humor existing between them suddenly gone. After a long pause, Jim asked, "How's he doing?"

Percy set his book down. "It's too soon to tell, I think. The doc's got him so drugged up he hasn't moved a lick, but I'll be right here in this chair all night. I'll let ya know first thing if anything changes."

"You going to be able to get some sleep?" Tom whispered.

"Ah, I don't know; probably not," Percy said, shrugging. "We'll see how it goes. I thought I'd do some readin'." He held up the book and pointed to the living room. "I hope you don't mind; found this on that shelf in yonder."

Jim waved it off. "You might have to read every one those books in there before this is over, so feel free to make yourself at home."

Percy nodded. "Thanks. I appreciate that, but y'all need to go on and get some rest. I'll make sure our boy here gets through what's left of this night just fine."

"All right," Jim said, "but, if you need anything at all, don't you hesitate to knock on my door...you hear?"

"Don't worry, I won't."

Jim and Tom said their good nights then made their way through the house to the front door, stopping to give each other a hug before Tom walked outside. It was a long embrace; each was glad that nothing had happened to the other. Before Tom stepped into the yard, he looked at his father and said quietly, "I love you. See you in the morning."

"It already is the morning, and I love you, too," Jim replied as he followed him onto the porch and watched him walk away. He stayed there, watching until his son entered the bunkhouse, thinking about how he needed to replace the dogs as soon as possible.

Aya lay in the swing, staring out into darkness that would soon be retreating, so Jim entered the house and closed the door behind him. Making his way through the quiet house to his own bed, Jim felt fairly confident that Chas would pull through but, for the first time in his life, he felt distinctly uneasy and uncertain about the coming days ahead.

CHAPTER 14

Tracks

J ennie Lue opened the door to her room as slowly and quietly as she could and entered the hallway in her stockinged feet, carrying her boots. Even though there was just a hint of morning light in the eastern sky, she had been dressed and ready to go for an hour now, and knew she would have to turn in early this evening because she hadn't gotten much sleep all night. There was no way she was going to stay here and learn from someone else what had caused the explosion the night before.

She set her boots down softly on the polished wooden floor and closed her bedroom door behind her, trying to keep the handle from clicking too loudly in the stillness of the house. After a silent, deep breath, she picked up her boots and, confident she had not made a sound, tiptoed toward the stairs. As she made her way down, she stepped over the boards she knew would moan when weight was brought upon them and stopped at the bottom, waiting for any noise that could indicate her parents were awake or aware of what she was trying to do. With a determined expression on her face, she set her boots down again at the front door and repeated the process of quietly opening the door, then backed out of the house as she gently closed it behind her.

"Going somewhere?"

"Oh, my God!" she said, as every muscle in her body convulsed at the sound of her father's voice. She turned around to find Turner sitting on the veranda, clad in his robe and slippers, smoking a pipe. She patted her chest.

"You scared the living daylights out of me! I nearly jumped out of my skin!"

Turner took a long puff and blew the smoke into the air before he set the pipe down on the side table. "I thought I'd find you out here this morning."

She closed the screen door and stammered, "What do you mean? And since when did you start smoking? I've never seen you do that before."

"Oh, that," Turner said as he eyed the smoke rising lazily from the bowl. "I've enjoyed a pipe for a number of years now. I just didn't want you to know I was capable of such a nasty habit. George is aware of it because he smokes those awful-smelling cigars all the time, and your mother gives us both plenty of grief over it, but that's neither here nor there."

She walked over to the chair next to her father, set her boots down on the porch and brushed some unruly hair from her face. "Why tell me about it now?"

"I just thought we should open up to each other," Turner said as he smoothed his mustache. "It's good for us not to have any more secrets between us."

"Okay…" she said, suspicious. "So…that's why you're out here?"

Turner pointed to the chair next to him. "Sit down. I'd like to talk to you."

Jennie Lue nodded, took her seat on the edge of the chair, folded her hands across her lap and asked in the most innocent voice she could muster, "About what?"

"Your mother and I had a long talk about you last night after you went to bed," he said, "and I have a pretty good idea where you're about to run off to."

"What do you mean?" She feigned ignorance. "I was going out for a ride. It's going to be a beautiful morning, that's all."

"Please, no more secrets, okay?" he said, and pierced her with his eyes to emphasize the point. She fidgeted in her chair just long enough for Turner to know he was on the mark. "*Okay*?"

She sighed as she turned away and looked into the distance before answering. "Okay then. What do you want to know?"

"Why would you want to sneak off this morning and not tell me or your mother where you're going?" he asked, as though his feelings were truly hurt.

"Because you wouldn't understand" she said, wiping a small tear that appeared on her cheek.

"Try me," he said. "Besides, I think I already know."

"No, you don't," she said.

"You were going to ride out to the Wallace place, weren't you?" he asked.

"No. I *am* riding over there just as soon as we're finished talking," she said.

"Why? We'll know what happened last night soon enough."

"Because I want to make sure no one over there is hurt," she said.

"You mean Tom, don't you?" Turner asked with a raised eyebrow. "You want to make sure *Tom* isn't hurt, am I right?"

Jennie Lue only nodded her head, so Turner continued, "There was always something between you two, wasn't there? Even when you were kids."

"I guess," she said, trying to downplay her emotions.

"Do you love him?"

Jennie Lue paused to look her father in the eyes, then collapsed into the back of the chair, knowing her short-lived charade was over. She stared into the distance for a while before she whispered, "I don't know…maybe…I think so."

"You know I won't approve, don't you?" he asked.

As another, much larger tear fell down her face, she said softly, "Yes, I know."

"I don't want you to go over there," her father said in a high-minded tone, as if laying down an unbreakable law. "It would never work out, and you could do a lot better for yourself. My God, Jennie, he just got out of prison." He shook his head. "No. I just won't have it. I *can't* have it."

"What do you mean *you can't have it*?" she asked, anger rising within her. "This has got nothing to do with you! It's *my* life, not yours."

Turner realized he might have gone a bit too far. "Jennie Lue, I just don't want you to get hurt."

"That's not it at all, is it?' she said. "You just don't want me to have anything to do with Jim Wallace's son. I don't think you've ever cared about how I feel."

"Jennie, there's no call for that," he said.

She wiped the tears from her face before she sat up straight and looked at her father with determination. "I have a question for *you* now. No secrets, right?"

Turner suddenly felt uneasy about the change of direction, but he leaned back and acted casual. "Sure; no secrets," he affirmed.

This time, it was Turner who couldn't have been more surprised. "Why have you and Jim Wallace spent so many years being enemies?" she asked.

"Oh…that's a long story. We don't need to go into that," he said.

"Yes, we do," she said. "I need to know. You yourself said we should have no more secrets, so you have to tell me, right now."

Turner reached over to the table, picked up his pipe and took another slow pull before blowing the smoke into the morning air and watching it lazily float away. "There's no reason to go into that, Jennie. It won't do anybody any good to go digging up the past."

"Then I'm leaving," she said and started putting her boots on with a vengeance.

"I forbid you to go over there," Turner said.

Jennie Lue shook her head and let out a loud disgusted sigh as she stood. "You say we should have no secrets with each other but what you really mean is I shouldn't keep any secrets from you." She tossed her blonde hair back as she stared down at her father, fire in her eyes. "You bring out that stupid pipe and try to make me believe that's a big secret between us? It's a bunch of bull, that's what it is. You think I'm...Jesus! I've always wondered why we never were that close, but now I know why."

She turned and stormed down the steps on her way to the barn as Turner stood and yelled, "Jennie! All right! I'll tell you."

She stopped and turned to face her father, who gripped the porch rail above her and said, "No secrets?"

Turner nodded. "Come back here. I promise."

She stared at the ground, summoning patience, then took a deep breath, walked back onto the porch and sat down with her father, her jaw set tightly. Although she wasn't nearly as worked up as she was a second ago, she still had an edge to her voice. "So tell me, why is it that you and Jim Wallace act like complete asses to each other?"

He let out a tired chuckle. "I guess that's one way to put it." He stroked his mustache and stared into the distance a moment before asking, "Do you remember playing with Tom and Buddy when you were little?"

She relaxed, sensing that her father was going to tell her the truth, then shrugged. "Some. Not much, though. I was just a little girl."

"Yes, you were," he said with a wistful smile. "Anyway, Jim and I used to be great friends, best friends even. We got to know each other as soon as your mother and I moved here, and we hit it off right away. We'd get together at least once a week for dinner and to watch you kids run all over the place. We had a lot of good times, but that was before the war."

"What does the war have to do with this?" she asked, perplexed.

Her father held up his hand. "Just…let me finish," he said. "Jim felt like he had to run off and join the cavalry. Of course, at the time there was a lot of pressure on people to fight, especially landowners like us. Jim was pretty gung-ho about the whole thing, but I didn't want any part of it. We started getting sideways when I refused to sign up."

She cocked her head to one side. "Twenty-some odd years later and you two can't get over that?" she asked.

Turner looked at her and, in a patient yet slightly irritated tone of voice, he said, "Let me finish, okay?" Jennie Lue nodded. "Believe me, there's a lot more to it," he went on. "Anyway, after Jim left, your mother and I would go over to the Four C's and do what we could to help out. You know, little things like washing clothes, helping clean the house, bringing dinner over and what not. Ruby had that Indian, who did a pretty good job of taking care of the property but, at the time, she didn't trust him at all and wouldn't let him anywhere near the house or her kids, so we'd drop by and help whenever we could." He took another pull from his pipe. "In the early fall of that year, that Indian…"

"His name is Aya," she said, indignant.

"Aya," Turner corrected himself, "Aya killed those four men right in front of the house, so your mother and I decided we should look in on Ruby and the boys more often than just once a week. So that's what we did. I guess that happened in September. Anyway, your mother took ill the end of October that same year and couldn't get around at all, so I started going myself."

"I remember that," she said. "What did Momma have?"

"Pleurisy," he said, staring into the past, "an awful thing it was; she couldn't do a blasted thing until the next spring, God bless her. But the doctor took good care of her and she finally came out of it okay. Anyway, we had all the help we needed around here while your mother was sick, but Ruby seemed to be hanging on by the skin of her teeth over there, so I did what I thought was right and went by to see her whenever I could."

Jennie Lue's eyes went wide. "Did you…and Mrs. Wallace?"

Turner sat upright in his chair and shook his head defiantly. "No! Of course not. But the gossip mongers in town thought otherwise because there was a lot of loose talk that Ruby and I had something going on between us." He leaned back as if dog-tired and took a deep breath. "When Jim got home in the spring, it didn't take long for all the loose talk to find his ears, and that was that."

"Didn't you try to reason with him?" she asked. "All you were trying to do was help out; that's all it was…right?"

"Yes," he said as he turned to look at her. "That's all I was trying to do. That's all I *did*, but Jim thought otherwise and, to this day, he believes I was in love with Ruby."

"What did Mrs. Wallace have to say about this?" she asked.

"She tried to tell Jim I was only there to help her out, but I guess he wouldn't have any of it," he said, "told me I broke his trust and he never wanted another thing to do with me."

"Does Momma know?" she asked.

Turner looked into her eyes, his look pained and exhausted. "I don't know. I believe so, but we've never talked about it. I told her that Jim and I got sideways over a piece of property, but yes, I think she knows."

Jennie Lue sat in her chair soaking in the story, not sure whether to believe there wasn't anything more to it than what her father had shared. She looked into the brightening blue sky and sighed, realizing it really didn't make a bit of difference when it came to what she wanted out of life. On the one hand, she was grateful he told her but, on the other, there was one more thing she wanted to know. Maybe it was out of reflex or curiosity, or maybe it was just to get even, but she couldn't believe the words that came out of her mouth when she asked, "Did you love her?"

"Ah! Damn it!" he said angrily as his pipe fell into his lap and then onto the wooden veranda, spilling glowing tobacco everywhere. He stood quickly, wiping the burning ash off his robe. He made way too much of a fuss over kicking the burning tobacco off the porch and into the yard, which kept his eyes away from Jennie Lue's for far too long. It was all the answer she needed.

"I'll be back sometime this afternoon," she said as she stood to go.

"Jennie…don't leave…nothing happened," he said meekly, turning his tired eyes to hers.

Jennie Lue wiped a tear from her face, turned and made her way down the steps into the yard without saying a thing. Turner stayed on the porch, but followed her around the corner as he pleaded forcefully, "Jennie! I will not have it! Please! You can't do this!"

She ignored her father and strode to the barn, not stopping to see if he was going to follow. She was hopping mad and hoped he would get the message and stay up at the house. When she got to the tack room and grabbed her saddle, she was grateful Cornelius wasn't around because she wasn't in the mood to see or talk to anyone. Once Pancho was ready, she guided him out of the barn and climbed into the saddle. Taking one last glance back up at the house as her horse fell into a trot, for a moment she thought she saw her mother staring from behind the kitchen window, but the image of her robed father, standing alone along the porch rail and watching as she rode off, was one she wouldn't get out of her head for days.

Although the story he told her was unsettling, she wasn't upset about what happened over twenty years ago. No, she was livid over the fact that her father didn't want her to see Tom for reasons that revolved solely around himself. It wasn't until she was halfway to the Four C's that she began to calm down. As she rode along in the warm, early morning sun, insecurity flooded over her, and she realized she was in an emotional "no-man's land" for the first time in her life.

After Henry was killed, she knew she could fall back on her parents for support but, after this morning, things would probably never be the same between her and her father, maybe her mother, too. There were no guarantees that Tom felt the same way about her as she did about him. But she did know one thing: no matter what the consequences, she had made a promise to follow her heart, and it was telling her to make tracks to the Four C's to make sure the man she had secretly loved all of her life was free from harm.

For the last five years, Tom's eyes had popped open before the break of dawn, no matter how little sleep he'd gotten. Even though it was now past sun up, it still seemed mighty early in the morning because he'd laid his head down only a couple of hours earlier. He stretched his tired muscles as he lay in his bunk, but sat up straight as he remembered the chain of events from the exhausting night before. He strained his ears for any commotion coming from the house, any signal that Chas was in trouble and needed help, but all seemed quiet over there. He lay back down, adjusted his head on the pillow and enjoyed the silence permeating the interior of the sunlit bunkhouse.

Jim built the simple, one-room log cabin bunkhouse mostly for Aya who, before then, had slept in the fields surrounding the house. It wasn't as big as the main house, or very well decorated, but it had all the creature comforts a ranch hand could want. Most cowboys working the big ranches around the state slept in tiny, single-room shacks that dotted the fields around the main house, but Jim never had any intention of building those. As a rule, a ccw hand didn't take care of anything except his horse so, after a while, those tiny shacks got cluttered and run-down, making the rest of the ranch look the same way. In addition, Jim believed that by having his men all sleep under the same roof, it would be easier to spot and get rid of the ones who couldn't get along with the others.

The bunkhouse stayed cool during the summer months, owing to the thick logs used for all four walls. The fireplace on one side heated the entire room nicely, even when the winter nights turned their coldest. There were eight bunks, two lined up on either side of the front door and four on the back wall, each with a small, locking cedar chest at the foot of the bed. Not that they were used much, but the end tables between the bunks held small lanterns, in case one of the hands might want to do a little reading or writing before turning in. A card table in the middle of the room had been the scene of many a game over the years but, more often than not, it was used for casual, sit-down conversations among the hands before it was time to kill the last light.

There had only been a few times over the years when all the beds came close to being full, and that was once every four or five seasons when they would sort the herd and gather the rest for a drive over to Waco.

Aya was the only man who had ever truly called this room home. He spent over twenty years in the bunk closest to the fireplace, but no one could tell by looking at his bed. It appeared as if he was ready to get up and leave any minute. He had a few changes of clothes in his cedar chest, but the only items he called his own were a bow and a quiver of arrows stored beneath his bunk, and a circle of feathers that he tacked to the wall above his pillow. Bear explained to everyone the night before that it was called a Dream Catcher, and was used to snare evil spirits that otherwise would enter a man while he slept and cause him to have an "ooltobakanko," or nightmare. Bear made it clear to everyone they should not, under any circumstances, poke fun at the idea because Aya believed he had another visit coming from the warrior who sent him here and could not afford to let some other evil spirit confuse him with a similar dream.

This morning was probably no different than most, because Tom knew chances were good that Aya's bed had not been slept in, which meant he had once again been outside all night guarding the ranch.

As Tom listened to the quiet, his first thought was to get up and go over to the main house to see how things were with Chas, but he decided to stay where he was a few moments longer and relax because, if there wasn't anything going on, he might as well enjoy the peace and quiet while he could. His mind wandered, though, and soon he was thinking of the mornings he had to drag himself out of a hole in the ground in a far-flung part of the state, work the deep aches out of his muscles with the first few swings of an axe or sledge hammer, then spend the rest of the day working, trying to eat whatever he could get his hands on and keep from ripping any new patches of skin off either hand.

Looking back on it now, it occurred to him how time didn't really mean much to any of the men he was imprisoned with because every day was the same. The five years he spent in prison had passed quickly, even though it didn't seem that way every morning when he woke up. It was common knowledge that getting up and getting to work was the key to survival. There were more than a few examples of men who wound up not making it out of prison alive because, for one reason or another, they simply couldn't face another day.

Tom recalled an incident of a man everyone only knew as Mosely who had just been released from the hospital inside The Walls and returned to the fields to split wood. Every inmate could tell by his sickly appearance that he had been sent back way too soon and had no business trying to fill a normal work quota. Regardless, the captain in charge of the work detail made no bones about his intense hatred for Mosely, and was heard several times saying he would kill him if he didn't get his work done. The rest of the inmates tried to absorb his quota the first day, leaving Mosely the easy task of stacking the wood, but the underfed men quickly started to fall behind in their own work, making them the subject of severe beatings. The second morning, Mosely begged the guards not to send him into the fields, only to be told by the captain that he would personally kick his guts out if he didn't get up and get to work. Even though he could barely lift his head, he was made to work the cross-cut saw, which was usually manned by only the strongest of inmates because of the tremendous stamina required to use it.

Mosely tried his best but, less than an hour later, he collapsed dead across the log and lay there for the rest of the day until the inmates carried him back to camp. That night, a handful of men buried his corpse where no one would ever find him, but Tom would never forget how the captain intentionally let him lay there all day in the hot sun as a warning to all who thought they might be able to talk their way out of a day's work.

When a prison official came out to check on the inmates a week later, it was everything Tom could do to keep from planting his axe in the back of the captain's head when he described Mosely as "healthy as a horse," saying he had no idea why he fell over dead. Tom had looked around at the other inmates who were close by and could tell they all had the exact same thought on their minds.

Tom scratched the top of his head and exhaled deeply, then sat up and put his feet on the floor, knowing it was time for him to get out of bed so he could get his mind off the fact that Mosely was only one of a hundred stories of men who died of "natural causes" during his time in prison. He felt the stubble of his overnight beard as he wiped the sleep out of his eyes, dressed quickly and walked out of the empty bunkhouse, leaving behind what was sure to be the only quiet part of his day.

As he approached the porch of the main house, he was greeted by his father and the other hands sitting out front, each with a cup of hot coffee. "I thought ya were gonna sleep all day," Bear greeted him with a smile.

"It isn't that late, is it?" Tom asked.

"It's about seven-thirty," Jim said as he took a sip from his mug.

"How's Chas?" Tom asked as he climbed the steps.

"The same," Percy said, "he ain't had time to get any worse or better, although I'm afraid worse is comin'."

"There's more coffee inside," Jim said, rubbing his bad leg. "Run on in and get a cup. Then we need to go over a few things."

Tom saw his father grimace as he massaged his leg. "You okay, Dad?"

"Yeah. Nothing I haven't gone through before," he said. "That run down to the bridge last night didn't bother me so much then, but my leg sure is barking at me now."

"Can I get you anything while I'm inside?" Tom asked.

"No, I'll be all right," Jim said, "just get you some coffee and come have a seat."

"Okay. Be right back," Tom said as he entered the house. He was soon back out on the porch and as he took a chair, a steaming cup in his hands, he noticed the heavy bags beneath Percy's bloodshot eyes. "You get any sleep?" he asked.

"Best ten minutes of my life," Percy answered with a tired smile.

Everyone chuckled before Jim said, "I think Percy and I are going to have to take turns keeping watch, which means you're going to have to take charge around here until Chas comes out of this. I'll watch him during the day, while Percy takes care of him at night."

Tom nodded. "Okay, and I'm guessing we have a bridge to rebuild first off."

"Yep," Jim said, "I want you to go into town and order the lumber from that fellow down at Old River Lumber. Tell him to deliver it today, if he can."

"Sure thing," Tom said. "Do you know what we need?"

"Yep." His father handed him a piece of folded paper that he pulled from his shirt pocket. "I went and looked around earlier. Wrote it all down."

"Where's Aya?" Tom asked, glancing at the figures on the paper before he folded it and put it in his pocket. "He's not in the bunkhouse. How come he's not here with y'all?"

Bear pointed toward the remains of Ruby's bridge. "He's down there. Been walkin' around the far side of that creek since sun-up."

"What's he doing?" Tom asked as he strained his eyes into the distance.

Bear shrugged. "Don't know. My guess is he's lookin' at tracks on the other side of that creek. 'Course, I'm not sure what good it'll do him; there's been people comin' by all mornin' lookin' and tryin' to find out what happened last night. Be mighty hard to see last night's tracks underneath all the ones laid down this mornin'." He looked at Jim, adding, "I didn't know you had so many nosy neighbors."

Jim chuckled. "Word around here travels fast."

Tom looked at Bear as he set his coffee cup on the small table. "You want to take a walk?"

"Sure," Bear said. "Why?"

"I thought we could ask Aya what he's looking at," Tom said.

"Fine by me." Bear stood and finished the last gulp of his coffee before walking off the porch with Tom.

"Tom, don't take too long," Jim said. "I need you to get into town and get that lumber ordered, and Bear's got breakfast to make."

"We won't. Besides, I don't know about the rest of y'all but, after last night, I'm not too hungry." Tom turned to look at his father. "I just need Bear so he can tell me what Aya's so interested in."

"All right," Jim said and waved them off the porch. "Let me know what you find out there, okay?"

Tom and Bear started to the creek. Neither said much on the way, and even less the closer they got to what remained of Ruby's bridge.

Shredded, charred lumber was everywhere. Pieces big and small lay across or stuck out of the tall wild flowers in every direction, some blown thirty or forty yards away. The closer they got, the more concentrated the fragments were, until they were practically walking over them with each step as they came to the bank of Cowhouse Creek.

"Damn," Bear said, "must a been a lot more than one stick a dynamite caused all this."

"I'm guessing maybe four or five. It's a wonder Chas is alive," Tom said as he looked at the mangled mess that used to be a bridge.

The main timbers were still imbedded in the bottom of the creek, but the tops were torn up as if ripped off by the hand of God. Although the bridge was roughly sixty feet long where it crossed the creek, there was nothing left, and it didn't take but one look to realize most all of the old wood was too busted up to be used for rebuilding.

Tom looked across to the far side to see Aya wave them over, so they climbed down the bank, waded around some busted timber clogging the shallow creek and pulled themselves up the other side. Aya was crouched on one knee, gently rubbing the dirt as Bear walked up. "Hicha…Sahmi?" Bear asked.

Aya stood, took a serious look at Bear and started talking so fast Tom knew he might as well stay out of the way for the time being. There was no way he was going to be able to understand a single word. He watched as Aya and Bear talked and surveyed the entire scene constantly, going back and forth in a language he didn't know. Although Aya talked about the bridge a little at first, his attention was focused on the ground, where he spent a great deal of time pointing out a particular set of prints. He then moved down the road apiece, only to stop and repeat the process. The grim expression on Bear's face never changed as they followed the marks on the dusty road until well outside the newly installed front gate.

When Aya finished explaining to Bear about the tracks in the road, he walked straight over to a small oak tree and used his outstretched arms to point out something else. He and Bear finished exchanging words as Tom joined them, then they walked down the road fifty yards or so where they stopped to examine a few more marks in the dirt. Finally, Aya stood and pointed back the way they came. The Indian held up both hands, saying words Tom would never be able to pronounce, but their meaning was loud and clear: something about last night didn't add up, and in a big way.

Bear stood rubbing the top of his head with a sour expression on his face before Tom finally had to ask, "Well? Are you going to tell me what he said?"

Bear took a deep breath as he turned to look at Tom with a clenched lower jaw. "Can't be for sure. There ain't enough proof to go accusin' anybody of anythin' in a court of law, but it looks like Buddy's tryin' to bullshit us pretty good about what happened last night."

The last thing Tom expected were those words to come out of Bear's mouth. "What?" he asked, stunned.

Bear took off his eyeglasses, cleaned them on the front of his shirt and squinted as he said, "Where do I start? Sheeez. Well, here, I guess." He put his spectacles back on and knelt, pointing out a track in the road. "Take a look at this here. This is the wheel track made by Buddy's wagon. And this hoof print was made by Curry's horse headin' to the bridge. You can tell by the mark Aya sawed out of the shoe yesterday when your daddy fired him. See that shoe print?"

"Okay," Tom said, recognizing the unique shape of the print as he knelt to take a good look. "So Curry's horse was here last night. So what?"

"Well, that's not what's important," Bear said. "The important part is, if ya take a close look at this track and all the others heading this way, the hoof prints are *on top* of the wagon prints, meaning Buddy's wagon was here before Curry's horse. Last night, Buddy said Curry was already here."

Tom got up and walked down the road, taking his time to eye every print in detail. Stopping after twenty paces or so, he turned and said, "You're right. They're all the same."

"Not only that," Bear said as he walked toward Tom, his eyes glued to the ground, "but either Curry's horse somehow miraculously followed the exact same path all the way down this road, or it was tied behind the wagon." Bear stopped to take a serious look at Tom, letting the point sink in. "You can walk as far back as you want, but the tracks don't change."

Tom felt the color drain from his face as he looked at Aya, who stood off to the side, quietly nodding to let him know there was no mistake. Tom took his hat off and scratched the back of his head before he asked, "What else?"

"Over here." Bear retraced his steps to the small oak Aya pointed out moments before. He used both hands to describe what Aya had told him. "This here is where Curry's horse was tied. Looks like Curry tied him up all right, 'cause there's only one set of boot prints here, but those prints don't start here by the horse; they start over there, like Curry got out of the wagon, walked the horse over here, tied him up and then went off yonder to the bridge. He smelled so liquored-up last night, I was wonderin' how he managed to stay in the saddle. But it looks like he never was. Looks like he rode here in the wagon with Buddy."

"Why in the world would Buddy be behind this?" Tom asked.

"I don't know," Bear said, "but come over here. There's one more thing." They walked back through the front gate to the blown-out bridge, eyes to the ground. When they got to the spot where Curry lay dead just a few hours before, Bear stopped, got down on one knee and continued. "If you'll look around, Curry's footprints are all over the place. That man was real drunk, bad drunk. It's a wonder he didn't fall on his face before he got here. Anyway, Aya's bet, and mine too, is that Curry was way too drunk to be firin' off shots in the dark that coulda come anywhere close to hittin' you or your daddy, which also makes the chances mighty slim he coulda lit that dynamite and thrown it on the bridge from here."

"You mean Buddy probably did it, don't you?" Tom asked. Bear shrugged. "How can we prove this? Against...my own brother...the sheriff."

"Probably can't," Bear answered, looking around. "Been too many people out here so far this morning messin' these tracks up. I don't know what ya should do. But I think ya need to tell your pa right off."

Tom walked back and forth, lost in thought, before he turned to Bear and said, "Not now. Don't tell him just yet."

"What do ya mean?" Bear said. "He's gotta know!"

"Give me some time to think about this," Tom said. He looked Bear in the eye. "Make sure Aya knows not to say anything, too, at least for now, okay?"

Bear took a deep breath, uncertainty in his eyes. "Well...okay. Whatever you want, but what are we gonna tell him when we get back to the house?"

"Don't lie to him; just don't tell him all of it. We'll say we found the prints from Curry's horse and it must have been one hell of a lucky throw to get that dynamite on the bridge." He paused. "We'll say there's been a lot of traffic up and down this road this morning and it's hard to tell exactly what happened; that's the truth." Tom's stomach turned at the thought his brother was responsible for all that happened last night. "Before we tell him all of it, I need to talk to Buddy. I need to be sure. I'm going to town this morning to order lumber, so I'll pay him a visit while I'm there. I'll know as soon as I ask if he's got anything to do with this. Then the three of us can sit down and have a talk with my dad when I get back. Fair enough?"

"Okay by me, I guess," Bear said with an unsure nod of the head. He turned to Aya and explained the plan. Aya wasn't thrilled about the idea, but consented, nonetheless. After Bear and Aya finished speaking, all three men made solid eye contact to let each other know they were in agreement, then turned and started toward the creek and back to the house. Before they had taken five steps, a women's voice called out behind them, "Tom! Tom Wallace, is that you?"

They turned to find Ms. Emma Lawton driving her one-horse buggy toward them, with Jennie Lue Sloan sitting next to her and Pancho tied to the rear.

Blondy Harbison pulled the reins on his horse, stepped down out of the saddle and into the dusty street in front of the jail. He tied his reins and walked onto the sidewalk, stopping to look in both directions at the early morning bustle of downtown Belton. The long blond locks sticking out from beneath his hat always seemed to catch the eyes of the girls, so he never missed a chance to see if he could spot a pretty one spying him from a distance, and this morning was no different. Sure enough, a young woman coming out of the general store a few doors down turned and gave him a cute little smile.

He knew it was a chance to introduce himself, so he grinned, tipped his hat and was about to make his way over when his attention was drawn to loud tapping coming from the front window of the jail. Buddy was on the other side of the glass, urgently waving him inside so, after a shrug, another smile and a disappointed look that said he'd like to run into her some other time, he turned and walked into the jailhouse to see what his boss needed.

Blondy was in his late twenties and had only been a deputy in Belton for three years but, in that time, he firmly established a reputation around town as being part lawman, part gunslinger, and a full-time ladies man. There was a long line of ex-boyfriends, husbands, fathers and brothers who couldn't stand the sight of his good looks or his long, blond curly hair. All would have paid a good deal of money to see a large caliber bullet exit through the back of his head, but none had the guts to try because of Blondy's lightning-quick right hand and his uncanny aim with a pistol. Being the deputy sheriff, knowing he was much faster on the draw than anyone else in this part of the country, made him believe he didn't have to give a damn about what people thought, making him all the more despicable to an ever-increasing number of men every time he grew bored with another heartbroken girl and tossed her aside.

The rumors about Blondy being run off by the sheriff in Fort Worth because of the shootings he was involved in didn't help his popularity, either. And, since coming to Belton, there had been a few more, which solidified his reputation as someone not to be messed with. Each time it happened, most townsfolk were just this side of forming a mob, but the unsolved murders were conveniently explained away by Buddy Wallace, who just happened to be appointed by the most powerful man in the county. There was plenty of talk in the barber shops over the last couple of years that it was high time people got up the nerve and demanded Turner Bell do something about his rogue deputy at the next town meeting, but the fear of Blondy's pistol always kept such talk strictly confined to the barber shop chairs.

"Mornin,' Boss. Whatcha need?" Blondy shut the jailhouse door behind him.

"Have a seat." Buddy waved his deputy to a chair. He sat behind his desk and fumbled with his keys until he untangled the one he needed, then locked a drawer and pulled on the handle twice to make sure the contents were secure before he looked up. "I guess you heard the explosion last night."

"Yeah," Blondy said with a curious smile. "How'd it go?"

Buddy leaned back in his chair and looked at the ceiling. "I guess it went pretty good. Most everything came off almost exactly like I told you it would." He shook his head and sighed with disappointment. "I had my chance to finish it off, but I missed." Buddy closed his eyes as the events from the night before ran through his mind, then sat up and drummed his fingers on the desk. "But it ain't all bad, 'cause they're probably over there right now thinking it was a good thing I came along when I did. Hah! If they only knew." A perverse smile crept across his face as he laughed. "Hell, you shoulda seen it! That bridge went sky high."

Blondy leaned back, appearing unfazed one way or the other with the news. "What about Curry?" he asked.

Buddy answered the question completely. "Curry who?"

"Good," Blondy said, nodding. "I got to hand it to ya, Boss, using Curry like that was smart, real smart. I bet that ol' drunk never had a clue, did he?"

"Nope." Buddy chuckled again. "That last drinking binge of his was one he never shoulda tied on. But anyway…listen, you playing cards tonight?"

"'Course," Blondy said. "Why?"

"Get here early. I'll tell you and George all about it then." Buddy got up from his chair. "Right now I have to run out to the ranch and deliver Curry's horse. He ran off after the explosion last night and turned up in front of the livery this morning."

He walked over to the hat rack by the front door, pulled his black Stetson from one of the hooks, ran his hand along the edges to make sure the rim was exactly in place and laughed. "I'm such a concerned son. I told 'em I'd give that horse to 'em as payment for the bridge I blew up. I mean, the bridge *Curry* blew up."

Blondy laughed. "I knew that Curry was no good," he said with mock sincerity.

"Me, too," Buddy said as he opened the door, "but hey…it's important while I'm gone this morning you make the rounds and tell as many people as you can what happened." He added with a wink, "At least our version anyway, right?"

"Sure thing, Boss," Blondy said, as he stood and followed Buddy out onto the sidewalk.

"And one more thing," Buddy said before he stepped into the street, "it might do us some good if you tell a few folks that it's kinda odd how it didn't take long for shit to splatter once my brother got out of prison. That ought to help liven things up around here."

"No problem. I'll get on it." Blondy grinned with a hint of malice. He watched as Buddy made his way over to the livery and, as soon as he was out of sight, Blondy started looking for the same pretty girl he had seen a few minutes earlier.

As he scanned the streets, he spied George Bell on the far corner, making his usual morning rounds talking to the shop owners. George spotted Blondy at the same time and offered a weak tip of his hat, but Blondy just stood there and stared until the mayor turned away. There were several reasons Blondy didn't care for George Bell. One was Blondy never liked anyone who was part of the "lucky sperm club" and George only had that job because of his father's influence, but he also considered George a sniveling government bureaucrat who got wealthier and fatter while doing nothing but sitting behind a desk and acting self-important.

Blondy also detected a familiar look of fear in George's eyes whenever he looked his way, the same expression most of the men he killed had in theirs right before he shot them dead. The greatest satisfaction he got from taking a man's life was the fear he saw in a man the instant before he lost his life. It was what made Blondy enjoy killing the most and the reason killing was a thirst he could never quench. Maybe one day, after the spineless excuse for a mayor's father was dead and gone, he'd get his chance to watch that look slowly fade from George's eyes and add his name to a growing list of souls he had taken from this world. For now, though, he could wait; there were a few other men on his list he had to take care of first.

Chuckling at the thought, Blondy started down the sidewalk toward the pretty girl with the shy smile he'd spotted earlier. An exciting story about an explosion, somebody getting killed and how he was going to protect the townspeople from such lawlessness might be enough to make her feel like he was just the kind of man she could give herself up to. Even though the day was off to a great start, Blondy Harbison felt certain it was about to get a lot better.

"Well, well," Miss Emma Lawton said with a broad smile as she pulled her buggy to a stop. She nodded to Bear and Aya before setting her gaze upon Tom. "If it isn't Mister Tom Wallace! It is so good to see you back home again." Without waiting for help, she was out of the wagon and on her feet, approaching Tom with outstretched arms. "Your father must be bursting with joy now that you're back. Come here, young man; let me put my arms around you so I'll know you're really home."

Tom had forgotten the embarrassment one can feel from a huge, grandmotherly-type hug in front of other people, but his chagrin evaporated when he stepped back and saw her genuine, kindhearted smile and the tears welling up in her bright blue eyes.

Emma Lawton was forty-five years old, and known around Belton as the most fashionably dressed woman in the county, a reputation she went through great pains to maintain. Of course, owning the finest women's clothing store in the city made it easy for her to justify wearing a fancy dress everywhere she went, no matter the time of day or night. Outlining her petite figure (which still turned the head of most every young cowboy in town), was a bright purple, bell-shaped dress with a white diamond pattern running throughout, outlined by black lacy trimmings along the bottom, the end of her short, ruffled sleeves and around her neck, which also sported a small white scarf tied into a bow. Soft touches of make-up highlighted her blue eyes and her olive complexion, shadowed by a solid purple bonnet sitting atop a full head of light-brown hair, tied up in back. Her hat matched the base color of her dress exactly and was highlighted by a large white bow on the side. She wore black lace gloves and carried a pocket fan in one hand with a purple velvet handbag in the other.

"Miss Lawton," Tom said politely as he stepped back, took off his hat and nodded. He glanced at Jennie Lue, who sat in the wagon trying to hide an empathetic smile with her hand.

Tom stuttered, "Good…good morning, ladies. Ah, what might bring the two of you all the way out here so early in the morning?"

"Why, that explosion we all heard last night, of course," Emma said as she looked past Tom at the ruins of Ruby's bridge for the first time. "Oh, my Lord!" she said, walking around to get a better look.

"What in the world happened?" Jennie Lue asked as she stepped out of the buggy. "Is everyone all right?"

"Well…" Tom said as he looked over the carnage, "not exactly."

"What do you mean, not exactly?" Emma asked anxiously. "Who's hurt? It's not your father, is it?"

Tom quietly answered, "No…no. It's Chas, Chas Kane. He was close to the bridge when the dynamite went off. Took a pretty good-sized chunk of wood in the shoulder. Looks like he lost the hearing out of one of his ears, too. We got Doc out here quick as we could, though."

"Is he going to be okay?" Jennie Lue asked.

"Too soon to tell." Tom sighed.

"Is everyone else okay?" Emma asked.

"Yes, ma'am," Tom said, "we're just tired, that's all. It was a long night."

"Who would do such a thing?" Jennie Lue asked, puzzled.

Tom glanced at Bear and Aya to let them know he wasn't going to let either woman in on their secret before he said, "It was Curry, Curry Hampton.

My dad fired him yesterday. I guess he didn't take it so well because he came back last night and tossed a few sticks of dynamite onto the bridge."

"Are you sure it was him? Did you tell your brother?" Emma asked.

"Yes, ma'am," Tom said, "we're sure. Curry's dead. Buddy killed him."

"Then he deserved it!" Emma said emphatically as she stared at the broken pieces of lumber laying everywhere. After a long moment of silence, she turned and asked, "Tom, is Chas…how bad is he?"

Tom looked at the ground before he answered softly, "Pretty bad. But we don't know for sure. Doc says he's got a chance if infection don't set in."

Ms. Emma turned to eye her buggy, then the ranch house on the far side of Cowhouse Creek and asked, "How does one get to the house now that the bridge is gone?"

"There's a crossing about twenty minutes south of here," Tom said, pointing. "I can ride down there and show you."

Emma looked back and forth from her buggy to the house a few times before she took off her gloves and said, "Nope. That just won't do. Tom, you know where to go. I want you to bring my carriage up to the house." She handed him her gloves, pocket fan and purse. "Take these with you."

"What? Ah…ma'am…what are you doing?" Tom asked.

Emma pulled her skirt up with both hands and started walking to the near bank of Cowhouse Creek, saying, "I'm going to the house. I'll meet you there."

"Miss Lawton!" Tom said as he gave everyone a quick look before starting after her, "You can't go that way! You'll be knee deep in the creek, and that dress of yours will be ruined. Let me take you around in the buggy. Please!"

Emma stopped in her tracks and turned to Tom as if she was considering the thought, then said, "I'll tell you what you can do for me, Tom. I want you to go into town and stop by Doctor Carrington's. Tell him to make a list of every kind of medicine imaginable that we might need over here. Tell him we need at least two weeks' worth."

"We have a few things up at the house…" was all Tom could say before Ms. Lawton cut him off.

"…and lots of bandages, rubbing alcohol and whatever else comes to that good man's mind." Emma thought for a moment before she finished. "Then get over to Will Weather's drug store, pile it all in the buggy and meet me back up at the house. Tell that new clerk working over there to put the tab on my account. And, if he decides to make a fuss over it, you tell him I'll take it personally and I'll tar and feather him myself before the day is out. You hear?"

"But, Ms. Lawton…" protested Tom.

"You get going now. Time's a wasting," she said as she turned and marched over to the steep bank and carefully started down the slippery slope, chunks of mud sticking to her fancy, laced-up leather, high-heeled boots with every step.

Seeing the lady was hell bent on wading through the creek, Bear quickly made his way down the embankment until he was in front of her, backing down with his arms outstretched as if he was going to catch her if she slipped and fell. He kept telling her to watch her step and be careful, but he was the one who needed help because his feet suddenly went out from under him and he tumbled into the water with a splash. She never lost her footing once.

Bear wasn't in his best mood by the time he finally stood up, knee-deep in muddy water at the base of the steep grade. Tom had to chuckle at the sight, because not only was Bear embarrassed, he was far dirtier than the lady he had been trying to help. Tom laughed, thinking maybe Miss Emma was the one who should have helped Bear down the embankment.

Tom, Jennie Lue and Aya all got a good chuckle out of the sight, but soon Ms. Emma had both feet in the water, the bottom third of her bright purple dress floating lazily behind her as she headed to the other side. Tom quit laughing long enough to point down at Bear and say, "You better go with her. I'll head into town and see Doc. And, when you get up to the house, make sure you tell Dad I'll take care of the lumber order while I'm there."

After taking a moment to watch Ms. Emma slosh through the creek, Bear tried to wipe some of the wet clay off his shirt with one muddy hand and rinse his dirty spectacles off in the creek water with the other before he shrugged and started up the far bank after Ms. Lawton without saying a word.

"She's quite a woman," Jennie Lue said as she and Tom watched Miss Lawton reach the top of the far bank.

"Yeah, I suppose she is," Tom said.

Ms. Lawton yelled at them from the other side. "Tom! One more thing! I want you to stop by my shop and tell my daughter to put together a satchel of clothes for me: work boots, jeans, old shirts and such. Tell her I'll be out here for a few days, and tell her what happened; she'll know what to do." With that, she turned and quickly marched up the road toward the house, the bottom of her soaking wet dress dragging along behind her in the dirt.

Tom and Jennie Lue got another chuckle at the sight, as Bear did everything he could just to catch up but obviously had no idea what he would do when he did.

With Miss Lawton and Bear well on their way up the road to the house, Tom looked at Jennie Lue and once again was struck by her petite figure as she stood there in her white straw hat, simple boots, slacks and a white shirt similar to the one she wore when he saw her the day before. Realizing he might have made her a bit uncomfortable by the way he was staring, he asked, "Well, Jennie Lue, would you like to ride into town with me?"

She looked up the road toward the house, then turned to him and smiled. "Yes, I would. If it's all right."

Tom hesitated. "People are going to talk when they see us together. You know that, don't you?"

She looked into his eyes. "I'm so sorry. I felt really bad about that after I got home yesterday. I owe you an apology," she said.

"For what?" Tom asked.

"For having any concern at all about what the townsfolk around here think I should or shouldn't do." She smiled and added, "Or who I care for."

Tom looked at the sparkle in her eyes and returned her happy smile. He nodded, "Thank you, but no apologies, remember?"

"I guess we'd better get going, then," she said. "No telling what Miss Emma might do if we're late getting back."

Tom turned to Aya, who was still watching Bear and Ms. Lawton in the distance. "Aya, can you take Ms. Jennie Lue's horse up to the house for us?" Aya went to the back of the buggy, untied Pancho and started lengthening the stirrups so he could ride the horse along the banks of Cowhouse Creek to the shallow crossing.

As soon as they were seated in the shiny black carriage, Tom looked at Jennie Lue and grinned. "You ready?"

"I certainly am," she said.

Tom no sooner had Ms. Lawton's raven-black horse and buggy turned around to head down the road into town when Jennie Lue nervously clasped her hands on her knees and slowly shuffled the soles of her boots back and forth along the floorboard of the buggy, saying in a light and sincere tone, "I'm sorry to barge in on you this morning uninvited and all, but...and I'm terribly sorry about Chas, but we heard the explosion last night. It came from the direction of your place...and... I just had to know you were okay."

Tom soaked in the sight of her shy, worried smile at length before he reached over, took her hand in his and said, "I'm really glad you came."

The gleam in his eyes told Jennie Lue all she needed to know. A sense of relief swept over her as she squeezed Tom's hand and wiped a small tear from her cheek. Neither knew what to say but, as she looked into Tom's eyes and saw the way he was staring back at her with his warm, handsome smile, Jennie Lue knew the feeling she had in her chest that instant had never been a part of her adult life until now, and there was no way she was going to let it slip through her fingers without a fight.

CHAPTER 15

Buddy's Dilemma

"What the hell is that?" Church said as he stood from his chair and set down what was left of his coffee. He squinted as he leaned over the porch railing, trying to make out the two figures who appeared to have crawled right out of the creek in the distance and were now marching up the dirt road leading to the house. "I don't know who it is," he added as he looked back at Jim, "but it appears you got a visitor...a lady visitor."

Jim and Percy stood and joined Church along the edge of the porch before Jim said quietly, shaking his head, "Emma."

"Is that Miss Emma? Emma Lawton, the fancy dress lady?" Church asked in disbelief.

"It is," Jim said with a sigh.

"I'll be damned," Percy said.

Church scratched the side of his head and asked, "Now what in the world would make that woman wade through a muddy creek? I almost can't believe my eyes. Ain't never seen her get anywhere near a mud puddle, much less walk through a creek like the Cowhouse."

"Well...knowing Emma," Jim said, "I betcha she just found out about Chas from Tom down there and is on her way up to the house to make sure the boy is okay."

Percy chuckled. "By the way she's marchin' double time, I would say that's a pretty good guess."

"Old Bear looks like he's doin' all he can do just to keep pace," Church laughed. "I might need to get inside and fetch him a glass of water so he don't keel over when he gets up here. Look at him! Whoowee, he looks like a pig that just finished rollin' 'round in a sty."

"He don't look happy, neither," Percy said as they watched Emma and Bear get closer to the house. The men chuckled at the sight, but erased their smiles as soon as Miss Emma Lawton got close enough to where they could make out the determination on her face.

Church and Percy tried to be neighborly, and walked down the steps to greet her with a "Mornin,' ma'am," but didn't get anything in return as she marched right past them as if they weren't there. Bear wasn't long on catching up, but stayed in the yard with his other co-workers as they watched Miss Emma make a beeline for the porch.

She stopped at the foot of the steps, looked up at Jim who was sipping on his coffee, and said judiciously, "Jim, I hope you can forgive me for showing up here this morning looking this way."

Jim lowered his cup and looked down at the bottom of her soaking wet, mud-caked dress. He nodded once to let her know he understood. "Emma. I'm bettin' you came out here to see about Chas."

"Where is he?" she asked. "I need to see him."

"He's in good hands," Jim said.

"What is that supposed to mean?" she asked, not so easily deterred by Jim's brush-off. "Do you really believe any of these dirty cowboys you have around here knows enough about medicine to save that boy's life?"

"Percy over there knows a thing or two about doctoring," Jim said as he pointed behind her.

Ms. Emma turned and glanced at Percy before she looked back at Jim and said in amazement, "The piano player? You mean to tell me you're going to let that child's hopes ride on 'a thing or two' the piano player knows?" She indignantly grabbed a handful of wet dress with each hand, lifted what she could off the ground, climbed the steps and headed straight for the door, saying loudly enough for all to hear, "This is nonsense. And I won't tolerate it." She stopped at the door and raised her eyebrows at Jim as if to say 'Are you going to open it?' before she looked back at Percy and added apologetically, "No offense. Mr. Goff, is it?"

"The name's Percy. Percy Goff. And none taken, ma'am," Percy replied.

"Where is he? I need to see him," she said forcefully to Jim.

"First room on the left," he answered as he opened the screen door and watched her march into the house. He glanced at his employees standing in the yard watching, then shrugged and followed her inside.

The cowhands stared at the door in wonder for a few moments before Church looked at Bear and asked, "What the hell happened to you?"

"What do you think? I slipped and fell in the damned water," Bear said in an offended tone. "And, if ya start makin' fun of me, you ain't gonna like your supper."

Church smiled at Percy and said, "I don't think either one of us would ever do that, would we? Well, at least not until after we eat, anyway."

"That's right. It's just like Church says," Percy added with a laugh.

He patted Bear on the back, then slung his hand in the air a few times trying to get the mud off his fingers as they all made their way back onto the porch. Percy was still chuckling as he sat down in a chair and added, "Let me guess. I'm bettin' the story goes something like this: you got yourself looking like a mud-covered sow 'cause you ran into some Injuns down there in that creek, but you were able to kill 'em all off with your bare hands and save poor Miss Emma's life. Am I right?"

Church chimed in with a laugh of his own as he pointed at Bear, "From the looks of things, I'd say Ms. Emma saved *him*."

Bear sat in a chair, making a vain attempt to wipe some of the dirt off the front of his shirt before he took his glasses off and laid them in his lap. "Well," he said as he raised both hands, "it weren't such a fuss. Those Injuns was big all right, but there was only ten of 'em."

Jim followed Emma through the house without saying a word. The lady in the ruined purple dress briskly made her way through the living room without so much as a glance at anything, paying no mind to the imprints of mud she left on the polished wooden floor.

Emma raised her hands to her face as she entered Chas's room. "Oh, my Lord!" she exclaimed. After moving alongside the bed and reaching down to check his forehead for a fever, she added, "You poor, poor thing."

Jim leaned against the door frame. After he had given her ample time to look over Chas's injuries, he said, "Emma, I don't think there's anything you can do. Me and the boys…"

"Don't you start with me, Jim Wallace," she interrupted, turning to him. "I've known this unfortunate child his entire life, and I will not stand here and listen to you tell me I can't do anything to help. I just won't have it."

"Emma…" Jim said, "I just don't know what else you can…"

"Have you sterilized this room?" she asked with raised eyebrows as she untied the chin strap of her purple hat, took it off and laid it on the dresser.

Obviously startled at the question, Jim stood straight and stuttered, "Well, no, not yet, anyway. We haven't had the chance."

Emma looked down at her soaking wet dress for a moment as if she noticed it for the first time. She sat down on the chair next to the bed and started untying her boots. "I'm assuming you have a bottle of liniment somewhere in this house? One that's mostly alcohol, rubbing alcohol that is, and lots of clean towels?"

Jim looked at the determination in her fiery blue eyes, realizing there was no way he was going to talk her out of doing whatever she had her mind set on. "Okay, what are we going to do?"

"We're going to make sure this boy makes it is what we're going to do," she said with certainty as she pulled off a boot.

"No, that's not what I meant," Jim said. "What I mean is, how are *we* going to go about it. Where are you going to sleep?"

"Is there something wrong with that bedroom next door?" she asked, as if Jim should have already figured that part out.

"No," he said with a tired chuckle. "I suppose that'll be fine. But, Emma, what about the neighbors?"

"What do your neighbors have to do with this?" she asked as she started untying her other boot. "Are you planning on letting them use that room as well?"

"No," he said, shaking his head with a grin, "it's just that…well, you know."

"No, I don't know." She sounded aggravated as she stood and picked up her muddy boots and set them outside the room. "What are you trying to tell me? That you don't think I should be here to help this child?"

"No, of course not. Don't be ridiculous," he said, "but if you're going to stay here, there's probably going to be some talk over it."

"Jim Wallace!" she said as she turned to look at him. "I can't believe it! You say I'm ridiculous, but *you're* the one being ridiculous. What are you worried about more, gossip in this town, or this boy's life?"

"Emma," he said as he walked across the room and reached out to hold her by the waist. "What am I going to do with you?"

She stood with anger in her eyes before she suddenly started to tremble, then she let out a sob, threw her arms around him and fell against him. "Oh, Jim! I'm so relieved you're all right! I was so worried."

Jim rocked her back and forth as he hugged her tightly. "It's all right, Emma. Everything's going to be okay."

They hugged each other for several minutes before Emma raised her head from Jim's chest, tears streaming down her cheeks, and asked, "You're not really worried about what people say about us, are you?"

"Don't be silly," he answered as he wiped her face. "I just want to make sure you know what's coming if you stay out here, that's all."

"Well, I don't give a damn what people say about us," she said defiantly as she tried to back away. "To hell with them! To hell with them all!"

"Emma Lawton!" he said, truly startled. "I've never heard you talk this way before!" He pulled her close and added, "But you're right…they can all go to hell."

She looked up at him and wiped another tear from her cheek. "Do you think I was too rough on that piano player?"

"Yes, I do," he chuckled. "You would have no way of knowing this, but he knows plenty about doctoring a man back to health. He was the one that helped patch my leg up in the war; he probably saved my life." He looked into her blue eyes and added, "I can tell you this, though, I'd much rather have you in the room next door than Percy. That's a fact."

She nodded and pulled away, gathering herself. "How did you both meet here in Belton?"

"That's a long story. Fate, I guess." he said as he watched her pretty smile creep back across her face. "How about I tell you over dinner?"

"Well, all right." She briefly looked into the mirror over the dresser and put her hair back in place. She turned and made a playful slap on Jim's chest. "But if I was the one who doctored you back in the war, you wouldn't have that limp of yours. Now, you want to go find that liniment for me? And don't forget, mostly rubbing alcohol. I have a lot of work to do."

"What are you going to do about a change of clothes?" he asked as he moved toward the door.

"I sent Tom and Jennie Lue into town to get my things," she answered.

"Jennie Lue?" he said. "What's she doing out here?"

"We ran into each other this morning on the way over here," she said as she put her arms around him again. "It seems she was just as worried about Tom as I was about you."

He smiled. "Hmm. I always did like her."

"Me, too," she said.

Jim leaned down and kissed her tenderly on the cheek. "I'll be right back with what you need."

"I'll be right here," she said, "and Jim...thank you for letting me help."

Jim had a hand on the door frame as he looked back, smiled and nodded once to let her know he was glad she was there before he left the room.

As he walked to his bedroom, he realized how good it felt to have Emma at the ranch helping with Chas, but the closer he got to his room where the medicine cabinet was located, his mood grew heavier. Walking through the door, he looked around at all of Ruby's favorite knick-knacks lined up neatly on every flat surface, and it occurred to him that the oak medicine box hanging on the wall had been dear to her as well. In fact, it could have been the most important thing in the house, because off those shelves came the ammunition she needed to care for her family. She took the notion seriously, always ready to pack it full of some brand-new kind of miracle drug that claimed to cure everything from diarrhea, colic, cramps, coughs, croup, neuralgia, gout, asthma, palpitations of the heart, bruises, sprains, burns, cuts, insect stings, chilblains, frostbites, toothaches, rheumatism and corns — and all with one dose.

Since Jim never trusted doctors, and didn't take any kind of medicine unless he absolutely had to, this was the first time he had turned the brass knob to open the small wooden door since Ruby's death. The brass hinges creaked as the door moved aside, the contents inside bringing back recollections of the various aches and pains that afflicted his family over the years, and of the different concoctions his wife always mixed to fight them off. Ruby had all sorts of remedies stacked neatly together on the two shelves, including Gargling Oil, Foot Tonic, Compound Oxygen, Caustic Balsam, Pond's Extract, Cod Liver Oil, Snake Oil, Eye Water, Fig Syrup and Worm Syrup.

His eyes came to rest on the label attached to a large bottle, which read *Moyer Bros. Laudanum*. Jim had put it back a day or two after Ruby died and never gave the drug another thought until now, but the act of turning the bottle over in his hands brought back painful memories of watching the once vibrant woman he loved slowly wither away, one agonizingly long day after another. Jim shook off his sorrow and carefully placed the bottle back in the cabinet behind the other miracle cures. He rearranged the others until he spotted one with a label that read *Mullin's Hornet's Nest Liniment — 66% Alcohol by Volume.*

"This ought to do it," he said to himself as he shut the door and locked the brass knob. As he turned to leave, a sad feeling swept over him. There were a million reminders of Ruby in this house and now there was another woman he cared a great deal for under the same roof. The feeling was an equal mix of sadness, happiness and guilt, which he knew was going to bounce around in his head and chest at all hours of the day for quite some time to come. He stopped at the hall closet to grab all the clean towels he could carry in one load, then poked his head into Chas's room to find Emma sitting in the chair, her hands crossed and a worried look on her face.

"Everything okay?" he asked

A nod was all she could muster, then she looked up with fresh tears in her eyes. "Jim, I'm so sorry. I didn't realize it until I was sitting in here by myself, but I don't belong here. This is Ruby's house."

"It's okay, Emma," he said, setting his armload of goods on the foot of the bed. He moved over, went to one knee beside her chair and took her hand. "Look at me. I want you here. I'm sure Ruby would, too." He brushed a stray hair from her face. "Chas needs you. Don't let that brain of yours get in the way of what's best for this boy, okay?"

Emma squeezed his hand. "Are you sure? I can leave right this second if you want me to. I'll understand."

Jim did his level best to try to hide the emotions he was feeling a short time ago as he answered, "No. I'm positive. In fact, I'd be mighty upset if you left."

She smiled and swiped at her tears with a clean handkerchief. "It's just that...I know I can help him."

"I know you can, too," he said. "In fact, I'm depending on it. So now about I get Percy to grab his things out of the room next door and you get to doing whatever it is you're so dead set on doing."

"Dead set on doing? You make it sound as if I'm hard-headed," she said with a small laugh.

"I don't know if I'd call it that," he laughed, "but, whatever it is, I like it. I don't want you to ever change a bit, you hear?"

Emma caressed Jim's face, gave him a short kiss on the lips and said, "Then you need to get out of this room right now so I can get started. And don't come back until Jennie Lue returns with my things. I've got to get out of this wet dress; no telling what kind of infectious diseases that boy could get from my clothes." She waved Jim away with the back of her hand. "Go on now. I'll leave my things outside the door."

Jim stood with a huge grin on his face. "I better get going, then. I'll try not to peek in here after you put your clothes in the hall."

"You better not!" she said with a smile.

He stopped at the door and looked back at her. "I hope you're okay with this, because I am...really. Don't worry about it, okay?" He lingered long enough to see Emma Lawton return his smile with an understanding nod before he closed the door behind him and headed out to find Percy. There was so much going on at the ranch right now, and every bit of it needed to be tended to at once, but the most important thing on Jim's mind was whether or not his feelings for Emma Lawton would be buried under an avalanche of the memories and guilt that seemed to be staring at him from every corner of the house.

"Come on, you ignorant pile of glue!" Buddy cursed the horse behind him. He had been in a foul mood since he left his office earlier because the charcoal-gray horse he was leading to his father's ranch turned out to be dumber than a box of rocks and didn't want to do anything except stop and sample flowers along the side of the road. Every time Buddy yanked on the rope to get the horse moving again, it would show its displeasure by moving up alongside and trying to bite the hindquarters of his palomino. Not only did Buddy have to deal with Curry Hampton's stupid animal, but his own horse would get riled up and try to kick the other one whenever Buddy wasn't paying attention.

"I should've shot you, too!" Buddy growled as he yanked the rope tied to the bridle of the stubborn animal as it tried to make a break for another bank of flowers.

Buddy was seriously second-guessing himself about heading out to the Four C's to give this brainless horse to his dad. The idea seemed like a good one last night, but now he was sure it would've been better to have charged his deputy with the task. Buddy paid Blondy Harbison damn good money to do an assortment of mundane things and, right now, he would like nothing more than to be sitting in his comfortable office chair with his expensive boots propped up on his desk, sipping a nice hot cup of coffee while someone else was out here in the hot morning sun dealing with this stubborn animal. The more he thought about it, the madder he got and, by the time Buddy was just halfway to the ranch, the only thing stopping him from putting a forty-five caliber bullet through the forehead of the stupid creature and leaving his carcass right there in the middle of the road was a plausible explanation for doing so.

Deep down, Buddy knew it wasn't just the dumb horse getting under his skin. This whole town was, or more accurately, this whole part of the country was, and it had been for a long time. It was either too hot and dry or too cold and rainy in central Texas, which was enough to make any sane man want to live somewhere else, but the idea of stomping around cow manure and horse shit for the next fifty years was what really made Buddy Wallace sick to his stomach. He envisioned himself as the kind of man who would enjoy seeing the world with a glass of fine whiskey in one hand and a pretty young girl in the other, and he had high hopes one day soon he would be able to afford to live such a life.

He had long been fascinated by incredible stories of men getting rich in California by just reaching down to pick up gold that was laying around everywhere, and of the beautiful girls working fancy saloons in San Francisco where a man with money was always treated like a king. In the east, tall ships sailed on a daily basis from the amazing city of New York, taking men no different than him to destinations like Italy, Spain, England and France. Buddy had no idea what he would do if he ever got the chance to see those countries, but that wasn't the point. He simply thought the names sounded good, and they were an awfully long way from Bell County, Texas, which was good enough for him.

His thoughts, and the stubborn horse he led, brought him back to how he couldn't understand why his father never seemed to have any ambitions, preferring to sit on that piece of land he called a ranch until he was too old to do anything else. Now it looked like his brother was back in town to carry on the family tradition, and Buddy couldn't for the life of him figure out why anyone in his right mind would want to call Bell County home. The only real reason he wanted to work in the sheriff's office in the first place was because it was the best ticket he knew of to get him off the ranch right away. In the beginning, he had high hopes it could lead to bigger and better jobs somewhere else, but now he was old enough to know he didn't want to wear a badge for the rest of his life. There were a lot of perks that came with the job, and the side money wasn't bad, but he had to pretend he cared about every little grievance from every little townsperson and was ultimately responsible for dealing with all the murderers, drunks, whores, cheats and liars that mankind had to offer in this tiny little corner of the world.

Thinking about it while trying to get Curry Hampton's pitiful excuse for a plow puller to the one place on earth he wanted to be away from the most made Buddy want to say the hell with it and make his way down to Galveston right then and there. There were plenty of ships leaving out of that port as well, and the idea he could be on one within a few days made him calm down. Still, Buddy knew there was work left to be done before he could enjoy life the way he wanted, so he yanked hard on the rope tied to the horse behind him once more, getting both animals headed in the same direction for the time being.

Moving slowly down the road, Buddy tried to simmer down by trying to convince himself the position he was in wasn't all that bad. If he wasn't the sheriff, he wouldn't have the opportunity he was faced with now. If everything went his way, soon he and some unknown pretty girl would be drinking champagne from fancy glasses in a hotel with a name he couldn't pronounce until he got bored with it all and started over in another town or country.

His job was what could make it all possible, so dealing with whining townsfolk might be a miserable thing to face, but it was tolerable, and nothing compared to dealing with the seedy underbelly of this job, which was the main reason he hired Blondy Harbison. There had been numerous occasions over the last few years when, for one reason or another, someone needed to be taken care of, and most of those situations were handled by his deputy, who was paid well to do that type of work. Although he didn't really have the stomach for it, Buddy was more than capable of shooting a man dead when needed — Curry Hampton was proof — but since he had a deputy who enjoyed killing, Buddy hardly ever got his fingers dirty when it came to getting rid of someone. Their partnership had earned them both a fierce reputation, which by now had spread across most of the state, and pity the poor soul who had the misfortune to stumble blindly into either one having badly underestimated the cold blood in their veins.

Of course, Buddy knew there would come a day when he would have to get rid of Blondy. If he didn't, there would either be a murder that would be his own or one he couldn't explain away, and either option was as bad as the other. Blondy wouldn't swing at the end of a rope before spilling his guts to any judge who would listen, which meant his boss would surely swing alongside him. Buddy chuckled at the thought, because there was no way he was going to allow himself to be the main attraction at a Sunday morning hanging. Blondy's quick right hand made everyone else in this part of the country nervous, but not Buddy because, even though he wasn't remotely close to having the same skills with a firearm as his deputy, he was confident he more than made up for it with smarts and planning. Buddy had already mapped out several ways to leave his deputy out in the cold and was absolutely sure, no matter what happened over the coming days, it would not be the other way around.

The calm he had gained over the last few minutes was quickly lost as the horse behind him made another lunge for a patch of wildflowers on the side of the road. Buddy yanked as hard as he could on the lead rope he held. The stubborn animal showed it wasn't happy about it by lunging at Buddy's horse with its teeth bared, only this time, it was Buddy's thigh it bit.

"You stupid son of a bitch!" Buddy yelled. Madder than he had been all morning, Buddy leapt out of his saddle as he pulled his pearl-handled revolver out of his holster. "This is it for you, you ignorant bag of shit!" Buddy raised the pistol and placed the end of the barrel next to the head of Curry Hampton's horse and cocked the hammer.

He was about to pull the trigger when he heard a wagon coming down the road. He glanced in that direction, instantly knowing now wasn't the time to kill the stupid creature causing him so much grief because Miss Emma Lawton's carriage was headed his way. He quickly put the pistol back in his holster and reached up to rub the side of the horse's head to make it look as if he was caring for it. Only as the buggy neared did he look up, trying hard to feign surprise at seeing Miss Lawton out here this early in the morning. He didn't have to pretend because it wasn't Miss Lawton he saw.

Sitting in Miss Emma's fancy carriage, Jennie Lue couldn't help but run her hand over the soft, dark-red velvet cushions. The black wooden canopy matched the shiny paint on the rest of the buggy, while the underside was lined with the same soft red material as the seats. Jennie Lue marveled at the amount of brass trim lining every outside edge and was admiring the craftsmanship of the oil lamps hanging on either side when she asked, "Have you ever driven a carriage this nice?"

She turned to Tom expecting an answer, but her question was quickly forgotten when she saw the expression on his face. His jaw was clenched as he stared down the road and Jennie Lue knew why as soon as she turned to look. Not a hundred yards away was Buddy Wallace, standing off to the side of the road. His presence made both their moods change drastically, the tension mounting the closer they got. After the buggy came to a stop, Tom took a second to size up the situation before he said stiffly, "Having trouble?"

Buddy tried to hide the shock of seeing Tom and Jennie Lue together. He squinted in the hot morning sun. "No, not really. Just trying to get this son of a bitch over to the Four C's. I'm havin' a hard time getting the damn thing to follow my horse. All he wants to do is eat flowers along the way."

Buddy looked down at his thigh to see the bite mark had left a sizable tear in his new pants, which was surrounded by a small blood stain and said, "Damned thing got me good, too."

He walked over to the side of the carriage, tipped his hat to Jennie Lue and said, "Miss Sloan. And how are you this fine morning?"

Jennie Lue answered him with a scornful look so Buddy turned to his brother. "Where are you and this pretty little lady headed?"

"Into town," Tom replied. "I need to order the lumber to rebuild the bridge and Miss Emma wants us to stop by the drugstore and pick up some medical supplies for Chas."

"Where is Miss Lawton?" Buddy asked as he rubbed the bite mark on his leg. He removed his hat to wipe the perspiration from his forehead.

"At the ranch," Tom said. "I guess you're headed that way?"

"Yep. Trying to, anyway," Buddy said as he pulled his shoulder-length red hair behind his ears and put his hat back on. He leaned against the front wheel of the carriage with a smirk on his face long enough for Tom and Jennie

Lue to get a bit uncomfortable before adding, "Um, um, um. I gotta hand it to you, brother, you ain't wasted any time since you got back, have you?"

"What's that supposed to mean?" Jennie Lue barked.

Buddy looked down at the ground and kicked the soil around a bit before he glanced back and forth at both of them. "Ah…nothing," he said. He wiped both sides of his handlebar mustache as he turned his gaze to Jennie Lue. "I have to tell you, though, I never thought a woman with a fine upbringing like yours would go for my brother. I mean, him being an ex-convict and all."

"I have a question for you, Buddy," Jennie Lue said as she leaned forward and stared at him with fire in her eyes. "Do you intentionally come across as an ignorant pompous ass, or are you really just not that bright?"

The insult didn't change the smirk on Buddy's face one bit, and Jennie Lue felt enraged as the sheriff looked her over from head to toe like she was one of the working girls at Dayna G's. He chuckled. "I wonder how the folks around this town are going to react to this. And does your daddy know? I bet he ain't gonna like this one bit, is he?"

She stared at the sheriff for a second before she shook her head in disgust and took one of Tom's hands in both of hers. "Actually, if you really want to find out how much we care about what anybody else thinks around this town, you might want to be at the opera house tonight."

"Why the opera house?" Buddy asked.

"Because Tom is taking me to see the Hanlon-Lees, the acrobat show," she said. She leaned toward Buddy as if it might help him understand her words better. "We have great seats. In fact, they're right down in front. So, if you stop by there later this evening, all of your little questions will be answered." She smiled at Tom, who had no idea what she was talking about and kept silent. She gently squeezed his hand to let him know she'd give him the details later.

"Uh-huh. I see," Buddy said slowly as he shook his head and eyed them. He grinned and said, "Well, now, I just may have to do that, then. I haven't had a good laugh in a while, and the show might not be all that bad, either."

She looked at Buddy as if he were truly the dumbest man she had ever met, then turned to Tom and said, "Oh, well, can't please them all. But we need to be on our way, don't we? We have far more important things to do than waste any more time here."

Tom never took his eyes from his brother, and his tone was far more serious as he said, "I think you're right, Jennie Lue. But give me a minute."

Tom hopped out of the buggy and walked to Curry Hampton's horse, which had moved off to the side of the road to munch on a patch of wildflowers. He grabbed the bridle rope and led the horse back to the carriage. "It's probably better if we take this horse back to the Four C's ourselves."

"Why's that?" Buddy asked. He followed Tom around to the back of the carriage. "What makes you think you can get this mindless pile of shit out to the house any easier than I can?"

Tom secured the reins to the back of the carriage before he looked up and said bitterly, "I got a tip for you. You don't pull Curry Hampton's horse behind another horse." Tom moved directly in front of Buddy and said with his face a few inches from his brother's. "Aya says it'll follow a wagon a lot better."

The comment caught Buddy completely off guard and, even though he tried his best to let his brother think he didn't know what it meant, the moment of silence that followed was all Tom needed to know that Buddy was indeed behind the events of the night before.

Buddy pulled a toothpick from the pocket of his shirt and stuck it in his mouth, never taking his eyes off Tom. He paused at length before he said slowly, "Now, since when did Aya start talking? He ain't said ten words in all the time he's been around. And how would you know what he was saying anyway?"

"I don't," Tom said coldly, "but Bear does. They've been talking up a storm ever since he got into town. Bear was married to a woman from the same tribe." Ice hung in Tom's voice as he added, "Small world, isn't it?"

Tom walked around his brother to the side of the carriage, climbed in and took his seat next to Jenny Lue as Buddy came up alongside.

"I guess you would be doing me a favor if you took this beast off my hands," Buddy said. He glanced down at the drying blood stain on his pants before he looked back at Tom. "I should get back to the office and tend to this, but be sure to tell Dad I need to talk to him. I'll be out to see him soon."

He took the toothpick out of his mouth, pointed it at his brother's chest and said, "Maybe you should try to talk some sense into him, about selling the place, I mean. If he's gonna keep stringing that barbed wire, I'm afraid there's gonna be more trouble — more *serious* trouble."

"Buddy," Tom said with disgust, "we already have *serious* trouble. Not that you ever pay any visits to Dad, anyway, but I can tell you right now it's not a good idea for you to even think about coming around the house anymore." He turned the carriage around in the narrow road to head back to the Four C's, and said loudly, "Not after last night."

"Well, I'll just see you two love birds at the show, then," Buddy called after them.

They traveled a few hundred yards before Tom took some deep breaths trying to calm down. He turned and looked into Jennie Lue's concerned hazel eyes and asked with a forced, weak smile, "So, are you going to tell me about this show I'm supposed to be taking you to tonight?"

She laughed, rubbed her hands together, and looked into her lap as though embarrassed. "I'm sorry. I know telling Buddy before I asked you wasn't a very proper thing to do, but I'd really like it if you could take me."

Tom's face lit up. "Jennie Lue Sloan! Are you asking me out on a date?"

"You don't mind, do you?" she asked.

"I thought we were getting together this Sunday," he said.

"Well…" she said shyly, "I wanted to ask you yesterday, when we almost ran each other over, but I didn't have the nerve. But we can go to the show tonight and still have a picnic on Sunday, can't we?"

"I don't see why not," he said, chuckling. "In fact, I don't think there's anything I'd rather do."

A smile spread across her face. "I was hoping you would say that." Then her expression changed to one of great concern as she looked back over her shoulder at Buddy, still standing in the road and returning her stare from a distance. "What was all that about? With Buddy, I mean."

Tom paused and glanced at her. "Are you sure you really want to know?"

After standing in the road and watching the carriage until it was out of sight, Buddy climbed on his horse and quickly made his way back to town, all the while trying to devise a plan that would change his run of bad luck. A thousand thoughts raced through his mind. He had been sure no one would know what really happened last night, and the fact that Tom, Aya and their new cook figured it out right away had shaken him to the core. Months of planning had gone into getting to where he was at this point, and now it seemed like everything might fall apart. He already had enough to worry about, like the railroad lines getting closer by the day, watching his back because of Blondy, and getting pressure from George because the people with the money were getting anxious. But now, if that wasn't enough, his brother and most likely everyone else at the Four C's, including his dad, were now firmly established as adversaries.

He slowed his horse to a trot on the outskirts of town but wasted no time getting to the jail where he jumped out of the saddle, tied the reins to the hitching post and stepped through the sheriff's office door, hoping no one caught a glimpse of his foul mood. He put his Stetson on the hat rack, sat down in his expensive leather chair, and put a fresh toothpick in his mouth. As he leaned back in the chair, he set his boots on the desk and closed his eyes, trying to imagine the perfect move that would take all his troubles and turn them into things of the past. Some of his best ideas had come from doing this exact same thing and, after fifteen minutes or so, a small smile crept across his face.

"Buddy...you're a genius," he said as he sat up, his boots banging against the floor. "We just might be able to pull it off."

He reached into his trousers to pull out a small key. Using it to unlock the drawer of his desk, Buddy yanked it open and looked into the bottom. He reached in and pulled out a seven-inch skinning knife with a polished handle made from the antlers of a deer.

Turning it over in his hands, Buddy started snickering. "Well, brother Tom, you might be the only person in the history of the world who would have been better off in the Texas prison system." He put the knife back in the drawer before locking it, then grabbed his hat off the rack and walked outside to see if he could find George Bell and Blondy Harbison.

The troubles that had consumed him only moments before suddenly seemed a lot more manageable now. He whistled a tune as he walked over to city hall. He now only had two things on his mind: one was the plan he had just come up with that would make his dream of getting out of this rat-infested town a reality, and the other was making sure everyone would arrive early for the card game scheduled for later in the evening. There, he would lay out his idea and make absolutely certain no one, including himself, would be responsible for any more mistakes, because it suddenly looked as if his dream was well within his grasp. Everything would happen quickly now.

CHAPTER 16

The Big Oak

As soon as they turned back to the Four C's to drop off Curry Hampton's horse, Tom began to tell Jennie Lue all he knew about the events of the night before. Deep down, he was more than relieved when they happened upon Aya just before they reached Cowhouse Creek. He knew there was no way he could keep the information about his brother from his dad if he saw him right now and, by turning Curry Hampton's horse over to his old friend, he wouldn't have to tell his father the bad news just yet. He did inform Aya he had seen his brother, though, and instructed him to tell everyone else at the ranch they should be ready for trouble in case Buddy decided to show up again. After feeling satisfied Aya knew what he was talking about, Tom and Jennie Lue turned the carriage back around and wasted no time getting into town.

Jennie Lue had far more questions about his brother than Tom could answer and, by the time they got to the outskirts of Belton, both were lost in silent speculations about what could be driving Buddy into madness. They stopped by Miss Emma's clothing store, told her daughter about Chas and why her mother wanted the satchel full of clothes, saying they would stop back by on their way out of town to pick it up after they ran the rest of their errands.

Moving through the streets, Tom could feel the eyes of most everyone gazing at them as they passed, and realized after they left Doc Carrington's office the people of Belton were going to have something to talk about for a couple of reasons. First, Miss Emma's carriage was easily recognizable, and the fact that she wasn't in it was cause enough to raise a few eyebrows. Second, there was a newly released ex-convict and Turner Bell's daughter riding along together, and most everyone in town had all the motivation they needed to spread the hot news from one end of the county to the other. Tom felt horrible about it. He looked at Jennie Lue and wondered if she had any idea how many times her name would be dragged through the mud after today, but the feeling left when she looked back at him and smiled, seemingly oblivious to the way the people in the street were staring.

Tom brought the carriage to a stop in front of Will Weather's Drug Store, where Jennie Lue climbed out quickly and stepped onto the sidewalk. "I still can't believe it. I never did like your brother, but I wouldn't have guessed in a million years that he could be behind something as awful as this," she said.

Tom set the parking brake and tied the reins before hopping out. "Jennie Lue! Shhhhhh! Don't talk so loud. Not here in town, anyway," he cautioned. He walked onto the sidewalk and stopped in front of her. "It's bad enough Buddy knows everybody out at the ranch has figured out what happened, but this town has a lot of eyes and ears, so be careful what you say. I don't want him to think you have any idea what's going on, okay?"

She looked around and noticed how most were returning her gaze with more than just a peculiar stare. She moved closer to Tom and whispered in his ear as she stood up on her toes, "Do you think they're staring at us because of what I said, or because you're here with me?"

He looked down into her worried eyes and said softly, "I'd bet the ranch it was because you're with me." He put his hand on her shoulder and pointed to the front door of the pharmacy, "But I don't care if you don't. What do you say?"

"I don't care one lick, Mister Wallace," she said as her worried look evaporated. "Let's go." They walked across the sidewalk and opened the door to the drug store, leaving behind a small handful of older women who immediately started whispering to each other, no doubt talking about the finest, first-rate gossip to come around in a long time.

The bell hanging over the door rang out as the door closed behind them, causing the young man behind the counter to ask, "What can I do for you two today?"

"I'm Tom Wallace from the Four C's," Tom said, handing the clerk a piece of paper. "Doc Carrington gave us a list of things to pick up. Miss Emma Lawton insists we put it all on her tab."

The twenty-year-old skinny clerk, who wore a white shirt along with matching white trousers, took the piece of paper, scratched the side of his head and slowly looked the list over before he raised his nose to Tom and said, "I know who ya are. You're that fella that just got out of prison, ain't ya?" He briefly glanced at Jennie Lue as if he couldn't understand why she was there before he continued. "There's a lotta talk around here about how it's mighty strange there was such a big explosion and a killin' out at your place so soon after ya got back. Heard that kid, what's his name, that retard…Chas Kane, that's it. Word is he got hurt real bad."

Tom tried not to lose his temper as he asked through gritted teeth, "What the hell is that supposed to mean?"

The clerk took an uncertain glance toward the windows of the store just to make sure the six or seven women standing outside were still looking in before he answered. "I'm just telling you what I heard. Deputy Harbison told me himself. Says everybody 'round here ought to keep a sharp eye on you "

"That's ridiculous!" Jennie Lue said. "Why in the world would anybody need to be worried about Tom Wallace? He hasn't done anything."

The clerk stood his ground, pointed at Tom and said, "'Cause everybody knows this fella just got out of prison for killin' a man in cold blood." Even though he could plainly see Tom was getting madder by the second, he continued, "Everything was pretty quiet 'round here 'til he got back. But now…all that dynamite went off last night. I knew Curry Hampton. Things like that don't usually happen in this town." He looked at Tom, shaking his head in condemnation. "All these goings-on do seem kinda strange now, don't they?"

"You can believe anything you want. I don't care," Tom said, "but we didn't come here to listen to your nonsense. We came for the medical supplies listed on that piece of paper. Personally, I wish we had gone someplace else but, since we didn't, I need you to get that pea brain of yours to think about filling that order…now!"

The clerk looked the list over and peered over the top of the paper. "My, my, this here's a lot of stuff. Looks like either Chas Kane is hurt real bad or…"

"Or what?" demanded Jennie Lue.

The clerk eyed them both carefully before finishing his thought, "Or maybe you folks out there at the Four C's are getting ready for more trouble.

Everybody knows all about the barbed wire you guys are stringin'. Gonna be a lot of free grazers spittin' mad about that."

Jennie Lue said slowly but emphatically, "Look, we're not interested in listening to your stupidity; we just need those supplies." She crossed her arms and added, "So if you don't mind, we'd appreciate it if you put these things together as fast as you can. We've wasted enough time, and we have more stops to make."

"I see," the young clerk said. "The only problem is, Miss Lawton ain't here to sign for all this." Emphasizing the point by setting the list on the counter and slowly pushing it toward Tom, he added, "Which means...I can't help ya."

Before Tom could respond, Jennie Lue put her hands on the counter and leaned over to get as close to the face of the clerk as she could. "Do you know who I am?" she asked.

The clerk was taken aback but nodded. "Do you really think there's going to be a problem getting your puny little bill paid?"

The clerk shook his head and stammered, "Well...well, no, ma'am, since you put it that way, I suppose not."

"Then why don't you get out from behind that counter right now and get to work?" she said, as she pushed the list back across the counter to him. "Put all of it on my daddy's bill if you have to," she added, "we need the supplies, and we need them *now*."

Before the skinny clerk could move, Tom asked, "What's your name?"

"Sam...Sam Webber," he said.

"Let me tell you something, Sam," Tom said. "You can put these supplies on Mister Bell's tab or you can put it on my father's account. It makes no difference to me, but it does to Miss Lawton. She told me to tell you that if you put up a fuss over any of this that she would be back over here this afternoon so she could personally tar and feather you." Tom stood up straight and crossed his arms before he added, "Personally, I'd like to see that. But I guess it's up to you."

Sam glanced at the list one more time before he looked at Tom and said, "Well...if I have to...I guess I can have this ready in about thirty minutes. Do y'all want to wait here or come back?"

Tom turned to Jennie Lue and asked, "What do you think?"

"We still have to get over to the lumber yard," she said. "Why don't we go order that wood and pick all this up on the way back? I don't want to stay in this store for a second longer than we have to."

"Sounds good to me," Tom said.

They turned and left the store, walking through a small group of old ladies standing under the sidewalk awning with holier-than-thou expressions, which didn't change a bit even though Tom and Jennie Lue gave them all a polite "hello" as they passed. Making their way into the carriage, Tom and Jennie Lue were on the verge of laughing out loud at the sight of the nosy old women, even though they were both madder than a hornet just a few seconds earlier.

Tom readied the reins and unlocked the brake, then he looked back and said sarcastically, "I hope you ladies have a good day." They watched the old women file inside the pharmacy and head straight for the clerk, unquestionably on a mission to find more juicy tidbits of information. Tom reached over and squeezed Jennie Lue's hand. "I told you so," he said.

She looked over and smiled. "Ah...what are you going to do?" They laughed as Tom guided the carriage into the street traffic, leaving the gossip mongers, the young clerk and the noise of the clanging doorbell behind.

"You know," Jennie Lue said as she took off her hat and shook her hair in the wind, "I don't know about you, but I'm glad we're done. I was getting pretty sick of being in that town."

"I agree," Tom said, reveling in the sight of Jennie Lue's locks blown about in the breeze.

They were headed back to the ranch after stopping by the Old River Lumber Yard, satisfied with the knowledge that their order would be delivered either late this afternoon or first thing in the morning. An expensive leather satchel full of women's clothes, along with a bag full of medical supplies, sat on the floorboard between them, proof they were able to accomplish the rest of their goals while in town.

"You'd think we both had an extra head growing out of our shoulders the way those people stared at us," he added with a smile.

Jennie Lue laughed at the thought and pulled her hair behind her ears and said, "Isn't that something! And why did that boy in the drug store try to blame you? Like you had something to do with blowing up your own bridge." She shook her head and added, "And the old man at the lumber yard said the same thing."

"Don't know," Tom said, turning his attention to a rabbit that suddenly jumped out of the way of the oncoming carriage and bolted into a thick stand of brush and trees.

They had veered off the road a half a mile back and were slowly making their way through a field of knee-high prairie grass and wild flowers on their way to the shallow crossing of Cowhouse Creek.

"I guess it's because I just got out of prison," he said. "I knew I'd have to deal with a few people looking at me like I was a leper after I got back, but I never thought they might think I was some sort of curse or plague or something."

She reached over and put Tom's hand in her own as she said tenderly, "I'm sorry, Tom. Looking at the way those people stared at you nearly broke my heart. You don't deserve that."

He smiled at her. "Well…maybe I do and maybe I don't. Either way, I don't care." He nudged her with his elbow and added with a sly smile, "I was watching *you*. There were a few times when it didn't look like your heart was breaking; looked more like your heart was telling you to run over and put some knots on their heads."

"You saw that?" she asked with a sly smile.

Tom chuckled. "I did."

"You weren't supposed to," she said, "but I can't help it. It just makes me so mad. How can people be so ignorant?"

"Look," he said, patting her knee, "they can all waste the rest of their days sitting around yapping about whatever they want; makes no difference to me."

She stared into the distance for a few moments before she turned to Tom and asked, "Can I…well…do you mind if I ask you a personal question?"

He shrugged and nodded. "Sure."

"I was just wondering," she said bashfully, "now that you're home, what is it you want? I mean, what do you want to do with the rest of your life?"

Tom gazed past the trotting horse in front of him and chuckled. "That's an interesting question."

She jumped in quickly, as if embarrassed, "You don't have to tell me if you don't want to."

Tom looked into her inquisitive eyes, smiling. "Do you mind if I show you something?"

"Show me what?" she asked.

"A place I know," he said. He slowed the carriage to a stop.

They had reached the shallow crossing, which was a wide, flat sand bar stretching from one side of Cowhouse Creek to the other. At one time, it was the only way to get to the Four C's until Ruby's bridge was built years ago. Tom pointed to the northwest. "We can cross here and head over that way up to the house…or," he added, pointing to the east, "I can take you a half-mile that way and show you my favorite place in the whole world."

She smiled at the idea before her expression changed. "What about Chas? Don't we need to get back right away?" she asked.

Tom glanced in the direction of the house. "I think Chas is in pretty good hands with Miss Emma right now." He looked over to the north and eyed a small thunderstorm rising out of the hot, late morning sky. "Looks like we might have a little rain headed our way but, yeah, I think we have a little time." Turning his attention back to her, he said, "Heck…it's not even noon yet, so what do you say?"

"You want to take me to your most favorite place in the whole world?" she asked, excitement in her eyes. "Is it pretty?"

"It's beautiful," he said, thinking as much about her as the spot he had in mind. "This will be the first time I've been back there since I went away and, I have to say, it would be an honor if you'd allow me to show it to you."

She blushed. "That was a nice thing to say."

They sat there smiling at each other without saying a word for a moment before Tom broke the silence. "Well?"

Jennie Lue was grinning from ear to ear as she said, "Let's go then. If you think it's special, then yes, I'd love to see it."

The horse didn't object to crossing through the shallow water and easily pulled the carriage up the gentle slope and into a rolling pasture on the southeast corner of the Four C's ranch. Neither said much during the short fifteen-minute ride but, after turning a corner in the seldom-used trail, Jennie Lue said, "Wow! What a beautiful oak!"

Tom only looked at her and smiled as he slowed the carriage to a stop, then hopped out and tied the reins. "What do you think?"

She sat in her seat for a long moment taking in the scenery before stepping down. "You were right. It is beautiful!"

The spot Tom had chosen was the top of a gently rolling hill covered with wildflowers and prairie grass, overlooking the point where Cowhouse Creek joined the Leon River a half mile downstream. They stood beneath a huge, old oak that was approximately fifty feet high, with branches and leaves forming an almost perfectly round ball as wide as the tree was tall. The base of the trunk was so big it would take three people holding hands to stretch their arms around it, and it rose fifteen feet in the air before the massive trunk split out into six or seven large branches. The tree was home to a hundred different birds and a half-dozen squirrels, who all stopped what they were doing to get a glimpse of the intruders now walking about underneath.

"I never knew this place was here. What do you call it?" she asked, gazing with awe at the vista spread before them.

"The big oak," Tom replied.

She gave him an embarrassed smile. "I guess that makes sense," she said.

He chuckled. "I used to come out here as soon as I learned how to ride good enough for my dad to let me on a horse by myself."

He walked up behind her, put a hand on her shoulder and pointed over her so she could follow the line of sight of his finger. "Right over there is where the Cowhouse Creek joins the Leon River and winds on down to Belton."

"You can see Belton plain as day from up here," she said.

"Yep," he said. He turned her shoulders a bit and continued, "Over to the northeast is the town of Temple. You can see the tops of a couple of the buildings if you look hard enough."

"I'll be," she said as she squinted. "You can!"

Tom walked down the gentle slope a few paces until he was out from beneath the massive, low-hanging branches and pointed. "Over there you can follow the Leon River until it runs out of sight." He turned and pointed again, "Our house is over that way...and over there you can see Cowhouse Creek as it flows in from the west." He walked back to Jennie Lue and asked, "Well, do you like it?"

"I love it!" she said as her eyes found his. She clasped her hands together in a plea. "Can we sit here for a few minutes?"

"I was hoping you'd say that," he said. He smiled as he sat down next to her at the base of the trunk.

Jennie Lue stretched her legs out, crossed her ankles and leaned her back against the huge tree as she took in the scenery. "Why do they call it Cowhouse Creek anyway?" she asked.

"You know where Pidcoke is, don't you?" he said.

"Sure," she said, as she gently punched his shoulder. "Most everybody knows where that little town is. It's about twenty-five miles northwest of here." She added with a smile and a shrug, "'Course, I've never been there but..."

"Neither have most people," laughed Tom. "Anyway, a few miles this side of Pidcoke, Cowhouse Creek runs through a big, long stretch of limestone." He leaned against the massive trunk, his feet flat on the ground and his forearms resting on his knees. "Over time, not only did the water flowing through there dig out the creek itself, but it also washed out a lot of the softer rock on either side. Some of the wash-outs are caves as big as a ranch house and, whenever a bad storm rolls through those parts, most of the cattle up there will get out of the weather by heading for those caves." He pulled a blade of grass from the ground and stuck it in his mouth to chew on before he added with a wink, "Hence the name...Cowhouse Creek."

She smiled as she took his hand in hers. "You know, I grew up not very far from here and I never knew that."

Tom pulled the blade of grass from his mouth and tipped his hat before he said, in an exaggerated southern drawl, "Glad I could be of help, ma'am."

She playfully elbowed him and said, "Stop it." Then she looked around again, breathing deep. "It is beautiful out here, though. Why didn't your father build the ranch house on this spot?"

"He bought this piece of property later on," Tom said. "It was a few years after the house was already built."

"This would be a wonderful place for a home," she said with a smile. She pointed to an area just off to the side of the big oak. "I can see it now. I'd put the house right over there...and have the front porch facing back the way we just came. That way a person could sit out in the back yard and enjoy this view every evening." She paused to let her vision sink in before she turned to Tom again. "Have you ever thought about building a home out here?"

Tom chuckled. "Only about forty million times over the last five years or so," he said and sighed. He chewed on the blade of grass and stared off into the distance. "Maybe one day," he added.

Jennie Lue took another slow look around at the scenery surrounding the big oak before she looked at Tom and said, "I bet it feels good to be back home."

"You have no idea," he said as he pulled the blade from his mouth and tossed it to the ground. "When I first went away, I would think about my mom and dad...and this spot...almost all day every day. But I had to force myself to stop. Felt if I didn't I would lose my mind."

"I'm sorry," she whispered, looking into his green eyes. "It's none of my business and I didn't mean to..."

"No, no. It's all right," he said. "I don't mind. In fact, I think you and my dad are the only two people on this earth I'd care to talk to about it."

"I followed what happened to you by reading what I could in the paper," she said, her voice heavy with regret. "I wanted to come back to Belton for the trial, to see how you were doing. But...I didn't think you'd care too much to see me."

Tom kept his eyes in the distance for a moment before he turned to her. "How can you say that?" he said. "You know...I never told anybody this before, but I used to think about what it might have been like if you had showed up to see me while I was rotting away in that jail." He paused. "And, to this day, I'm sure it would've been a lot like seeing an angel from heaven."

"Even though I was married?" she asked with surprise, "You really mean that?"

"Yes, I do," he said. He picked a small twig off the ground and idly tossed it at a red wasp that had flown in a little too close. After the insect buzzed away, he said, "My dad told me about what happened to Henry on the train back from Huntsville. Must have been a terrible thing. I want you to know I'm very sorry about what happened to him," he said.

She offered him a weak smile before she looked into the distance and said with a quiver in her voice, "Thank you, but..." She gazed into nowhere for a long moment before she turned to look at Tom with a guilt-ridden look on her face. "It all seems like such a blur now."

"What do you mean?" he asked.

She wiped away a small tear. "The whole thing...the wedding...moving to Austin...Henry's death...moving back home...everything. The last eight years have added up to a whole lot of nothing, and it seems like I spent all of it like I was in some kind of a trance, like I was numb inside."

"How can that be?" he asked. "That sounds like something I'd say about being in prison. You had a life. A good one, I bet."

Jennie Lue sighed deeply before she gave up her darkest secret. "I want you to know: I feel awful about Henry. I feel like it's my fault he's dead."

Tom had a perplexed expression on his face and shook his head. "Jennie

Lue, correct me if I'm wrong, but didn't Henry get robbed and shot after leaving our place? They found the guy who did it and hung him, right?" he asked. She just nodded as she wiped more tears from her face. "Well, how in the world could you be responsible for that?"

"Because…maybe if I was a better wife he would have been home most nights and not out on the town all the time like he was. Maybe he would have been home that night." She added with a tired shake of her head, "In the beginning, I thought I would learn how to…but…I never did love Henry. I never did."

"I…don't quite know what to say," Tom said. This time he was the one who was uncomfortable. "You know…you don't have to tell me any of this."

"It's just that I saw you in town the day Henry and I left for Austin," she confessed, looking into her lap as if ashamed. "You were standing on the sidewalk in front of that shoe store as we passed by. I knew you were there, but I didn't want you to know I saw you." She sat quietly for a moment as if trying to gather the right words. "My father wanted me to marry Henry. I didn't want to, but I was young and stupid and thought he knew best, so I married him. Henry's father is the biggest banker in Austin and my daddy did his best to convince me the marriage would be the best thing that ever happened to me. As I got a little older, though, I found out my father wanted my marriage into that family to be the best thing that ever happened to my father." She looked at him, regret etched in every part of her face. "It was the worst mistake I ever made. And I've waited a long time for a chance to tell you this, Tom. I'm very, very sorry."

Tom let go of her hand so he could put his arm around her shoulder and pull her close. "We've both made our fair share of mistakes, haven't we?" he said.

"I suppose," she said. "But yours was an accident. I made mine on purpose. That's a big difference, you know."

Tom chuckled loudly.

She pulled back, confused. "What are you laughing about?"

"Jennie Lue…you are something else," he said with a smile. "You do realize I walked into Dayna G's that day on purpose, don't you? Maybe what happened to me was inevitable because I was in there so much. And not once did anybody ever put a rope around me and drag me through those doors. I walked in all by myself every time."

She nodded as she dried the last of the tears. "After I left, I asked George about you every now and then. He told me he saw you in those types of places on a regular basis." She laughed softly. "I think my brother was born for hanging around working girls and brothels, but I never thought you would end up the type."

"You know, my father told me that once, too," he said as he pulled his arm from around her shoulder. He stared into the distance and heaved a few deep breaths. "I didn't listen to him. At the time I thought, 'what would he know?' He had to be the most boring man on the face of the earth. But looking back on it now I realize he knew a hell of a lot more about life, and about being a man, than I ever could. My mother never said anything about it, but I know she didn't like it at all."

Jennie Lue nervously rubbed her hands together and held her breath as she asked hesitantly, "I hope you don't think I'm rude for asking, Tom, but what happened in Dayna G's? I've heard a couple of different versions of the story, but what really happened that day?"

"Wheew! Now, there's a question," he said, shaking his head. "What a day *that* was."

She squirmed against the tree and said meekly, "Never mind. I'm sorry. I don't have the right to ask you that question."

"Oh, don't worry about it," he said, and gave her a gentle pat on the thigh. He turned to look into her bright hazel eyes before he said with a chuckle, "I don't mind. Geez, it was a long time ago, and besides, about five years ago I learned a truly troublesome question isn't one somebody asks you; it's one you have to ask yourself." He tapped himself on the chest with his finger. "And the only way to find the answer is to dig deep down, right here."

"I think you're right about that," she said with a small sigh. "God knows I've had some really tough ones to answer about myself these past few months, but still, you don't have to tell me if you don't want to."

"No, it's okay," he said. "It's all in the past now."

She looked down into her lap. "It's just that, I worried about you for so long and...well...I've always wondered. So if you don't mind, I'd really like to know."

Tom raised his eyebrows. "You were worried about me?"

"Don't be silly," she said, returning his gaze. "Of course I worried. I didn't sleep a wink for I don't know how long after I heard about it."

"Really?" he asked, genuinely surprised. He stared into her troubled eyes. "Well, if you really want to know, I used to play a lot of cards. And I'd heard about this fella by the name of Jim Conner who came into town and he was talking it up, saying he was the best card player there ever was and nobody in this town could beat him. I've always been a pretty good player myself, so I let it be known I was highly offended by his loud mouth." He chuckled ruefully. "Seemed like he was insulting everybody around these parts. Acted like he thought we were all nothing but a bunch of idiots."

"Is that why you were there that night?" she asked.

"That was why I was there every night," he said. He shrugged. "Contrary to popular belief, I didn't go in there for the girls so much."

"That's not what my brother…" she started.

"Your brother…hah! He never did know a damned thing about me," he said, irritated at the thought of George Bell. "He doesn't know a damned thing about playing cards, either. Anytime I was running a little short of folding money I could always count on George to be sitting at one of those tables just begging to give his pile away to anyone who knew the difference between an ace and a deuce."

She shook her head and sighed. "That's not surprising. I swear, the only reason my brother got to be the mayor is because he's the biggest liar in Texas, always has been." She laughed. "He's told me for years that he's the best card player in town and he'd always take you and everybody else for their money."

"Hardly," he said with a chuckle. "We would all let him win a little every now and then just to keep him coming back, but I guarantee you, he lost twenty dollars to every one he ever made." Tom held up his index finger. "There's a really important rule when it comes to playing cards."

She smiled at his animation and asked, "And what rule is that?"

"Rule number one," he said with a grin, shaking his finger, "you never kill the chicken; you only pluck it. That way, you can pluck him again and again just as soon as his feathers grow back. Fortunately for me, George's feathers grew back pretty quick."

She laughed at length as she realized her brother fit Tom's description exactly before she finally caught her breath. "That sounds like George! It really does."

"Anyway," he continued, "I got into a game with that Jim Conner fellow and, even though we were the last two players at the table and it took me until almost sun up, I finally had the last of his money piled up in front of me."

"Is that why the fight got started?" she asked.

"Never was a fight," he said, shaking his head. "Heck…when we got up from the table, I didn't even know he was mad. From all appearances, he was a perfect gentleman, said it was a pleasure to play against somebody who truly understood the game. I even took him over to the bar and bought us both a shot of whiskey as a toast." He looked at Jennie Lue and added with a sigh, "Later on, I found out I took him for every last penny he had."

It was more of a question when she said, "I heard both of you were drinking all night."

"If you're asking me if I was drunk," he said, obviously uncomfortable with the memory, "the answer is yes, definitely." Tom dropped his head a bit and paused for a moment as if he was replaying the event in his mind before he looked back at Jennie Lue. "But next thing you know, I turned to walk out the door and I caught something out of the corner of my eye. I don't know if it was movement in the mirror behind the bar or from one of the lights behind me…or maybe it was my guardian angel looking out for me, I don't know. But when I turned, I saw Jim Conner and he was charging me…only a foot or so away, and he had that knife. I'll never forget; it had a polished handle made out of a deer antler." His hand was a fist as he raised it in the air and continued, "All I knew was he had that knife in his hand and it didn't take a genius to figure out he was going to plant it as far into my back as it would go."

"I heard rumors there was a knife," she said. "What happened to it?

He shook his head. "Don't know. I remember I spun around, grabbed his arm and tried to throw him to the floor, but he half caught his balance and flew headfirst into a corner of one of those heavy wooden tables they have in there. He went down in a heap and, even though it only took me a minute to realize he wasn't going to get up, when I looked around, the knife was gone."

"Who do you think took it?" she asked.

"Don't know that, either," he said. "There were only a few people in there at the time — Gil the bartender, a couple of the girls who had come downstairs to get a cup of coffee, and my brother."

"Buddy was there?" she asked.

"Yep. He had just walked in," Tom said, scratching his cheek. "I suppose he still starts every day off with a free cup of coffee from that place."

"And he didn't see what happened?" she asked.

"Nobody did," he said with a shrug. "At least, that's the official version, anyway. It all happened so fast. And everybody there said they were looking at something else because nobody had a clue the fellow was even mad in the first place." Tom took in a deep breath, then exhaled slowly. "I guess it was fairly easy for the judge to think I had it in for that man, seeing how my own loud mouth had been flapping for a couple of days before it happened. I suppose the bottom line is, there was no proof it was self-defense and there was no proof it wasn't, but there was a dead man on the floor, and somebody had to pay. In the end, I reckon I got what I deserved."

"I'm sorry, but I don't believe that, Tom. I don't believe it at all," she said, clearly upset. She sat quietly for a moment. "There's something I need to tell you," she said, determination in her voice, "something you should know."

"What's that?" he asked.

"The other night, my brother…" she started, "well, we both know that whatever comes out of his mouth is at best a skewed version of the truth, but he said Buddy wanted you to go to prison. He said your brother didn't help you because it would make the townsfolk realize he was all business, that by sending you to prison it would help his career or something." She looked up at Tom. "Could that be true? Can Buddy be that heartless…to his own brother?"

Tom sighed and played with a few blades of grass before he answered "I don't know. I've asked myself a thousand times why Buddy didn't do more to help but, for the life of me, I have no idea." He contemplated what they shared and turned to her. "Seems to me we both have brothers that are a little off center, like their staircases don't reach the top floor."

"I agree," she said. "I've never been able to figure mine out. He's always been harmless, mostly, but Buddy, on the other hand…well, I really think there's something wrong with him. Like he's just plain mean."

"I know. He's always had a little of that in him," he said, "but it seems to me he's gotten a lot worse since I got back."

"I hate to tell you this," she confided with a smile, "but your brother has been a jack ass for some time now…not just since you've been back."

Tom chuckled. "I suppose you're right, but I wish I knew how many times over the last five years I've thought about things, especially Buddy, and how they might have turned out different if I hadn't gone into Dayna G's that day."

"I don't think Buddy would have turned out different," she said with conviction.

"Maybe you're right" he said, and sighed.

They sat quietly. Jenny Lue knew she couldn't say anything that could add insight to Tom's thoughts about his brother, so she changed the subject. "Why did you start hanging around saloons in the first place?"

Tom laughed. "You sure ask a lot of questions," he said. He paused a bit. "Looking back now, I guess I didn't know what else to do. I was lost inside. After you left, I didn't care about much of anything or anybody anymore, including myself. Don't get me wrong, I'm not saying what happened to me is your fault 'cause it's not...not even close. It's just that, even though you and I never had the chance to really get to know each other, I always felt like...like when you moved to Austin, I lost something, something that was a part of me, something I wouldn't ever be able to find again."

He turned back to her, saw the caring look in her eyes and smiled. "After spending a lot of time thinking about it over the last five-and-a-half years, I want you to know, I've made a very important promise to myself."

"Do you mind if I ask what it is?" she asked.

This time it was Tom who gave up his deepest secret. "Well...it's two parts, really. First, I promised myself if I ever got out of prison alive, I would come home and live the rest of my days just trying to do the right things. I want to look back when I'm on my deathbed and be able to say I lived a good life, that I was a good man." He paused, contemplating his words. "And secondly, I swore that if I ever got lucky enough to find that girl again who held that missing part of me in her hands, I would damn sure do a lot more than just stand on some sidewalk with my hands in my pockets watching her ride away for good."

"I guess we've both made a mess of things then, haven't we?" she whispered.

"What do you mean?" he asked.

"Well, you made a mistake and went to prison," she said, "and I married myself *into* a prison. That's how I always thought of it, anyway."

Tom adjusted himself against the tree and took her hand in his. "You don't have to talk about it anymore. Besides, it's all in the past. It doesn't matter now."

"I suppose," she said. "But I guess what I'm trying to say is, I'm never going to make that kind of mistake again."

Tom's heart sank and a large knot formed in his stomach as he let go of her hand. He did his best to hide his emotions by looking into the distance. After a long moment he picked a small branch off the ground and flung it as far as he could. "I don't blame you. I probably wouldn't want to get tied down again, either, if I had gone through something like that."

She looked at him, puzzled, then playfully smacked him on the leg. "That's not what I meant, you fat-head," she said. She paused, as if what she needed to say was the most important thing in the world. "What I'm trying to say is that I'm never going to let anyone else decide what's best for me again. Do you know what I mean?"

Tom's spirits lifted as quickly as they had sunk. Relief was written on his face as he looked at Jennie Lue and said, "I think I know exactly what you mean."

"You know, it's interesting that you told me you've made a promise to yourself. Because I have, too," she said.

"You know I'm going to die if you don't tell me what it is, don't you?" he teased.

She clasped her hands together tightly and smiled nervously. "I promised myself from now on I would live my life on my own terms, and no one else's, not even my father's." She paused a moment before she added, "With Henry, I had a chance to listen to my heart and didn't, and I paid a big price. I've promised myself I'll never do that again."

Tom smiled. "Listen to your heart, huh?"

For a moment, she thought he was making fun of her so she dropped her hands in her lap and asked, "Yes. Why? Do you think that's stupid or something?"

"No, not at all. It's just that…" Tom paused a long moment, summoning his courage. "Do you mind if I ask what your heart is telling you now?"

Jennie Lue said nothing, but took off her white straw hat and set it on the ground. She reached over and did the same with his, then leaned in close and kissed him softly on the mouth. The kiss was brief and light, but the electricity Tom felt race though his heart at the instant her lips touched his was something he wouldn't have thought possible if it hadn't just happened.

He stared into her shining hazel eyes. "Wow," he said, "there must be a God. All my life, I've prayed that might happen."

"Really?" she asked.

"Only since I was old enough to know what a kiss was," he said with a smile. "I guess it's kind of funny, isn't it? How we're like two peas in a pod?"

"How do you mean?"

"Well," he said, "the way I see it, we've both just got out of our own kind of prisons, carrying promises to ourselves that aren't too far from being the exact same thing." He winked at her. "And I have a little advice for you, if you want to hear it."

"Okay," she said.

"My experience tells me," he said with a grin, putting a finger close to her chest, "that you should *keep* listening to your heart."

The moment that followed was brief, but their beaming smiles were all it took to let them each know there was nothing either wanted more than to be with each other constantly in the coming days.

She leaned in close and whispered, "I believe you're right." She kissed him again. This time, the kiss was much more passionate and lasted far longer than the first, lighting a burning fire in them both. She finally put a trembling hand on Tom's chest and gently pushed him away before softly kissing him once more. She leaned back against the tree and fanned her face while catching her breath. "Whew! I think…I think we need to stop."

Tom laughed and leaned back against the tree. "You're probably right about that."

"You're not mad, are you?" she asked.

He reached down, picked up his hat and returned it to his head before he said, "I'd have to be out of my mind to be mad about kissing the prettiest girl in the whole world."

Jennie Lue looked into his green eyes and smiled. "That was another nice thing to say." Her expression suddenly changed as she looked down and said softly, "Tom, I've been meaning to tell you…I'm terribly sorry about your mother."

"Me, too," he said, "and thank you." He looked off into the distance. "After everything that's happened, if I had just one wish, if I could only change one thing in my past, I would have been here to see her before she died."

"I'm sure she knows that. And I'm sure she's happy you're home now." Tom reluctantly nodded.

"Do you think she'd approve of me?" Jennie Lue asked.

Tom chuckled, picked up a small stone and tossed it into a patch of blue bonnets. "Oh, yeah."

"You really think so?' she asked.

"I'm absolutely sure she would," he replied. He shook his head and laughed softly. "But knowing her, the first thing she'd do, after being so thrilled to hear the news, would be to smack me on the side of the head and ask why it took so long for me to come to my senses."

Jennie Lue laughed. "Well, then, maybe we both need a good wallop. God knows it took me a while." She smiled at him before leaning over to rest her head on his shoulder. After a long moment of silence, she asked with deep concern in her voice, "Tom, what are you going to do about Buddy?"

Tom's thoughts were quickly pulled back to an awful reality. He had no answer to the troubles with his brother and sighed heavily. "My brother. I don't know what I'm going to do about him. I really don't have any idea. You know, right before she died, my mother wrote a letter for me to read after I got out of prison. My dad gave it to me as soon as we were on the train out of Huntsville."

"Really?" she said. "That must have been hard for you."

"Yep," he said sadly. "It was."

"Do you mind if I ask what she said?" she asked.

Tom shook his head, then turned to stare at the growing thunderstorm on the horizon. "I don't mind. She said she was happy I was coming home and all...and that I needed to look out for my dad. But she also asked me make peace with Buddy. Told me my father was upset with him for not helping out at the ranch, and she understood how I might hate my own brother after everything that happened, but she didn't want to leave this world worrying about whether or not her family could get along with each other. Made me promise I'd do everything in my power to let it all go and make amends with him."

Tom shook his head. "She said she prayed every night that, if I made things right with Buddy, maybe my dad could, too. But it sure doesn't look like it's going to work out that way."

"Is that why you haven't told your father yet?" she asked.

"Yeah," he said. "I was holding out that maybe Buddy didn't have anything to do with it. I wanted to go into town and talk to him first to make sure. I didn't want to tell my dad until after I looked into Buddy's eyes. Well, now I know. I'm certain Buddy blew up our own bridge...and he fired those shots, too."

She put her hand on his cheek. "I'm so sorry, Tom. I wish there was something I could do."

"Me, too," he said, kissing her hand and smiling at her. "But right now, the only thing I know to do is to tell my dad the truth about last night. In fact, we should get back to the house so I can get it over with. Outside of that, I don't have a clue."

He glanced to the north at the storm cloud growing bigger by the minute and moving directly for them.

Tom stood as if his bones ached, then bent down to take her hand. "I'd much rather stay here with you for the rest of the day," he said, "but that storm's coming, and we need to get those supplies back to the house. I guess we'd better get going."

Jennie Lue held his hand as she stood, then reached down to pick her hat off the ground and brush off the loose blades of grass before she put it back on. As they left the trunk of the great oak, she took one last long look around. "Thank you for showing me this, Tom. It's beautiful. Can you bring me out here again? Before Sunday?"

"How about tomorrow?" he said. "I have a lot of work to do with the bridge and all, but I could probably skip dinner, and maybe meet you out here around six o'clock?"

"That will be our second date in two days," she said with a smile.

"It's a good thing, too," he said, laughing.

"Why do you say that?" she asked.

"'Cause I don't think I could have waited that long to see you again," he said. They started walking back to the buggy.

"My, my," she said with a grin, "aren't you full of nice things to say today." Tom shrugged, a bit embarrassed. "Six o'clock it is then. Maybe we can talk about how great the acrobats were. I'll bring a picnic basket. How would you like that?"

"That would take care of my dilemma about skipping dinner," he said as they neared the buggy, "and I'd like that very much. What are you going to bring?"

"If I tell you now it won't be a surprise," she said, winking.

They climbed in the carriage and Tom took one last look around. "I'm really glad you like it out here. It means a lot to me."

"Thanks. It means a lot to me, too."

"It seems my calendar gets more jam-packed every time I see you," he said. His grin let it be known that he was more than pleased with their time together.

"Oohh," she pouted, "I don't mean to."

"Jennie Lue, you really are something else," he said. "I'm only kidding and, just to let you know, I don't have anything planned for Thursday, Friday or Saturday or all of next week or the week after, in case you were wondering."

She smiled a little as she answered, "I'll keep that in mind because my own schedule is wide open. But tell me, where do you want to meet tonight? I could be out front of the theater…say about seven-thirty?"

Tom turned to look at her as if he didn't understand. "Don't ask me to meet you out in front of the theater. I could never do that," he said. "I'm going to pick you up in front of your daddy's house, nice and proper." Jennie Lue's big, worried sigh let Tom know there was a problem. "Your daddy probably isn't going to like me showing up over there, is he?"

She took another deep breath "Probably not."

Tom took the reins, then hung his head. "Son of a gun. I'm sorry. I didn't think about that." He looked over at her. "It's okay. I'd rather pick you up nice and proper, but I'll meet you any old place at any old time. You just name the spot and I'll be there."

Jennie Lue pondered their situation, then turned to him, the sound of determination in her voice. "Can you be at the Double T tonight, say, about seven o'clock?"

"But what about your father?" he asked.

"He'll just have to get over it," she said with a casual shrug, but her tight-lipped expression gave way to a sly smile. "The sooner the better is what I say."

"I don't have a problem with that," he agreed. He wore a huge grin. "Jennie Lue, I like the way you think."

There would never need to be another word spoken between them about what Turner Bell or the rest of the people in Bell County thought about their relationship because, at that precise moment, the looks in their eyes said it all. For the first time, there were no doubts about their future together and both knew the promises they shared were as firmly entrenched as the roots of the big oak tree they had been sitting under. In the place of their doubts was a strong, unspoken feeling between them that nothing or no one was ever going to stand in their way again.

"Are you ready, Jennie Lue?" he asked, "really ready?"

She leaned over, gently put her hand on Tom's cheek, and whispered, "More than you know."

Tom smiled. He popped the reins and the buggy pulled away from the tree. Soon they were talking about their date set for later on that night and about their rendezvous at the big oak the following afternoon. Even though Jennie

Lue sat close to his side, making him feel like the luckiest man alive, Tom thought it ironic that a thunderstorm was heading straight for them because he couldn't shake the sinking feeling that dark days lay on the horizon. There was no rhyme or reason why Buddy would do something as cowardly as what he had done, but the worst part of all was imagining the look on his father's face when he told him the dreadful news.

Tom tried hard to listen to Jennie Lue's every word along the way as she talked about how exciting the acrobats were going to be and what she could do to make their date that evening a memorable one, but all the while his mind was on the words he must choose to make his father's shock as painless as possible.

Soon the ranch house came into view and he saw Church, Aya, Bear and Percy down at the creek, working hard as they gathered shredded lumber off the ground and loaded it into the work wagon.

"Those fellas need to hurry up and get back to the house before this storm hits," Tom said, looking again at the turbulent black clouds rolling across the sky. "I guess after the rain passes, we'll get back down there this afternoon and finish it up," he added. He brought the buggy to a stop in the front yard next to the hitching post where Jennie Lue's horse was tied. Tom hopped out quickly, made his way to the other side, took Jennie Lue's hand and helped her step down. She was looking at him with sympathy. "Unfortunately, what I need to do now is tell my dad."

"Tell me what?" came Jim's voice from the house as the front door opened.

Jennie Lue glanced up at Jim standing on the porch and said, "Hello, Mister Wallace. It's nice to see you again."

Jim put his hands on the rail and leaned in. "Why, Miss Jennie Lue! What a pleasant surprise. I hope you plan on staying for lunch."

Jennie Lue looked at Tom for a moment and then back to Jim. "I appreciate the kind offer, Mister Wallace, and I'd love to, but I'd better be going."

"You're more than welcome to stay," Tom said. "That storm's almost on us." He looked back into her eyes. "It'd probably be best if you stuck around here for a while. Besides, I'd really like you to."

"By all means," Jim said. "We have plenty of food. Miss Lawton is here, in case you don't want to hang around a one-legged old man and a bunch of dirty cowhands all by yourself."

She bit her lower lip nervously as she pondered the options, then shook her head. "No, thank you. I'm sure I can get back home before the rain starts if I go now. Thank you, anyway." She stood on her toes and gave Tom a quick kiss on the cheek before she whispered, "I'm sorry for what you have to do. But I can't wait for tonight."

"Me neither," he said softly before they both walked over to Pancho. Jennie Lue untied the reins from the hitching post and climbed into the saddle.

"I'll be there. Seven o'clock sharp," he said.

She looked down from the saddle and smiled. "I'll be waiting for you." She turned her attention to Jim. "Mister Wallace, can I take you up on your offer some other time?"

"You bet! Any time, as far as I'm concerned," he said. "Sorry it can't be today."

"Me, too," she said. She turned to Tom. "Good luck. I'll see you this evening."

Tom had both hands on his hips and a gleam in his eyes. "You have no idea how much I'm looking forward to it."

She turned her horse and put it into a gallop away from the house and the approaching thunderstorm, leaving Tom standing there to watch her until she was out of sight.

Jim had a smile on his face as Tom made his way over to the buggy, grabbed Miss Emma's satchel bag in one hand and the bag of supplies in the other, but his expression changed quickly as Tom walked toward the porch and neared the bottom of the stairs.

"I told you not to go into town again without wearing a sidearm," Jim said sternly, pointing at his son's hips.

Tom glanced down at his waist and up at his father. "Oh. Sorry about that. I guess I forgot with Miss Emma and Jennie Lue showing up this morning like they did. It won't happen again."

"See that it doesn't," Jim said. "And, while we're on the subject, I want you to get your gun out of that cedar chest in your room. Clean it up good and run some rounds through it this afternoon. It's been a while since you did any shooting and, after last night, I need you to be sharp. I've already pulled a few of the other guns and all the ammunition you boys will need." He looked skyward at the approaching thunderstorm. "Maybe after this rain passes you can round everybody up behind the barn and can get in some target practice."

"Sure thing," Tom said as he started up the porch stairs. "After all this time, it'll be interesting to see if I can still hit anything."

Jim shook his head in wonder, recalling events in the past. "Well, you were about the best I ever saw and, besides, once you know how, you don't forget it."

"Hmm," Tom said tiredly, "I don't know about that, but hopefully it won't take too long before I get the feel of it again."

"I guess you'll find out this afternoon, then, won't you?" Jim said.

"I guess so," Tom said, as he got to the top of the steps and looked around, not quite sure what to do with the bags he carried.

"How did your trip with Jennie Lue go?" his father asked, grinning.

Tom couldn't hide his elation or the smile that spread across his face. "Great! It was really nice. She asked me to go see that show tonight at the opera house, the one with all the acrobats."

"Really?" Jim said, raising an eyebrow. "That should be fun. I'm sure you'll have a nice time. Just make sure you keep a pistol on your hip, you hear? I don't want to worry about you."

"I will," Tom promised, setting the supplies by the front door and pulling up a chair.

Jim pointed at the bag. "Did you get everything?"

Tom took his seat, but his smile had been replaced by a troubled look, "Oh, yeah. Everything and then some is in those two bags, but I need to talk to you, Dad. It's important."

"Uh-oh," Jim said with a playful smile, "you and Jennie Lue planning on getting married already?"

Tom shook his head and said with a sigh, "Nope. Not even close."

Jim looked at his son and immediately knew that whatever the conversation was going to be about was serious, so he looked around at the porch and said in an entirely new tone, "Okay. You want to talk out here?"

"Sure," Tom said, slumping into the backrest of his chair.

Jim started for the front door. "Let me get a fresh cup of coffee and I'll be right back. You want one?"

"No, thanks. I'll take a glass of water, though, if you're going," Tom said.

His father went inside and Tom sat looking over the porch railing and down to the creek watching his friends finish up their work. A huge knot formed in his stomach that made him anxious to get the bad news about his brother off his chest. The few minutes Jim was gone seemed like hours, leaving Tom's mind to sift through a multitude of thoughts about how his life was going to play out and how everything was turning out so much differently than what he expected just a short time ago.

He wondered how in the world he could be so excited about his life, to look forward to so much after finally coming home and having a chance to be with Jennie Lue after all these years. He was elated. At the same time, he was filled with dread; his gut instincts told him something bad was lurking right around the corner. Just six short months earlier, he didn't know if he would live long enough to get home alive, much less get the chance to kiss Jennie Lue Sloan beneath the big oak but, if someone had told him his own brother would blow up Ruby's bridge and take shots at him and his father, he would have said that was just as impossible. It seemed as if the Lord and the devil were competing for his soul. On one hand, he believed Jennie Lue Sloan was truly an angel sent from heaven and, on the other, it felt like whatever his brother was up to could only be something dreamed up by the devil himself.

As the first smell of rain came rolling across the fields, Tom knew the time was at hand to say what he needed to say. He could hear his father's footsteps approaching but, as the wind violently shook the tops of the trees and the first loud crack of lightning split the now-darkened sky, the last thought he had before Jim walked onto the porch with a cup of coffee in one hand and a glass of water in the other was that he couldn't wait for the evening ahead. Little did he know, though, that the next time he saw Jennie Lue Sloan, events in his life would once again take an unexpected turn and their night on the town together would turn out far worse than either could have ever imagined.

CHAPTER 17

Tin Cans and Miss Emma

"Is there anything in particular you like about me?" the pretty young brunette seductively asked as she sat down in Buddy's lap and ran her fingertips over the exposed upper portion of her ample breasts. She leaned in close and whispered in his ear, "What I mean is, why would a real man like you be interested in spending any time with someone like little ol' me?"

Buddy took his time to take in the perfumed smell of the girl in his lap and looked her over from her pretty little head to her toes before he flagged down a waiter and said with a laugh, "I can think of two good reasons right off."

The brunette put her arm around his neck and playfully smacked him on the chest as she squirmed in his lap. "You are soooo baaad," she said, laughing.

"Maybe I am, and maybe I'm not. Maybe I'm somewhere in between," Buddy said with a sly grin as he reached down and squeezed her behind. He noticed the way she had applied just the right touch of make-up to accentuate the delicate lines of her face. "But, if you're interested in finding out, you could start by having a few glasses of champagne with me and we'll see what comes up."

"Stop it," said the girl with a laugh as she squirmed again. "I could tell as soon as I saw you that you were my type."

"And what type is that?" Buddy asked as he squeezed her butt again.

She leaned in close. "Well, you look like you're the kind of man who appreciates the finer things in life."

"What you mean is, I'm the kind of man that has money, ain't that right?" Buddy swallowed the last of his champagne.

"Is that so bad?" asked the girl with child-like innocence. She twiddled the hair on the back of Buddy's head and rubbed his inner thigh as she continued, "A girl like me can only dream of a handsome, rugged man like you taking care of her." She paused a moment as she gazed at him with enchantment in her eyes. "…and of the ways a girl like me could take care of a man like you."

Buddy stared at her with a confident grin. "And how would you go about that?"

"Well," said the brunette as she leaned over to whisper in his ear, "we could take a bottle of champagne upstairs and I could show you." She reached out and softly turned Buddy's face toward hers and gazed into his eyes. "Or is there something else you'd rather be doing right now?"

Buddy chuckled a bit and said, "Well, now, there is one other thing I'd rather do than to go upstairs with you."

The girl sat up straight on his lap as if she was offended. "And what would that be?" she asked, pouting.

Buddy pointed over at the bar. "That pretty blonde thing you were sitting with earlier. I was thinking about how nice it would be if we took her upstairs, too."

The brunette glanced at the bar, then back at Buddy. "What's the matter? You don't like me?"

Buddy winked at her. "Honey, I didn't say that. 'Course I like you. I just think I'd like you a whole lot better if you brought your friend along." He squeezed her butt again and added, "What do you think about that?"

"I might be more than you can handle," she whispered. "How do you know you'll need another girl?"

Buddy shrugged. "I don't know. But it sure would be fun to find out, wouldn't it?"

The brunette bit her lip as she looked back and forth from Buddy to the attractive blonde at the bar. A sly smile crept across her face. "I could probably arrange it. But we'll need more than one bottle of champagne and the price will be double," she said.

"I'm way ahead of you," Buddy said. He reached into his coat pocket and pulled out a wad of crisp, brand-new bills. He peeled off two and handed them to her. "That ought to be enough to get this shindig started, don't you think?"

The pretty brunette's smile grew as she reached out, took the money and put it in her brassiere with a giggle. "I knew you were my type. What room are you in?" she asked.

"Three-eleven," Buddy said, putting the rest of the wad back in his pocket. "How long will it take for the both of you to get up there?"

"Five minutes. Is that all right?"

"Perfect," Buddy said. He watched as she stood from his lap, and he gave her a playful slap on the rear.

She put a hand on her hip and sashayed through the lavish hotel lobby over to the bar where she started talking to the blonde girl, who looked back at Buddy with a seductive smile.

Buddy was imagining this evening was going to be one he wouldn't forget for quite some time, but his daydream was suddenly brought to an abrupt end by the sound of the bell above his office door.

He opened his eyes and sat up straight in his chair, his boots coming off his desk. He was about to yell a few profanities at whoever it was that just ruined the best dream he'd had in a while, but the words got stuck in his throat when he saw his father in a yellow rain slicker heading straight for him.

"What the hell is going on, Buddy?" Jim demanded as he stopped in front of the desk.

Even though Buddy was still a bit groggy after being abruptly dragged out of his dream, the last thing he expected was his father standing in front of him. However, he was well accustomed to the practice of putting on a poker face. No one would have guessed he was even the least bit flustered as he put his hands behind his head, leaned back in his chair again, groaned a couple of times and took a moment to stretch before he answered sleepily. "I'm not sure what you mean. What are you talking about?"

"You know what I'm talking about," Jim said. He put his hands on the desk and leaned over, his jaw clenched with anger. "I'm talking about last night! I'm only going to ask you once more. What happened at the creek?"

"Am I missing something?" Buddy asked as he slowly sat up. He played with his red mustache, giving the impression of utter confusion. "You were there, Dad. You know what happened. Why are you coming in here asking me?"

Jim could barely control his anger. "Because I just had a little chat with Tom, Bear and Aya. First thing this morning, those boys went down to the creek and checked out the tracks you and Curry left behind last night." He took a deep breath and exhaled slowly, but anger was still seething in his voice. "Aya would bet his life it was you who blew up the bridge and did all the shooting. I want to know right now why he's wrong. I can't imagine how you could possibly do such a thing, but I'm not leaving until I find out the truth!"

Buddy stood abruptly, acting as though he couldn't believe his ears. "Aya said *what*?" he said as innocently as he could.

Droplets of water clinging to the sleeve of Jim's slicker splattered all over Buddy's desk when he slammed his hand down, yelling, "Don't play stupid, Buddy! You hear me? Tom already told me about his run-in with you this morning!"

"Yeah...I saw Tom...and Jennie Lue," Buddy said, "so what?"

Jim stared at his son, carefully looking for the slightest bit of uncertainty in his eyes, but finding none, he breathed deeply and asked, "Why was Curry Hampton's horse following your wagon? You told me you rode up on him by chance, after he was already there."

Buddy leaned back, chuckled once and shook his head before he said apologetically, "I'm sorry. I guess I should have told you the truth last night."

The answer wasn't what Jim expected, which caused him to drop his guard and ask in a calmer tone, "And what would that be?"

Buddy pulled a toothpick out of the pocket of his crisp white shirt and put it in his mouth. "Look, Dad, I'm sorry. I guess I wasn't thinking. I just didn't think it would matter. I didn't want you to know I brought Curry, so I told you a white lie last night. The truth is, I came up on Curry on the road not far from the house. He was mumbling something about going to see you, to set things right." Buddy knew his father was trying to spot even the smallest hole in his story, so he looked him dead in the eyes. "But he could hardly even stay in the saddle, so I told him it'd be best if I took him the rest of the way." Buddy sighed heavily. "I tied his horse behind the wagon, he climbed in the back and next thing I knew, he was passed out cold."

The relaxed response from Buddy caught Jim off balance so he straightened up. He eyed his son with mistrust. "If Curry was out cold, why did you stop outside the gate? Why didn't you just come on through and up to the house?" he asked.

"Hmm," uttered Buddy as he pulled the toothpick from his mouth, "now I wish I hadn't done it. But the simple truth is, I had to stop and take a leak." He opened his hands innocently. "I went into the bushes to relieve myself and the next thing I knew, I heard Curry get up out of the wagon and stumble around. So after I put my pecker back in my pants, I turned around and saw him trying to get back on his horse, but he was so drunk he couldn't get in the saddle. I was finally able to grab the drunk son of a bitch and prop him up against the wagon, but when I did, his horse got loose and went off to the side of the road to chew on some of those damned flowers." Buddy shook his head regretfully. "I went to get the stupid animal, and that was the biggest mistake I made in all of this because, shortly after that, all hell broke loose."

"You didn't see him with dynamite in his hands?" Jim asked. "How could you miss that little detail?"

"I don't know," Buddy said quietly, hanging his head. "It was dark. I guess it was in his saddle bag. After it was all over, I knew he wasn't trying to get on his horse at all. He was just trying to get to those sticks." He paused a bit before he looked up at his father. "Anyway, he must have seen me coming out of the bushes and tossed it behind the sideboard of the wagon where I couldn't see it. After I went off to fetch that stupid animal of his, he must a grabbed it and lit out on foot for the bridge. And, well…you know the rest."

"Are you saying it was your prints where the horse was tied?" Jim asked. "Aya said it looked like Curry was the one stumbling around over there."

"We can go over there right now if you want and I'll show you those prints match my boots exactly," Buddy said defiantly.

Jim walked over to the window and watched the light rain dancing on the puddles in the muddy streets outside. He took a deep breath and exhaled sharply, as though trying to expel his frustration, then he turned back to Buddy. "We'd have done that by now if it hadn't rained."

Buddy shook his head and looked at his father. "Well, the rain's not my fault, too, is it?" Sensing he might have gone a bit too far, he added, "I can't help that now, can I?"

"No. You can't," Jim said. He looked for any sign of wavering in Buddy's eyes; he was still a long way from convinced. "Why were you in the wagon in the first place? How come you weren't on that fancy horse of yours?"

"He'd thrown a shoe!" Buddy exclaimed, as if he couldn't understand why his father hadn't thought of it before.

Jim eyed Buddy for what seemed like an eternity. "So you made up all that other stuff just because you didn't want me to think you were responsible for Curry being there?"

Buddy nodded. "I'm sorry, Dad. I should have told you the truth."

"Damn right you should have," Jim said. "Now you got everybody at the ranch, including your brother, thinking you're responsible for what happened to Chas. And I got to tell you, none of them are too happy right now."

Buddy stood up. "I'm sorry, Dad. I can get out there right now and straighten this all out," he said.

Jim rubbed his chin for a moment and shook his head. With uncertainty in his voice he said, "No, no. It's best if I explain it to them. But you need to stay clear of the Four C's for a few days. .give everybody a chance to cool down."

Buddy walked around to the front of his desk. "You sure?" he asked.

"Yeah," Jim said, nodding. "I'm sure."

Jim moved to the door and Buddy followed. "How is Chas? He gonna be all right?" Buddy asked.

"Too soon to tell," Jim said. He pulled open the door and they both walked out onto the sidewalk. Jim glanced up and down the street, then turned to his son. "Buddy…I'm sorry I barged in on you like this, but so help me, don't you ever lie to me again. You hear?"

Buddy dropped his head slightly and nodded. "I'm sorry. Really, I am." He reached down deep to summon all the sincerity he could muster and stared at his father. "I just wasn't thinking," he said.

"All right, then," Jim said. He stepped down into the muddy street and untied his horse from the hitching post, making sure he had his foot securely in the stirrup before he grabbed the saddle horn and climbed on. As he pulled on the reins and backed his horse away from the sidewalk, he looked down at his son. "I'll see you in a couple days," he said.

"Sure thing," Buddy said, raising his hand in good-bye. He watched his father turn his horse. "Where you headed to now?" he called out.

"Got a few errands to run," Jim said loudly, putting his horse into a trot.

As he urged his horse down the muddy street, Jim couldn't put his finger on why the conversation didn't sit so well with him. For all appearances, Buddy was telling the truth and he desperately wanted to believe him. He prided himself on being able to spot the difference between an honest man and a liar, but there was something about Buddy's too-quick answers that seemed a trifle odd. The issue about the footprints bothered Jim as well, because Aya hadn't made a mistake like that in all the time he had known him. Even though Jim returned Buddy's wave as he went down the street, he thought it best to head over to the livery and have a talk with the blacksmith.

Maybe he'd know something about the shoe that was supposed to have come off Buddy's palomino.

Buddy heaved a sigh of relief and smiled as his father rode away. It wasn't every day someone could pass off a story like that to Jim Wallace and get away with it. Although Buddy's expressions were sincere as he waved at his father from the sidewalk, he wasn't thinking about anything except how smart he was to have covered every little detail of his story after he had the good luck to run into his brother and Jennie Lue Sloan earlier in the day. He felt his luck was changing and everything could now fall back into place because, if he hadn't met them on the road, he never would have known they were on to him and he wouldn't have had enough time to come up with a story that explained everything away from the night before.

He laughed as he walked back into his office and closed the door behind him. Not only had he just spun his best lie ever, but he knew where his father was now headed. He had that part covered, too. The fellow who owned the livery was a man by the name of Milo Hollman, and he just happened to owe Buddy a good deal of money from a card game and was eager for that obligation to be off his back. Buddy had paid him a visit, and Milo didn't hesitate a second when told all debts would be forgiven if he were to show a twisted horseshoe to Jim Wallace and claim it came off the right front hoof of Buddy's prized palomino. The liveryman repeated the instructed story over and over until Buddy was more than convinced his father would swallow the minor detail hook, line and sinker.

The loud crack of gunpowder as it exploded and the kick of the pistol in his hands were strange sensations for Tom, even though he had been shooting for so long he couldn't remember the exact age at which he started.

Standing behind the barn with the rest of the hands while shooting target practice brought back the memory of being six or seven years old, and finally talking his father into letting him fire one round out of a small, pearl-handled derringer his mother kept in her purse whenever she went to town. He could still recall turning around to see the amazed look on his father's face after the small medicine bottle ten feet away exploded into a thousand pieces. It didn't take long to convince his dad to get the lessons started after he fired three more shots and shattered every other bottle he aimed for. Tom would never forget how proud his father was of him that day.

Through the following years, Tom took every word of advice his father offered about firearms and the respect they deserved with utmost seriousness. His father taught him well. There were many instances before Tom went to prison where men showed up wanting to pick a fight because, no matter how hard he tried to keep the word from spreading about his talent, it didn't work. Tom never got sucked into gun play or flaunted his skill with a pistol, but he won the blue ribbon at the county fair every year and every other shooting contest around the county, making it hard to keep his reputation from spreading.

Today, taking his first target practice in almost six years, it was a different story. "Damn!" he said as he looked at the gun in his hand as though something was wrong with it. He glanced back at the rest of the hands standing behind him. "How in the world could I have missed that?" he said.

"'Cause you ain't no good at this," Bear said, laughing. "Hell, even I could hit *that*."

"Yep," Church said, shaking his head, "It's a shame, too. I can remember the time when you used to be halfway decent."

"Oh, yeah?" Tom said, dropping the pistol to his side and pointing at the target. "Let me see what you boys can do. Go ahead. Show me what you got."

"All right, then. Step aside," Bear said. He moved up to the makeshift firing line and took his stance, then glanced behind him at Percy and Aya. "Watch and learn," he said.

He adjusted his glasses and took a long moment to stare at a row of tin cans sitting on top of a few bales of hay ten yards away, then pulled out his pistol and fired, making one of the cans violently jump into the air before it spun back to the ground with a loud clunk. He turned back to the others, grinning. "How'd ya like that?" he asked everyone as he holstered his gun, obviously proud.

"Not bad," Church said in his gravelly voice as he stepped up to take his turn. "I woulda never thought you were that quick but, I have to tell ya, I've seen little old ladies draw faster than that."

"Little old ladies? Ya think so, do ya?" Bear looked insulted. "Tell ya what, let's back up another five paces. Everybody gets six shots at six cans, and we'll just see who knows what they're doin'. How 'bout that?"

"What's the bet?' Percy asked. He cracked his knuckles, intrigued by the new wager.

"As long as it isn't too much, I'm in," Tom said, holstering his gun. "But you fellas ought to take it easy on me. I don't have much money; I ain't got paid in over five years." His friends all laughed.

"Tell ya what we'll do," Bear said, as the laughter died, "the guy who hits the most cans the quickest gets a beer, paid for by everybody else." He looked around and nodded. "What do ya say?"

"I'm gettin' thirsty just thinkin' 'bout it," Church said with a chuckle.

"I'm in," Percy said. He pulled his pistol from his holster and spun the cylinder, making sure it was fully loaded.

Bear turned to Aya. "How 'bout you? Holitcha ittamayya...isna?"

Aya crossed his arms on his chest and asked, "Sahmoosi?"

"Biya," Bear answered, pointing to the rest of the hands.

Aya unbuttoned his vest, pulled the left side open and patted the grip of the small revolver he always kept in an inside pocket. Tom was well aware it was the same gun Aya used to kill the last man in the front yard those many years ago.

Aya rocked back on his heels and shook his head as he buttoned his vest. "Ankobi...hollochi," he said.

"Suit yourself then," Bear said. He looked around at the rest of the men. "Aya don't drink no more, and he don't appear to like putting rounds through that peashooter underneath his waistcoat if he don't have to, so he's gonna sit this one out."

Tom looked at Aya and asked, "You sure?"

A simple nod from his friend was all the answer Tom needed before he looked at the rest of the men and said, "Well, beer it is, then." He watched his friends make sure the chambers in their guns were full of live rounds as he asked, "Who's first?"

"I'll go," Church said eagerly. He spun the cylinder of his pistol and walked over to a spot five paces behind the previous one. He put the pistol back in his holster, rocked his head from side to side as he tried to pop his neck, then rapidly opened and closed his right hand before he took a stance and drew. The six shots he fired were in rapid succession and, when his turn was over, four tin cans lay on the ground. He looked at Bear and Tom and said, with more than a little sarcasm in his raspy voice, "You ladies want to quit now? I'll understand if ya do."

"Not bad," Percy said, nodding, "'Course, that'll get ya last place at the county fair."

Bear walked to the spot where Church had just fired from and said, "Speakin' of ladies, I do believe my momma could draw faster than that." He waited until Church set all the cans back up on the bales of hay before he added, laughing, "That was pretty good shootin' for a blind man."

"What's that supposed to mean?" Church asked as he took a place next to Tom.

"Well," Bear said, "I figure four outta six is what a blind man could do from this close."

"Really? Ya think so?" Church said, chuckling. He pointed at the cans then crossed his arms. "Well, come on and show me how it's done then, mister eagle-eye...or is it mister four-eyes?"

"Now don't go makin' fun of my glasses," Bear said as he cracked his knuckles. "Ya ought to watch your words, 'cause after I get finished here you're probably gonna want to buy 'em off me." There was a groan from Tom and Church before Bear took his stance and drew. His six shots were fired just as quickly as his friend's, and when the smoke cleared, there were five cans on the ground.

"Looks like we might have a winner," Church said as he walked over to retrieve the cans and put them back up.

"Not yet, we don't," Percy said as he stepped up to take his turn. "At least, not until I get finished shootin', anyway."

As soon as Church finished setting the cans back up and was out of the way, Percy drew and fired all six rounds. Once again there was one tin can still sitting on top of a bale of hay. "Son of a gun!" Percy said, putting his gun back in his holster. "I can't believe I missed that last one."

"I can," Bear said, "I guess the two of us will have to keep going." He held his gun in the air with one hand and let the spent cartridges fall out. "Sorry ya ain't no good at this, Church. But me and Percy here'll go ahead and settle this up now." Bear pushed his old worn-out hat down to fit more snug and looked at Percy. "Or should we let Tom here waste our time and his ammunition first?"

Percy was chuckling at the comment as he walked back from the bales of hay and stood next to Bear. "I suppose we ought to let him shoot, seein' as how his daddy's our new boss and all," he said.

"Oh, yeah, I guess you're right," Bear said with a shrug as he reloaded his gun. "I didn't think of that."

Church gave Bear a nudge with his elbow and nodded his head. "That's why you're not the brains of this outfit."

Tom had taken his stance and was trying to focus on the targets when he turned to his friends. "Will you guys shut up? I'm trying to concentrate here. Hell, I thought we were having a shooting contest…not a bull-shitting contest."

Bear had his gun back in his holster and was leaning on his heels. "I'm confident I could win either one," he said with a straight face.

Tom chuckled as he turned to face the targets again. "I'm sure you could win the bull-shitting contest hands down but, right now, I'm going to see if I can beat the three of you out of a cold beer."

He tried to focus on the cans but was having a hard time. His mind had been on other matters ever since he told his father about Buddy out on the front porch earlier. The fact that the storm came in across the fields at the exact moment he sat down to talk to his dad was not lost on him, and added to the dreadful thoughts running through his mind ever since. To make things worse, Aya, Bear, Church and Percy had all gotten out of the weather and back up to the house before Tom had a chance to finish telling his father what he knew about the night before. The awful conversation was prolonged considerably because everyone had a chance to add their own two cents, and none of it was good.

Jim listened intently and never once gave an indication he either believed the story or not, but he asked a lot of questions before walking into the house without a word after everyone said their piece. All the hands stayed on the porch, assuming Jim was inside contemplating the situation, but they soon knew the only reason he went inside was to get his rain slicker, then leave through the back door to the barn. He took everyone by surprise when he raced by the side of the house on his horse. It was painfully clear to all he was hell-bent on a mission to find out exactly what Buddy was up to. The rain was coming down sideways and flashes of lightning were far too close and frequent, but the skies of Texas never had and never would produce a thunderstorm big enough to stop Jim Wallace from the conversation he was about to have with his son.

The storm blew through just as quickly as it arrived and, even though the sweet smell of fresh rain hung in the air and the warm rays of the sun were now shining down everywhere, thoughts of his brother sent a chill through Tom as he looked at the cans lined up neatly on the bales of hay. He shook his head trying to clear his mind, then locked the fingers of both hands together and stretched them out over his head as he took a deep breath.

"Geez…sometime today would be nice," Bear laughed.

"Have we got time to take a nap?" Church asked as he lit up a smoke.

"Ya'll give him a break," Percy said. "Let him take his time. He ain't gonna be in this much longer."

Tom turned to his friends, his arms outstretched. "You guys just give me a minute. It's been a while, you know," he said.

"Ya already had a darned minute," Bear said. "I just hope ya don't need a whole day. Your daddy told me you were pretty fast, but I tell ya, I don't know where he got that from."

"Okay, okay…I'm going." Tom turned to face the targets. He stood still for what seemed like less than a second, then in an instant, all six rounds were spent from his gun and all six tin cans tumbled wildly through the air. Tom stood frozen as all the cans came to rest, then spun the emptied Colt on his trigger finger sharply and slapped it back into his holster. Turning to face his astonished friends he said apologetically, "I reckon you fellas owe me a beer."

"Damnnnnn!" Church said, open-jawed.

"That was mighty impressive," Percy said, shaking his head.

Bear pointed at Aya as if he was at fault. "You knew he was gonna do that, didn't ya?" Aya got the gist of what Bear was saying and answered his question with a wink and a rare grin. Bear turned to Tom. "I thought ya said ya ain't had no practice."

"I haven't. Not for almost six years, anyway," Tom said. He stared at the cans on the ground as if he couldn't believe it himself, then shrugged. "I'm just as surprised as you fellas are. I don't know what happened."

"I'll tell ya what happened," Bear said, "ya beat me, Percy and ol' Church here out of a beer. Man, oh, man; I didn't see that comin'."

"Me, neither," Church said, as he walked to Tom and gave him a clap on the shoulder. "Looks like you ain't lost nothin since ya been gone. That's about as fast as I ever seen."

"I was lucky, that's all," Tom said. "Blind squirrels find acorns, too."

"Weren't nothin' blind about that," Percy said with a chuckle.

"You fellas want to go one more?" Tom asked.

"Hell, no," Church said. "I seen ya shoot like that before. 'Course, I didn't know you'd be that good now." Church turned to Bear. "And don't let him talk ya into it, either. You'll owe him your whole paycheck 'fore it's over."

"Whooooh! I can see why," Bear said with admiration. He reached out to shake Tom's hand. "I know when I'm outclassed! When can I buy ya that beer?"

"How 'bout tonight?" Church asked. "Bear and I are goin' into town this evening. We got plans to meet up with some pretty girls over at Dayna G's, but ya can come along if ya want."

Tom looked at Bear and smiled. "You're going to see that little girl... what's her name?"

"Jessie," Bear said proudly. "I must a worked my magic on her pretty good the other day."

"Word is, she wants to see him real bad," Percy said, as if he couldn't understand it.

Bear scratched the side of his face as he said, "Yeah. And it probably won't take long 'fore she quits me, neither, but it'll be fun while it lasts."

"You need to be careful," warned Tom, "Jessie is Buddy's girl, isn't she?"

"Not from what I hear," Bear answered. "Besides, I got it on good authority he always plays poker on Tuesday evenin' 'til midnight, and I'll be long gone before he gets outta his game. I can sneak in and out the back of Dayna G's, and the only people that will ever know I was there will be that pretty little gal I'm goin' to see, and Church, here."

"You sure about that?" Tom asked.

"Yep, I'm sure" Bear said. "Your brother will never know. So, ya wanna go?"

"Nah," Tom said, shaking his head. "You guys go on. I have my own plans."

"Uh-huh," Bear said with a grin, "I bet you're gonna see that pretty little girl you was with earlier today, ain't ya?" Tom's smile was all the answer Bear needed. "Well, well...good for you. 'Course any ol' idiot could tell the two of ya ought to be together."

Tom tried to downplay the subject. "We're just going to go see a show, that's all. And that means the two of you don't have to buy me that beer today."

"I'm good with that," Church said.

"Me, too," Percy said. "I'd rather owe ya than pay ya any old day."

"You'll have your chance to even up soon enough," Tom said, grinning. "It just won't be tonight, that's all." He pointed to what remained of the two boxes of cartridges. "What do you say we run through the rest of these shells and then head on up to the house? We ought to check in with Miss Emma to see how Chas is doing."

Bear was already walking back to reset the cans. "Fine by me," he said. "If we're in a hurry to fire off all these shells, we ought to let you shoot 'em, Tom. The way you handle that gun of yours, we could be up at the house in a matter of minutes."

Tom smiled at the compliment and felt good about the fact that, after all this time, he was still good with a pistol. As he took his turns at the tin cans, it occurred to him that, even though he was a lot skinnier now than he was six years ago, it probably wouldn't take too long to become the crack shot he once was because of all the work he did with sledge hammers, hoes and picks while he was in prison. He might not have accomplished anything else in all that time, but he did spend every ounce of energy he had in his arms and hands on a daily basis and could tell he might turn out to be even faster with a pistol than he was before if he just put in a little practice. The gun in his hand felt good and his quickness was far better than he expected, but try as he might, he didn't hit more than four cans when he attempted to duplicate his previous beer-winning, quick-draw accuracy.

After the last shot was fired, and the good-natured ribbing started to die down, Tom made sure the spent cartridges were picked up off the ground, knowing his father would want every shell accounted for and would more than likely have them all reloaded before the end of the day. Years ago, he didn't understand why those seemingly worthless, empty brass casings could be so important, but Tom now understood his father was only being loyal to a very important truth. The small armory hidden beneath his bedroom floor was an exhibit to the fact that, although it was possible for a person to have too little ready ammunition, he could never have too much. The idea of being well armed brought Tom's thoughts back to the events of last night, and before the men even rounded the barn on their way up to the house, he was lost in thought trying to figure out how in the world he and his father could settle things with Buddy — and why they had to in the first place.

"Hey, Tom, ya all of a sudden come up deaf now?" Church asked, playfully nudging his friend on the shoulder.

"Sorry," Tom said as he turned and looked at the cowboy, knowing he must have missed a joke or two aimed at him. He shrugged. "I guess I didn't hear you. But I'm assuming it had something to do with you fellas being upset over owing me a beer. Am I right?"

"Damn straight you're right," Bear joked. "I feel like I just got took. I fell for it, too. Hell, the last time I got took that bad was when I lost all my clothes in a game of strip poker with a little old lady back in Huntsville."

"Bear," Tom said slowly, as if he didn't understand, "correct me if I'm wrong but, if you were playing strip poker with a lady, weren't you *trying* to lose your clothes? Or get her to lose hers?"

Bear hung his head and snickered before he looked up. "Well…sorta. But that ain't how I got took."

Church took a deep puff of his newly lit cigarette and said hoarsely, "I'm dyin' to hear this one."

"I'm afraid to ask, but I know somebody will," Percy said, as he sidestepped a pile of manure. "How exactly did you get took? She steal your money or something?"

"Oh, no. It was way worse than that," Bear answered.

"Worse than stealin' your money?" Church asked.

"A lot worse," Bear said. "Ya see…first off, I was a little drunk at the time."

"Ya don't say?" Percy said sarcastically.

"Will ya let me tell the story?" Bear said. "Like I was sayin', I'd been drinking a bit and wound up at this old woman's house and we started playing cards for our clothes. Naturally, I lost every chance I got and, to make a long story short, we wound up in the hay as soon as I got naked."

"So far, it doesn't sound like you were taken at all," Tom said. "Sounds to me like you had it planned all along."

"I'm getting to that," Bear said, waving his hand. "The problem was, well, there was two problems, really. The first bein' that woman was butt ugly, and the second was she snored like a grizzly bear."

All the men were laughing when Tom asked, "But I still don't see how you got took. You knew she was ugly going into the deal and all you had to do was leave when she fell asleep, right?"

Bear pointed his finger at Tom and nodded. "Now you're gettin' somewhere. Ya see, I didn't find out 'til after it was too late that she hid my clothes…all of 'em! That's how I got took. I guess she wanted to make sure I stayed 'til mornin', but I couldn't stand it! With all that snoring goin' on, I had to leave. As God is my witness, that woman had them window panes rattlin' in their frames, I swear she did."

"So what'd ya do?" Church asked, still snickering.

"I left, plain and simple," Bear said. "I couldn't get away from all that snorin' in that little old house, and did I mention she was butt ugly?" He shuddered at the thought. "I didn't want to wake up next to that." He snapped his fingers. "So I lit out. Ran all the way back to the restaurant naked as a jaybird. Used alleyways as best I could, but I didn't have a stitch of clothes on the whole way there." Bear chuckled and shivered. "Woo! It was damn cold that night, too."

There was laughter all around as Percy asked, "I bet ya scared the dickens outta anybody unlucky enough to be awake at that hour, didn't ya?"

Bear answered with mock seriousness, "Well, everythin' came out all right 'cause one of them old ladies in town who loved to gossip caught sight of me 'in all my glory' and most every widow in town suddenly wanted to play cards with me." Bear chuckled, obviously proud of himself, and added with a wink, "I must've lost a wagon's load worth a clothes over the next two or three months."

Laughter and loud groans came from the group as they neared the back of the house, but all the friendly banter stopped when Miss Emma stuck her head out the back door and pleaded, "Tom! I need you and Mister Percy in here, right now." Every man was struck by the fear and sadness in her eyes and the quiver in her voice. "He's taken a turn for the worse."

As Tom raced into his brother's old room, he was caught off balance by how different Chas looked now than he had the night before. Even though it was obvious he was loaded up with morphine, unaware of anything around him, there was no doubt the young man was in serious trouble. Every few seconds, an unintelligible word or moan escaped his lips and his skin was more ashen than Tom would have thought possible. At first glance, the water on Chas's face seemed as if it might have come from the wet towel Miss Emma was using as she tried to cool him down, but it didn't take long to realize it wasn't water at all. He was sweating profusely, his body temperature high enough to drench his bedding. Tom watched as Percy knelt at the side of the bed and pressed the back of his hand against the swollen, bandaged shoulder of his injured friend.

Tom couldn't help but notice the work Miss Emma had done to his brother's old room since she arrived earlier that morning. Up until the night before, the last person to be in there was his mother, and no one would have called it dirty or unkempt. But the dusty, stale smell that creeps into every nook and cranny of a room no longer in use was replaced by the unmistakable odor of rubbing alcohol. Everything appeared to be in its place, but Tom was certain Miss Emma had wiped clean or scrubbed every square inch because there was not a trace of dirt or dust anywhere.

Miss Emma had made no bones about the fact that she was there to clean things up, but he found himself impressed that she could do so much in such a short period of time and still be dressed the way she was. She paced the floor, her light brown hair perfectly in place, and the soft blue dress she had changed into not only seemed to glisten in the sunlight coming through the window, but also didn't seem blemished with even the slightest speck of the dirt or dust that she had meticulously banished from the room.

Not a word was spoken between the three of them as Percy gingerly started pulling back the large bandage covering the wound on Chas's shoulder. Tom turned his eyes away; he had seen enough trauma to last a lifetime and couldn't stand the thought of seeing more. His gaze fell again on Miss Emma, who stood frozen, her clasped trembling hands covering her lips. For the first time, he noticed she no longer appeared to be the strong-willed woman he had always known. Her usual, staunch disposition had given way to run-away tears and Tom thought she might faint dead away when she softly cried out, "Oooh, God!" as Percy finally pulled back the gauze, exposing a stitched, jagged wound oozing blood from the middle of a dark, melon-sized, purple-and-black bruise.

Tom quickly moved to her and reached out a steady hand. "Miss Emma... are you all right?"

"No," she said. She turned and buried her head against his chest and sobbed uncontrollably. Tom would never forget the brief tender moment. Not only did Miss Emma's robust determination match his mother's, but her deep compassion did as well, making her the only other woman he ever knew who could do so. The fact that she and his father would be perfect for each other wasn't a stretch of the imagination by any means, but he was astounded at how swiftly he welcomed the idea and somehow knew in his heart his mother would, too.

Emma pulled away and tried to regain her composure. She stared out the window as she furiously wiped tears from her face. "Tom, Mister Goff...I mean Percy, I'm sorry you two had to see me like this," she said between sniffles. She was drying her face with a handkerchief that appeared out of nowhere, with a few fresh sobs escaping. "I shouldn't have come," she said quietly. "A lot of good I turned out to be...crying like a little school girl."

Tom tried to console her as best he could. "Miss Emma, it's okay. I know I can speak for every man here when I say we're all glad you're here to help."

"Yes, ma'am. He's right, ya know," Percy said as he stood and turned to her. She only nodded her head to acknowledge the compliment before he looked down at Chas. "Seems to me this boy woulda been a sight worse off if ya hadn't cleaned up this room like ya did. Besides, I got good news." He pointed a lazy finger at Tom. "I remember your daddy when I first laid eyes on him. He was a lot worse off than this boy is now, and look how he turned out."

Miss Emma wiped the last tear from her face and asked with a half-laugh, half-cry, "I thought you said you had good news!" The tension in the air was replaced by light laughter from everyone as Miss Emma added, "Jim Wallace has got to be the most bull-headed man the good Lord ever put on this earth ... and you call that good news?"

"Well, I can see your point," Percy said with a smile. "I can't guarantee this boy won't turn out to be any less stubborn, but I think he's got a lot more than a fightin' chance to pull through this." Their brief moment of levity was replaced by seriousness as he looked down. "But we got us some tough work ahead."

Ever since she had called them into the house, Tom had an uneasy feeling that Chas's injuries were proving to be more severe than what Miss Emma could deal with, but he was relieved and more than impressed when she looked Percy in the eyes and asked, "What do you want us to do?"

"Well, first thing we need to do is break this fever, but we can't move him too far," Percy said, as he pretended not to know that Miss Emma just put him in charge. "Tom, ya think you and a couple of the other fellas can round up a wash tub and set it in here next to the bed? Looks like our friend Chas here's gonna need a real cold bath."

"I'll get right on it," Tom said, turning to leave the room.

"While you're at it," Percy called after him, "we need to get somebody to man that water well pump. We're gonna need a steady supply of cold water."

Two hours later, Tom leaned against the door frame watching Miss Emma let out a huge sigh of relief as she folded a new set of fresh sheets across Chas's chest. Everyone else had gone out to sit on the front porch, but the relaxed mood they were in now was a far cry from what it was not long before. It had taken a combined effort, with very few words spoken during that time, but Chas was now doing much better and sleeping comfortably due to the hour-and-a-half cold bath he didn't even know he took.

Worried looks and grimaces were on everyone's face as they carefully lifted him off the bed and lowered him into the tub, and it took another shot of morphine to keep the young man from moving about too much once they got him in the cold water but, after an hour or so of bailing the warm water out and pouring fresh cold water in, he finally started to come around, even though at one point Tom wasn't sure if they were making any headway because his fever seemed too high to break.

"Why do you think his fever came on so fast?" Tom asked as Miss Emma smoothed the fresh sheets tenderly around her charge.

"I wondered about that myself," she whispered. Standing straight and turning her attention to Tom, she added, "No way to tell for sure. Percy said he might have been walking around with a cold for a few days, but who knows."

Tom ran his fingers through his hair as he let out a deep breath. "For a while there, I was afraid we weren't doing any good."

Miss Emma let out a small, tired chuckle. "Don't tell anybody, but I was thinking the same thing." She sighed, took a look around the room, and noticed the noon sun had moved on; the sunlight coming through the window was creeping toward Chas's bed. She walked over and pulled down the shades. "I'm afraid that's not the last time we're going to have a scare, though."

"You're probably right," Tom said. He watched her look around the room, making sure everything was clean and in its proper place. "Is there anything else I can do?" he asked.

She looked down at Chas, put her hands on her hips and said with resignation, "No, I don't think so. At least for now, anyway."

Tom felt about as tired as Miss Emma looked and had no intention of opening up a new can of worms, but when Miss Emma turned to walk out of the room, Tom surprised her and himself when he said, "Miss Emma, I just want to tell you how happy I am that you're here. I know my father is, too."

She stopped in her tracks to look intently into Tom's eyes. Immediately seeing the answer she was looking for, she clasped her hands before her chest and stepped back over to the window, her back to him. "Can you shut the door please?" she asked. After hearing the latch on the door click, she asked, "Did your father tell you?"

"No," Tom said.

She turned and faced him. "Then how did you know?"

Tom sheepishly glanced down at the floor before he looked up and said with a smile, "Well, Miss Emma, it's as plain as day." He shrugged. "Heck, I don't know how anyone could miss it."

New tears were in her eyes. "Tom, please don't be upset. We were going to tell you, I promise. I know it's only been a year since your mother passed on, God rest her soul, and…and…" She was asking for acceptance when she added without the slightest hint of pride, "I'm so sorry."

Tom stood there a moment, then walked over and hugged her gently. Neither said a word for what seemed like an eternity. Tom finally looked down at her and said, "But, Miss Emma, you know how ornery and bull-headed my father is." Miss Emma coughed on a small chuckle as she pulled away and wiped tears from her face as Tom added with a laugh, "Do you know what you're getting yourself into?"

"Yes," she answered quickly but sincerely, "I do." She turned away. "Damn, this is the second time today I've made a fool of myself in front of you, And now I'm cursing, too " She clenched her fists. "This has been a disaster! I could think of a million ways to introduce myself more properly than this."

"I can't," he said with a smile.

His answer caught her off guard but, in the silence that followed, a look of happiness appeared on her face. "Really? You mean that?" Tom nodded.

She asked with renewed hope in her eyes. "You really don't mind?"

"Miss Emma…" he said, trying to choose his words carefully, "not only do I not mind, but I can't think of any one thing I'd rather see happen around here."

"*Any* one thing?" she asked, drying the last of her tears and more at ease. "What about Miss Jennie Lue Sloan? I've seen the way you two look at each other."

Tom laughed. "Okay. Fair enough. Make that two things I'd like to see happen." They exchanged a look of understanding for a moment before their conversation was ended by the sound of hoof beats in the front yard and muffled greetings from the men on the porch.

"Sounds like your father is home," she said, as she took one last look at Chas.

Tom reached to open the door. "When do you want to tell him I know?"

There was genuine relief on her face along with a smile as she answered, "Maybe we'll get the chance later this evening. I know he'll be happy you're not upset about it."

Tom nodded. "I don't know why the two of you thought I'd be upset. I think it's great, and I know my mother does, too."

"You're a good son, Tom Wallace," she said, with admiration in her eyes. "And thank you very much."

"No, thank you," Tom said sincerely, "for looking after my father." They gave each other a smile. "Come on. Let's go see what he has to say about Buddy."

As they left the room and walked through the house, Tom couldn't help but feel the apprehension build in his chest as to what his brother had to say about the night before. But there was also a part of him that couldn't wait for later in the evening when he and Miss Emma could tell his father the good news about their heart-to-heart talk. Just before they stepped out on the porch, he and Miss Emma glanced at each other once more and silently shared their secret with a quick, tender smile, then turned their attention to Jim as they walked out among the rest of the hands.

At the time, Tom had no way of knowing the conversation he was looking forward to would quickly become insignificant to other events at hand but, as everyone took a seat, he could tell the tension on the porch was thick enough to cut with a knife and noticed, just before his father started talking, it was so quiet he could have heard a small hat pin hit the wooden flooring.

CHAPTER 18

The Night of the Show

Tom pulled back on the reins and slowed Clever to a gentle trot as the evening sun slipped below the blue horizon, causing the high clouds painting the western sky to glow bright orange and gold. He was in a hurry to see Jennie Lue and had made good time coming over from the Four C's but, after turning into the entrance leading to Turner Bell's huge white house, he was having second thoughts about getting there so quickly.

All afternoon he thought about their plans for the night and what a wonderful sight it would be to finally see Jennie Lue emerge from her front door wearing some type of fancy, flowing dress but, as the carriage moved farther down the private road, the excitement within him gave way to the dreadful prospect of having to shake hands with her father. Tom was well aware Turner Bell would be none too pleased about him coming to pick up his daughter, and the idea caused something akin to nausea to race through his insides as he made his way up the perfectly smooth winding path. He tried his best to shake off the feeling by looking around at the beautiful scenery that made up the Double T Ranch.

Behind the wooden white-washed fences lining each side of the road were hundreds of fat cattle grazing and extremely well kept horses that came up to stare at him as he passed. Moving closer to the house, he could hear the sudden baying of what would no doubt be a hardy hound as he passed a small pecan orchard, the branches heavy with an infinite number of unripe pecans.

He gave himself time to build his courage by traveling up the road as slowly as he could but, the closer he got to his destination, the worse his anxiety became. As he neared the front yard, every room in the house seemed lit up. For an awful moment, he thought he saw Turner Bell waiting for him on the veranda but, as the carriage came to a stop, he could tell it was only a shadow cast from one of the many outdoor lamps lit to keep the evening darkness at bay.

Tom tied the reins and reached over to grab the gift in the seat next to him before stepping down out of the carriage to scratch the ears of the now-friendly dog that had crawled out from under the porch to see if he was friend or foe. He walked up the stairs, made his way to the polished wooden door and took a moment to make sure the suit he was wearing was perfectly in place before he exhaled deeply and knocked three times.

At first, there didn't seem to be anyone home. He listened for any sound coming from the other side of the door but, hearing none, he moved over to one of the front windows and was about to peek in when he heard what sounded like movement upstairs. He quickly hid his gift behind him, stepped back in front of the door and held his chin up as he listened to the sound of footsteps coming down the stairs. His heart nearly pounded its way out of his chest by the time the door opened and Jennie Lue presented herself with a beaming smile. "Hi! Come in. And don't you look handsome!" she said, holding the door wide.

Tom spent quite a bit of time trying to get the only suit he had ever owned looking like new. He shrugged off the compliment by tugging on the loose-fitting jacket. "I don't know about that. It used to fit pretty good. Guess I'm still a little skinny these days."

"Don't be silly! You look really nice," she said as she looked him over from head to toe.

Tom wanted to change the subject, but he was also trying to be proper when he took off his hat and presented his gift. "Jennie Lue," he said with a grin as he stepped into the house, "I brought this for you."

"A posy! They're beautiful!" She brought the flowers to her nose and inhaled deeply before she closed the door and looked up. "Thank you so much! Did you pick these yourself?"

"Yes, ma'am," he answered proudly. Standing with his hat in his hands, he pointed at the base of the small bouquet. "When I was little, my mother taught me how to tie those stems into a handle. She used to tell me one day I'd meet a beautiful girl and would need to know how to do that proper." He took a moment to take in the sight of Jennie Lue and nodded. "She was absolutely right."

"Why, Mister Wallace! Aren't you a silver-tongued devil?" she said as she took in the aroma of the fresh-picked flowers once more. "Let me put these in some water. I'll be right back."

Tom watched her walk across the polished hardwood floor and disappear into the kitchen before he looked around. It seemed as if he and Jennie Lue were the only ones in the house, which at first brought a sense of relief that he wasn't going to have to shake hands with Turner Bell, but the feeling didn't last long when he realized her parents hadn't come out to meet him because they didn't like the idea of their daughter going into town with Jim Wallace's son, who also happened to be a newly released ex-convict.

He paced the floor, trying to drive the thought from his mind when Jennie Lue came out of the kitchen and walked back to him. She gently pulled out each side of her skirt and curtseyed before turning around to give him a full view of her new dress. "Do you like it?"

Tom smiled as he took in the sight. Her handbag matched the soft yellow dress she wore, which was trimmed with light blue, English cotton lace at the end of her tight-fitting sleeves, along the base of her skirt and around the slender lines of her neck. Her blonde hair was tucked up beneath a small yellow bonnet, and just the right touch of make-up perfectly accentuated the gleam in her hazel eyes. "Well? What do you think?" she asked.

Tom was at a loss for words, but managed to say, "My goodness, Jennie Lue. I do believe you are the prettiest sight I've ever seen."

"Then mission accomplished!" she said cheerfully. She stood on her toes and kissed him on the cheek. "Are you ready?" she asked.

"Yes, ma'am," he said. He glanced around the house, leaned in close and asked with a whisper, "What about your father? I can't say I was looking forward to it, but don't I need to shake his hand or say hello…or something?"

Jennie Lue waved the idea away. "We're not going to worry about him," she said, rolling her eyes. She moved to the door. "He *said* he had important business to take care of in Austin and left this afternoon, but I know he was just using the trip as an excuse to avoid seeing you tonight. Come on; let's go."

Tom let out a small sigh of relief and reached for the door. "I can't say I was really excited to see him, but now I feel a little disappointed."

"Oh, well," she said, as if she didn't have a care in the world, "we're not going to worry about him, remember?"

She was about to step out onto the porch when her mother's voice called out, "Tom? Could you please wait up a minute?" Judy Bell walked out of the kitchen wearing a light beige summer dress, looking ready for a night on the town even though she rarely went anywhere. She took off her eyeglasses and patted her hair as she came into the foyer, smiling. "My, my...Tom Wallace. Look at you! It's been a long time."

Tom nodded, "Mrs. Bell."

Judy walked over to Tom and gave him a polite hug before she held her hand waste high and said, "Seems like I haven't seen you since you were this tall." Trying in vain to cover the truth, she became serious. "Pardon my manners. I'm so sorry, but my husband had to tend to an urgent business matter in Austin; otherwise, he would be here to see you two kids off."

Tom glanced at Jennie Lue before he told his own white lie, "I'm sorry to hear that, ma'am. I was looking forward to seeing Mister Bell."

With relief in her voice, she said, "Well, there will come another time when we can all get together. Maybe I can talk Jennie Lue into inviting you over for a Sunday dinner sometime soon. How would that be?"

Tom looked at Jennie Lue. She was smiling at her mother appreciatively. "I'd really like that," he said.

"Good, then," she said, clasping her hands. "You two work it out and let me know, all right?" She moved to hold the door for them. "Now you kids run along. I know you don't want to stand here all night talking to me."

"Yes, ma'am," Tom said with a broad smile.

Judy looked at her daughter. "What time will you be home?"

Jennie Lue glanced at Tom before she looked back at her mother and said, "I don't know. It's a two-hour show; maybe eleven-thirty or twelve?"

Judy's furrowed brow and set jaw let Tom know she wasn't pleased with her daughter's answer. "I'll have her home by eleven o'clock, ma'am," he offered.

Judy took her daughter's hand, gave it a loving squeeze, looked at Tom and said, "Oh, heck. Y'all go have some fun. Why don't you just have her home by midnight? I'm sure that will be just fine."

"Midnight it is then," he said.

Judy shooed them out saying, "Take good care of her, Tom. Y'all run along now." They were off the porch and walking down the steps when she called after them, "Have a nice night, but be careful!"

"We will," Jennie Lue said as she stopped by the side of the carriage. Before she stepped in, she looked back. "Mother…thank you very much."

Judy Bell stood in the open doorway and answered with a loving, proud smile before she softly closed the door and left them alone in the yard.

"I like your carriage," Jennie Lue said as Tom helped her in. "Is this yours?"

"No," he said as he walked around to the other side and climbed in. "It was my mother's. This is the first time it's been used since she died."

"It's really nice," she said.

Tom popped the reins, turned the carriage around and started back the way he came. "Thanks," he said. They moved down the smooth road. "It took me a while to get it out from behind all the wire my father has stacked up in the barn, and the rest of the afternoon to get all the dust and muck cleaned off. I'm glad you like it."

"I do," she said as she looked it over. The one-bench, apple-red buggy was by no means as nice or as new as Miss Emma's, but the carriage rolled over the road almost as smoothly and the lack of a canopy made it a pleasure to look at the brightening stars as they came out to take their turn in the night sky. She enjoyed the breeze on her face and the sights of the Double T as it slowly fell behind them. "I think it was sweet of you to pick me up in this."

Tom chuckled. "I couldn't see picking you up in that beat-up old work wagon. Besides, if my mother was still alive, she probably would've cleaned it up herself if she knew I was using it to take you out on the town."

Jennie Lue smiled. "You really think so?"

"I know so," he said.

The appreciative smile on her face was suddenly replaced by a look of concern as she turned sideways in her seat, placed her hand on Tom's leg and said, "I hope you forgive me but, if I don't ask, I'm going to burst. How did it go with your father?"

Tom looked into her face, then turned to stare ahead. He shook his head slowly. "I don't know how he did it, but Buddy explained everything away, as if we're all out of our minds to think he might have been responsible."

"Really?" she said, as if that was the last thing she expected to hear. "How can that be?"

"Well," he said, "I know my father wants to believe him. And I guess deep down I do, too, but something about his story just doesn't add up."

"Something about his story?" she asked. "How in the world could your brother have a story that explains away everything that happened last night?"

Tom took a deep breath. "Maybe I should start at the beginning…"

He told her about his conversation with his father on the porch and how he took the news, his ride into town in the middle of the storm and how he came back in the afternoon madder than a hornet at Buddy for not telling the truth, but obviously relieved his son wasn't responsible for the injuries to Chas.

Jennie Lue listened intently as Tom spoke and quietly turned to look into the distance after he told her everything he knew. There was a long moment of silence as she mulled the story over in her mind. "What do you think?" she finally asked.

"I already told you what I think," he said.

"It is possible, though…isn't it?" she asked.

He looked into her confused eyes. "I suppose," he said, "but I just can't believe Aya got it wrong about those boot prints."

"What does Aya think?" she asked.

"He doesn't say much," he said, "but I can tell he's upset. Aya doesn't get this type of thing wrong…at least, I've never seen it."

"Everything else seems possible," she said quietly.

"I know! That's the hard part," he said. "Just when you think you might have Buddy figured out, he comes up with something that makes you think *you're* the one that's crazy, not him."

"Now what?" she asked.

"I suppose the only thing we can do now is watch him like a hawk," he said. "Other than that, I don't know."

Neither said anything until the red carriage was halfway to Belton and Jennie Lue said, "Let's talk about something a little more cheerful."

They started talking again and didn't stop until Clever came to a halt in front of the livery, which was just down the street from the opera house. The ride only lasted twenty minutes but during that time, they effortlessly discussed a whole host of other things like Jennie Lue's father and mother, her brother George, the railroad and what it might mean in the coming years, Tom's parents, Chas, Miss Emma Lawton, rebuilding Ruby's bridge and their plans to get together in the coming days. Along the way, Tom felt that, even though he and Jennie Lue never truly had the chance to get to know each other until now, the connection between them was incredibly strong, in spite of being neglected for so long. He thought it was as if their need to soak in one another after all this time matched the thirst of a man wandering in the desert who couldn't drink enough water after stumbling upon an oasis, but little did he know it was far stronger than he could ever imagine and would surprise everyone in Bell County within the next twenty-four hours.

"It's about time you showed up," Blondy Harbison said from his seat at the table as the front door to the sheriff's office swung open.

"Sorry I'm late, fellas," Milo Hollman said as he rushed in. He quickly took off his old, dirty black hat and put it on the rack by the door before he took a seat next to George Bell and said, "I forgot you guys said the game was gonna start early tonight. Why'd y'all do that, anyway?"

"We gotta break the game up a little early," Blondy said. "Got some things to tend to later."

"Oh," Milo said. He looked as though he was going to ask what that might be, but changed his mind and reached into his pocket to pull out his money. Milo Hollman was forty-five years old and had been a liveryman in Belton since anyone could remember. He stood six feet four, weighed close to three hundred pounds and had a face that only his mother could love but, because of his grizzled looks, he rarely had any late payments for the work he did at his livery, even though he was the type of man who wouldn't hurt a fly. His wife, on the other hand, was only five feet tall, uglier than he was, meaner than a rattlesnake and had no qualms about letting everyone in town know she ruled her husband with an iron fist.

All this was well known around the card table, which caused George to ask, "Your old lady wouldn't let ya out of the house early, would she?"

Buddy and Blondy laughed as the liveryman tried in vain to defend himself. "That's not it. I just forgot about the time, that's all."

"Sure ya did," George said, as he rolled his eyes and started shuffling the cards, a slight tremble in his hands. He, Blondy and Buddy were all fairly certain that Milo's wife wouldn't let him out of the house early to play cards and, since the three of them had a lot more on their minds than tonight's game, they used the time to pass around the bottle of corn whiskey sitting in the middle of the table and discuss their plans for later on in the evening.

George was by far the most concerned of the group. The railroad was getting closer by the day. He had finally raised the one hundred thousand dollars necessary to ensure the rails came through the Four C's but, as he informed Buddy and Blondy, the men with the money arrived in town earlier in the afternoon and had given him an ultimatum. The buyers told him they still wanted the property and there was more than enough money in the deal to make everyone in the room rich, but they were tired of waiting and, if they didn't have a signature on the contract by noon Saturday, their agreement was off. Even though they had all sworn to stick together from the very beginning and ride out their plan to the very end, the air in the room was heavy and their dispositions were much more serious now than they had ever been.

When Buddy unveiled his plan, George protested fiercely because he didn't approve of violence unless there was no other way around it, and it had taken a few extra shots of whiskey to calm his nerves before he finally agreed.

Blondy tried to act like he didn't care one way or the other and said he was just looking forward to doing what he did best, even though it was clear he was lost in his thoughts.

Buddy appeared as if he was more than confident the evening would play out as planned and his chance to see the world the way he wanted was finally at hand, but he also felt a small twinge of guilt because, once again, he would be using his brother as a pawn to make his plans come to fruition. The feeling didn't last long, though, because Buddy never did put much stock in a conscience and had developed a powerful urge over the last two days to see the expression on Tom's face the instant he realized that his life with Jennie Lue Sloan would be forever out of reach. When the time came, he was going to make sure he was there to see that.

"I saw your pa today," Milo said as he glanced at Buddy.

"How'd that go?" Buddy asked.

"Oh, fine," answered Milo with a sly smile. There was no doubt he was letting Buddy know he had held up his end of the bargain. "He just stopped by to say hello, then went on his way." As he settled down to play, Milo Hollman would never have guessed he just missed some heated arguments among his friends, and had no idea behind each of their friendly smiles was the same intense feeling a gambler gets the instant he rolls the dice when the last of his money is on the table. He grabbed the bottle of whiskey and filled the shot glass of each man. "Gentlemen, here's to cards…cheers!"

They all emptied their glasses in one gulp before Buddy leaned over to Blondy and whispered, "You probably don't want to drink too much. I heard those boys are over at Dayna G's right now."

Blondy set his glass back down. "Don't you worry about me. I know what I gotta do."

Buddy glared at Blondy and said through a clenched jaw. "We're going to have to be there in an hour and a half."

"I can tell time, too," Blondy said as he returned the stare.

"Everybody in?" asked George uneasily, trying to change the subject and ease the tension. He began to deal the cards.

"Of course we're in," Buddy said, and tossed his ante on the table, "we're all in."

"Bear! It's time to go!" Church whispered as he stood in the upstairs hallway of Dayna G's and tapped on one of the bedroom doors. He listened in vain for any sound of movement on the other side before he knocked again. "Come on! We gotta get outta here."

"All right, all right!" Bear's voice said through the door. "I'll be out in a minute."

"Hurry up then!" Church hissed before he stepped to the far side of the hallway and leaned against the wall. He had already said his goodbyes to Ida Griffin who had a room just down the hall. Even though she had been a working girl at Dayna G's for a number of years, Church was sure he was in love with her because she was the only woman who ever gave a damn about him.

Ida wasn't good looking by any stretch of the imagination and was extremely overweight, but they had grand plans to start a family as soon as he landed a job that paid enough to support her without spending all his time on the trails. Even though Church was certain they had a bright future ahead, for the time being he had to be content with sneaking in and out of Dayna G's to see his girlfriend over the last few months because, if there was one thing the owner of this place despised, it was one of her girls falling for a broke, unemployed cowboy and giving her services away for free. Since everyone in town had known for some time that Church Davis was a perfect example of what Dayna hated the most, he had to take great precautions whenever he stopped by so she would have no idea he had been around. He normally didn't get here until three or four in the morning, but now here he was, trying to sneak out without being seen at ten o'clock, which made him more than a little nervous as he stood in the hallway.

Church had arranged things with Ida so that she and Jessie Moore were both 'feeling ill' and not up to working tonight, but this also happened to be the busiest time of day and he didn't want to be spotted out here in the open. He impatiently stepped back to the door and whispered, "Bear! This ain't funny! *We gotta go!"*

"I'm comin', I'm comin'," Bear said from the other side.

Church could hear the faint sound of muffled voices as he nervously waited, but soon Bear stepped quietly out of the room carrying his boots in one hand and his hat in the other. "It's about time you got outta there! Come on," Church said as they moved down the hallway to the back stairs.

Bear put his hat on and was following Church as he said, "I'm sorry about that, but whew! What a girl that one is. I gotta get back here as soon as I can."

"Hush up! Neither one of us is gonna get the chance if we get caught," Church said. He waited for Bear to put his boots on before opening the back door. He took a quick look outside to make sure no one was in the alley, then turned back. "Come on!"

They quietly made their way down the wooden stairs outside. As soon as they reached the bottom in the back alleyway, Bear put his hands on Church's shoulders. "I gotta tell ya," he said, "I owe ya big. That Jessie Moore is a notch on my pistol I'll never forget."

"Shhhh!" Church said as he pulled away from Bear and waved at him "We still got to get to our horses. We ain't outta the woods just yet."

"I'm just sayin'," Bear said, "I ain't even hardly left yet and I'm already so lathered up to go back I could piss my pants."

"Bear! Ya gotta be quiet, ya hear me?" Church whispered as they crept along the alley. "Dayna's got spies all through here lookin' for fellas just like me and you, so hush up."

"As a matter of fact," came a voice from the darkness, "I been out here waitin' for the both of you."

Normally, Church would have sprinted if someone made any noise out here in the ally but this time he and Bear stopped in their tracks at the unmistakable sound a pistol makes when it's being cocked.

"Who are ya?" Church asked, raising both hands in the air. He turned and tried to make out the figure in the shadows.

There was no immediate reply, so Bear asked, "Why ya waitin' for us?"

"So I can kill you," the man said from just a few feet away.

Even though Bear had spent his entire life giving a cocked pistol the utmost respect, he was caught totally by surprise as the first shot exploded from the barrel of the gun. The alley was illuminated for the briefest of moments because of the flash but, in an instant, he saw Church Davis fall backward out of the corner of his eye and the face of the shooter, Blondy Harbison.

Bear instinctively reached for his gun, but long before he could get it out of his holster there was a second loud flash, causing him to feel like he had been kicked by a mule as the forty-five caliber bullet slammed into his chest. His legs crumpled beneath him as he collapsed onto his back and, after he got over the initial shock of what just happened, his first thought was he couldn't see very well because his eyeglasses were missing. It didn't take long, however, for Bear to realize the night was rapidly getting darker because this day was going to be his last. The taste of burnt gunpowder in the back of his throat and the labored breaths bubbling through the hole in his chest were clear indications of a mortal wound and caused him to panic at first but, as he struggled for air, he soon relaxed and smiled slightly. Bear saw images of his wife and son appear out of nowhere, looking exactly as he remembered. They were there to greet him and wore happy, understanding looks on their faces, but the last expression on his face was not a peaceful one; it was one of confusion. As he turned his attention to the man who killed him, he couldn't understand why he saw so much hate in his eyes.

Bear's lips moved slightly as he tried to talk, but his life was too far gone for words to come, so he went to his grave without knowing why he had been shot down, or why the kid with the long blond hair stepped out from the shadows and laughed until the darkness overtook everything and a gentle evening breeze carried his last breath away.

"Have you ever seen anything like this in your life?' Jennie Lue asked, her eyes alive with excitement as she took a sip from her glass of wine.

"No, I haven't," Tom said with a smile as he looked into her eyes. "And the show's not bad, either," he added. They stood in a small corner of the crowded lobby, enjoying a glass of wine before the final act.

She held her glass delicately with both hands and laughed. "You know what I meant! I was talking about the show. Isn't it amazing?"

Tom took a sip of his wine and set the glass down on a small table. "It really is. I wonder where they come up with the ideas for a show like that."

"Who knows?" she said. "I was wondering how they can do all those tricks without killing themselves." She took another sip. "I just can't get over it that none of those people were hurt in the first act, when that stage coach broke in half, and they did it right on stage with that horse running around and everything."

"I know," he said, shaking his head. "And how can all of them fly off the stagecoach and land in those chairs smoking their cigarettes like nothing ever happened?" He moved close to Jennie Lue so an older lady in a huge dinner dress could pass. "We even knew they were going to do it because of the picture on the front of the program, but I still can't believe they pulled it off."

"And all the juggling!" she said. "How did that man put all that food on those plates and toss them up in the air without spilling a single thing?"

"It's a mystery," he said as he shrugged, "but, if he ever gets hurt doing this, I'm sure he can get a job anywhere as a waiter in one of those big city fancy restaurants."

She laughed. "I'm sure you're right about that!"

"And what about the last act?" Tom said, "they had that rail car cut open where you could see all the people inside…"

"…and the wheels were spinning so it made it look like it was moving," she said, finishing his thought. She took a deep breath. "Tom…thank you so much for a wonderful evening! I'm having a great time."

Tom picked up his glass and clicked it against hers. "No…thank *you*. This is the best night of my life."

They smiled at each other and took a sip to finish their toast, but were startled by the loud voice of an usher. "Two minutes!" he called out.

"I guess we should head back to our seats," she said. "I can't wait to see what they do for the last act."

"Me, either," he said, setting down his unfinished glass, "you ready?"

She set her glass on the table and put her arm through Tom's. "Let's go."

They chatted happily as they made their way down the aisle to their front row seats and never once showed the slightest concern over the whispers and stares directed their way. As they settled into their chairs, they talked about what astounding acrobatic feats might await them in the next act, but the biggest shock of their lives wouldn't come from the actors in the show. It would be delivered by George Bell.

Before the lights dimmed, signaling the beginning of act three, George hurried down the left center aisle, forcefully made his way through the people sitting in the same row until he stopped next to Tom and leaned over to whisper in his ear. The sight of the overweight mayor moving through the opera house as quickly as he did caused a hush to fall over the crowd, but the silence didn't last long because Tom immediately jumped from his chair and ran out of the building with a horrified look on his face, followed closely by Jennie Lue Sloan and her brother, who was gasping for air and wiping his forehead with a handkerchief all the way back up the aisle. Act three didn't start for another five minutes because of the commotion that followed, but the rumors started immediately and only got bigger as they passed from one person to the next.

Not everyone would agree about what happened in the opera house that night because some would say Tom looked like a man who had gone mad. Others would argue they saw him run out with his gun in his hand. There was one story circulating that he took Jennie Lue Sloan out at gunpoint and another that he even fired a couple of shots in the air before he left the building. But there was no doubt in anyone's mind that serious trouble always followed Tom Wallace, and it was just a matter of time before it found him again.

Most of the circumstances surrounding the events of the evening became known by the next morning but, by then, the facts had been distorted and didn't mean much anyway because for the next two days the citizens of Belton, Texas firmly believed Tom Wallace deserved to swing from the end of a brand-new rope.

"Oh, my God," Tom said under his breath as he ran around the corner of the alley and saw the sprawled figures of his two friends. The alley was lit up by lanterns carried by the small crowd that gathered, which enabled Tom to realize immediately Church and Bear were dead and there was no longer a chance that George Bell's shocking story wasn't true.

After leaving the opera house, he and Jennie Lue ran over to the livery to get the carriage, then raced through the streets hoping there had to be some kind of mistake but, as he knelt down and looked at the lifeless expressions on the faces of his friends, the truth hit him in the stomach like a run-away train.

Jennie Lue was only a second behind Tom. Tears were already streaming down her cheeks and her voice was cracking with emotion when she came up beside him and said, "Oh, Tom!"

Everyone there could easily see the chest wounds of the two men so Tom stood, wrapped his arms around Jennie Lue and whispered in her ear, "There's nothing we can do."

"What happened?" she asked to no one in particular. "Why...who did this?"

Tom glanced around at the people standing there only to see a blank, "I don't want to get involved" look on every single face.

"Did anybody see anything? Please! Anybody?" he pleaded. Suddenly the people who had just been so interested in the bodies of the two men decided they had other things to do. Without a sound, the crowd dispersed, making their way back to wherever they were before the shootings, leaving Tom to yell even louder, "What the hell happened here? Somebody had to see something!"

Tom made eye contact with an older man who was a shop owner on the other side of the alley. "You there! This happened right behind your store. Where is everybody going?" A blank stare was all the answer he got, but the old man did something next that Tom didn't understand. The old shop owner never said a word, but he tried to convey a message by staring straight into Tom's eyes and tilting his head to the left once, then set his lantern down slowly before entering the door to his shop and closing it behind him. Everyone else had carried theirs away, but the old man's lantern illuminated the back alley just enough.

"They're all leavin' cause I told 'em to, prison boy," came the voice of Blondy Harbison as the last person in the crowd disappeared from sight. He had been waiting in the shadows behind Dayna G's for Tom and Jennie Lue to show up ever since George went to spread the news. He had a smug look on his face conveying his eagerness to finish his night's work.

Blondy hadn't planned on the small lantern behind the old man's store, but considered it a minor detail and welcomed the idea that the night's festivities would be a lot more fun if he could actually see the look in Tom's eyes the moment the bullet found his chest. As Blondy took his stance in the middle of the ally, the dull light from the lantern plainly lit the smirk on his face. "Looks like your friends there had a bad day."

Tom was by no means a lawman experienced in unraveling a crime but, as soon as he came around the corner and saw Church and Bear lying on the ground, he could tell they never had a chance. His first thought was his friends made the mistake of assuming Blondy Harbison wouldn't shoot because he had no reason, but Tom knew different, and quickly tucked the right side of his coat behind his pistol.

He stepped away from Jennie Lue and said in a voice seething with hate, "You shot them in cold blood, didn't you?"

"It's like this," Blondy said, tapping the badge pinned to his shirt, "I'm a deputy sheriff and those two fellas are dead. Any questions?"

"Why? Why did you kill them?" screamed Jennie Lue.

"Boss's orders," Blondy said with a shrug. "Sad thing it was, too. Their girlfriends are mighty broke up about it. Hell, I didn't know a couple of whores could carry on about anybody that much. Took us forever to get 'em back inside." He spat on the ground. "You know, watchin' 'em caterwaul like they did almost made me shed a tear myself." He gave Tom a baleful grin.

Tom slowly moved to the center of the alley. "Looks like you got over it pretty quick," he said.

Blondy acted proud and smiled. "Yeah…I did. Some people say it's a gift." He shrugged. "People die all the time. So what? Besides, I can't think about it too much. My work's not done. You're here…and we got one more little thing to take care of before I get to call it a day."

"You've been waiting for me, haven't you?" Tom said. He squared his shoulders at Blondy, who was barely twenty feet away. The deputy sheriff nodded.

"You killed them just to get me out here," snarled Tom. "Why not shoot me down in the dark like you did them?"

Blondy chuckled and pointed at the light. "I was going to, but I didn't figure on that lantern bein' there. That old man's gonna have to pay for that."

A huge grin spread across his face as he laughed. "But I gotta admit it'll be a lot more fun this way."

Jennie Lue was frantic as she stood off to the side and watched. Her hands were rolled up in a ball next to her chin as she cried and pleaded desperately, "Tom! Come back over here! You don't have to do this! Please!"

Tom never took his eyes off Blondy. "Stay back, Jennie Lue. You're wrong. I don't know why but, if it's not here, it'll be somewhere else."

Blondy chuckled loudly and shook his finger at Tom. "You know, you're absolutely right about that." A sudden serious look came over him. "I hear you're pretty fast at them county fairs, but this here's different. Them little balloons tied up on those boards don't shoot back, now do they?"

Blondy looked for a flicker of hesitation or fear in Tom's eyes but, after seeing none, he decided to draw, thinking his experience at this deadly game was still a huge advantage. He either had one too many shots of whiskey at the card game, or he underestimated his adversary, or both, but the next thing Blondy Harbison knew, he was standing in the street with a red blood stain spreading across the front of his shirt. Wobbling on his feet with a stunned expression, he squinted his eyes and tried to see if the shot he fired had found its mark, but Tom Wallace stood in front of him without a scratch.

"I'll be a son of a bitch," Blondy said. He made one last attempt to raise his pistol to get off another shot but, before he could get the gun above his belt, his strength left him completely and he fell backward into the dirt.

Tom would never be able to recall the split second it took him to put a bullet through the chest of the deputy sheriff but, because of the lantern he was able to see and would never forget the look in Blondy Harbison's eyes the instant he decided to go for his pistol. As he slowly holstered his gun, the thought occurred to him that the last ten minutes might be part of some crazy nightmare but, as he turned to Jennie Lue who rushed to him with her arms outstretched, he realized there was no chance of that. She raced into his arms and held on tightly until she pulled away with tears streaming down her face. "Are you all right? You're not hurt, are you?"

"No. He missed. I'm fine," he said. He held his trembling hands up for Jennie Lue to see before he took a deep breath and nodded. "I'm okay. I just can't believe this is happening." He exhaled deeply once more to calm his nerves before walking over to Blondy Harbison, who lay coughing on the ground. "Why did you do it?" he asked.

The front of Blondy's shirt was almost completely soaked in blood, and more oozed out of his mouth. He laughed and answered slowly between coughs, "I…already told ya…boss's orders." He coughed again, his words labored, "Hah…looks like…today's the day…I get to dance with the devil." He chuckled. "I'll let him…know you'll be comin soon though."

Tom stared as Blondy exhaled for the last time and his eyes glassed over, then reached for Jennie Lue as she fell into his arms again. "Why would Buddy be behind all this?" he said.

They were both startled by the sound of a pistol being cocked and the sheriff's voice. "I'm not behind nothing except you, and I need you to put your hands in the air!"

They turned to see Buddy ten feet away, his gun pointed at Tom. A small crowd of people behind him were gathering in disbelief that Blondy Harbison had finally met his match. Buddy never lowered his gun as he walked up and pulled Tom's out of his holster but, after stepping back, he looked down at Blondy and said, "I gotta hand it to you, Tom. I'm impressed. I didn't think you could take him."

"What the hell are you up to?" Tom asked, hatred in his eyes.

"What am 'I' up to? I was going to ask you the same thing," Buddy said, glancing around at the three dead men. He took his time to make eye contact with some of the crowd. "Looks to me like you just killed a deputy sheriff." He looked back at his brother, shook his head and feigned sadness. "Tom… how could you do it?"

CHAPTER 19

A Pocket Watch and Knife

Tom wiped the sweat from his forehead and squinted up at the blazing sun, now climbing its way to the noon sky. His hands were already bloody, his new black and whites were drenched with sweat and he was breathing heavily after spending his first morning back on the chain gang, driving spikes along the railway line. He took a moment to glance around. Two of the guards on horseback were talking about him as they pointed his way, so he lifted the twelve-pound five-and-a-half into the air and crashed it down onto a spike.

He kept his head down and worked as hard as he could, hoping the guards' interest would pass, but it didn't take long for him to realize the worst when the armed rider he feared most came up behind him and said, "I'll be a son of a bitch! If it ain't Tom Wallace!"

Tom nearly fainted when he turned around to see Jack Pruitt staring back. "Welcome back! I been waitin' for this day, and I didn't even have to wait long." He laughed maliciously.

"Boss, I'm sorry about what happened in Huntsville," Tom said quickly, desperation in his voice. "It was all a mistake…my dad…"

Pruitt leaned over in his saddle. "Shut up, boy! I already told you what was gonna happen if you ever came back here, so you and me is gonna go for a little walk." He pointed at a nearby shovel and nodded toward a bank of trees. "I want you to grab that and head off over that away. We got a hole to dig."

Tom's heart raced as he slowly made his way over to pick up the shovel. He wondered if he could get close enough to hit the guard with it, but Pruitt kept himself at a safe distance. Tom moved as slowly as he could, but the walk to the trees didn't last long and soon they were into the grove and away from the eyes of the work crew. Jack Pruitt pulled his horse to a stop and yelled, "All right, boy! This spot looks good. Start diggin."

"Boss...I..." started Tom.

"Hush up!" snapped the guard. "You already know what we're here for and I ain't got all day. Get to it!"

Tom exhaled deeply and accepted his fate as the first shovel full of dirt was removed from what would soon be his grave. He took his time digging the hole as thoughts started racing through his mind. The first was he hoped to see his mother right after he fell, but his mind turned to how he was going to miss his dad fiercely and prayed Miss Emma would take good care of him.

Tom had never once contemplated what sort of regrets might go through a man's mind just before he died, but all he could do was think about what had come to matter the most to him. As the last shovel full of dirt was tossed aside, he tried to focus on all the good things that had happened in his life. A smile came across his lips when he decided the best was the kiss he shared with Jennie Lue beneath the big oak. When he stood to face Jack Pruitt's gun, the only thought on Tom's mind was how the life he wanted so desperately with Jennie Lue was now lost forever, along with the children they would never have.

Jack Pruitt laughed. "I'm gonna send your daddy a letter and tell him you was tryin' to escape. I wonder how he'll take the news that it was me that shot ya down."

"Boss...please..." Tom pleaded as held up his hands.

"You ready, boy?" Pruitt asked with a sneer.

Tom watched him pull the hammer back, and there was a loud bang as the gun went off. He suddenly found himself sitting upright on a jailhouse bunk, covered in sweat. He rubbed the sleep from his eyes, realizing it had all been a dream and the sound of the gun was actually the front door to the sheriff's office slamming shut. He had been alone in this cell for twenty-four hours or so, but hadn't been able to sleep much because he was always awakened by a different version of the same dream.

He stood and looked out the barred window. It was dark outside, but he had no idea what time it was or how long he had been asleep. It seemed like an eternity had passed since his father stopped by earlier in the day, but now Tom wished he hadn't because his father looked as if he had aged ten years in one day. Jim told him he would hire a good lawyer and everything would be taken care of because Jennie Lue had seen the whole thing, but they both knew a deputy sheriff had been killed by a man who had just been released from prison, and there was more than a good chance a jury would not believe anything Jennie Lue Sloan had to say.

He heard his brother whistling a tune in the next room and could see him through the hallway door every now and then as he moved around his desk, but conversation with Buddy had been non-existent to this point, even though Tom had been trying hard to get his attention.

Tom sat down on his bunk, leaned back against the cold brick wall and glanced at the other empty cells before yelling, "Buddy! When are you going to talk to me?"

The whistling in the next room stopped, causing Tom to get up and look through his cell bars at Buddy who was once again sitting at his desk, fiddling with something from the bottom drawer. Instead of ignoring his brother as he usually did, Buddy put whatever it was back and secured the lock before spinning around in his chair. Tom knew Buddy was coming to talk and, since he didn't want his brother to know he had been watching, he quickly returned to his bunk and listened as the sound of the sheriff's boots on the wood floor drew near.

Buddy walked into the hallway where the four cells were lined up, stopped in front of Tom's and said with a smile, "How ya doin' in there, brother?"

Tom stood and walked over to his cell door so he could look into Buddy's eyes. "What the hell is going on, Buddy? What the hell are you in such a good mood for?"

Buddy pulled up a chair from the hallway, sat down and pulled his long red hair behind his ears. "Oh, no reason. It's just been a great day, that's all," he said. He leaned back and crossed his hands behind his head. "I got some news for ya. Looks like Dad sold the ranch so he could come up with the money for some big city lawyer to defend you."

"He did not," Tom said in disbelief.

"Sure did." Buddy grinned. "He signed the papers this afternoon. All we need to do now is wait for the money to transfer."

"Shit," Tom said under his breath as he hung his head. He took a few deep breaths before he looked up at Buddy. "That's what all of this has been about, isn't it…selling the ranch?"

Buddy's only reply was a slow, malicious wink.

"What do you have to do with all this?" Tom asked. "What do you have to gain that's worth killing people over?"

Buddy pulled a toothpick out of his pocket and put it between his teeth. "Ya see, Tom, it's like this. We got the railroad coming through here in about a month, so George and I convinced some mighty powerful people in Austin it should go right through the middle of the Four C's." He had a huge grin on his face. "Looks like they're gonna divide that property up and sell it off piece by piece."

"George is in the middle of this, too, isn't he?"

Buddy nodded. "He has a purpose, but hell, Tom; they're talking about making a whole new town over there, with the railroad going right through the middle. It's gonna wind up being bigger than Belton will ever be. Might even name it Wallaceville, after me…how 'bout that?"

Tom gripped the bars, his knuckles turning white. "You set all this up just so you can make a little money? Is that it?"

Buddy laughed. "Oh, it's more than just a little money. These fellas want to pay us a finder's fee for settin' up the deal, plus I get a percentage of every lot that gets sold after the line gets laid down." Buddy chuckled and moved the toothpick to the other side of his mouth. "I really don't know how I'm gonna be able to spend all that money."

"So you don't care about killing my friends?" Tom asked hatefully.

"I didn't kill 'em, Blondy did," Buddy said with a shrug.

"You sent Blondy out there to kill them…and me, too," Tom said, disgusted.

"Well," Buddy said as he slowly stretched in his chair, "I didn't figure you'd take Blondy, but it didn't matter to me either way. Dad would've wound up sellin' the Four C's if you had lived or died."

"So you have to kill people over it?" Tom said as he shook his head. "You couldn't think of any other way to pull this off?"

"We were down to the wire, Tom," Buddy said. "The buyers told us we had to get the contracts signed by the end of this week. Hell, it's Dad's fault, anyway. I gave him plenty of chances to sell, *but no*, he wouldn't do it. We tried everything, rustling cattle…"

"That was you? *You* were stealing cattle from your own father?" Tom asked.

Buddy shrugged and acted like he couldn't understand why Tom didn't see his side of things. "Tom, the Four C's is way too much property for Dad to handle; he's getting old. Sellin' it would be the best thing for him, so yeah, I did it so he'd get tired of it all and just give up."

"What about Turner?" Tom asked, "Were you stealing from him, too?"

"Yeah, but that didn't work, either," Buddy said. "We did our best to make it look like Aya was responsible so we could string him up or run him out of town, but old man Turner's probably just as stubborn as Dad, maybe more. I tried plenty of times to get Turner to press charges, but he never did; said we had to have more proof."

"You tried to pin all that on Aya?" Tom asked. "They would have hung him!"

"Yep," Buddy said, "but none of it worked." He sat up in his chair and cracked his knuckles. "So...here we are."

"Why blow up the bridge?" Tom asked. "Why kill Curry Hampton if you'd already planned on setting me up?"

Buddy laughed. "'Cause I didn't know exactly what I was going to do until yesterday, that's why." He pointed at his temple. "But I'm smart. Before I saw you and Jennie Lue out on the road, the only thing I knew to do was make trouble and blame it on the free grazers. But when you told me you and Jennie Lue were going to that show, everything fell into place. There's a new girl over at Dayna G's that wants me pretty bad, so I already knew those two loser friends of yours would be there last night."

Buddy clapped his hands and rubbed them together. "I knew you'd be getting out of prison and coming home soon, and I gotta tell you, the timing was perfect. I figured I could always come up with something and use you as my ace in the hole." Buddy smiled. "Everything worked out fine, and now the Four C's is sold. I'm going to be a rich man, Tom."

There was venom in Tom's voice as he said, "Buddy...you're a son of a bitch!" Buddy only laughed. "Why not just kill Dad and be done with it?" Tom continued, "Why not take the property that way?"

"I would've if it came down to it, but we don't have to think about that now, do we?"

Tom shook his head in disgust. "How can you even think up something like this? How can you live with yourself?"

"Actually, I sleep pretty good at night," Buddy said. He stood and stepped closer to the cell. "You see, that's where you underestimate me, Tom. You have to understand. I wouldn't have cared if that old boy in the bar killed ya five-and-a-half years ago and I didn't care at all when you got shipped off to prison, so what makes you think I'd care if somebody came along and killed you now?"

"What happened to you?" Tom asked, shaking his head. "What happened to the brother I used to know?"

Buddy chuckled, took the toothpick out of his mouth and pointed it to his heart. "I've always been right here. You just never knew who I really was, and I'm *really* tired of this shithole of a town," he said.

Buddy started back to his office as Tom yelled, "You're not going to get away with this! I'll tell Dad to stop the sale; I'll tell everybody everything."

Buddy stopped and looked back. "The only thing you're gonna do is either swing from a rope or spend the rest of your life working on a chain gang." He rubbed his hands together, then held them in the air as if he had just washed them. "Me? I didn't do nothing. Blondy shot those friends of yours, and you killed him over it. Who do you think people are gonna believe? Me or you?"

He pointed his finger at Tom. "There is one good thing, though; you'll always be remembered as the man who killed Blondy Harbison. I'm proud of you for that. Whew-wee! That was worth watching." He grabbed his crotch and grinned. "And don't you worry about Jennie Lue Sloan, either. I'll make sure all her needs are taken care of."

Tom felt ready to scream when the sound of the bell above the sheriff's office door interrupted them. The short time it took Buddy to get to the door seemed like hours as Tom listened intently for the sound of a friendly voice and his heart skipped a beat when he heard Jennie Lue's as she said, "I'm here to see Tom."

"I'm afraid you can't," he heard Buddy say. "Visiting hours are over and you're not immediate family, so I have to say no."

Tom tried to catch a glimpse of her but all he could do was listen as she said, "Please, Buddy! I know you and I have had our differences in the past, but...but I'm willing to start fresh if you are." Tom couldn't believe the tenderness in her voice. "Please, Buddy, I'll do anything you want if you'll just let me see him for a few minutes."

"Anything?" he heard Buddy ask. Tom could tell Jennie Lue's answer must have been a nod and felt his heart break in two when Buddy added, "All right then."

Tom hadn't been able to see her since he'd been placed in his cell, and would have given anything for the chance but, after hearing her conversation with Buddy, he suddenly felt like he had nothing to live for. He stepped away from the bars and waited for her to come into the hallway as he heard Buddy say, "Before you go in there, let me look in that purse of yours." There was a short pause before Buddy finished. "Okay. You got five minutes."

Jennie Lue came into view as she moved into the hallway and up to his cell. She hesitated before asking, "Tom...are you all right?"

Only seconds before, Tom didn't know if he wanted to see her or not but, as soon as he saw the sadness and worry in her eyes, they were both reaching through the bars hugging each other as tightly as they could.

"I'm sorry," he said, tears streaming down his face.

She pulled away and wiped the tears from her cheeks. "Everything's going to be okay, Tom," she said. She pulled the chair in front of the cell, sat down and set her purse in her lap. "I just had to see you."

"I know. I heard," he said.

"Don't worry about that," she said with a smile. "I'd rather kill myself than let that happen."

Tom sighed with relief and smiled affectionately. "I'm awfully glad to hear it. But don't kill yourself, okay?"

"That's not going to happen, either," she said with a grin.

"Good," he said. He ran his fingers through his hair and sighed. "What time is it? It's late, isn't it? I've been asleep."

"I don't know," she said as she looked around at the other empty cells, "probably around ten-thirty or so."

Tom took a moment to admire her bonnet, which matched the pale blue dinner dress she was wearing. "It's late for a pretty girl like you to be out, and you're awfully dressed up to be visiting somebody in jail, aren't you?"

She looked down at her outfit before she looked at him. "There's a reason for that, but I don't have time to go into it." She leaned in close and whispered, "Have you been able to find out what's going on?"

Tom took a deep breath and nodded before quietly telling her everything Buddy had told him. Jennie Lue listened intently until Tom finished, saying, "Yep. All this is about using me so Buddy and George can get the railroad to go through the middle of the Four C's and get rich in the process."

"You're kidding!" she whispered. "All of this for *that*?"

"Uh-huh," he said with a sigh. "Buddy's been trying to get my dad to sell the place for a while, and now it looks like he's finally pulled it off."

"I'm so sorry, Tom," she said, as she reached through the bars to take his hand. "I heard your father signed the papers this afternoon."

"Who did you hear that from, George?" he asked.

She shook her head in disgust. "As a matter of fact, yes," she said.

"Figures," he said. "They're both in it up to their eyeballs."

"Have you seen him? Your father?" she asked.

"Yes. He came by earlier today. He looks old," he answered. "He's sold the ranch so he can hire an attorney Says he'll take care of everything, but..."

Jennie Lue shook her head. "No...don't do that, Tom. Don't give up. Everything is going to be taken care of, you'll see."

A soft smile crept across Tom's face. "I sure wish I had your attitude." He squeezed her hand. "What about your father? What does he think about all this?"

She shook her head. "He's been acting like an ass. He tried to tell me how something like this was bound to happen and how it's the best thing for me. But all he's really done is prove how ignorant he really is."

"Don't say that," Tom said. "He's your father."

"Well, it's true!" she said. "I told him I was coming to see you tonight, but he wouldn't have any of it so I had to get Cornelius to bring me." A soft smile came to her face as she shrugged. "Of course, it gave me an idea, so... it worked out better this way."

Tom smiled. "I want you to know something...," he began.

They both jumped when Buddy's voice bellowed from the next room, "Your five minutes is up! Come on outta there!"

Jennie Lue stood from her chair and looked back over her shoulder before turning back to Tom. "I'm not going to let anything happen to you, Tom," she said, "I promise."

"Well, I know your daddy has a lot of pull in this county," he whispered and gave her a tired smile, "but I doubt even he could get me out of this mess. They got me hemmed in good."

She glanced at Buddy who was walking toward them, then turned back to Tom. "My father's not going to have anything to do with this," she whispered. Just before Buddy got to the cell, she took a deep breath, stared deep into Tom's eyes and mouthed the words, "I love you."

Tom's heart jumped. He wanted to tell her the same thing but before he could, Buddy walked into the hallway and stepped between them. He looked at Jennie Lue and said, "I kept my end of the bargain. Now it's time for you to keep yours."

Tom was in shock and would have killed Buddy if he could, but he was taken by complete surprise when Jennie Lue looked up at his brother and asked, "Where would you like to do this?"

Buddy glanced at Tom, then turned to Jennie Lue and said with a smirk, "Why not right here? It'd be kinda weird with Tom watching and all, and I'm not so sure he'd enjoy it, but I know I would."

"Fine by me," she said, as she set her purse and hat on the chair.

"Don't do it, Jennie Lue! Please!" Tom begged through the cold iron bars.

Jennie Lue answered him with a vacant stare as she put both hands behind her back and unbuttoned the back of her dress while Buddy moved in close to grab her breasts with both hands. Tom couldn't bear to watch, but he didn't turn away. His only thought was to lure Buddy close enough to where he could strangle him with his bare hands. He was almost out of his mind as his brother unbuttoned his trousers and put both arms around Jennie Lue so he could pull her close, but Buddy suddenly stood straight and froze as she said, "I think we're done now."

Tom had no idea why his brother started backing away from her so quickly, but relief washed over him when he saw the derringer she pointed directly at Buddy's heart as she forced him to back up across the hall. Without taking her eyes off the sheriff, she said, "Tom, grab his gun."

"Pretty clever hiding that gun beneath your dress, but you're making a big mistake," Buddy said as Tom reached through the bars and took his pistol.

Jennie Lue glanced at the lock to the cell door and demanded, "Open it."

Buddy knew by the look in her eyes there was a good chance she might pull the trigger, so he reached for the keys on his belt and turned to unlock the cell.

As soon as the door swung free, Tom stepped around his brother into the hallway and asked Jennie Lue, who still had her derringer pointed at the sheriff, "What are we going to do with him?"

"I don't know," she said. "I hadn't thought about that."

"You're not going to get far," Buddy said, his hands in the air. "Every lawman, bounty hunter and anybody else looking to make a buck will be after you." Buddy sneered. "I'll make sure there's a hefty reward."

Tom swung his right fist as hard as he could and caught Buddy flush in the nose. Not only did the force of the punch shatter the cartilage and bone in his nose, but the back of Buddy's head slammed into the iron bars behind him, causing him to drop to the floor like a sack of rocks. Tom dragged him into the cell, leaving a bloody trail on the floor but, after his brother was locked inside, he and Jennie Lue found each other in a strong embrace.

"Are you okay?" he asked as he held her at arm's length.

Her hands were trembling as she answered, "I just wouldn't be able to stand it if I lost you again."

"It's all right," he said, holding her face in his hands. "I love you, too."

"Oh, Tom!" she sobbed. She turned to look at Buddy sprawled out on the floor of the cell and asked, "Is he dead?"

"No," Tom said as he glanced at his brother. "He's not going to feel very good when he wakes up, though." He looked back at her. "And he's going to be mad as hell. I can't believe you did this. What were you thinking?"

"I had to do something!" she said. "Everybody in this rotten town can't wait to see you hang."

The thought made Tom unconsciously rub the side of his neck. "Well, then, I guess we're going to have to leave here. You know that, don't you?"

She nodded quickly. "Of course I know that, and I've got it taken care of. The carriage is right outside. I'm pretty sure we can get out of here without much fuss." She smiled. "Have you ever been to Mexico?"

"No. Not yet, anyway," he said with a chuckle. "What about Cornelius? Where's he?"

"I sent him to the livery," she said. "I didn't want him to be involved, so I told him I wanted him to look at a horse that's for sale over there."

"You would go through all of this? You would give up your family… everything, for me?" he asked.

She looked into his eyes. "I already did. I told you I wasn't going to let anything happen to you."

"You're something else, Jennie Lue Sloan," he said, shaking his head in wonder. He handed her the keys to the jail. "Here, put these in your purse. We don't want to make it easy for Buddy to get out of there." After the key ring was at the bottom of Jennie Lue's bag, he smiled. "Okay, let's go."

They made their way to the gun rack where he pulled off his holster and strapped it on, then moved to the front door where he grabbed his Stetson off the hat stand. They were about to exit out onto the sidewalk when he stopped. "Wait a minute. I need to see something."

"We don't have time," she said.

"It'll only take a second," he said as he walked around Buddy's desk. He tried the drawer, but it was locked. He looked for something to pry the drawer open but finding none he went back to the gun rack and pulled a shotgun off the wall. He went back to the desk and used the weapon as a battering ram. The wood splintered as the twin iron barrels smashed into the desk, taking only three hard blows before the lock gave way. Tom dropped the gun on top of the desk before he yanked the drawer open. "Oh, my God!" he said.

"What is it?" she asked as she came to see.

"Look at this," he said as he reached in and pulled out a hunting knife with a handle carved from the antler of a deer. He held it up to Jennie Lue. "This is the knife Jim Conner tried to kill me with five-and-a-half years ago. Buddy's had it in his desk all this time." He turned the blade over in his hands and was about to say something else when he glanced at Jennie Lue, and knew something else was wrong.

As if in a trance, Jennie Lue reached into the drawer and pulled out a gold pocket watch. Tears streamed down her face. "This was Henry's. I gave it to him."

"Are you sure?" Tom asked.

"I'm positive," she said as she gently opened the watch. "Look." She handed Tom the timepiece.

A small picture of a younger Jennie Lue was tucked inside the cover. "That means Buddy had him murdered, too," he said.

"There must be a dozen things in here. They all must be some kind of horrible mementos," she said as she stared at the contents.

Tom glanced around the room. He grabbed Buddy's empty saddle bags from the end of the gun rack and emptied the drawer into it. "We have to take this, all of it. This may be our ticket out of this mess." He threw the bags over his shoulder. "Come on. Let's get out of here."

"Let me go first," she said as they got to the door. "I'll let you know if it's clear before you come out. There shouldn't be many people out there. Just act natural." She stood on her toes and kissed him once before she smiled, opened the door and walked across the sidewalk to the carriage.

Tom watched her settle into her seat as she scanned the street for signs of danger. His heart was racing as she finally nodded once. He stepped out of the office door and tried to act as if he didn't have a care in the world, but fully expecting their plan to fail when someone recognized him and sounded the alarm. It seemed an eternity passed before he was in the carriage and they were moving down the street and out of downtown Belton. He was sure their luck wouldn't hold as he hid his face from a few prying glances, but no one on the nearly deserted sidewalks recognized them as they left the outskirts of town and made their way into the safety of darkness.

"What do we do now?" she asked.

"Let me have the reins," he said. He immediately put Pancho into a fast trot. "First thing we have to do is get rid of this buggy, so we've got to get to the ranch before Buddy does. I'm sure that will be his first stop." He glanced at her dress. "You can't ride in that. Do you have any other clothes?"

"You need to give me a little credit," she said. "I have a saddle in the back, along with a change of clothes." She carefully climbed over the front seat to the back. "I thought it might be best if I changed on the way. Don't turn around unless I tell you, okay?"

Tom laughed. "What happens if I can't help myself?"

"You'll wind up with a knot on the back of your head," she said.

Tom laughed again, but couldn't turn around to look if he wanted to because they were moving down the bumpy dirt road far faster than he would under normal conditions. Even though the half-moon hung directly overhead and partially lit up the night, he was forced to rely on the eyesight of the horse as they raced toward the Four C's while he prayed the animal didn't stumble.

He smiled at Jennie Lue as she climbed back into the seat next to him wearing a shirt, boots and pants, but all of his attention was quickly brought back to the dangers at hand as he steered Pancho home. Once they were on the other side of the shallow crossing, he relaxed a little because he knew this stretch of ground like the back of his hand, but neither said a word until the carriage came to a stop in front of the house.

Candlelight cast a soft glow from the windows of the front room as Tom asked, "Can you stay here and get Pancho saddled?"

"Of course," she said.

"All right," he said as he grabbed the saddle bags and jumped to the ground. "I'll run back to the barn and get Clever ready."

She watched Tom disappear around the corner of the house as she quickly made her way to the front of the carriage. She deftly unhooked Pancho from his collar and belly band and was in the process of removing the reins and blinders when she was startled by Jim Wallace's voice.

"Jennie Lue?" he said, "what are you doing out here at this hour?"

She turned to look at Tom's father and was struck by the way he seemed to have grown old overnight. She took a deep breath. "Mister Wallace, Tom's out back in the barn." She glanced up at Miss Emma who walked out onto the porch in her robe. "We're leaving," she said.

The expression on Jim's face was a mixture of sudden hope and horror as he realized what was taking place. "Did you do this?" he asked.

Jennie Lue's eyes welled up as she nodded and held Pancho by his bridle, so Jim came down off the porch as quickly as he could and limped around the corner of the house on his way to the barn. When he was out of sight, she looked at Miss Emma. "If I didn't do anything they would have either killed him or sent him back to prison. I couldn't let that happen."

Miss Emma stepped off the porch, walked up to Jennie Lue and gave her a loving hug. She held her at arm's length before she pulled away. "If you two are going to take a trip, I guess we'd better get some things together."

Jennie Lue was just as grateful for Miss Emma's smile as she was for the supplies as she squeezed her hands and said, "Thank you! Thank you so much."

Tom had thrown his saddle onto the back of Clever as he stood in his stall and was pulling the belly strap tight when he heard Jim say, "Tom! What's going on?"

Without taking his eyes off his task, he said, "Jennie Lue and I are leaving, Dad." When the strap was secure and tight, he turned to face his father. "This is the only way out for me. I have to go."

Jim looked as if he was about to collapse. "I already hired an attorney, Tom. Please give me a chance to get this all sorted out. If you leave now, they'll hunt you down. They'll find you and kill you."

Tom stepped over to his father and held him by the shoulders. "It's too late for that, Dad. But, before I go, I have to show you something." He knelt down and lifted the saddle bag off the stall floor and turned it upside down, spilling the contents onto the dirt. He looked at his father who was already on one knee reaching for the knife. "Jennie Lue and I found this in Buddy's desk."

Jim appeared to be in shock as he turned the knife over in his hands. "Is this is what I think it is?"

Tom spread out the rest of the contents on the ground as he nodded. "Yes. He had it all along."

Jim looked as if he had no life left in him. "These last five years, you should have never been gone."

Tom put a hand on his father's shoulder and picked up the pocket watch. "It gets worse. This belonged to Henry Sloan. Buddy must have had him killed."

Jim took the watch from Tom and opened the cover to reveal the picture of Jennie Lue. "Before they hung that black kid, everybody in town wondered what happened to this watch. Henry made a point to show it off whenever he came to town. Loved to tell everybody how expensive it was." Jim took a deep breath and pointed to the objects on the ground. "Do you know anything about the rest of this?"

Tom looked down and shook his head. "No, but it's a safe bet that all of it has something to do with folks who have been killed around here." They looked over the rest of the contents, which included a straight razor, purse, belt buckle, sheriff's badge, hat band and leather wallet. "Any of it mean anything to you?"

Jim put an elbow on his knee as he reached over for the sheriff's badge. "This was Bennie Leak's. They said he killed himself." He put it back on the ground and pointed at the straight razor. "And that must have been that barber's; talk was he got robbed and killed on the way home one night. Must have been three years ago. Never found out who did it." He pointed at the belt buckle. "And that was Curry Hampton's."

"Yep, you're right," Tom said with a nod.

Jim opened the empty wallet and tossed it on the ground. "I'm not sure who this belonged to and I don't know about that hat band, either, but I'd be willing to bet that purse belonged to that working girl over at Dayna G's." He rubbed his forehead before slowly getting to his feet. He looked at Tom with a grim, sad look in his eyes. "They found her in bed with her throat cut from ear to ear. Awful thing it was. She was bound and gagged; couldn't have made a sound if she wanted to."

Tom put all the items back in the saddlebag. "I bet nobody ever found out who did that either, did they?" he asked.

"No, but now I think we know who did," Jim answered. He dropped his head to his chest, then slowly looked up at Tom. "Why is Buddy trying to add you to his collection?"

"He wants the ranch. It's why Church and Bear are dead," Tom answered as he stood. "Buddy and George have this plan to get the railroad to come through the middle of the Four C's. They're going to make a whole new town out of this place and get rich in the process." Tom stood and tossed the saddlebag onto Clever's back. "His plan was either to kill me or set me up so you would sell the ranch." He spit on the ground. "It's all about the money."

Jim looked at Tom as if he was crazy. "The railroad? The railroad's not going through here."

"What?" Tom asked. "What are you talking about?"

"You remember that friend of mine I paid a visit to before we left Houston?" Jim asked.

"Yeah," Tom said, "what about him?"

"He works for the railroad that's coming this way," Jim said. "He's the one who's been deciding where those tracks get laid. They're not coming through the Four C's at all, or even Belton. Those tracks are going down a few miles east of us, then up through Temple."

"Are you sure?" Tom asked.

"'Course I'm sure," Jim said.

Tom took a deep breath. "Then all of this has been for nothing…"

"Looks that way," his father said. He reached over and yanked the saddle bag off the horse. "Let me have this."

"What are you going to do with it?" Tom asked.

"I don't know," Jim said, "but I can do a lot more with it here than you can with it out there."

Tom pondered the thought, then looked at his father and nodded. "Okay. But you need to be careful. Buddy told me he even thought about killing you to get the ranch." He pointed at the saddlebag. "From the look of things, I wouldn't put it past him."

"I think you're right," Jim said. He threw the bag over his shoulder. "But you need to get going. Don't worry about me."

Tom walked Clever from his stall. "Look, Dad, whatever you do, don't sell the ranch, okay? It's what Buddy's been trying to get you to do all along."

The sadness in Jim's eyes was now replaced by anger. "I already signed the papers."

"Tell them you changed your mind," Tom said as he walked Clever out of the barn. "Just don't sell the ranch."

Jim grabbed his son by the arm. "Tom…you don't have to go! I've got you a good attorney, the best. Why don't you and Jennie Lue hide out in the powder room until I get this all sorted out? They won't find you there. You and I are the only ones who know about it."

Tom shook his head. "No, we have to leave. One thing you can't do is find a way to erase the tracks Jennie Lue and I left on our way here." He chuckled. "You'd have to shoot a bunch of people to keep them from ripping the place apart looking for us. Nah, it's best we make ourselves scarce. We'll figure a way to get in touch after we're safe."

Jim knew his son was right, but asked anyway, "Are you sure you need to leave? Are you sure you want to do this?"

Tom looked into his father's eyes and smiled. "You know, I asked Jennie Lue the same thing, and you know what she said?" He shook his head in wonder as he added, "She said she already did. Isn't that something?"

Jim took a deep breath as he accepted his son's decision. "Okay, then. Where are you going?"

Tom looked south, then west before he answered with a shrug, "Probably west."

"You have to go deep, then," Jim said. "Everybody with a gun this side of the Rockies will be looking for you."

"I know," Tom said. "I'll be careful."

"And remember, you killed Blondy Harbison," his father continued as they walked away from the barn. "Not only are you going to have to worry about the Texas Rangers, but there's a whole lot of men out there who would love the chance to kill you just for the status, let alone the reward money." He gazed into Tom's eyes to see if there was a chance he would change his mind, but saw none. "You can't defend yourself out there with just a six shooter," he said. "I'll run into the house and get what you need. I'll meet you by the porch."

"Thanks, Dad," Tom said as he led Clever around the side of the house. "Don't worry; everything will be all right. Just don't sell the Four C's."

"I know," Jim said as he headed for the back door, "you told me."

Ten minutes later, Tom and Jennie Lue were standing in front of their horses saying their farewells. Percy and Aya had come out of the bunk house to see what the commotion was all about and quickly pitched in to help gather everything Tom and Jennie Lue might need for their trip. On each saddle horn hung a small dried ham alongside two canteens and there was a sheathed, thirty-caliber rifle attached to the sides of both saddles. They both had gun belts on their hips with Colt forty-fives in the holsters, and there was plenty of ammunition tucked away in the saddle bags that hung next to the bedrolls tied to the back of their saddles. Tom figured they could make it into the Rockies before having to stop and resupply because they each had money, a change of clothes, rain slickers, plenty of matches, jerky and anything else they could think of that might come in handy for their journey.

Tom walked up to Percy first and shook his hand. "Percy, I'm sorry I didn't have the time to get to know you a little better."

"Me, too," Percy answered with a smile, "but I know enough, and you're a good son." He glanced at Jennie Lue as he patted Tom on the shoulder. "Y'all be mighty careful out there. We want to see you two back here safe and sound."

"We will," Tom said as he smiled and nodded. He moved to Aya, who as usual hadn't spoken a word, and gave him a hug. Aya had tears running down his face as he finally stepped back and shook Tom's hand vigorously, but there was deep pride in his eyes as he pointed at him and Jennie Lue and used his fist to tap his heart.

Tom choked up as he said, "I'll miss you too, Aya."

Aya poked Tom's chest with his finger and said, "Be...strong." He then hugged Tom once more and whispered in his ear, "Be...smart...safe."

Tom pulled away and nodded before moving over to Miss Emma. They gave each other a polite embrace before he pointed at his father. "Take good care of him for me."

Emma glanced at Jim and smiled. "I'll do my best. He's kind of ornery, you know." She nodded at Jennie Lue. "And you take good care of her. She loves you very much."

Tom seemed embarrassed as he wiped away a tear. "I know. I love her, too."

He walked to his father and held him close. "I love you, Dad. Whatever you do, just don't sell the ranch, okay?"

Jim was doing his best to act strong, but his eyes were welling up as he nodded. "All right, Tom, all right. You two need to get going, now; it's time."

All were silent as Tom and Jennie Lue climbed into their saddles but, before they turned their horses away to begin their journey, Jim said, "Promise me you'll write as soon as you can. Let me know where you are."

"I promise," Tom said.

Tom and Jennie Lue's tearful farewell ended as they put the horses into a trot but, before they disappeared into the darkness, Tom called out: "Tell Buddy we went south to Mexico!"

"I'll get this straightened out, son…I promise!" his father called.

There wasn't a dry eye among them as the sounds of hoof beats grew fainter in the distance. Miss Emma walked over to put her arms around Jim.

Percy scratched the top of his head and kicked the dirt, saying, "I sure am sorry, Mister Wallace. This is a hell of a thing." He walked onto the porch and collapsed in one of the chairs. Aya took a deep breath as he nodded at Jim, an oddly determined look in his eyes, then turned and quickly made his way back to the bunkhouse.

Jim and Miss Emma stayed out in the yard long after the sound of horses faded completely and never said a word as they succumbed to the sickening feeling in their stomachs. When they finally turned and made their way up the steps into the house, they were so lost in their thoughts they didn't even notice Percy as they passed him on the porch.

After the house went quiet and the crickets regained their control over the noises of the night, a dark dreadful feeling settled over the ranch. For the next twenty-four hours, sleep at the Four C's was a luxury only Chas could afford, but anger, grief, shock, longing and a whole host of other demons were cheap and in abundant supply.

No one at the Four C's had any clue as to what the future might bring and only Aya had any idea what to do next, but they all owned stock in the anguished, unspoken belief that, if Tom Wallace and Jennie Lue Sloan got lucky over the next few days, and didn't get caught or killed, it was highly unlikely either one would ever be able to step foot onto the Four C's again.

CHAPTER 20

Cowhouse Creek

Percy watched Jim smooth the saddle blanket on the back of his horse and asked, "What ya gonna do?"

"I'm going over to go see Jennie Lue's father. Maybe I can get some help out of him," Jim said as he turned and walked over to his saddle, sitting atop a bale of hay. "If not, I'll have to go after Tom and Jennie Lue myself."

"What about Buddy?" Percy asked.

"Well, he's gotta know Tom took everything out of that drawer," Jim said. "He'll come by here first. When he does, you make it clear I don't want him around while I'm gone."

Percy raised an eyebrow and slowly shook his head. "That's your boy, Jim. He grew up here. He ain't gonna pay attention to anything I have to say."

"There's a shotgun by the front door," Jim said, "he'll pay attention to that."

Percy cocked his head and nodded. "That ought to do it."

Jim took a hard look at Percy. "Buddy's done enough harm, but only use it if you have to."

Percy exhaled deeply. "That's a tough thing to ask of a man, but I'll make sure he don't do nothin' 'til you get back."

"Good," Jim said. He grabbed his saddle and walked back to throw it over his horse. "Where's Aya?" he asked.

"Don't know," Percy said. He pushed the stall door open for Jim. "I think he lit out not long after Tom and Jennie Lue left."

Jim finished securing his saddle and saddle bag, then led his horse out of the stall. "He's probably around here somewhere. It's his way of looking after the place." They stopped just outside the barn. "I want you to make sure he knows I need him to keep an eye on the cattle 'til I get back."

"Yes, sir." Percy smiled. "I'm not sure how much he'll understand, but I'll do my best."

Jim grabbed his saddle horn and carefully stepped up onto his horse before he looked down at Percy. "I need you to take care of the place, plus Miss Emma and Chas. I might be back before noon or a week from today, I don't know. I'm not sure where all this is going to lead."

"Don't worry about us," Percy said. "I'll make sure everything is fine around here 'til you get back."

Jim sat up straight in his saddle and glanced around in the darkness. "It's kind of funny how things work out sometimes, isn't it? Fate's the damnedest thing." He looked down at Percy. "When my leg was busted up, I didn't even know you, but I was depending on you to save my life. Here we are, twenty some years later, you haven't been here three days and I'm counting on you again."

Percy chuckled and reached up to shake Jim's hand. "You're right; fate is a funny thing, but you just get on out there and make sure Tom and Jennie Lue get back in one piece."

"Thank you," Jim said. "I don't how I can ever repay you."

Percy chuckled. "You just keep that piano of yours tuned up and we'll call it even. Maybe throw in a steak every now and then. How 'bout that?"

Jim smiled. "That's a deal." He turned his horse away from the barn. "There's a letter on the kitchen table I signed giving you permission to keep everybody off the property while I'm gone. That might come in handy if I don't make it back here quick." Jim tipped his hat. "And tell Emma I'll be back as soon as I can."

"She don't know you're leavin?" Percy asked.

"No," Jim said with a sigh. "I didn't want to wake her."

"You didn't want to wake her?" Percy asked with a wry smile. "You sure it wasn't 'cause you didn't want to listen to her give you the devil on why this might not be such a good idea?"

Jim laughed. "I always did like you, Percy," he said. "Wish me luck." He kicked his horse in the sides and galloped away.

Percy looked into the darkness that swallowed Jim Wallace. "Somethin' tells me we're all gonna need plenty of that," he said softly as he shook his head and started back to the house.

"I swear…when I find you, Tom, I'm gonna break every bone in your body," Buddy said as he rubbed the side of his head. He had just cleared the shallow crossing on his way to the Four C's and was taking a moment to massage away some of the headache caused by his crooked, black-and-blue nose. "Then I'm gonna have some fun with your girlfriend," he added, as he kicked his horse in the sides.

Two hours ago, he woke to find himself locked in his own jail. After yelling through the window at the top of his lungs, it didn't take long to attract the attention of a young man who came in and set him free. Although the situation was a bit embarrassing, Buddy decided to use the event to his advantage and sent that same young man out into the streets to spread the word that Tom Wallace and Jennie Lue Sloan were now fugitives wanted by the law. The next thing he did was head over to the house where the telegraph operator lived and left word that, as soon as the office opened, he needed a wire sent to Austin so they could send a Marshall to watch over things while he was gone. He also told him to make sure every town in Texas knew there was a thousand dollar reward out for Tom Wallace, dead or alive. He had no idea where the money would come from, but he would worry about that detail later. It would be far better to owe somebody for killing his brother than to have Tom running loose with enough evidence to put a noose around his neck. There was also Jennie Lue Sloan to deal with and Buddy wasn't going to lose any sleep if she caught a stray bullet before this was over, but the idea he could settle that score his own way would consume his thoughts throughout the rest of the day.

He paid a visit to George Bell's home, but afterward wished he hadn't. The mayor's first reaction was to panic but, after a heated conversation about what to do if Tom and Jennie Lue showed up in town somewhere, he seemed to settle down. George assured him the money for the railroad was in his office and he would take care of his end of business first thing this morning as planned, but there was an odd look in George's eyes as Buddy left that made him more uncomfortable the more he thought about it. He tried to shrug it off, but it stuck to him like glue.

He knew George had always been a weak coward and it was no surprise he was showing his true colors now, but there was a feeling in his gut that if he didn't take care of his brother and get back into town soon the mayor would wind up doing something stupid, and he'd be better off to keep on riding and never come back to Belton again.

As soon as he crossed Cowhouse Creek, he started thinking about what would happen if Tom and Jennie Lue were still at the ranch, and his adrenaline started flowing when the house came into view. The place was lit up, allowing him to plainly see Jennie Lue's carriage parked out front but, as he drew closer, he realized his plans for a quick resolution was not going to happen here because her horse was missing and they most likely were, too. He had been going over the story he would tell his father about what took place at the jail, but those thoughts left his mind when he arrived at the porch and was greeted by Percy, who stood along the rail with a shotgun leveled at his chest.

"What the hell is that about, boy?" Buddy growled.

"Your daddy told me not to let nobody in this house 'til he gets back," Percy answered flatly.

"So I guess he ain't here?" Buddy asked. Percy didn't say a word or move a muscle. "Did he say where he was going?" Once again, silence was his answer, so he looked around and noticed Miss Emma was watching from one of the windows.

"You know Tom and Jennie Lue are wanted by the law now, don't you, boy?" He stepped down out of the saddle and walked over to look in the carriage before he turned his attention to Percy. "And since I'm the law, I'm gonna have a look around."

Buddy started for the stairs but didn't get far because he was stopped in his tracks by the sound of both barrels being cocked. "I got something to tell ya, sheriff, and ya might want to listen close," Percy said. He pulled the butt of the gun up to his shoulders and took dead aim at Buddy. "I'm absolutely sure your daddy was talking about you when he said nobody."

Buddy stared at Percy with malicious eyes before he nodded. "Let me see if I got this right...a black man staying with a white woman in the house I grew up in is gonna tell me what to do. Is that how it is, boy?" There was no answer from Percy. Buddy rubbed his chin and laughed. "Wheeew! People 'round here are gonna love that one."

He stood, biting his lower lip and thinking about reaching for his pistol before he finally backed down and chuckled. He turned and walked away from the house before looking back at Percy. "That was a bad mistake you just made, boy. After this is over, I'll make sure you pay for it." He stopped and knelt down to look over the hoof prints surrounding the carriage. "People forget sometimes I can be a mean son of a bitch, but I always remind 'em in the end." He stood and looked at Percy. "I'll make sure you go to your grave thinking about that."

"Hate to disappoint ya, but the last thing I think about won't be you," Percy said. The shotgun was still aimed squarely at Buddy's chest. "Might turn out to be the other way around. And just to let you know, I wouldn't care one way or the other if I watched you bleed out right now."

"Is that so?" Buddy asked. He stood and walked back to the porch. "That's mighty bold talk comin' from a two-bit, washed-up old black man."

Percy didn't bat an eye as Buddy stopped near the bottom step. The barrel of his gun remained steady as he said, "If you take one more step, I aim to sit in the shade the rest of the day and watch the flies shit in your eyeballs. Understand, *Sheriff?*"

Buddy glared at Percy, then chuckled and pointed at the ground. "All this dew on the ground is gonna make it pretty damned easy to track 'em." He laughed again. "You be sure to tell my father I should have all this wrapped up soon." He pointed at Percy as if his hand was a pistol and fired his finger. "Then I'll be back for you."

He turned, climbed back on his horse and rode off, never looking back at the Four C's or the decisions he made that brought him to this point. Buddy had given the idea plenty of thought and now knew, one way or the other, it was time for him to leave Bell County for good. He was more than ready to kill his brother and get his hands on the money from the ranch because then he could leave Texas a rich man. But, if things didn't work out that way, it wouldn't be such a bad deal to start over in a town like San Francisco or Carson City, Denver or Salt Lake or Los Angeles — anywhere, just as long as it wasn't here. He'd much rather spend the rest of his life living in style, but Buddy was content knowing that, no matter how all this turned out, he was either going to leave this God-forsaken part of the world today, or sometime within the week after he was paid.

The thought also occurred to him maybe he wouldn't catch up to Tom and Jennie Lue until years later in another town, but that wouldn't be so bad either because killing them then would be just as enjoyable as killing them now. With any luck, though, he'd catch them before the end of the day, and his brother would spend his last moment on earth watching Jennie Lue get what she had coming. Even though the pain from his broken nose had given him a pounding headache, he started whistling a tune as his horse broke into a gallop because he knew there would be plenty of satisfaction in taking his time with that.

Jim arrived at the Double T just before daylight to show Turner the contents of Buddy's desk drawer. After a brief conversation, they were in the saddle and on their way into town. At first Turner didn't believe Buddy or George could be involved in the events of the last few days but, after seeing Henry Sloan's pocket watch with his own eyes, he knew he had to do everything in his power to make sure Tom and Jennie Lue made it back home safe.

The first thing they did when they got into Belton was to stop at the sheriff's office but, as expected, Buddy was nowhere to be found. The next was to go by the mayor's office, where all they found was an empty, open safe and a few stories from nosy office workers about how George Bell took off in his wagon an hour or so before. They were no doubt curious as to why Jim Wallace and Turner Bell were seen together for the first time since anyone could remember, but there was no answer to that question because the two men turned and walked out of city hall just as fast as they walked in. Lastly, Jim and Turner paid a visit to the telegraph office where they sent a wire to a friend of Turner's in Austin who was a captain in the Texas Rangers.

As they hurried out into the street and climbed on their horses, each hoped that before another hour passed, every lawman in the state would know, even though Tom Wallace had killed a deputy sheriff, he and Jennie Lue were not guilty of anything. Neither said a word about it all morning, but they both knew what Buddy would try to do next and were well aware the only real option they had left was to ride west as fast as their horses would take them. Jim had a good idea where Tom would try to bed down later that evening, but the idea was quickly overshadowed by the sickening realization they were two hours behind Buddy and he had a far better chance to get there first.

They raced by the Four C's as they picked up the trail of Tom and Jennie Lue. Percy and Miss Emma were standing out on the porch as they went by, and even though Jim felt Miss Emma deserved some kind of explanation for his leaving this morning, he knew there wasn't time. He would have felt a lot better if he could have seen the worried yet understanding look in her tear-filled eyes as she held her hand up to wave goodbye, but he had his eyes glued to the ground and his full attention directed at the hoof prints in the dirt as he and Turner rode past.

He and Turner had said little to each other all morning. Jim knew not much was being said because this was the first time in years they had been around each other for any length of time and neither knew what to say for fear their differences would boil to the surface and get in the way of the task at hand. Ten hours later, after riding in the hot Texas sun, they were both tired and irritable as they stood by their horses and let them drink from a small stream.

Both men were covered with a fine layer of the grit they picked up along the way, and Jim had chuckled to himself more than once at how Turner's ragged looks seemed to get progressively worse as the day wore on. Jim was used to coming back to the house at the end of every long, hot summer day looking like he had lost a fight with a large dirt pile, but Turner was the kind of man whose idea of hard work was to find Cornelius to get one of his prized pair of boots shined up to his liking.

As they watered their horses, Jim noticed that Turner's brown-and-gray handlebar mustache was now just a small mass of unkempt hair with a fair shade of dirt to it. He figured it was a good bet the shirt and pants he wore would be burned in the trash barrel as soon as he got back home. The sweat-soaked, dust-covered derby on Turner's head hadn't done a thing to keep the sun off his red face and more than likely would join the rest of his clothes in the fire as well.

The boots he had on this morning were so polished a man could see his face in them but, as the sun dropped closer to the western horizon, they were scratched up from heel to toe and just as dull as the ground they had been covering. When they first started out, Jim thought there was a real possibility

Turner might not be able to keep up with him as the day passed but, as the sun dipped toward the western horizon, Jim secretly admired the way Turner handled himself and his horse thus far.

"I sure hope you know what you're doing," Turner said, as he took off his hat and wiped his brow.

Jim took a long swallow from his canteen. "I do," he said.

"I do? That's it?" Turner said. "I do? I've been taking your lead all day and you haven't once tried to explain to me why we quit following their tracks..." Turner pulled out his pocket watch and glanced at it. "...four hours ago! Why is that?"

Jim put his canteen back in his saddle bag. "I know where they're going... that's why."

"Did they *tell* you where they were going?" Turner asked.

"Nope," Jim said.

Turner put his hat back on and took a deep breath. "Okay, then. So tell me, where are they headed? Or, to be more precise, where do you *think* they're headed?"

Jim looked into the distance and pointed. "Just this side of Pidcoke. I figure we're only about three or four miles from there."

Turner shook his head in exasperation. "*Pidcoke*? We broke off their trail for that?" All Turner got for an answer was a nod. "You mean to tell me you think Tom and Jennie Lue are going to ride into a town, I don't care how small it is, walk into a hotel and not expect to get caught? Are you crazy?"

"They're not going into town," Jim said.

Turner's frustration was apparent. "Then what the hell does Pidcoke have to do with anything?"

"Turner," Jim said, "I'm sure Tom is going to try and bed down somewhere just this side of Pidcoke, along Cowhouse Creek where the washouts are set back in the limestone." He checked to make sure the billet strap was tight beneath his horse before adding, "It's a full day's ride to get there from Belton and a perfect place to hole up for the night. We might be able to get there before Buddy if you can just keep up, all right?"

"Jim Wallace, you've always been a stubborn son of a bitch!" Turner said as Jim climbed back onto his horse. "What about what I think they're going to do? Did you ever consider asking me about that?"

"Not really," Jim answered, "but I get the feeling you're about to tell me."

Turner ignored the remark as he shook his head and pointed to a ridge in the distance. "I think we need to head north, over there." He climbed onto his horse and grabbed his reins. "If we can get to the top of that cliff we might get lucky and either find them or, at the very least, catch sight of them."

"They're not headed that way," Jim said as he settled in his saddle. "Besides, we can't just hope to get lucky."

"Damn it! Would you listen to me?" Turner said. He thrust his finger at Jim. "If I was them, I'd head to the high ground over there. It'll be getting dark soon and, if they were up on that ridge, they could see anyone coming or going for miles."

Jim took a deep breath and said, "Turner, you don't know what you're talking about."

"I don't know what I'm talking about?" Turner yelled. His horse was startled and almost bolted, but he kept the animal in place by yanking back hard on the reins. "You ass! You haven't known what you were talking about since before you got back from the war. Do you ever think about that?"

Jim's face was red with anger. "Don't you start with Ruby, Turner! I'll climb off this horse right now and whip your ass if you even think about bringing her up, you understand?"

"Oh, yeah. That will help things," Turner said angrily. "Here we are out in the middle of nowhere trying to find our kids and you're more worried about whipping my ass over something that didn't happen twenty years ago!"

"Damn it, Turner!" Jim yelled. "I told you not to talk about it!"

"Talk about what?" replied Turner. He was pointing at Jim, so mad his finger was shaking. "About how Judy and I helped Ruby all those years ago, or how you've been such an ass to my whole family for all this time?" Turner jabbed his finger at Jim one more time. "Is *that* what you don't want me to talk about?"

Jim opened his mouth to speak but, before he could get the words out, the crack and echo of a rifle shot in the distance startled the men and their horses.

"Where did that come from?" Turner asked.

"Over there," Jim said, pointing in the direction they had been traveling for the last four hours. They glanced at each other as their long-standing feud vanished, replaced by the dreadful feeling they might already be too late. In that instant, they both knew whatever happened in the past meant absolutely nothing compared to what they were faced with now, so they kicked their horses in the side and sped off toward Cowhouse Creek as a succession of four more shots echoed from the same location as the first.

Lasco Potts and his son Enos had been riding all afternoon, searching every piece of property west of Pidcoke in the hopes they might get lucky enough to catch a glimpse of the infamous killer and the rich girl with him who were on the run from the law. They had no solid reason to think Tom Wallace or Jennie Lue Sloan were heading their way, other than they were probably trying not to be seen. Since Pidcoke hardly qualified as a populated area, it wasn't a bad bet the two outlaws might be somewhere in the area.

The news had traveled fast around town this morning after the wire came in describing how the sheriff was almost killed in his own jail, and since neither one had a nickel to their names nor the prospects of any legitimate work at all, Lasco and his son had set out on their old mules to see if they might strike it rich by capturing or killing the most celebrated killer to come out of Texas since Billy the Kid himself. They had done a little bounty hunting before, and anyone listening to them talk when a jug of whiskey was being passed around might think they were seasoned veterans, but the truth was, they were only successful in tracking down a few people in the last ten years and even then those 'outlaws' were mostly town drunks who didn't show up for a minor court case.

Born in Pidcoke fifty-five years earlier, Lasco never left and was unsuccessful at making any kind of living although he tried his hand at most things, the latest being a failed attempt at carpentry. He couldn't work for anyone for very long because, if he ever had any amount of money in his pocket, it would either wind up in the cash box at the only saloon in Pidcoke or at the small feed store where it was invested in corn for his still. He was a short, skinny man with long white hair and a beard to match who'd spent the last few years wondering if his son Lee would have been sent off to prison if he had been a better father, but the answer to that question was never answered. At the end of every day, Lasco always managed to bury the thought underneath a series of long pulls off a cheap jug of whiskey.

Enos was the spitting image of his father, only younger, and grew up thinking living in a broken-down, one-room shack drinking homemade, rot-gut whiskey until passing out every day was the normal thing to do. Both of them believed there would come a day when one big break would land in their laps and they could finally leave this town for a better life in a big city somewhere. Even though bringing in Tom Wallace was extremely risky, and it would be a gross understatement to say Lady Luck would have to be on their side, their hopes were high today that this was their day.

"Whatch ya think, Pa?" Enos asked as they pulled their mules to a stop at the top of a small bluff overlooking Cowhouse Creek meandering through the limestone twenty feet below.

Lasco pulled off his tattered hat and wiped sweat from his brow with his sleeve. "Don't know, son. I kinda liked our chances when we set out this morning, but maybe they ain't headed this way after all. Texas is a big place, ya know."

Enos scanned the countryside on the other side of the creek. "Ya ain't thinking about quittin' that easy, are ya, Pa?" He pulled the Colt from his holster and spun the cylinder to make sure all the chambers were loaded. "'Cause I aim to find 'em and go down in history as the man that kilt Tom Wallace."

Lasco chuckled and spat on the ground. "I'd slow down a bit there if I was you."

Enos raised his eyebrows. "He's wanted dead or alive, ain't he?"

"That's what they told me the piece of paper said," answered Lasco as he scratched the top of his head, "but tryin' to make Tom Wallace dead ain't gonna be easy."

"Well, you ain't figurin' to take him alive, are ya?" Enos asked.

Lasco looked at his son and chuckled. "Nah. That wouldn't be such a smart idea." He rubbed the neck of his mule before adding with a wink, "Ain't no glory in bringin' a man in alive."

"Good," Enos said, "'cause I was thinkin' the exact same thing."

"Well, we'd best hope we get the perfect chance," Lasco said with a sigh as he put his hat back on. He pointed at his son's pistol. "That old Colt Model Two ya got there was a fine weapon twenty-five years ago, but it ain't now. Even if you're lucky, you're only gonna get one shot off with it against a man like Tom Wallace."

"One shot's all I'm gonna need," Enos said, holstering his gun.

"I hope you're right," Lasco said, shaking his head. He looked into the distance. "I really hope you're right." He glanced at the setting sun before turning his eyes to Enos. "Well, I'm plumb out of ideas. We're almost out of daylight and, if we don't find 'em today, we ain't gonna find 'em at all. So what do ya think, south or north?"

Enos looked to the south, then turned in his saddle to face north. "Your call, Pa, whatever ya think."

"Well, I dunno. Maybe we ought to head up to…" Lasco began. He stopped speaking because of the faint noise moving toward them, which they both recognized immediately as the sound of horse hooves moving through shallow water. The soft echoes bouncing off the narrow limestone walls on either side of Cowhouse Creek quickly made Lasco and his son realize that if Tom Wallace and Jennie Lue Sloan were indeed heading their way, fame and fortune might finally be within their reach but, as he and his son scrambled off their mules and hid them in a thicket of brush, their minds were on a different subject entirely. After climbing down the embankment to take concealed positions on either side of the water, the only thought going through their minds was if the man who shot Blondy Harbison was just a few yards away and headed right toward them, they better not make even the slightest mistake.

"How are you doing?" Tom asked as he turned in his saddle.

Jennie Lue took her eyes off the creek below and said with a tired smile, "I'm okay. It's been a long day, but don't you worry about me."

Tom nodded. "You're an amazing woman, Jennie Lue Sloan. Did I ever tell you that?"

"So far, about a hundred times today," she said with a laugh, "but I still love you."

"And I love you, too," he said before turning his attention back to the meandering creek in front of them.

They had been riding nonstop since they left this morning, but Tom realized early on they should have left Pancho at the Four C's and taken one of his father's horses instead because Jennie Lue's started to play out early in the afternoon, causing them to slow down to an uncomfortable pace throughout the rest of the day. Both of them had sore necks from looking over their shoulders to see if anyone was following but, since they couldn't ride fast, Tom had been careful to stay in the brush or creek beds whenever he could, hoping no one could see them or follow their tracks even if they were close by. He knew their best bet was to get to this stretch of Cowhouse Creek before sunset so he could find a big enough washout somewhere in the limestone to use as a place where he and Jennie Lue could bed down for the night. After a hard, seventeen-hour ride, it now appeared their first day as fugitives would shortly be behind them.

Tom looked at Jennie Lue and smiled. "While I was in prison, I always wondered what it would be like to be on the run but, I have to tell you, I never, ever thought I'd be hunted by my own brother."

"We're not on the run, silly," she said. "We're on our way to a new life."

Tom nodded. "You're an amazing woman, Jennie Lue Sloan. Did I ever tell you that?"

"Geeze, would you shut up already?" she said.

"Sorry, but I just can't help myself," he said with a shrug and a smile. "What's the first thing you're going to do after we put these horses up?" he asked as they made their way around a shallow bend in the creek.

"That's an easy one," she said as she rubbed the back of her neck. "I'm going to wash my face, brush my teeth, and then…and then, well, I don't know. I haven't thought that far ahead."

Tom laughed. "Now that you mention it, I hadn't either." He pointed to a washout just beyond the next bend in the creek. "But it looks like we need to start, because right there is where we're going to stay the night."

"Really?" she said, in a lively tone Tom hadn't heard since early this morning.

"That might be the place," he answered.

A flood of relief swept over them as the anxiety they shouldered all day vanished, replaced by the excitement of knowing they could finally relax for the first time that day.

Tom breathed a heavy, grateful sigh. "I think we made it," he said. A second later, Clever suddenly stopped in his tracks, snorted and perked up his ears as if something up ahead wasn't quite right.

Jennie Lue realized something was wrong as soon as she saw Tom reach down to put his hand on his gun. She pulled reins on Pancho as she whispered, "What is it?"

Tom put his left index finger over his lips and mouthed "Sshhh" as he listened and watched his horse intently scan the creek in front of them, looking for whatever it was that spooked him. After the longest two minutes of the entire day, Clever shook his head and snorted again, then bent down for a drink of water. Whatever startled him was gone. Tom wasn't quite so sure and listened for any sounds coming from the washout ahead that could be cause for alarm but, after another long moment, he too let his guard down. He gently kicked Clever in the sides, saying, "I guess it was nothing. Come on; let's go get some rest."

"You sure?" she asked, riding alongside.

"Sure as I can be," he said. He tried to convince Jennie Lue with his tone of voice everything was all right but, as they slowly made their way up the creek bed toward the washout only twenty yards away, the look in his eyes told a different story. His reflexes did, too, when a large snapping turtle, sunning itself on the bank twenty feet in front of them, lunged into the water with a splash that startled them both. Tom's gun was out and cocked in less than a second but, when he realized what happened, he looked over at Jennie Lue and laughed. "I knew something was wrong," he said. He put his gun back in his holster. "That damned turtle was just waiting to bushwhack us, but I guess he got scared."

Jennie Lue laughed and said, "I'm glad I have a big strong man to protect me from all these mean old turtles."

"Is that some kind of an insult?" he asked indignantly.

"Ohhhh, nooo," she said. "You only had me scared to death." A shudder went through her. "And all over a turtle."

"Wrong! Don't move!" came a booming voice from just to the left of them. Both Pancho and Clever nearly threw their riders as Lasco Potts and his son Enos jumped out from the rocks on either side of the creek, their guns drawn and ready. They sized each other up in silence.

"I know who ya are and, if ya don't take that six-shooter a yours and throw it to the ground nice and slow, I'll blast ya right off that horse," Lasco threatened.

Tom held his reins with both hands, knowing he had little chance of going for his gun, but Lasco could tell he was thinking about it. "Even though I don't want to see it happen, if ya make a move for that pistol, my boy standin' on the other side right there is gonna put a hole in your lady friend," Lasco said.

Tom could see indecision in their eyes because Enos briefly looked at his father as if to say shooting a woman hadn't been part of their plan, but knowing he would have to make two perfect shots against men who already had their guns cocked, and Jennie Lue would get killed if he didn't get them

359

off just right, Tom slowly reached for his pistol and tossed it on the ground before raising his hands over his shoulders. He looked at Jennie Lue. Despair had overcome the bright look that was in her eyes just a few moments ago, and he knew that, unless something completely unexpected happened, the plans they had for a life together would remain forever a dream.

"Pa! We did it! We did it!" Enos yelled as he rushed up to grab the nose band of Pancho's bridle. His pistol was shaking in his dirty hand, but it was still aimed at Jennie Lue. "What we gonna do now, Pa?"

Lasco paid no attention to his son, keeping his eyes on Tom. "I know who ya are, but do ya know who I am?" he asked.

"No," Tom said as he shook his head, "I don't."

Lasco paused for a moment to stare into Tom's eyes, but finally raised a finger at him. "You're the one who wrote that letter, ain't ya?"

Tom gave Jennie Lue a perplexed look before he turned his attention back to the old skinny man with the gun. "What letter?" He shook his head. "I'm not sure what you're talking about."

"You knew my boy," Lasco said. "You didn't save him."

Tom still had his hands in the air, but the thought suddenly occurred to him they believed he was someone else. "Mister, I don't know who you think I am, but I'm pretty sure you've got me confused with somebody else you're looking for."

"Nope," Lasco said, "ain't no confusion here today. You're Tom Wallace, ain't ya?"

Whatever thoughts Tom had about getting out of this mess with a simple case of mistaken identity vanished with the sound of his name, but his stone face kept his emotions from showing. "I've heard of him, but who might you be?"

"My name is Lasco." He pointed at his son. "That there is my son, Enos, least the only one I got left. Either one a them names ring a bell to ya?"

Tom slowly dropped his hands onto his saddle horn as the break he was hoping for presented itself. He nodded. "Yes, they do. You're Lee's father, aren't you? You're Lasco Potts."

"Keep your hands in the air, son," Lasco said. His pistol was not shaking and was pointed directly at Tom's chest. "I want ya to tell me what happened to Lee and why ya didn't do nuthin' to save him."

Tom glanced at Jennie Lue again and it was plain to see by the look on her face she had no idea what was going on. There was a strange combination of hope and despair in her eyes as he raised his hands back in the air, looked back at Lasco and answered, with sadness in his voice, "It was at the rock quarry. We were having a problem getting a rope under one of the big stones so we could haul it up out of there and we kept telling the guards we needed a few more minutes to get it secured. I don't know why, maybe they thought they were being funny, or maybe one of the guards up there decided he was tired of waiting, I don't know. But, before we knew it, the slack came out of the lift rope and that stone got away from us. It didn't get an inch off the ground before it swung around and pinned Lee up against the side of the quarry." Tom took a few deep breaths. "I'm sorry, Mister Potts, but everything happened so fast, Lee didn't have a chance to get out of the way."

Lasco nodded his head slightly as he accepted the story, but continued to hold his gun on Tom. "They said he died in prison, at Huntsville. They buried him there. You're tellin' me he died somewhere else. How can that be?"

"That stone crushed his right leg bad," Tom said. "They should have gotten him to a doctor right away, but they didn't. They didn't care. They finally got him back to Huntsville after a week or so, but it was too late. He died the next day." Tom could tell the story had no impact on the way Lasco Potts was pointing his gun at him, so he added, "I went to visit him at the cemetery before I came home."

The moment that followed was an exchange of glances from everyone there. Jennie Lue was looking at Tom in the hopes his story would be enough for the men to let them go. Enos glanced back and forth with panic in his eyes, worried the story they just heard might be enough to make his father let their one and only chance at fame and fortune slip through their grasp. Tom never looked away from the skinny old man, hoping he would see enough compassion come into his eyes that could mean he was about to let them leave unharmed.

Lasco had other ideas. "I'm sorry, son. I know ya was a friend to my boy and all, and I give ya my word ya can rest in peace knowin' we'll treat the little lady here with respect, but I need the money," he said, ice in his voice.

Jennie Lue shouted, "No!" as Lasco prepared to fire but, before he could pull the trigger, Lasco was knocked off his feet, as though swatted down by an unseen giant hand. A split second later, they understood what happened as the echo of a rifle shot filled the air.

Tom and Jennie Lue fought to gain control of their surprised horses as Tom turned to where the shot came from. He turned his attention back to

Enos and yelled, "Don't shoot!"

Enos's face was a mixture of desperation and confusion. "Pa! Are ya okay?" he shouted. His father had fallen onto his side and was trying to drag himself out of the water and onto the bank of the creek, but his agonized, labored movements made it clear his wound was severe and life was leaving him quickly.

Both Tom and Jennie Lue feared Lasco's son might start shooting, so they stayed in their saddles, their hands still raised. "Please! Don't shoot!" Tom pleaded, as Enos clumsily tried to keep his attention and his pistol pointed at them as he scrambled sideways across the creek. He only got halfway to the other side before a hole appeared in the middle of his brow and the back of his head exploded in a spray of blood, causing him to fall lifeless into the shallow waters of Cowhouse Creek.

Tom looked at Jennie Lue. "Get out of sight!" he yelled as he jumped out of the saddle, yanked his rifle out of its sheath and sloshed his way over to Lasco. When he rolled the old man onto his back, Tom could see his wound was fatal. There was a large hole in the middle of his shirt and his long white beard was now stained bright red from the blood coming from corner of his mouth. He grabbed Lasco by the arms and dragged him up the bank before looking across to the other side of the creek at Jennie Lue, who was crouching behind a boulder twenty yards away. "Are you okay?" he called to her.

Jennie Lue was visibly shaken, but she nodded and answered, "Yes."

Tom desperately scanned the area for signs of the shooter, but his attention was brought back to Lasco as the old man asked through labored breaths, "What? What the hell happened?"

"I don't know," Tom said.

Lasco coughed up a mouthful of blood and grabbed Tom by the arm. "They bury my boy proper?" he asked with difficulty.

Tom nodded. "He's in a good spot, Mister Potts. I went to see him before I came home. Carved his name on his cross, too." Tom waited for the old man to quit coughing before he added, "Lee was a good man. I'm sorry he didn't make it."

"Me, too…me…too," Lasco said. Then his strength failed him completely and a blank, glazed stare came over his eyes.

Tom took a deep breath and leaned back against the rock he was hiding behind before glancing over at Jennie Lue. "I want you to stay put until I figure out what's going on, okay?" he said. Jennie Lue nodded.

He tried to size up the situation. The shots had definitely come from behind them, but everything happened so fast that he didn't know how many shooters there were or where the shots had come from. The one thing he did know was that they couldn't risk exposing themselves; Lasco and his son had been gunned down by someone who didn't miss much.

Jennie Lue was trying to be calm, but there was fear in her eyes. "What do we do now?" she asked.

Tom was desperately trying to come up with an answer when they were startled by the sound of his own name. "Tom! Are...you...okay?" came the voice in broken English.

Relief and excitement filled them both as they looked out from behind their hiding places to see Aya making his way to them, fifty yards downstream. He held his rifle in the air as he carefully climbed down the steep embankment, but dropped it to his side once he reached the bottom and started running to them.

Tom looked at Jennie Lue. "Get the horses," he said, then ran to meet his old friend. Even from a distance there was a troubled look on Aya's face Tom didn't understand and made him slow as he drew closer. Initially, Tom thought Aya was worried and trying to reach him in a hurry because of what just happened but, when another shot rang out and Aya tumbled hard to the ground, it suddenly became clear another shooter was out there and Aya must have known it.

Tom ran up to his friend and grabbed him by the arms to pull him out of the line of fire, but never had the chance because another shot rang out. He suddenly felt and heard his femur snap in two as a bullet slammed into his left thigh. He watched the world spin for a brief moment as he fell backward. The searing pain that followed nearly made him pass out, but he managed to turn over on his belly and crawl in front of Aya to see if he was still alive. His friend was breathing, but had an exit wound just under his right collarbone and was bleeding profusely from a large gash on the side of his head from where he landed on the hard limestone floor of Cowhouse Creek.

Tom shook his friend and yelled, "Aya! Aya!", but there was no movement or response. He turned to look for Jennie Lue, hoping he could warn her to stay away, but she had already made her way down the creek and was kneeling beside him before he could say a thing.

Tears flowed down her cheeks. "Oh, my God, Tom...are you all right? Tell me you're all right."

"Get out of here!" he said through clenched teeth as he held his leg. "They're going to kill us!"

"I'm not leaving you," she said. She looked at his leg. "Let me see." She pried his hands off to see how bad the wound was only to see a large amount of blood spurt out onto the ground. She realized he would bleed to death if she didn't find a way to get a tourniquet on his leg, so without thinking, she started taking off her belt.

"What are you doing?" he asked, desperate for her safety. "You need to get out of here!"

"I'm not leaving you," she said, her determination clear. She stripped her belt off in a matter of seconds and wrapped it as tightly as she could around Tom's thigh. "The first thing we need to do is stop that bleeding." Content she did the best she could and the flow of blood had eased considerably, she asked, "Where did the shots come from?"

Tom had to let a fit of pain pass before he could answer. "Over there," he said, nodding his head. "I'm not sure, but it had to be from over there, from the other side of the creek."

Jennie Lue looked off in that direction but, after a moment, she glanced back at Tom and said, "I'm going to go get the horses. I'll be right back."

"No!" Tom shouted, as he reached up for her hand.

Jennie Lue got to her feet and turned to run back up stream but didn't make it ten feet before another shot rang out. She heard what sounded like a bumble bee whiz passed her nose and nearly jumped out of her skin as the bullet slammed into the limestone wall just in front and to the right of her head. Bits and pieces of rock sprayed out from the wall and stopped her dead in her tracks. She knew whoever pulled the trigger was not going to miss the next time.

"Stop it!" she screamed at the top of her lungs as she shook her fists in the air and turned to look for the shooter. Her tears were flowing as she yelled, "Who are you?"

"My, my, my. If it ain't Miss Jennie Lue Sloan out here in the middle of nowhere," came a voice she and Tom recognized immediately. They looked to the other side of Cowhouse Creek to see Buddy Wallace start down the embankment thirty yards away, a rifle in one hand and his pistol in the other. There was dried blood all over his mustache and down the front of his shirt from his crooked, swollen nose. The devilish look in his eyes was magnified a great deal by the dark purple-and-black bruises covering most of his face.

"Fancy meeting you two here," he added with a laugh as he reached the bottom of the creek. "Small world, I guess."

The fear and worry in Jennie Lue's eyes was replaced by anger. Without thinking, she marched toward him in a rage. "You son of a bitch!!" she screamed, but stopped suddenly as Buddy cocked his pistol and aimed it squarely at her chest.

"You need to stay right there," he said. "I ain't gonna waste another bullet." He walked over and took her pistol before throwing it and Tom's rifle into the creek. He took a moment to make sure his brother didn't have a gun in his holster before moving over to Aya and tossing his rifle into the water as well. There was a smirk on his face as he looked down at Tom. "I didn't really want to kill Aya, seeing as how we grew up with him and all. And he did save me some trouble by shooting those other two fellas up the creek but, you know, sometimes you do what you have to do." He inspected the bullet wound in Tom's leg and laughed. "You know, Tom, you busted up my nose pretty good, but *that's* gotta hurt. I guess today's not your lucky day, is it?"

Tom struggled to rise but fell back onto the ground, saying between set teeth, "Let Jennie Lue go, Buddy. It's only me you want."

Buddy leaned his rifle against a large boulder, but his pistol was still pointed squarely at Jennie Lue as he walked in front of her. "You're wrong, Tom. I came here for more than that." He tried to smooth his bloodied red mustache and pushed his hair behind his ears. "A lot more."

"Tom's hurt bad; he could die! I'll do whatever you want if you let him live," Jennie Lue said as she took off her hat, her blonde curls falling around her neck. She quickly unbuttoned her blouse and dropped it to the ground. Buddy couldn't take his eyes off her as she fumbled with the laces of her simple corset and pulled it off. She glanced down at her chest before looking into Buddy's eyes. "This is what you want, isn't it?"

A huge grin came over Buddy's face. He turned to Tom and said with a laugh, "I bet you never thought I'd be there when she showed you her tits for the first time, did you, brother?"

"Stop it, Buddy! Please!" Tom pleaded through his pain. "Just get on your horse and ride off. Mexico…California…anywhere. I gave Dad the knife and Henry's pocket watch. I told him about the plans you had for selling the ranch. He knows everything. It's over, so just leave!"

"Looks like I'm gonna have to now…thanks to you," Buddy said. He shook his head and spit on the ground. "I've been out here all day chasing you two, trying to figure out how I could come up with an explanation for having all that shit in my desk drawer but, for the life of me, I can't think of a Goddamned thing."

He paused and took a deep breath. "Son of a bitch! Took me almost a year to get the old man to sign the ranch away. Hell, I had it all worked out. I was going to be a rich man. You even killed Blondy for me so I could keep his share, which was damned impressive, by the way. Now everything's all gone up in smoke."

"Why?" Tom asked.

"Why what?" Buddy said.

"Why did you have to do all this?" Tom grimaced in pain. "What happened to you?"

"You just don't get it, do you, Tom?" his brother answered. "You'd probably be happy as shit growing old in Belton, wouldn't you?"

"What's wrong with that?" Tom said.

"Everything," Buddy said, shaking his head. "I can't stand the thought of it. Nope. That's not for me. I want something better. I want to see what the whores are like in San Francisco and New York…maybe even Paris."

"You're willing to kill people, even your own brother, for whores?" Jennie Lue was aghast.

"Jennie Lue, you sure have a way with words," Buddy laughed. "Hell, I never thought of it like that, but I guess you're right."

"Why did you have to kill Henry?" she sobbed.

"I didn't kill him, Blondy did," he answered. He thought about it and shrugged. "But, if you must know, that night the son of a bitch went over to the Four C's trying to cut me out of the deal. That was a big mistake on his part."

"Why don't you just leave? Leave while you can," Tom begged.

"Ah, don't you worry. I will," Buddy said. He turned to Jennie Lue. "But it ain't over just yet."

"She doesn't have anything to do with this, Buddy!" Tom yelled.

Buddy raised his eyebrows. "Oh, but she does! And I owe her a thing or two." He walked to Jennie Lue, reached out and cupped her right breast as he stared into her eyes. "What to do, what to do," he said with feigned confusion. He glanced at Tom. "I know! I got an idea." There was excitement in his voice and he reached to twist the soft curls of her hair. "We'll play a game."

"What kind of a game?" she asked, swatting Buddy's hand away.

"A game we all three can play," he said, laughing. "You see, Tom, the rule is this," He stared at Jennie Lue's breasts, "if your girlfriend rides me like a wild horse and makes me pop before you bleed to death, I'll let you both go."

"You're a son of a bitch!" Tom roared.

"Oh, no," Buddy said with a look of mock disappointment. He looked at Jennie Lue and shook his head. "Looks like we have a sore sport over there." He paused for a moment, then smiled. "How 'bout you? You wanna play?"

"Why are you doing this?" she asked, tears streaming down her cheeks.

"'Cause it'll be fun!" Buddy yelped. "You see, if you don't act like I'm the best fuck you ever had, I ain't gonna shoot my load and the last thing Tom will see on this earth is me having my way with you." An evil grin spread across his face as he winked. "And, if you're as good at it as I think you are, then Tom will spend the rest of his life thinking about how a real man turned his girlfriend into a cheap whore. Either way I win." He laughed uncontrollably as the thought entered his mind. "Hell, if Tom does live, I bet after today you'll want to close your eyes and pretend it's me on top every time you two go at it. Hell, you might even name your first boy after me. Hah, I'd like to be there for that conversation!"

His smile quickly disappeared as he reached down and picked up a large rock with his free hand, then walked over to stand next to his brother, a crazed look in his eyes. "But I think we need to make it a bit more interesting, and Jennie Lue, I can see you need some motivation." Buddy suddenly bent over and slammed the rock down onto Tom's right forearm.

Tom's loud, painful scream was mixed with the sound of bones breaking.

"Stop!" Jennie Lue screamed as she ran to kneel beside Tom and glanced at his crooked, broken arm. She looked up at Buddy and sobbed, "All right, Buddy! Just stop it! Please!"

"Fantastic!" Buddy flashed a demented grin. "Looks like we have a deal!"

Tom screamed in agony as his brother reached down and yanked the belt off his leg, but could do nothing as Buddy pointed his pistol at Jennie Lue's head. "Let the games begin."

Jennie Lue knew that Tom couldn't squeeze his leg hard enough with just one hand to keep from bleeding to death. He would die soon if she didn't do what Buddy wanted. Tears ran down her face as she watched Tom start to pass out. She ran to a rock, sat down to pull off her boots, pants and underwear as quickly as she could. She vaguely heard Tom's weak pleas to stop, but was already in some sort of a trance as she knelt in front of Buddy and began unbuttoning his trousers. Even though she had been married to Henry for over seven years, she didn't have much experience with sex and didn't have any idea what to do next, but she prayed Buddy wouldn't last long and this would all be over in time to get Tom to a doctor.

"Lookee here, Tom," Buddy said with a huge grin as Jennie Lue reached into his pants. "You ought to thank me, you know. Your girlfriend turned out to be nothing but a whore after all."

Jennie Lue was in such a daze that she barely heard Tom's faint cries for his brother to stop, but would never forget the moment when an echo of a gunshot registered, snapping her out of her trance. She looked up to see complete surprise on Buddy's face as he slowly turned to find out who shot him in the back. The last image Buddy Wallace had on this earth was smoke lingering out of the barrel of Aya's pistol as he stared back with the same cold, steely-eyed glare he had in his eyes long ago in the front yard of the Four C's Ranch.

Aya had come to, and managed to reach the revolver in his vest pocket before his strength left him. As Buddy fell sideways to the ground, Jennie Lue stood and looked as if she didn't know where she was, but her eyes quickly came to rest on Buddy, who was lifeless at her feet with a small, bloody hole in his back. Her trembling, clenched fists instantly came up to her cheeks as she started crying and shaking uncontrollably.

"Over there!" Turner said when he and Jim saw the palomino.

Even from a distance, they could tell it was Buddy's horse, and rode over as fast as they could, a sickening feeling in their stomachs knowing they might be too late. The horse was tied to a small tree thirty yards off to the side of the creek, but Jim and Turner rode straight up to the side of Cowhouse Creek and from their saddles caught sight of what was happening below. They were both horrified at the scene playing out in front of them and immediately realized what needed to be done, but it was Jim who acted first. He grabbed his rifle from its sheath and with one smooth motion cocked a shell into the chamber, focused the sight at the end of the barrel squarely on

Buddy's chest and clicked the safety off. Tom, Jennie Lue, Aya and Buddy were only fifty yards away. If it had been anyone else, Jim would have pulled the trigger without thinking, but that was still his son he had the rifle leveled on, which caused him to pause.

"Shoot him!" Turner growled. "What are you waiting for?"

Jim took a deep breath and silently asked God to forgive him but, before he could take his shot, a puff of blue-white smoke appeared from where Aya was sprawled out in the creek bed, and the sound of the gunshot reached their ears a split second later. As it turned out, Jim never had to pull the trigger because Buddy Wallace suddenly fell sideways against the limestone wall before dropping dead to the ground.

CHAPTER 21

A Prayer For Ruby

J im looked up as a gust of wind rattled the leaves in the huge, old oak tree, then looked back at Turner. "I'm glad you came," he said.

"Me, too," Turner replied as he looked into the cemetery. "I'm sorry everything turned out this way."

Jim nodded. "I appreciate that, Turner. I really do. It's still hard for me to believe Buddy was responsible for all this." He took a deep breath. "I don't know where I went wrong."

Turner rested his hands on the wrought iron fence surrounding the Wallace family plot as he dropped his chin to his chest and sighed. "I know how you feel. I thought I raised George better, too."

"Any word from him?" Jim asked.

"Nope," Turner said as he looked up. "There was a rumor he was spotted up in Colorado a week ago. Before that, somebody said he was in Virginia. But I don't know where he is. I'll probably never know." He squinted into the blue sky and watched a small, white cloud slowly float past. "What ever happened to those land grabbers, anyway? The ones you signed the ranch over to?"

"Never heard another thing from 'em," Jim said. "Turns out they were trying to bamboozle George and Buddy out of the money. Guess they high-tailed it soon as word got out that the railroad wasn't going through here. Probably thought they'd get strung up if they stuck around any longer."

"The railroad never was going through here, was it?" Turner asked.

"Nope. It was going through Temple all along," Jim answered with a sigh. "George and Buddy got conned into thinking it was, though."

"They weren't the only ones," Turner said as he scratched the back of his neck. "Me and a few local shop owners got skinned pretty good, too."

"We all got skinned pretty good," Jim said, as he contemplated the three new graves in the cemetery. "Some for a lot more than just money."

"I'm…I'm sorry," Turner stuttered, "I didn't mean to…"

"Don't worry about it, Turner," Jim said. "I know what you meant."

They stood in silence for a moment, then Turner pointed at Ruby's headstone. "I like what you did for Ruby. This is a nice place for her."

"Yeah," Jim said, smiling at the memory of his wife. "She always did like it here. She used to come down here with a blanket and spend all day. I asked her why, once." He waved at the countryside surrounding them. "She used to say it was the prettiest place on earth and from here she could see everything in the world that made her happy."

A moment of silence followed before Turner said, "Jim, nothing ever happened between us. As God is my witness. You have to know that, don't you?"

Jim stared at Ruby's grave. "I know," he said. He turned to look Turner in the eyes. "It's just that there was a lot of talk going around town. She never said it out loud, but I'm sure it was the reason Ruby hardly went into Belton anymore." He sighed as he shook his head. "I felt so bad for her, like I was such a fool."

"Maybe you should have discussed it with me," said Turner, "instead of listening to all the idiots around this town who don't have anything better to do than talk about people they don't even know."

Jim nodded. "You're right. You're absolutely right. I'm sorry."

Turner stared at Ruby's headstone as his eyes teared. "She loved you more than anything. And I don't want you take this the wrong way…but I miss her."

Jim put his arm around Turner's shoulder. "Yeah, I miss her, too."

Turner's eyes were glued to Ruby's headstone. "I swear, I never had a friend like Ruby in all my life," he whispered. He looked at Jim, then smiled. "Except for you, maybe, before you went off to the war and got stupid. I didn't know the correct procedure for fixin' a busted leg was to remove the brain."

Jim laughed. "Don't push it!" he teased. "It's been nice being friends with you and Judy again, so don't go spoiling it now."

"Yeah," Turner said, grinning, "it's a shame we let all that time get by us, but I got an idea on how we can make up for it."

"How's that?' Jim asked.

"I have a sweet little business deal you might be interested in," Turner said with a wink. "Could make the two of us a lot of money."

"Oh, geez, here we go," Jim said.

"Seriously…we'd be partners," Turner said as he put his hand on Jim's shoulder, "hear me out."

"Tell you what," Jim said, "knowing you, it'll probably be some kind of cockamamie scheme, but I'll listen. And maybe we even can do something, but not right now. If any of the women up at the house get wind we're talking business they'll shoot us before we get a chance to step back on the porch."

Turner smiled. "You're probably right, but I can tell you that you won't be sorry. How about if I come back here tomorrow afternoon? Just you and me will sit down and talk?" He held his hand out. "What do you say?"

Jim took Turner's hand and shook it firmly. "Sounds good. Tomorrow, then."

"Fair enough," Turner said. He stepped away from the fence. "Speaking of the ladies, why don't we head up there and see how they're getting along?"

"There's a good idea. Percy ought to have dinner ready soon and I'm starving," Jim said. He paused to take a last look at the new headstones in the family cemetery, then turned and joined Turner for the walk back to the house.

"My, my!" Emma said, glancing at the screen door, "Look who's up and around!"

Everyone applauded when the screen door opened and Chas Kane slowly walked out onto the porch. He had lost a lot of weight from being bedridden for the better part of a month, and had to support himself with a cane, but he wore the biggest smile of his life when he said, "I thought I'd join y'all out here for a spell."

Judy Bell sat closest to the door so she stood up quickly and helped Chas settle into her chair, saying, "We were all wondering how long it would take before you got sick and tired of lying in that bed."

There was a sheepish grin on Chas's face as he adjusted his new eyeglasses and said, "Mrs. Bell, I was sick and tired of lyin' in that bed as soon as I got in it!"

"But here you made it all the way out by yourself," Emma said.

"Yes, ma'am," Chas said proudly. "I'm getting better every day. I got to." There was laughter from everyone as he added, "I got to get down to the river pretty soon and do some fishin'. Them catfish are probably thinkin' they got it made since I got laid up."

"Child, how are you planning on catching fish with just one arm?" Judy asked.

"Don't know that yet. But I aim to figure it out." Chas smiled. He pointed at Tom, who sat in a rocking chair next to Jennie Lue. "Tom there still has one good one. Between the both of us, we still have two good arms."

Tom laughed and tapped the cast on his leg. "Yeah, but I only got one good leg right now. I don't know how much help I could be."

"You'll be good as new in no time," Chas said. "But lookee here, I got somethin' to show ya'll." He reached down with his right arm and straightened the fingers of his left hand. His arm was wrapped tightly in a sling and looked as if he would never be able to use it again by the way it limply hung against his side, but another round of applause went up as everyone on the porch saw the first two fingers move ever so slightly.

"That's fantastic!" Tom said as he adjusted himself in his chair. He rocked his left foot back and forth because his leg was itching from being in a cast for three weeks and his right arm had been giving him fits for the same reason. He was still trying to get comfortable as he asked, "How long you been able to do that?"

"Since yesterday," Chas said with a broad grin. "I figure pretty soon I'll be able to earn my keep 'round here."

"Just make sure you get well first," Tom said. "We still have a lot of wire to hang. There will be plenty for you to do once you get back on your feet."

"You need to take your own advice," Jennie Lue said as she playfully slapped Tom on the shoulder. "You need to take it easier on yourself, too."

"You try to do too much now and you'll wind up with a limp just like your father," Emma chimed in as she nodded at Jennie Lue. There was laughter all around as she added, "With your bad left leg and your father's bad right, the only way either one of you could walk a straight line would be to lean the two of you up against each other."

"All I did was go down to the creek to see how the new bridge was coming along," Tom protested. "I didn't help build it; I just watched. There's a big difference."

"*Two days in a row*?" Jennie Lue said, her eyebrows raised.

Tom smiled. "Well, maybe it was a bit much, but I did stay in the wagon the whole time, and Ruby's new bridge sure turned out nice." He shrugged. "I just wanted to get some ideas, in case we wind up building our own across the shallow crossing."

"Where our house is going to be? Over by the big oak?" Jennie Lue said with a bright smile.

"Exactly," Tom said, reaching out to take her hand. "Heck, we're getting married in two weeks! I have to start thinking about these things."

"Aw, that's nice," Jennie Lue said. "I guess I forgive you for being so pig-headed."

"You two didn't hear it from me," Judy jumped in, "and when Turner tells you, make sure you act surprised but, if I don't tell somebody, I'm gonna burst."

"What, Momma?" Jennie Lue asked as she leaned forward in her chair.

Judy Bell looked around at everyone on the porch. "If any one of you utters a single word about this I'm going to beat you with a stick! Everybody understand?" There was a round of nods before she continued, "As your wedding present, Turner's going to…"

"Shhhh!" Emma said, "Jim and Turner are coming!"

Everyone went quiet as they looked to see the two men just a few yards away from the house, and an awkward silence remained as Jim started up the steps. "What's going on here?" he asked.

Emma came to the rescue as she stood and brushed off the front of her expensive red dress. "Why, Jim Wallace, sometimes you're just not too bright, are you? Chas walked out here onto the porch for the first time in a month all by himself, and you didn't even notice."

Jim walked over to Chas and patted him on his good shoulder. "All right! That's great! How do you feel?" he asked.

"Pretty good, Mister Wallace! I'll be back to work lickity-split."

"Not until I say so, you won't," Jim said, smiling.

"Chas can move his fingers!" Jennie Lue said.

"Really!" Turner said as he joined them on the porch. "Can you do it again?"

"Sure! Lookee here," Chas said, and they all watched his two fingers twitch.

"Doc Carrington said he wouldn't ever be able to do that again," Percy said as he opened the screen door and walked onto the porch. "Shows ya what he knows."

"That's just terrific," Jim said. He looked around the porch. "Where's Aya?" he asked.

"He's been out working all day," Percy said. "All the little stuff that's been needin' to be fixed 'round here. I saw him down at the barn a little while ago."

"Go down there and tell him.. " Jim began, but stopped at the sound of a horse coming around the side of the house.

They all watched as Aya led his horse into the front yard. He stopped and slowly waved an outstretched hand from the west side of the property to the east as he said in his deep voice, "Mister Jim, everything fixed. I go now."

Jim stepped out to meet his old friend. "What do you mean? Where are you going?"

"Warrior spirit...come again...in dream," Aya said with tears on his cheeks and great sorrow in his eyes. He choked up before adding with great difficulty, "I kill Buddy...warrior say...I go home now...to my people."

"Are you sure?" Jim asked, not comfortable with the thought of the Four C's without Aya. "This is your home. This will always be your home."

"No, Mister Jim. Spirit say I have woman there. She wait for me," Aya said slowly. "Spirit say she give me three sons. I will call first one Bear," he said and wiped the tears from his face.

Jim could tell by the determination in Aya's eyes the time had finally come for him to leave and he knew there was absolutely nothing he could do about it. Years ago, he had been powerless as he tried to run Aya off when he first showed up at the Four C's and Jim was struck by the irony that he was just as powerless now when it came to keeping him from leaving.

He walked up to his old friend and wrapped his arms tightly around him. The long hug that followed brought a tear to every eye on the porch, but soon, Aya pulled away and walked over to stand by his horse.

"Is your shoulder going to be all right? Do you need anything?" Jim asked.

Aya gingerly touched his shoulder and shook his head no. Then he looked over at Tom and Jennie Lue, tipped his hat and nodded. "Be happy," he said, "have many babies."

"Thank you, Aya. You're a good man. Thank you for all you've done for my family," Tom said, and he raised his left hand in goodbye. "Be careful."

A fresh tear rolled down Aya's cheek as he waved goodbye and was about to climb into his saddle when Tom grabbed his crutch, struggled to his feet and yelled, "Wait! I have a question for you. How is it you can speak English all of a sudden?"

Aya chuckled and tapped the side of his head. "I listen good...for long time."

"Well, listen to this," Tom said as he balanced on his crutch, "we're about to eat and you have to stay for dinner. You can leave first thing in the morning."

Aya took a deep breath and looked into the distance to mull the thought over.

"Please, for me and Jennie Lue," Tom said. "It's going to be dark in a couple hours, anyway. What do you say?"

Aya looked at the hopeful faces lining the front porch, then nodded and led his horse up to the porch rail. He tied the reins, looked up at Tom and smiled. "Okay. Tomorrow, I go." A cheer went up from everyone as Aya climbed the steps. He embraced everyone there before he looked back at Jim. "Mister Jim...thank you."

"No, Aya. Thank you," Jim said as he stood in the yard. He put his hands on his hips and sighed heavily as he watched Miss Emma come off the porch and join him. He put his arms around her and said softly, "I can't believe Aya's leaving. I just can't believe it. And today was going to be such a great day."

"It still is, silly," Emma said with a smile. "He's going home! That's a wonderful thing." She could tell by the look in Jim's eyes her words didn't do much to ease his sorrow, so she held him tight and whispered in his ear. "Tell you what, why don't we go back up there and tell everyone the news. Maybe that will make you feel better."

Jim looked into Emma's eyes and smiled. "I think that's a great idea, but are you sure you want to do it now?" The twinkle in Emma's eyes and the quick nod of her head was all the answer he needed. "Come on then."

They turned and walked back up the steps as Jim said, "Everybody...not to take anything away from Tom and Jennie Lue's upcoming wedding and all, but Emma and I want you all to know we're getting married, too."

Another round of cheers and applause erupted as Judy ran over and grabbed Emma's hands. "That's just wonderful! We have so much to do!! When's the big day?" she said.

"We haven't figured that part out just yet," Jim answered.

"This is all so exciting!" Judy said as she held Emma's hands and looked back and forth between the two couples. "First Tom and Jennie Lue...and now Jim and Emma!"

"This is great news," Percy said with a wide smile. "Why don't we all go inside and have a toast? And a roast I hope ya'll will brag about for days. I got supper just about ready."

"Mister Jim says you're a pretty good new cook," Chas said as he stood. "Is that right?"

"I reckon," Percy answered as he helped Chas through the door. "He ain't run me off yet."

"Good, 'cause I like you, Mister Percy," Chas said seriously, "and right now, I'm so hungry I think I could eat anything."

Percy chuckled and said, "Well, come on then," and motioned everyone inside.

Judy Bell stood slowly, looked down at Tom and Jennie Lue and hid her mouth by pretending to fix the hair on the side of her head as she mouthed the words, "I'll tell you later."

They both nodded discreetly before Tom looked at his father and said, "Dad, we'll be just a minute. There's something I want to show Jennie Lue."

"You two take all the time you need," Jim said as he stopped in front of the screen door, "You have plenty of that now."

"Thanks, Dad," Tom said before Jim disappeared into the house, leaving them alone on the porch. Tom reached into his shirt and pulled out an envelope.

"What is it?" Jennie Lue asked.

"The letter my mother wrote, the one I was telling you about," he said and held it out for her.

"I can't read that," she protested, "it's too personal."

"No, I want you to," he said as he gently waved the letter at her. "Please take it."

Her hands trembled as she took the envelope and slowly removed the letter inside. She didn't move a muscle or say a word until she read the letter entirely. There were tears in her eyes as she handed it back to Tom. "That was beautiful. She was sitting right here when she wrote it, wasn't she?"

"Yeah," Tom said. He pointed to Cowhouse Creek. "She was probably sitting in that same rocking chair you're in now looking at a sunset just like this one. See how the light is bouncing off the water down there?"

"Ah...it is," she said, wiping a small tear from her cheek. "I guess her prayer came true then, didn't it?"

"Well...not all of it," he sighed. "I did come home in one piece, and I figure I'll be working this ranch 'til the day I die, but I didn't do too well on mending fences with Buddy."

"Buddy was hopeless. You have to know that, don't you?" she said as she gently squeezed his hand.

Tom sighed. "Probably beyond hopeless, if truth be known."

"He really was," she said reassuringly. "Promise me you won't go kicking yourself over it. Can you do that for me?"

Tom nodded. "You're right. Besides, he's buried right next to Momma and she's looking after him now. If anybody could straighten him out, it would be her."

Jennie Lue laughed, which made Tom ask, "What's so funny?"

"Because here we are, talking about a prayer your momma had for you," she said with a chuckle, "but, if she's got to deal with Buddy, I think we need to say a prayer for *her*."

"You're right about that!" he grinned. He looked out into the distance. "I just wish I could have done something to turn Buddy around, to save him from himself."

"You promised me you wouldn't do that," she said. She put her arm around his shoulder and kissed him on the cheek. "Besides, the most important part of Ruby's prayer came true; you *did* meet the right woman. And we can start thinking about having those children the day we get married."

"Why, Jennie Lue Sloan," he said, raising his eyebrows, "it sounds like you're looking forward to that."

She leaned over and kissed him on the lips. "Oh, yes...I can hardly wait."

"Me, neither," he answered. "But I think we need to get inside before your daddy gets suspicious."

"Too late," she said, as she hopped up from her chair and helped him to his feet. "He already is."

"Uh-oh," Tom said with a grin, "He's on to me, is he?"

"I'm afraid so," she said with a laugh as she helped Tom get his balance. She looked out toward the cemetery. "It sure was nice of your father to bury Church and Bear out there."

"Yeah," Tom said. "I guess The Cowhouse Creek Cattle Company has its own version of Peckerwood Hill right here."

"Don't think of it like that," she said, frowning.

"Oh, I'm not, really," he said as he slowly limped his way to the door with Jennie Lue on his arm. "They're buried where they're supposed to be, with family." He stopped as she reached out to open the door. "And speaking of that, are you ready to start a family with me, Mrs. Jennie Lue Wallace?"

"I'm not Mrs. Wallace just yet," she said.

"I know, but it sure does have a nice ring to it, doesn't it?" He smiled.

She kissed him softly. "It sure does."

"Are you ready to grow old with me?" he asked.

"Positively absolutely," she said, as she put her head on his chest and held him tight.

"I guess Momma's prayer was certainly answered," he said, as he gently rocked her in his arms.

She looked up. "It sure was," she said.

They kissed each other softly once more, then stepped inside the house, arm in arm, to join the celebration as the setting sun's reflection danced on the waters of Cowhouse Creek.

THE END

Notes to the Reader

The idea for this book came to me over the course of a few months and, if it wasn't for my wonderful wife, I never would have written it, but after three years and 'The End' finally appeared on the last page, I felt there were a few more thoughts I had to include.

When my wife Lori and I started doing research for this book, I had every intention of keeping the historical facts surrounding Huntsville and Belton intact but, as the story progressed, I had to make a few minor changes regarding Belton and the reason why the railroad lines passed the town over.

After they took fifty thousand dollars from local businessmen, the Gulf, Colorado & Santa Fe Railway made the townspeople of Belton believe they were going to lay tracks right through the middle of town but, at the last minute, the rails were laid down to the east and went through Temple instead. Belton filed a suit seeking their money back plus damages and eventually won but, by that time, most all major commerce was going through Temple, ensuring that Belton would never become the great city the people envisioned in the years following the Civil War. In 1882, a second set of tracks was laid just to the north of town, which went west to Lampasas, but that line also connected in Temple, which made the new tracks virtually useless when it came to economic benefits for the local businesses of Belton.

However, the history of Huntsville is accurate. I was lucky enough to locate a website called *Walkercountytreasures.com*, which posts quite a few rare pictures of the town in the 1880s. Anyone with a few minutes to spare would do themselves a favor if they were to look it over.

I would also like to give special thanks to a man by the name of James Patton, who works at the county clerk's office and knows the history of Huntsville like the back of his hand. He guided me around the town, pointing out where places like the old railway depot used to be, the location of Felder's General Store, the spot where Aunt Jane's Place stood, the lot where The Keep Hotel was and Robert Tilley's train tracks that still lay in ruins just to the south of The Walls. It stands to reason Huntsville looks nothing like it did back in 1880, but if you stand along those washed-out, dilapidated tracks with a clear line of sight up the hill to The Walls, it doesn't take much imagination to feel the suffocating presence the prison would have on a man's soul, shackled to other inmates on Tilley's train as it rolled around the bend to show the imposing, red brick walls as they came into view. Although the only 'death chamber' for the Texas prison system is located within The Walls and executions are carried out there more than any other place in the country, the unit is now used strictly to house inmates who are about to be discharged.

There is a dark side to the history of the state that I only touched upon as I wrote this book. That subject will be the basis of another story another time, but I want to make it clear to everyone that I love the state of Texas and always will. I was born in Marshall, I've lived in Houston most all my life and I can't imagine living anywhere else but, if a man went to prison in Texas around the turn of the century, there was a good chance he might not make it out alive, even if he was sentenced for something as trivial as stealing a chicken.

Like most states in the south, Texas adopted the Pig Laws of 1876, which made stealing any livestock grand larceny punishable by up to five years in prison and, since there were plenty of uneducated, unskilled black migrants moving into the area on a regular basis, the state used those laws to scoop them up and put them to work on the railroads. At the time, there was no such thing as an oversight committee and it was not uncommon for the state to hire guards who were not a better example of humanity than the inmates themselves. There was a great need for the commerce the trains brought with them and almost a sense of nationalism to get the rail lines down as fast as possible, no matter the expense, which ultimately turned out to be the people no one knew or cared about. Every inmate knew the worst thing that could happen to them was to either get sick or severely injured because work on the tracks didn't stop for anyone.

I took my family to ride the Texas State Railroad, a refurbished oil-fired locomotive that runs back and forth between Rusk and Palestine on tracks laid down by prisoners in 1881, and would recommend the experience to anyone who has ever wondered what it was like to ride in a passenger car behind a belching steam engine. But as the train moved along, it was hard not to think there might be unmarked graves off to the side of the tracks of poor souls who fell victim to the philosophy of the time that it was far easier to bury a convict than to take the time and manpower to get him to a doctor. Unfortunately, digging holes for dead inmates was a lot more common back then than people today might think.

Which brings me to Peckerwood Hill. There are well over two thousand documented graves in what is now called Captain Joe Bird Cemetery, but it is impossible to know exactly how many people have been laid to rest there. Unbelievably, the state didn't keep written records until as late as 1974, making identification impossible for hundreds if not thousands of forgotten names. My wife and I were humbled as we walked the grounds, not only because the old, weather-worn crosses were far too many to count and the cramped graves on which they stood seemed to go on forever, but when we met in the car and talked about the experience, we both felt a need to name all the characters in the story by using the names on some of the crosses. The main reason I did this was so that some of these long-forgotten names could be uttered once again, and maybe there could be some positive attention drawn to the cemetery itself. Peckerwood Hill struck me as being the most depressing cemetery I've ever been in and the idea that I could somehow make a few people remember those forgotten souls, while shedding a little light on a very dark spot in the history of Texas, seemed the right thing to do.

There are a few names in the book that were not taken from the cemetery. Jim Wallace was a good friend of mine who recently passed away and I chose to use his name only because I thought it sounded perfect for the character in the story. His wife's name was Ruby Nell Wallace and I chose her because, even though she passed away July 8th, 1986, Jim Wallace never remarried and carried around his wedding ring on his keychain until the day he died. It's hard not to like a guy like that.

I don't know how the name Bear came to me, but I fashioned that character out of another friend I worked with as a bartender some time ago. I used the name Tom because it was simple and I named Buddy after a kid in my neighborhood who at one time put himself in charge of pissing everybody off up and down the street. I guess every neighborhood has a nuisance like that, but I can happily add that particular kid was able to straighten himself out with the help of a basketball coach who lived nearby. At least there was a happy ending when it came to the real Buddy, but not for the thousands who died at the hands of the Texas prison system over the years.

My wife and I wrote down names we chose from the graves that were legible (there are hundreds of decrepit crosses that have nothing on them at all) and took them to Jim Willet, who is the director of the Texas Prison Museum in Huntsville. I owe him a great deal of gratitude because he was kind enough to look up the information in his database, even though some had been dead for almost a hundred years. We did not want to use the names of inmates who were executed — those crosses are marked with a simple X — and we did not choose any name for any reason other than it sounded interesting. As it turned out, their crimes ranged from murder to bootlegging to stealing a pig. I'm not trying to say that some, if not most, didn't deserve their fate, but the list speaks for itself. Out of the thirty-two random names used for the book, only nine were over the age of thirty, with the youngest being sixteen.

There is no way of knowing how many people died or where they were buried during the chain gang years of 1875-1925, but early in my research for this story, it became clear it was seldom any inmate died of old age. When I started writing *Ruby's Prayer*, I only wanted to tell a story that had been rattling around inside my head but, as the pages grew and I began to understand what is was like to be incarcerated in the Texas prison system those many years ago, I felt I needed to finish this book as a prayer for all the people who died away from home and at far too young an age in an era when there was nothing anyone could do about it, and very few who cared. These are some of those:

Turner Bell: Age 33. Black male convicted of murder. Died 7-19-1918

Judy Bell Burse: Age 27. Black female convicted of murder. Died 1-24-1929

Jennie Lue Sloan: Age 22. Black female convicted of murder. Died 6-14-1941

George Bell: Name and inmate number does not match. No record. Died 9-11-1915

Chas Kane: Age 22. Black male convicted of burglary. Died 10-15-1918

Church Davis: Age 46. White male convicted of manufacturing intoxicating liquor. Died 6-5-1932

Percy Goff: Name and inmate number does not match. Died 6-11-1914

Blondy Harbison: Age unknown. White male convicted of transporting liquor. Died 8-31-1927

Emma Lawton: Age 24. Black female convicted of burglary. Died 12-20-1918

Lee Potts: Age 45. Black male convicted of murder. Died 8-7-1929

Curry Hampton: Age 16. Black male convicted of forgery. Died 8-7-1912

Cornelius Love: Age 20. Black male convicted of burglary. Died 10-18-1918

Isaac Norton: Age 66. Black male convicted of theft of hogs. Died 6-14-1911

Thelma Williams: Age 18. Black female convicted of assault with intent to rob. Died 9-1-1923

Berta Wortham: Age 29. Black female convicted of theft from person. Died 2-26-1936

Gilmer Mure: Age 22. Hispanic male convicted of burglary. Died 3-7-1911

Bennie Leaks: There are two graves in Peckerwood Hill that claim to hold the remains of this man and no one knows which one he is in or who is in the other. He was black and convicted of murder, age unavailable. Died 8-12-1945

Zeb Coleman: Age 21. Hispanic male convicted of assault and rape. Died 5-15-1919

Barney Lee: Age 23. White male convicted of murder. Died 6-8-1925

Moses Henry: There are two graves in Peckerwood Hill that claim to hold the remains of this man and no one knows which one he is in or who is in the other. He was an 18-year-old Hispanic male convicted of burglary. Died 9-28-1916

Owen Ayers: Age unknown. Black male convicted of burglary. Died 12-31-1933

Jessie Moore: Age 33. Black female convicted of burglary. Died 10-18-1918

Ida Ruth Griffen: Age 49. Black female convicted of murder with malice aforethought. Died 8-10-1938

Arthur Danley: Age 25. White male convicted of robbery. Died 9-27-1920

Walter Carrington: Age 20. Hispanic male convicted of burglary. Died 12-14-1917

Sam Webber: Age 69. White male convicted of burglary. Died 7-30-1945

Jim Conner: Age 39. Hispanic male convicted of burglary. Died 6-24-1911

Milo Hollman: Age unknown. Black male convicted of arson and 1st degree murder. Died 3-6-1912

Leonardo Hernandez: His inmate numbers are on the grave marked Arthur Thomas, meaning no one is sure who's buried there. Wherever he is buried,

Leonardo Hernandez was a 22-year-old Hispanic and died 10-17-1918.

Charley Cobb: Age unavailable. Hispanic male convicted of theft over fifty dollars. Died 4-16-1948

Will Weathers: Age 34. Black male convicted of burglary. Died 9-30-1918

May they all be forgiven and rest in peace.

Ronald H. Keyser

The first picture is of the chain gang. I didn't spend a great deal of time in the book discussing the "pig laws," as they were called at the time, but you can tell from the photo there were far more blacks working the rail lines than there were whites. The uneducated, recently freed slaves coming into Texas looking for a place to start a life were scooped up, given a five-year sentence for as little as stealing a chicken to eat, then sent off to work on the railroads in conditions that were deplorable at best. Notice the tattered, dirty clothes that every man in the picture is wearing.

The second picture is of Doorman's Saloon. This is my favorite because I was a bartender for years. You can tell by the way the two men behind the bar are dressed that they were men of standing and took the profession seriously. Not much has changed, either, because if you look at the back bar carefully, you can see pour spouts that are identical to the ones still used today in almost every bar in the country. What's more, on the back bar you can see a bottle of Grand Marnier and Galliano, liquors still bottled the same way. This picture was taken in 1890. The building is still there, but now houses a clothing store.

The picture of Felder's store is interesting because it truly is a snapshot into the past. The young boy in the upper left-hand window reminds me of me. I would have wanted to be there if I was going to be in the picture. Also, everyone on the sidewalk is very serious about the picture as well. You can tell the second floor is the home of Mr. Felder, and I believe the man downstairs to the left is Mr. Felder himself. I'm also assuming the young man in the window is his son.

The next three pictures are of The Walls Unit. The first is a picture of the front, which was only seen by people going in for business, or by the inmates when they were released. The second picture is the west gate, which is where the inmates entered the facility, and the third is a view from the yard where inmates were rousted to before they began their day's work.

The next two pictures are of the old Huntsville Depot and Tilley's train. The picture of the depot was taken in this spot because it purposely shows The Walls directly over the roof. The depot was torn down years ago but, if this picture was taken from the same spot today, The Walls would still be clearly visible. I also like the picture of Tilley's train. Even though the train is a blur, you can see the black smoke belching from the engine. The depressing part, though, is this picture was taken from the south wall of The Walls Unit looking directly down the hill. How many souls watched the same sight for years and years as they waited out their time to go home on that same train?

The Silas Baggett House was constructed in 1886 and named after a wealthy businessman, Silas J. Baggett. I modeled Turner Bell's home in Ruby's Prayer after this beautiful structure, which is now a bed and breakfast called the Morning Glory Inn. Ele Baggett, the second son of Silas and Ellen Warren Baggett, built his family home directly across the street; and it is a mirror image of his father's home. Both are still magnificent examples of 1800s Victorian architecture.

A crew in east Texas late 1800s-early 1900s. It was common for poor people, including Blacks and Chinese, to work the rails for meager pay. Prisoners would have been wearing black and whites. Pictured is the type of terrain chain gangs were subject to in east Texas and Huntsville, Texas areas.